GREENBANKS

Persephone Book Nº 95
Published by Persephone Books Ltd 2011
Reprinted 2016 and 2021

First published by John Murray in 1932
© The Estate of Dorothy Whipple
Afterword © Charles Lock 2011

Endpapers taken from a worsted cotton damask
designed by Alec Hunter for St Edmundsbury Weavers c.1930
© Francesca Galloway

Prelim pages typeset in ITC Baskerville by
Keystroke, Wolverhampton

Printed and bound in Germany by
GGP Media GmbH, Poessneck on Munken Premium
(FSC approved)

9781903155851

Persephone Books Ltd
8 Edgar Buildings
Bath BA1 2EE
01225 425050

www.persephonebooks.co.uk

GREENBANKS

by

DOROTHY WHIPPLE

✱✱✱✱✱✱✱

with a new afterword by

CHARLES LOCK

PERSEPHONE BOOKS
BATH

CHAPTER ONE

I

THE house was called Greenbanks, but there was no green to be seen to-day; all the garden was deep in snow. Snow lay on the banks that sloped from the front of the house; snow lay on the lawn to the left, presided over by an old stone eagle who looked as if he had escaped from a church and ought to have a Bible on his back; snow lay on the lawn to the right, where a discoloured Flora bent grace-fully but unaccountably over a piece of lead piping that had once been her arm. Snow muffled the old house, low and built of stone, and of no particular style or period, and made it look like a house on a Christmas card, which was appropriate, because it was Christmas Day.

Inside the house, the clocks were striking one, and life was concentrated into two rooms. In the kitchen, Mrs. Sam bent her burning face over the ovens, pre-paring dishes for Bella and Lizzy to carry into the dining-room. Sam, gardener and coachman, sat on a chair by the table, waiting for his turn to come. His mouth watered and he made facetious remarks from time to time, but the women took no notice of him, making remarks of their own:

'Drat it, that's hot!'

'Mind them plates now.'

'Missus wants more bread sauce.'

'Here, give me them Brussels—quick!'

In the dining-room, nineteen people were gathered round the expanded table. The leaves which had been taken out one by one as the family diminished were all put back to-day to accommodate the returned Ashtons and the husbands, wives and children they had added unto themselves. It was a confusing, if hearty, scene, and Louisa Ashton, serving the vegetables, the gravies, the sauces, all she termed the 'etceteras', was a little bewildered and kept calling her children and her children's children by the wrong names.

'Letty—Laura—I mean *Rose*, dear me! This is yours, dear? Is it you who doesn't like gravy? You do like gravy? Why, yes, of course. What am I thinking about?'

Maids did not wait at Elton tables in 1909, but Bella stood behind her mistress's chair to carry the plates to their destinations.

At last they were served, and Louisa, waiting for her own plate to be sent down by Robert, could sit back and smile round on them all.

On the wall above Robert Ashton at his end of the table, and on the wall above Louisa at hers, hung their portraits done in oils, by goodness knows whom, at the time of their marriage. In the picture, Louisa was fair and young, with a round bosom, a trim waist and a tranquil, trusting gaze. Louisa at the table was old, her hair was grey, she had no waist—not that she was fat, but her figure was gone past redemption —the trusting look had given way to a wise one, made wistful by a slight lift of the eyebrows. Louisa, as far as looks went, compared poorly with her portrait; but Robert surpassed his. He was handsomer than ever, improved by the grey at his temples, by the closer modelling of cheekbone and nostril, and by the short pointed beard he now wore. This beard always poked slightly and his lips had a half-smile as if he had a secret joke with his own self. The young Louisa had been immensely attracted by this hint of something smilingly held back ; but somewhere, early on in their married life, she had given up hope of sharing her husband's secret amusement. Perhaps one time it had been Miss Minty, perhaps another the girl in the Empire bar, perhaps now it was the woman at Wellford. Robert had been out driving this morning ; he had probably been to see her, even though it was Christmas Day. Her thoughts turned on this for a moment, then returned to her happiness. What if Robert was too gay for his age—which was fifty-six and also hers? What if her life with him had been nothing like she had hoped ? At this moment, it did not matter ; she was happy. Her children and grand-children were gathered round her, enjoying the dinner she had prepared with such care. Laura, the only daughter left at home, had done the decorations, the crackers, the tree, the imitation frost and snow, the flowers, but Louisa had seen to the foundation, the food. She was a great housekeeper and derived a deep pleasure from looking after the bodily needs of other people. Their souls she dared not interfere with.

Bella brought her plate, and Louisa helped herself to the etceteras. She sat in the buzz of talk, comfortably quiet. At her side, Rachel Harding, aged four, who had clamoured to ' sit next to Grandma ', was now perched on a high stool, feeding herself with a spoon over a bib of turkish towelling. Louisa looked with tenderness on the small, dark head. This was her favourite grandchild, who fortunately lived within

twenty minutes' walk of Greenbanks and could be
seen every day.

The child, feeling her grandmother's gaze, raised
her eyes, which were remarkable and lovely, being a
clear light grey with a dark ring to the iris and dark
lashes and brows. She considered her grandmother,
then removed the spoon from her mouth, and, in
spite of gravy and potato, smiled widely. Louisa
bent her head and smiled back. Both wrinkled their
noses slightly as if to say : ' Isn't all this nice ? '

Ambrose Harding noticed this exchange of confidence, and a mixture of paternal pride and jealousy
made him wish to share in it. He leaned forward
over the table.

' Rachel,' he said. ' Rachel.'

She turned her face to her father, all inquiry.

' You're not eating nicely. Wipe your mouth.'

Rachel looked abashed, but laid down her spoon
and scrubbed obediently with the bib. She looked at
him to see if it was all right now, and he smiled at
her. But she did not smile back, only applied herself
to her dinner. He was annoyed that what he had
intended had not come off, and looked round for his
wife, who was really the proper person to be seeing
that the child did not plaster herself with food like
that. But Letty was laughing and talking at a great
rate on the other side of the table, entirely forgetful,
in the company of her sister from London, of her
daughter, her husband and her sons.

Ambrose, with conscious care for them, looked down
the table at Dick, next to a cousin from London, and
then at the twins, David and Roger, sitting side by
side, stuffing silently. Ambrose was slightly outraged
by their bulging cheeks and swallowings.

'Letty mustn't let the twins be greedy,' he thought.
'I must see to it.'

There was always a great deal for Ambrose Harding
to see to. He slumbered not neither did he sleep in
his vigilance over the speech and manners of his family
lest any Lancashire trait should creep into either.
Ambrose had been fourteen years in Elton, but his
spiritual home was still Ealing, whence he had come
as Clerk to the Income Tax Commissioners at the
age of thirty.

'He's a barrister,' Letty had remarked with pride
after a dance years ago at the Assembly Rooms, where
the newly-arrived young man had singled her out for
attention. There were no barristers in Elton ; lawyers
in plenty in the little black row of offices known as
King's Place, but no barristers.

'Mr. Harding has been called to the Bar,' said
Letty, putting on airs to her sisters and imagining a
personal summons from Her Majesty to some awful,
probably golden, barrier that mere lawyers were not
allowed to approach.

Ambrose was, as well as a barrister, a personable
young man, tall, fair, scrupulously dressed. Also he
came from London and spoke beautifully. This was
enough to attract the twenty-year-old Letty at first
sight, and as the acquaintance progressed, she was
further attracted by the fact that he was 'solid'.

In reaction from the vagaries of her own father,
Letty desired a husband who was, above all things,
solid. She married Ambrose and if, as the years went
on, she found him increasingly solid, she reminded
herself that it was what she married him for.

It was queer, it was frightening, she thought, how
in life you got what you wanted. Men, for instance,

who admired above everything else, beauty in women, married beauty and, more often than not, found themselves with nothing but beauty. She married for security, and she was inclined to think she had security and nothing else. Not much fun, anyway. Ambrose was too solid for fun. But she had forgotten him for the time being, and she too was happy.

The dinner ended at last in crackers and confusion, and Rachel found to her indignant amazement that she was expected to have her afternoon sleep as usual.

'But it's Christmas Day,' she protested to her mother.

'I know, darling, but you would never keep awake until Jenny fetches you to-night, if you didn't have a nap now.'

''Course I would. Is *she* going to sleep?' She pointed hopefully at her cousin Margery who came from Birmingham and wore a pink silk dress.

'Oh no,' said Margery's mother. 'She is seven and a half.'

Rachel cast a baleful look at Margery for being seven and a half and permitted herself to be led upstairs and put under the crimson eiderdown on her grandmother's mahogany bed.

It was dark when she was waked and taken down to the drawing-room. There, her mother and her aunts were sitting round the fire with their silk skirts turned back from the heat. They had been joined by Aunt Alice, who was a great-aunt, although she looked smaller than the others to Rachel. Rachel was taken on her grandmother's lap, where she yawned like a little cat and would not speak to Margery.

Ambrose Harding had spent a wretched afternoon, wandering from room to room without being able to

settle anywhere. He was now smoking a cigar, looking from time to time at the butt and remembering
anew that, although good, it was not one of his father-
in-law's best.

All the men of the family seemed to be out. It
was just like them, he reflected. Always bent on
their own affairs ; no consideration for others. Perry
Blackwood was playing with the boys in the billiard-
room, but Ambrose had no wish to join them. Earlier
in the afternoon he had run Robert Ashton to ground
in the morning-room, but although Ambrose had
chosen as a topic of conversation the state and prospects of the timber trade in which Robert Ashton,
being a timber merchant, ought to have been interested,
his father-in-law had shortly afterwards excused himself and gone from the room. Joy, whose hand is
ever at his lips bidding adieu, might have been used
to typify Robert Ashton in the presence of Ambrose.
He smiled, he listened, replied and went. There was
nothing for it after that but for Ambrose to seek the
company of the women in the drawing-room ; he
found it very dull, for they did nothing but talk of
old times.

Rachel, now properly awake and ignoring Margery's
plea to come and play house, slid from her grandmother's lap and went to re-examine the decorated
drain-pipe that stood between the piano and the
windows. The drain-pipe was painted reseda green
and covered with scrap pictures of ladies all bustle
and bosom, of pug dogs with red bows on, and children
in voluminous clothes playing with hoops and balls.
It was as good as a picture book to Rachel.

'Fancy that dreadful thing being there still ! ' said
Rose. 'I should turn it out, Mother, if I were you.'

'No,' said Louisa tranquilly, 'it does for Charles to throw his cigarette ends into when he's playing the piano. If there isn't something there, he throws them into the curtains. You know he burnt my best pair.'

'Does he still play the piano?' asked Thomas's wife, May. 'What does he play now?'

'Oh, just chords, I think,' said Louisa.

'Chords!' repeated May in astonishment.

'Yes, chords up and down, you know how he does,' said Louisa. 'He plays a few pieces too.'

'The tuney parts, I suppose,' said Rose. 'And stops when he comes to the difficult bits.'

'Yes, he stops then,' twinkled Louisa.

'He would,' threw in Ambrose significantly.

Louisa glanced at her son-in-law. The absence of expression in her glance was in itself a comment. Ambrose was always getting at Charles, as if Charles wasn't worth fifty of such as Ambrose, worthy though he was, hard-working, good father and husband and all that—you couldn't love him as everybody loved Charles.

'Charles,' said Ambrose, with a sarcastic inflection in his voice, 'Charles has the artistic temperament without the art.'

He was rather pleased with the way he put it, and smiled round on the women. But only Thomas's wife smiled back out of politeness; she was not really one of the family and did not therefore resent criticism of Charles.

'Let's have the photograph albums out,' said Rose suddenly.

Somebody remembered this source of fun every half-dozen years, and it was hailed with delight.

' Oh, yes ! Mother, where are they ? '

' I think they're on the last shelf of the dining-room bookcase, and bring my spectacles from behind the biscuit-barrel, Laura, will you ? '

Laura returned with the albums, massive with brass clasps and backs of stamped and padded leather. Rose took one on her knee and opened the stiff pasteboards, decorated round the inserted prints with painted sprays of rose and maidenhair, forget-me-not and lily. The others drew their chairs close and smiled in anticipation. Ambrose went on smoking over their heads ; these old photographs were nothing to him.

' Oh, goodness,' cried Rose. ' Here's that one of us at school.'

They went off into peals of laughter at the sight of Rose and Letty, in the uniform of a Belgian convent : long skirts, ribbons from the back of their hats, crosses on their breasts and freckles on their noses.

' Letty's hair is drawn back so tight, she looks Mongolian. How did you blink your eyes, Letty ? ' asked Laura.

' Wait a minute,' said Letty. ' Where's that one of you with those long needlework frills half-way down your legs ? '

There were fresh bursts of laughter, at which Ambrose frowned slightly.

' Oh, to think I ever went about like that,' wailed Laura.

' I don't know what you're laughing at,' remonstrated Louisa mildly. ' You all looked very nice, I'm sure.'

' Look at Charles cast away on that skin mat ! Look at Thomas in that dreadful check dress and those oily curls ! Oh, here's father ! '

They bent over a photograph of Robert Ashton, beardless then, in a wide-brimmed straw hat, standing among his friends, making them look stolid and commonplace.

'Oh, he was handsome,' breathed Laura. 'He was beautiful, Mother. Weren't you mad about him?'

'Well,' said Louisa uncomfortably, 'I suppose I was.'

She reflected momentarily that if he had been less handsome and she had been able to keep him to herself, the children would not have been what they were. They would have been less handsome too. They did not get their looks from her, she reflected; their father's type persisted in them and reappeared in most of the grandchildren.

'Who's this?' asked May.

They leaned to look.

'It's Kate Barlow.'

'Oh!' said the others. The exclamation, though short, was significant. The sisters leaned lower.

From the glossy print a young face looked back at them; dark, unsmiling eyes; full, clear-cut unsmiling lips; the hair, dark and smoothly parted, and the delicately hollowed cheeks gave an added gravity to the face.

'Who'd have thought it,' commented Rose, 'to look at her!'

'How old would she be here?' asked Laura, lowering her voice because of Ambrose. 'Would this be taken before or after?'

'Oh, before,' said Letty, shocked at the idea that Kate Barlow would have her photograph taken *after*.

'Poor girl,' murmured Laura.

'I suppose no one ever hears anything of her now,' said Rose.

'No,' answered Louisa, and sighed.

She had never forgiven herself for being too late to help Kate Barlow. She felt too that she was somehow responsible for the disaster that had overtaken the girl. At any rate, she had chaperoned her to the Infirmary Ball where Philip Symonds noticed her for the first time.

Kate was the only child of an elderly father and a young mother, who died when Kate was six years old. The child had roused Louisa's pity from the days when she came to parties at Greenbanks, an odd little creature in outlandish frocks, who was very shy and difficult at the beginning of a party and very excited and reluctant to go home at the end. She was not quite contemporary with any of Louisa's daughters, being younger than Rose and Letty, and two or three years older than Laura, but Louisa always invited her to the Greenbanks parties and picnics, because she felt that if she did not, the child would never get any fun at all.

When Kate was eighteen, Louisa paid a visit to the dark house, all its front obscured by a great sycamore tree which grew so close that its branches pressed almost against the windows, to ask Mr. Barlow's permission to bring Kate out at the Infirmary Ball, the foremost social event of Elton.

She remembered that visit ; the pallid cranium of Mr. Barlow the only light thing in that dark room, where everything was of a dull, deep red ; his eyes were narrow behind pince-nez and his long, dry hands never still. A polite, proud, strange man she had thought him, and hoped she would never have to visit him again. He had been hard to persuade, but at last he had consented.

Kate went to the Infirmary Ball, and Louisa who had no daughter to bring out that year, Laura being still at school in Belgium, sat among the matrons and watched her protégée with pride. She had been pleased when Mr. Symonds, who was what Louisa called to herself 'rather a swell', looked after Kate by bringing up young men, and taking her into supper himself. Poor innocent Louisa had thought him most kind.

'What was his wife like?' asked May.

'Oh, years older than he was—I suppose he would be about thirty-eight then,' said Letty. 'She had a purple complexion, and always knew everything. You know the type.'

Compared with his wife, thought Louisa, how pale, lovely, young and diffident Kate would seem!

'He was good-looking, wasn't he?' put in Rose. 'I used to be rather fascinated by him myself. He was charming; but he was a cad.'

When discovery threatened, Philip Symonds scurried back to safety, back to his wife. He must have told her everything, because they combined forces superbly to carry the thing off. He himself went about smiling, going out of his way to speak to people, making sure that they were friendly towards him, being more than ever hail-fellow-well-met with all and sundry. His wife increased the number of her luncheons and dinner parties; she had always given a good many, making such a business of it that although you never got anything decent to eat, you came away feeling you had attended a considerable function.

Scandal was slow to reach Louisa's ears. When she at last heard of this one, she did not believe it. People jumped to such wild conclusions from such insufficient premises. She was sure there was nothing in it. She had however just made up her mind to speak to Kate, when she saw her, about the advisability of giving people no occasion for talk, when she was told by her friend Mrs. Brewster that Kate had given birth to a child.

Louisa again could not believe it ; but Mrs. Brewster hammered the tale home to such effect that Louisa, the hesitant, the diffident, went again to the dark house behind the sycamore tree.

She asked for Kate, but was received by Mr. Barlow. He smiled with his narrow eyes through his pince-nez and said he regretted his daughter's absence. She had left the town, he said.

' The modern fever of independence has reached even Elton, Mrs. Ashton,' he said, speaking through his almost closed teeth. ' My daughter wishes to earn her own living. I have not stood in her way. She wished to go and she has gone.'

Louisa, who could be obstinate, asked how Kate was earning her own living.

' She has taken a post as a companion,' he replied.

' And when did she go ? ' asked Louisa.

' She went yesterday,' replied Mr. Barlow with his smile. ' You have missed her by one day. Unfortunate, is it not ? '

Louisa asked for Kate's address. But after a pretended search in a hideous burr-walnut bureau, he said he had mislaid it.

' I will let you have it when I recover it, Mrs. Ashton, and now if you will excuse me . . .'

The address never came. Louisa wrote two or three times to the Sycamores, but had no answer.

'And her father didn't leave her one single penny when he died, dear,' said Aunt Alice, laying a hand on May's knee. She loved a tale like this; it was a pity, for Aunt Alice, that the story of Kate Barlow was really wrung out long ago and could not afford much excitement now.

'What happened to the child?' asked May.

'Nobody knows. They said it was taken out of the house the night it was born. They say it was a boy,' said Aunt Alice. 'And now Philip Symonds is dead. He died three months ago.'

'Poor girl,' said May. 'What a sad business it has been!'

Bella came to say that tea was ready in the dining-room, and they all trooped out, leaving the album open on a low chair to be resumed later. In the firelight, the face of Kate Barlow now leapt from the page, now sank into obscurity.

II

Ambrose opened the door of the dining-room where the shrunken table had been pushed into the window, and said it was time for the children to go home. He was not heard in the uproar. Charles was being a bear on all fours, and the children baited him with shrieks of delighted terror. He had nothing but a folded newspaper for defence, but managed very well, thwacking their legs and backs and mingling his growls with their yells.

'David! Roger! Dick!' cried Ambrose sternly. 'Do you hear me? It's time to go home.'

The game stopped. The twins stood panting, their

sailor collars twisted from back to front. Rachel
made another little rush at her uncle, who suddenly
and unaccountably was a bear no longer and took
no notice of her.

'What time is it?' asked David.

'I said it was time to go home,' said his father,
and added with one of his anti-climaxes, 'As a matter
of fact, it is quarter-past eight.'

An expression of disgust came over the twin's faces.
Quarter-past eight and Christmas night! This
wouldn't sound well if repeated to their friends.
On Shrove Tuesday it was how many pancakes you
could eat, and on Christmas night it was how late
you could stay up.

'Come along,' said Ambrose.

'But I don't want to,' said Rachel, coming to
explain. 'I went to sleep this afternoon, and I
aren't a bit tired now.'

'Jenny is here for you, darling,' said Letty, drawing
her aside.

'Why is she? Why did she come?' Rachel
tore herself out of her mother's hands and rushed
through the baize door into the kitchen. There,
sitting with Bella and Lizzy, was Jenny, waiting.
The kitchen was very comfortable with the firelight
shining on the *Pears Annual* pictures of ' Cherry Ripe '
and the little girl in the white satin bonnet.

'Why did you come, Jenny?' asked Rachel, with a
frown.

'Because your ma told me to,' said Jenny shortly.

'Now then, what have you to say to that?' asked
Bella.

Rachel looked at the three maids. They were too
much for her. She blinked her eyes at them, and

went out of the baize door again. Her mother caught her and took her upstairs to put on her outdoor things.

When they were on, there was everybody to kiss ; prickly cheeks of uncles, smooth cheeks of aunts, the wrinkled cheek of her grandmother, where she lingered and whispered : 'Will that girl be going back to where she lives soon ? ' meaning her cousin Margery. When she came to Aunt Alice's cheek, Rachel thought it was like kissing dough. She had once kissed dough on its round floury top ; not only kissed, but bitten it and got into trouble. She was tempted now to try Aunt Alice's cheek with her teeth, but remembered the trouble and desisted.

The boys shook hands according to their father's instructions. They all, Rachel included, felt it was a dreadful thing that they should be made to go home in the middle of the festivities.

'And did you see those jellies and creams and things waiting ? ' asked Roger indignantly. 'They're going to have another party now we've gone.'

He was right. There was another party. Charles's friends arrived, and Laura's, and people to see Rose and Thomas.

After cards, there was an impromptu set of lancers in the dining-room with someone playing the piano from the drawing-room. Ambrose leaned against the door to watch the dancing. Laura danced with Cecil Bradfield, returning to him from Corners as if she had been separated from him for a month. Letty had Percy Brewster for a partner, and was enjoying herself immensely, her eyes alight, her hair rolling on her neck. Once Percy swung her out so that she kicked the sideboard. Ambrose winced, but when, at the end of the set they broke away and galloped round the room, Ambrose could stand it no longer.

'Excuse me, Brewster, if I take my wife away,' he said, bringing them to a halt. 'Letty, you know you are not allowed even to run for a tramcar.'

'But this isn't running for a tramcar!' protested Letty indignantly.

'You mustn't do it,' said Ambrose relentlessly, and taking her by the arm, he led her out into the hall and said it was time they were going.

'Well, you go,' said Letty, pinning up her hair. 'I'll come later.'

'Of course I shan't do that,' said Ambrose. 'If you insist on staying I shall stay with you. But there really isn't anything to stop for, is there, Letty? You can't dance in that room, and you can see these people every day of your life.'

'Oh, all right, all right,' said Letty. He would keep on until she gave in. She knew if she went back to the dancing he would hover round the door to say : 'Letty, don't you think it's time . . .'

She put on her things and in her turn kissed everybody good-bye.

'All this kissing,' said Ambrose testily, waiting at the front door.

By and by the party ended. Guests went. Chairs were restored to the places, wines and cigars consigned to their cupboards, the floors remained strewn with crackers and remnants of jollity. Robert Ashton stayed down to smoke a final pipe ; Louisa went upstairs at last.

She turned up the gas, making two illuminated blanc manges appear in suspension above the dressing-table. She moved about the room as she undid the innumerable hooks and eyes set down the front of her braided bodice. From the crowded day behind her, events, words, faces rose again. She talked to herself as she had not been able to talk to anybody all day. Fancy Ambrose gibing at Charles again ! She would have liked to say something caustic to him, but her policy was not to say anything, to let remarks like that slide away without the emphasis of a quarrel, so that nobody would notice when Charles wasn't really working at the timber yard. She herself would speak to him, though she did not expect to do much good by that. Charles worked by fits and starts, but Jim and Ambrose would not admit that he worked at all. They were unjust ; they did not understand him.

And had Robert really been to see the woman at Wellford in the morning ? Louisa was not jealous now, not bitter—all that was over, but she was humiliated. She and Robert were getting old ; surely it was time to be decent and settled ? Poor Kate Barlow, she thought with another leap of the mind ! The victim of just such another pleasant rake as Robert. There seemed to have been several of them about at one time ; as if it had been the fashion for men to be like that.

She put on her maroon dressing-gown and went to the bathroom ; but Jim called out that he was inside, and when she went back later, Charles was there, and later still Laura. She made these patient journeys as she had done for years ; in the intervals, she took off her ' switch ', a piece of false hair she wore coiled on the crown of her head, and put it away in a drawer ; she knelt down by the bed and said her prayers. She tried the bathroom door again, but Thomas had got there before her. And Robert was coming upstairs now and must not be kept waiting for his turn. Louisa reflected, with good humour, that it was quite like old times.

CHAPTER TWO

I

WHEN Christmas Day was past, the family tide, which had then been at the full, began to recede from Greenbanks. Thomas took his wife and child back to Birmingham ; Rose withdrew with her husband and sons to Sydenham Hill. The table in the dining-room shrank to accommodate only Robert and Louisa, Jim, Charles and Laura ; and Greenbanks returned to the normal.

Robert spent his evenings at the club and elsewhere. Jim was a mere lodger, coming in and going out, and that was all. Louisa knew nothing about him. She spoke to him in an apologetic voice. She saw to his erratic meals, darned his socks, asked no questions, received no information and was frequently staggered to remember that he was her son.

Charles was different. Although he was twenty-six, Louisa lived very close to Charles. Every morning she had to go several times to his room to get him out of bed.

'Time to get up, Charles,' she would say mildly the first time.

'Charles, are you up?' she would inquire more pointedly the second.

At the third visit she would seize his dressing-gown and shake it urgently. 'Now, now, now, get up at once ! Jim has gone. Your father is down. I've run your bath. Come, love, quickly !'

At last he got up and allowed her to help him into his dressing-gown. When he caught sight of himself with ruffled hair and unshaven chin, he sang inquiringly :

'Why was I born so beautiful, why was I born so young ? '

Then he kissed her and padded away to the bathroom, while she went down to keep his breakfast hot, as unobtrusively as possible, so that no one would remark on it.

Charles was of an inventive turn of mind and spent most of his evenings at home, making things : a patent chair no one would sit in because it was too reminiscent of the dentist ; a folding bed he carried out into the garden on warm nights ; a contrivance for turning the gas off and on at the top of the stairs by pressing a button at the bottom. He was so pleased by this idea that he extended it to all the rooms, and after weeks of labour, everyone could now turn the lights off and on from bed or chair.

'Just when we're going to have electricity put in,' commented Jim.

When Charles was not contriving something in the old nursery, whistling and banging in his shirt-sleeves, he was in the drawing-room playing stumblingly on the piano. The marvel of it was, thought Louisa, that with all his persistence thereat, he never became any more proficient. His hands on the keys made her laugh with tender amusement ; they were as stiff and inadequate as a couple of pork chops.

'Now, listen, Mother,' he would call out to her as she sat by the fire with her knitting. ' Listen ! I've got it now.'

He played a few bars in triumph, then ceased abruptly.

'Wait a minute. I'll begin again. Now listen.'

He began again, carried it a little further and stopped once more.

'No, no, wait a minute. That was bad. I'll play it really well this time. Now listen.'

'I'm listening, dear,' said Louisa, giggling into her knitting.

She loved these evenings when she and Charles were together and alone in the drawing-room. She was happy and secure ; something in her that had been kept tight all day from old habit expanded into ease. She felt the relaxation of the mother of a large family when the children are at last in bed. Her children were grown up, but she still kept herself taut during the day to deal with Robert and Jim. Now they were out : the velvet curtains of a faded reseda green were drawn, and the firelight was warm on the carpet whose terra-cotta garlands were almost merged into the silver-green background.

'That was very nice, dear,' Louisa would say, turning her knitting. 'Do play it again.'

Sitting in the drawing-room, listening to Charles blundering about on the piano was not to Laura's taste. She spent a good deal of time in her bedroom in mysterious occupations ; stitching lace and silk together, writing letters perhaps or reading them, probably dreaming. She had begun to appear daily at Letty's house to take Rachel for a walk in the afternoon. Letty asked no questions, being only too glad to be relieved of her daughter. When the boys were on holiday, the small house in Beech Crescent was uncomfortably full.

Rachel went with her young aunt into the Park. She liked best the ducks on the pond, but Laura liked the Italian garden and there they went. Rachel began to understand that when they reached this garden someone called Uncle Cecil would soon appear. When she saw his tall figure approaching down the sanded paths, she rushed towards him and had a few moments swinging on his hand before they reached Laura.

'Run along, darling,' Laura always said, and Rachel ran on in front with reluctance, looking back very often to watch Uncle Cecil bending his head to Auntie Laura, while she looked up at him.

'Run along, darling,' said Auntie Laura, smiling quite kindly all the same.

The Italian garden was rectangular and secluded, with a steep grassy bank crowned with lime trees on one side, and a high hawthorn hedge on the other ; one end was enclosed by an ancient summer house of brick and tile, damp and echoing and rather frightening to Rachel, who ran in at one side and out of the other very fast, just to say to herself that she had done it. At the other end of the garden was a delicate group of birch-trees standing on the grass where the stream was. It was towards this that Rachel ran on a winter afternoon, drawing the lovers after her.

She stepped on to the grass in spite of the notice saying, so she had been told, that she must not. She glanced round to see if they were looking at her, and as they were not, she stole to the edge of the stream and looked into the shallow, tumbling water. She glanced round again, but they were standing under the trees absorbed in each other, so Rachel leaned over and touched the water with her gloved fingers.

'Now that bit of water that I touched,' she said. 'It's gone swirling away. It's probably out of the Park gates by now.'

She looked about for something to throw into the water to see how fast it ran. But there was nothing ; no twig, no leaf at hand, and she was afraid to go in search of any in case she should be noticed and told to come off the grass. She therefore carefully collected saliva in her mouth and spat into the stream. It was very satisfactory. She saw her little bubble whirled away between the stones for several yards.

'It stuck together for quite a long time,' she observed, and looked round to see if Auntie Laura had noticed anything   Auntie Laura seemed to think there was something dreadful about spitting a little into streams.

But Laura was not looking at Rachel. She was looking up into Cecil Bradfield's face, her hand was against his cheek and his arms were round her. Rachel felt strange to see them so, almost as if it were sad. She leaned against a tree and gazed at them. There was a deep yellow light low down in the sky, and the rest of the world was going very dark. Perhaps something was sad, because Laura suddenly wiped her eyes on the handkerchief sticking out of Cecil's pocket. Rachel's lower lip drooped, but all at once, Laura laughed and kissed Cecil again, and called out :

'Come here, darling, and say how d'you do to your new uncle.'

Rachel ran to him.

'Is he a real uncle now ? ' she inquired, clasping his legs.

'Yes, he's a real uncle now,' laughed Laura, clasping his arm.

The lovers kissed each other again, and then they bent to kiss Rachel. Everything was suddenly very happy. They did not tell her to run on in front any more, but let her swing on their hands between them. She loved them both so much that she confessed about spitting into the stream.

'But I won't do it again,' she promised hastily. 'I won't do it again, Auntie Laura.'

Laura had no time to be cross, because Cecil said at once :

'I used to do that—specially on bridges.'

He really was a splendid uncle to have, thought Rachel, leaning backwards and looking up at him with love.

II

After this there was no further need for Laura to take her niece into the Park. Louisa therefore came to Letty's assistance by taking Rachel on visits to Aunt Alice or on shopping expeditions into town.

Aunt Alice was the sister of Robert Ashton and had been a widow for more than thirty years. Rachel did not enjoy the visits to Aunt Alice. The chairs had cold, slippery covers, the blinds were half down and the windows further darkened by curtains falling from above and pot-plants growing up from below. In the gloom, Aunt Alice sat and talked about Mrs. Parsons having had three hats already this winter, or rumours that Mrs. Joicey's girl was turning out very flighty. In the kitchen old Betsey sat by the fire reading a book on dreams through steel spectacles.

Rachel sighed and fidgeted in Aunt Alice's house, until her grandmother said it was time to go and then she recovered her spirits immediately.

Shopping was different. Rachel loved shopping with her grandmother. She liked going to the pork butcher's where everything was so clean ; Mr. Belton in a white coat and a cloth cap, Mrs. Belton in a white coat and a black hat, the floor sanded and the window full of pork that looked as if it had just been scrubbed. On Thursdays, they took the pork out of the window and put a vase of lilies in.

At Gibbs', the grocer's, there was a smell of coffee and spices and Mr. Gibbs leaned on the counter and discussed rheumatism.

At Miss Siddle's, the confectioner's, it was so warm and pleasant you felt you never wanted to come out. On the counter were two trays of toffee, yellow sugar and black treacle, with a little silver hammer waiting to break it up. Miss Siddle always talked so much that you thought she was going to forget to give you a piece of the yellow toffee, but she always remembered in the end.

Louisa enjoyed shopping too. She was, by circumstance, the ideal customer ; she had a full purse and a large family. But she had, by nature, endeared herself much further to the Elton shopkeepers. She had her favourites behind the counters ; besides Mrs. Belton, Mr. Gibbs and Miss Siddle, who were old friends, there was the nice young man at the bacon counter and the poor girl in the wool shop who was always having colds.

One February afternoon, she went, with Rachel by the hand, into the wool shop and found Miss Barton again with a white face and a red nose.

'Miss Barton,' she cried. 'Have you got another cold?'

'Yes, Mrs. Ashton,' admitted Miss Barton with a shamefaced smile.

'But it's serious. You can't go on like this. You'll have no constitution left. Now if I go into the chymist's next door and get a bottle of Cod Liver Oil Emulsion, will you promise to take it?'

'Oh, Mrs. Ashton, I shall be all right.'

'Will you take it?' repeated Louisa firmly.

'Yes, I'll take it, Mrs. Ashton, but I wish you wouldn't . . .'

'Will you be getting me four ounces of that heather mixture I had last week? Yes, that one. Come along, Rachel, we'll just go to the chymist's.'

'Why do you say "chymist", grandma?' inquired Rachel, lowering herself from the chair on to which she had just climbed. 'Mummy says "chemist".'

'Bless me, here's another beginning to pull me up! I say "chymist" because I'm old-fashioned, I suppose.'

'Like humbugs?' asked Rachel, following her to the door.

On the tin at home, it said, so the boys told her: 'Old-fashioned Humbugs.' She tried to make out the points of similarity between humbugs and her grandmother. The problem lasted until the emulsion was bought and presented with instructions, and they were again out in the streets. Then Rachel gave it up abruptly.

'Where are we going now?' she asked.

'I just want to call in King's Place,' said Louisa. 'And then, if you're a very good girl, I might take you to the Mikado Café for tea.'

' I are good,' Rachel assured her earnestly, trotting up King's Place with renewed energy.

It had been a brilliant afternoon, though the sun had now gone. The day was taking on a last significance, marking every cobble in the paved street, every small brick in the old house-walls, throwing into relief the march of iron railings, spiked and black and very cold to the hand, and the two plane trees standing like pagodas, tasselled, against the darkling sky.

The street was empty. Rachel's feet made a light, quick patter, Louisa's hardly any sound at all, because she wore flat shoes and did not nowadays lift them very high. Lights began to show in office windows.

As they advanced, a woman came out of an office a little higher up the street and turned towards them. The revealing light illumined her face. Louisa came to a startled halt.

' Why—Kate ! Kate Barlow ! '

The woman recoiled ; then recovered herself.

' Oh ! . . . Mrs. Ashton,' she said reluctantly.

There was a silence.

' Fancy seeing you after all this time ! ' breathed Louisa, laying a hand on the other's sleeve. ' How are you, my dear ? '

The warm anxiety in her voice made it more than a conventional inquiry, but Kate Barlow chose to treat it as such.

' I'm quite well, thank you, Mrs. Ashton,' she said, smiling faintly and looking down at Rachel while she was being looked at by Louisa.

She looked thin and shabby and somehow old, although she must still be under thirty, thought Louisa.

'Are you here for long, Kate?' she asked, her eyebrows high with distress.

'No, only for the afternoon,' replied Kate, still looking at Rachel, who gaped upwards in return.

'How is Letty? And Laura?' she asked suddenly, as if it had just occurred to her that they existed.

'They are very well,' said Louisa, dismissing them. She didn't want to waste time on them. If she did not make haste, Kate would disappear as she had disappeared before, leaving Louisa full of uncomfortable compassion. But all she could think of to say was :

'This is Letty's little daughter.'

'Oh!' said Kate, smiling in a twisted fashion at Rachel. Rachel did not like the smile and moved out of range behind her grandmother.

'We've thought about you very often, Kate,' said Louisa, trying again. 'In fact, we were only talking about you at Christmas-time.'

Kate smiled again ; her smile implied that she knew what they would be saying about her. Louisa was distressed, as if she had made a blunder.

'I wrote to you two or three times, Kate, but I had no answer.'

'I don't remember hearing from anybody after I left Elton,' said Kate.

'Could you come and have tea at Greenbanks, dear?' plunged Louisa.

'Thank you, but I haven't time. My train goes in twenty minutes.'

'Can't you take a later one?'

'My time is not my own,' Kate reminded her, raising her dark eyes and looking full at Louisa for the first time.

'Could you come again?' asked Louisa.

'I'm afraid not.'

'Are you far away? Where are you?' Louisa was getting desperate.

'I'm in Bradford?'

'What are you doing there, dear?'

'I'm companion to an invalid.'

'Are you happy there, Kate?'

'It's a good place, as places go.'

'Will you give me your address?'

Kate hesitated. A flicker of reluctance passed over her pale, closed face.

'9, Victoria Terrace,' she said at last.

'9, Victoria Terrace,' repeated Louisa, very relieved to have got that much out of her. 'And now shall we walk towards the station with you?'

Kate hesitated again. Louisa realized that she thought she would escape notice more easily if she were alone, and said hurriedly:

'Perhaps we shan't walk fast enough for you—an old woman and a little girl don't go very fast. Good-bye then, Kate.' She took Kate's hand in its cotton glove between both her own. 'And remember,' she said, smiling to make it seem a joke or something light, 'I mothered you to balls and parties in the old days; I'm ready to do the same in any other way now. Good-bye, dear. I wish you'd . . . but never mind, perhaps you think I'm an interfering old thing. But I'm here if you need me, anyway. Good-bye.'

'Good-bye, Mrs. Ashton,' said Kate, moving off at once.

Louisa stood where she was, looking after her. The strange, awkward girl wouldn't allow you to do anything for her, wouldn't allow you to approach her—and she had suffered, you could see. . . .

The lamplighter came up the street, lighting the lamps. Kate's figure passed out of the last custard-yellow effulgence. Louisa sighed and turned away. She noticed that the office out of which Kate had come was Mr. Hind's, the lawyer. She wondered, suddenly, if Philip Symonds had left Kate some money.

'And so he ought,' thought Louisa burningly. 'It's a poor amend, anyway.'

Rachel, who had been very quiet, began to clamour for the Mikado Café and Louisa was obliged to keep her promise and take her there. She sat with lights in her eyes and music in her ears, sadly preoccupied with that last sight of Kate going away under the lamps to continue to be companion to an invalid.

CHAPTER THREE

I

ALTHOUGH Louisa took Rachel off Letty's hands as much as possible, it was not enough. Letty was expecting a baby in December and was depressed about it. She did not want any more children ; four, with twins among them, were enough, she told her mother tearfully. She was fretful, impatient and unfit to cope with Rachel, who was a rover by nature and always getting into the wrong houses and gardens.

So Rachel was sent to a small school chosen, not for the qualifications of its mistress, who indeed had none, but for its proximity to Greenbanks. The Misses Wilson's school was in Elm Street and not more than fifty yards from the gate of Greenbanks.

Every morning now, Rachel was taken in the tramcar by her father. She sat among the business men, clasping a pencil box with a rose on the lid and two pencils inside, her eyes widely on the world, listening to the strange conversations :

' I went out in forty and came home in forty-two —not bad, eh ? '

' Well, I did the ninth in four myself ; a marvellous approach, by George, I wish you'd seen it.'

' I told him. I told him months ago what would happen. I saw it coming.'

Rachel was sure they were all very clever ; they probably knew everything in the world, she felt.

When she left the business men, she went into Elm House school and sat in what had been the front drawing-room, doing pot-hooks under the supervision of Miss Patty, or pushing a needle threaded with wool in and out of a pricked card and seeing, with pride and mystification, a cat emerge from the pricks. When the bell rang at eleven o'clock and the little girls went out into the garden to play, Rachel found it possible to run into Greenbanks and get biscuits from the glass barrel on the dining-room sideboard. She climbed on to a chair to do this, and if Auntie Laura came into the room she complained about the upset and the crumbs, but grandma never minded.

Often in fine mornings, when he was not going round by Wellford, Robert Ashton took Louisa and Rachel with him in the dog-cart when he went into the country to inspect timber or to sell it. The Misses Wilson made no difficulty about allowing Rachel to go ; there was no rigidity in their rules, everything was pleasant and accommodating.

When Rachel received the welcome summons, she would close up her pencil box with joy and emerge at the front door, struggling crookedly into her coat.

' Oh, Grandma, where are we going ? Are we going to where you lived ? Or are we going to where the little bridge is ? '

' I don't know yet, love. Grandpa will tell us. Let me put your hat on.'

' Will you tie a knot in my elacstick, please ? '

Louisa would bend, a stiff figure all of a piece in her mantle and full skirt, to tie yet another knot in the flaccid elastic dangling under the childish chin. Rachel chewed her hat elastic, sometimes audibly. When she ran down the hills in which Elton abounded, she held the elastic between her teeth like a bit and let the hat fly off behind.

Robert Ashton waited at the gate of Greenbanks, handsome in his square bowler hat, discreetly checked suit and yellow driving gloves. Behind him the solid house seemed to breathe with a gentle rise and fall of curtains at open windows. The street was full of sunlight on those days.

Rachel took her place between her grandparents, the plaid rug, which sometimes set up a furious tickle on Rachel's legs, was tucked in, and with a word to Tom, the shining black cob, they were off with a clatter, clatter, clatter over the paving-stones of Elm Street, and a fine free bowling over the wide road that ran out of the town into the country.

Louisa and Robert talked in a desultory fashion ; Louisa often thought they could not have talked at all if Rachel had not been there. Rachel kept a sharp look-out all round : those hens, she felt she could draw them, they were shaped like the quarters of an orange ; a little tree like an umbrella blown wrong side out ; a stile nobody fat could get through. How awful to be stuck in a stile and never, never be able to get out ! A black wood where dragons, witches, toads and all damp, dark things might be, and she flying safely past it with her grandmother ! She chewed her hat elastic delightedly.

When they went round by Titburn village, they called for the butter to save Mrs. Simpson the trouble of bringing it in. They all got down, and Rachel had a piece of currant pasty, a glass of milk and a look into what she and Mrs. Simpson called the ' shipp'n ' but what her father said must be called the cow-shed. Then Mrs. Simpson, a comfortable woman but strangely shaped with a waist under her arms, arranged the yellow boats of butter in a lidded basket, and they climbed back into the dog-cart and went bowling on again.

Rachel always went to midday dinner at Green-banks. She sat on the high stool next to her grand-mother, and ate whatever was put before her, only too glad to escape the carrots and custard and other dreadful mixtures with which Uncle Charles constantly threatened her.

Charles was a tease, but now to Rachel's relief, he mostly teased Laura. He arrived at table with crochet-work draped round his neck, or produced, as a handker-chief, some piece of silk and lace. Laura shrieked at the sight of them and rushed to rescue her precious handiwork. They fell over the furniture and scuffled. Once Laura would have flown into a real passion, but now she was too happy to be cross.

For months Greenbanks had basked in her happiness. She was radiant, lighted up from within. She was always singing under her breath as she went about the house ; even in the streets, her mother could hear Laura singing to herself as they went along to-gether. She included everybody in her happiness : her mother, Charles, Letty, the maids—even Rachel came in for a share of Laura's notice and began, under the treatment, to develop an affection for her young aunt.

Then something went wrong. One night, Cecil Bradfield banged the front door with unusual violence. The next morning, Laura was pale and tight-lipped. She did not sew at her trousseau that day. Louisa watched with anxiety, but dared not inquire. She hoped it was nothing but a lovers' tiff and would be made up that night when Cecil came as usual. But he did not come. Laura spent the evening in the drawing-room with her mother and Charles. She was very lively, teasing Charles about his music and playing it herself. But every time steps crossed the hall, Laura became very still. By half-past ten, her cheeks, so pale in the morning, were blazing. She said good night and went away, singing.

When Cecil came the next night, Laura was out.

The breach became serious so quickly that no one at Greenbanks realized what was happening. Laura, proud, silent, ridiculous, carried it off without a word. Louisa tried a few tentative inquiries, but was met by cold looks and evasions. When anything was wrong, Laura's eyes said plainly : 'Leave me alone ; it's nothing to do with you.' She was hot-headed, stubborn, spoilt, but the prettiest of them all and so endearing when she was happy that everyone loved her.

Rachel was the small and helpless witness of the only sign of distress that Laura gave.

One November afternoon, Laura took Rachel home from Greenbanks by way of the Park and the Italian garden. As they went along by the hawthorn hedge, Rachel saw someone standing under the trees by the stream and called out delightedly : ' Uncle Cecil ! Uncle Cecil ! '

Laura gave one wild look and hurried Rachel up the steps out of the garden.

' Be quiet, be quiet ! ' she said sharply.

' But it's Uncle Cecil,' protested Rachel, pulling backwards. ' See ! It's Uncle Cecil ! '

' You mustn't call him Uncle Cecil,' said Laura, almost running.

'But you said he was a real uncle.' Rachel was
bewildered.

'He isn't. He isn't.'

Rachel craned upwards and saw that she was crying.

'Oh, Auntie Laura, I want him to be a real uncle,'
she said, beginning to whimper herself. 'I love him.'

Laura pressed the back of her free hand to her lips.

'You mustn't love him,' she said. 'Not now. I
don't.'

'But I do,' wailed Rachel loudly. 'I *love* Uncle
Cecil.'

'Oh, don't,' said Laura desperately. 'I can't bear
it. Oh, do be quiet. I'm not cross, darling, but I
can't bear any more. Oh, I must go away. I can't
stand this. I must go away.'

And when Rachel returned to Greenbanks after the
week-end, she was gone ; on a long visit to Rose at
Sydenham Hill. So Rachel went out in the afternoons
with her grandmother. It was winter now and very
cold. Rachel put her hand under her grandmother's
warm velvet mantle and took her by the arm. Ladies
took arms. Rachel wished to be a lady quickly. Her
ambition at this time was to have a pair of stays like
Auntie Laura's with suspenders attached thereto.

II

Letty's baby—a girl—was born two days before
Christmas, but lived only one week. Letty had not
wanted this child, but when it was born she loved it
with passion and fought desperately for its life. When
it died, she let go abruptly and was very ill.

For days, it seemed to her that she had sunk to the
bottom of a deep pool where she might have lain
drowned and at peace if it had not been for the black,

monstrous shadows that passed and re-passed on the
surface of the water overhead. They were the familiar
things of life, but looked at from below, they were
terrifying.

When, without knowing why or how, she emerged
from this nightmare pool and found herself on the bank,
nausea took the place of terror. The familiar things
of life were still there, and she was, she whispered to
herself, so sick of everything.

She lay in the front bedroom of the house in Beech
Crescent and let the days slip away. The fire crackled
softly in the grate, but she could not see it. On the
pale-blue wall facing the bed hung an enlarged photograph of herself in her first ball dress, with a trail of
roses on one shoulder and her hair piled high. The
young smiling Letty of that day gazed ceaselessly at
the sick woman in the bed.

'You didn't think you'd come to this, did you?'
asked Letty. 'You weren't going to live a life at all
like this, were you? No. Well, you see you've got to.'

She spoke vindictively to the portrait as if it were
getting its deserts.

When Ambrose came to exhort her to make an effort
at recovery, she drew up the sheet to keep out the
smell of his tweed suit, and wished she could close
her ears to the sound of his voice. She lay mute, not
looking at him. When he went away, she wept weakly,
not lifting her hand to wipe away the tears, but letting
them trickle down each temple to the pillow, which
they made damp and uncomfortable. She didn't like
him to be there, but when he was not, she felt he ought
to be ; at least *someone* ought to be there, *someone* ought
to help her. This unwarrantable assumption still
persisted in Letty.

Except Rachel, who was out of sight at Greenbanks, her children had at present no charm for her. When Jenny called Dick and the eldest son of the house called back : ' I can't come, I'm engaged,' it didn't sound amusing to the listening Letty, it sounded pompous. She noticed too that he had a habit of beginning a sentence with : ' By the way . . .' If no one noticed him he began again : ' I said by the way . . .' Was it an echo of his father ?

She felt she could never again cope with her family ; all those corrections, holes in socks, everlasting meals, colds in the head, tidying up, tarnished silver . . . and if she started having another baby she would go mad. . . .

' Is there something wrong with me ? ' she asked in alarm. ' This is no more than other women have to put up with. Why don't I like housekeeping ? '

She thought of her mother who loved it, who snatched opportunities from every season : seville oranges for marmalade in January, strawberry, raspberry, plum as they appeared ; who hailed the first spring cabbage with delight and presented early garden peas in triumph to her family ; who used up unripe tomatoes in chutney and excess of mint in jelly for the winter mutton ; who always had a pot of this or that to give to friends when they called.

And her mother, Letty knew, always washed Charles's socks herself out of very love. Other socks could be done by the maids in the wash-house, but Charles's socks were done secretly in the bathroom and their drying supervised by Louisa, who frequently went to turn them and pull out the toes so that they should be just right for her boy.

' Why can't I be like that ? ' Letty asked herself.

Her mother lived for and through other people, but Letty wanted something for herself. That was it, she decided ; and she couldn't help it, either.

'When are you going to get up, love ? ' inquired Louisa, who called round every day with Rachel.

'I don't know,' said Letty. 'I'm in no hurry to begin things again. I'd rather lie here and let them pass over my head.'

'That's because you're so weak. If you'd take your food properly you'd feel different.'

'I'd like to go right away and stay by myself somewhere. I don't know where—in a little town hanging over the sea,' mused Letty, thinking of the posters she had seen at the station, 'or a lake. Where there would be people going up and down, but I would be by myself. I'd like that.'

'Would you, love ? ' said Louisa.

Letty turned her eyes from the wan sky and smiled. Her mother never said much, but the tones of her voice, the expressions of her face were infinitely comforting. Letty's misery lifted a little.

'You need a change of air,' said Louisa.

Perhaps Letty had something of her father in her. Perhaps she was restless and wanted an expedition of some kind. Robert was always making expeditions ; to Paris, to Italy, to London, and if he could not get as far as that, to the Isle of Man, to Windermere, even to Blackpool. Louisa had once longed to go on these expeditions too, but it always happened that she had just had, or was just going to have Thomas, Jim, Rose, Letty, Laura, Charles, or the two other babies who had died. And now the wish to travel had left her ; she was rooted at Greenbanks.

'Perhaps Ambrose would take you to Southport for

a little. It's nice and mild there at this time of the year. Shall I suggest it?' she asked.

But perhaps Letty was not like her father after all. She at once repudiated the idea of going to Southport with Ambrose.

'No, Mother, no. I shall soon be all right.'

And as if to prove it, she sat up for tea for the first time.

III

Letty did not want to go to Southport with Ambrose, but when, in the spring, he suggested that she should go with him to London for two or three days, she accepted with alacrity. Ambrose would have business in London, and London, even with Ambrose, was always London.

Louisa offered to have the three boys with Rachel at Greenbanks. She looked rather frightened as she suggested it. She felt she was getting too old to cope with the boys. On their visits to Greenbanks, she had the air of some gentle puss baited by riotous puppies who meant no harm, but were very disturbing. She thought, however, that it was good for husband and wife to go away together, and had an idea that if she had been able to go away with Robert, he would not have got into such ways. Letty would also see Laura and bring news of her ; she had been away a long time now, and Louisa was anxious.

Letty dispatched her family to Greenbanks and with pleasurable excitement packed the valise for herself and Ambrose. She put in a silk and lace boudoir cap with ear flaps which gave her, when she put it on, the air of a mild Roman legionary. In this cap she hoped to sit up in the hotel bed and drink early-morning tea.

She hoped very much that Ambrose would run to early tea ; it was a shilling, but it made such a difference. Somehow, drinking what she called her ' first cup of tea ', hopes for the day sprang up fresh and strong, and if there were worries she even rather enjoyed them. This mood hardly ever lasted beyond getting out of bed ; but if she had no tea, it seldom came at all.

Letty packed the valise with joint necessaries, but she packed her own capacious handbag for herself. She put into it her secret savings, her knitting, a small packet of raisins that had come as an advertisement, a few almonds from the kitchen as an accompaniment thereto, a map of the Underground Railway and her inseparable companion—a combined corkscrew, knife, gimlet, nail-file and scissors. The contents of this bag, strangely enough, gave Letty a sense of exhilaration. It was very heavy when full, and she was careful to keep it out of Ambrose's way.

It was such a long time since she had been away alone with Ambrose that she felt strange when the train went off with them sitting in opposite corners of the compartment. Ambrose began at once to go through his papers. Letty looked with interest at her fellow-travellers.

There was an anæmic young woman with pale eyes, pale lips, and when she smiled, long pale pink gums. ' She reminds me of veal,' thought Letty. The young woman had a young man, with such thick lenses to his glasses that they gave his face an illuminated look. ' And it isn't really worth it,' thought Letty. In the remaining corner was a woman with a very tame face, in the coat of some very wild animal.

Letty wriggled farther into the corner with the pleasure

these reflections afforded her. When she had finished looking at the people, she looked out of the window at the uglinesses that stretched from Elton to Wigan, Warrington and beyond. Then the train bore her away from these into a country silver with blossom and willow, and white water-crowsfoot on the ponds, silvered sheep and lambs in pale-green fields, powdered with daisies. A sweet pleasure flowed into Letty. The world was lovely, if only you had time to realize it. Lovely—this spring—in spite of everything.

An attendant appeared at the door.

' Anyone for lunch, please ? '

This inquiry was the signal for the occupants of the carriage to look stonily out of the windows, glance malevolently at the attendant or otherwise convey to him that they never, in any circumstances, ate.

All except Ambrose, who said : ' Two first service.'

Letty turned in amazement from her preoccupation with the landscape. How nice of him ! She had not expected it. She smiled at him, but he put on an expression of nonchalance and importance and went on with his papers.

By and by they were summoned to lunch and made their swaying way to the restaurant car. It was pleasant to sit in a corner and go through lunch from soup to cheese and watercress. Letty leaned back between the courses, enjoying the sensation of speed and change, which not only filled her with pleasurable anticipation, but were enjoyable in themselves. Ambrose exchanged opinions on the state of trade with his neighbour. Letty was glad he had someone to talk to.

Talk made Ambrose earnest ; it fired him with a

desire to put the world in order. An opportunity to do this, in a small way, presented itself immediately and he took it without flinching.

The waiter came for payment ; he made out a slip and Ambrose paid. Letty relapsed comfortably again, but Ambrose watched the waiter.

'Excuse me,' he said, leaning across to the woman next to Letty. 'Did he give you a bill ? '

The woman said " No."

'I thought not,' said Ambrose. 'And yet you see it says here that one is to see that a bill is presented for all payments. I've been watching the fellow. Waiter ! ' he called.

Letty looked startled.

'You didn't give this lady a bill, I think,' said Ambrose.

The woman blushed. The waiter, without expression, rapidly made out a bill and as rapidly removed himself.

'Thank you,' said the woman.

Ambrose bowed.

The people at the next table after refusing coffee thought the better of it and took it. The waiter came again for payment.

'He hasn't given bills for that coffee, you see,' said Ambrose, still alert.

'I shouldn't trouble any more, Ambrose,' murmured Letty.

But Ambrose again called the waiter.

'I think it better to give a bill in each case,' he reminded him gently.

The waiter, expressionless as ever, went away. Returning, he laid a little stack of papers before Ambrose.

' You're so keen on bills, sir, perhaps you'd like the lot.'

' Insolent fellow ! ' said Ambrose, preparing to leave the table. ' But I don't mind him. I made him do his duty anyway.'

' You did,' said his neighbour admiringly. ' There ought to be a few more people like you about.'

Letty, by her hot blush as she extricated herself from the reluctant plush, did not appear to agree with him. And back in her compartment once more, neither the people within it nor the landscape without afforded her the same pleasure as before.

IV

Their hotel was in Bloomsbury ; there were Biblical pictures on the staircase and notices in the bedrooms to say no intoxicating liquors would be supplied. The bed-linen was of a strange, thick whiteness ; Letty was sure that clouds of chalky dust would rise when she got into bed. London roared under the windows, but in the public rooms, the people all looked as if they came from the provinces. Letty was disappointed not to see anyone more dashing.

The first night, they went to a play. They sat in the precipitous upper circle, and Ambrose read the *Evening Standard* while waiting for the curtain to go up. Letty looked round. Women in twos, threes and fours enjoying an evening out ; boys and girls in love ; chocolate boxes and best frocks; conversation and laughter. Letty's face was wistful as she observed them. Ambrose was deep in his paper ; strange how he talked when she wanted him to be quiet and was quiet when she wanted him to talk. Perhaps he felt the same about her. Still she couldn't bring herself to say to him : ' Have you ever seen such a face as that woman's, third from the end ? ' which was what she wanted most to say at the moment.

The curtain rose.

As the first act unfolded, Letty became uneasy. Ambrose would never approve of the way the heroine was going on. She was right. During the interval, while other people drank lemonade and ate ices, Ambrose expressed his disapproval.

' Preposterous,' he threw out, looking furiously at the people who remained unmoved around him. ' Monstrous.'

Letty, her eyebrows raised deprecatingly, felt for some time as if it were her fault the girl on the stage had gone to the bad. But during the second interval, she was goaded out of this apologetic attitude.

' But, Ambrose, the young man hasn't been much better. He admits that, doesn't he ? And if there are no children, I can't see that it is worse for her than it is for him.'

The subject was anonymous between them ; their life together was full of such anonymities.

Ambrose drew back his head in horror.

' Not worse for a woman than a man ! Letty, I'm surprised at you ! More—I'm concerned that my wife and the mother of my children should hold such lax views. Not worse for a woman than a man ! Of course it's worse. Public opinion . . . it has always been punished more severely. . . .' Ambrose spluttered. His views would not come out. He could not lay hands on them. ' Well, anyway,' he said, turning in triumph to Letty, ' take a case in point : Who suffered most, your friend, Kate Barlow—a woman, or Philip Symonds, a man ? '

'Kate, of course, poor girl,' cried Letty, ' and because she had no money. That's why. If she'd had money like a man, she could have kept her baby and gone where no one knew her. It's because she had no money that she's suffered as she has, and money makes a difference to public opinion, I admit.'

Ambrose shied away from the mention of money, which was a source of conflict between himself and Letty.

'When a woman has once taken the downward step, she goes to pieces altogether,' he said sententiously.

'Rubbish,' said Letty hotly. 'Mother saw Kate Barlow last year, and she's not gone to pieces, but is keeping herself as best she can by being companion to an invalid. This girl in the play isn't going to pieces either, you'll see.'

'That's why I say it's a preposterous play,' said Ambrose. 'I'm ashamed to be present at such a play with my wife.'

'Oh, don't worry about me,' said Letty. 'I know all this and more.'

'You know nothing,' said Ambrose severely. 'That's the only redeeming feature of your appalling views. Ignorance. You've lived a sheltered life, thank goodness. But as a wife and a mother, you ought to uphold a strict moral standard whether you understand why or not.'

'Not at a play! Not at a play!' broke in Letty wildly.

She turned from him and pretended to be absorbed in watching the attendant with trays of ices, but really she was saying to herself: 'Oh, I'm tired of all you say. I'm tired even before you begin . . .'

Ambrose went on talking, but she did not listen.

He gave her, more and more frequently, the same flat exhausted feeling she had when she tried to carry a mattress downstairs unaided ; that exasperating feeling of not being able to get hold of the thing properly and of wanting to give up at every step. But of course you couldn't give up ; you couldn't sit down in the middle of the stairs with a great burden like that ; you had to carry it the whole way, until you could put it down somewhere final.

When the curtain went up again, Ambrose pished and pshawed audibly, until a woman in front asked him to be quiet. Letty was both indignant with the woman and furious with Ambrose. Her enjoyment of the play was ruined.

As they came out of the theatre, Ambrose saw their bus approaching and hurried Letty into it. She would have liked to walk about a little among the lights and the crowds, but Ambrose would not have seen any sense in that and she dared not suggest it.

She felt happier when she heard him order early tea, and got out her boudoir cap to be ready. She knelt on the bed to say her prayers, because she did not fancy the carpet. Ambrose gazed at her in a puzzled fashion, but she did not explain.

' Good night,' she said, laying her head on the chalky pillow.

' Good night,' replied Ambrose, following suit.

v

Ambrose's appointment was not until two-thirty the following day. He therefore accompanied Letty in the morning. They walked about Regent Street, Oxford Street, Bond Street and Piccadilly, but without pausing to look in the shop windows, except the silver-

smiths in which Ambrose was interested. The most
tantalizing bargains kept occurring to Letty's eyes :
a sweet, cheap little frock for Rachel, and a marvellous
line of sandshoes for the boys at half the price she had
to pay in Elton. If only Ambrose would see that he
could save by spending a little money in advance !
But she knew he would not ; his budget rules were
rigid. She repressed the bargain-hunting fervour and
followed him wherever he led. But what a waste of
good shop windows and places where you could have
coffee and a rest ! If only she had been with someone
else, or even by herself !

' You must lie down and rest this afternoon while
I am out,' said Ambrose, when they had partaken of
mutton and boiled potatoes in the deserted dining-
room of the hotel.

' I'm not so tired now,' said Letty.

' No, but you ought to take care of yourself. Go
upstairs and lie down,' he urged.

' I'll see.' Letty would not commit herself.

' You'll have a late night to-night with Rose and
Laura and Perry. Who's the man they're bringing
with them ? Have you heard of him before ? '

' No.'

Rose had suggested a meeting in London. It was such
a long way out to Sydenham Hill, she said. Rose, Letty
knew, did not like to put herself out by entertaining.

' Well, I should go and lie down,' said Ambrose
again. ' They'll think I don't look after you if they
see you looking so tired.'

' We've done a good deal of walking this morning,'
Letty reminded him.

' Yes, quite enough for one day. You go and rest.
I must be off.'

She watched him through the swing doors, and gave him five minutes to get out of the way. Then, in spite of her aching feet, she escaped into the streets like a child coming out of school. She was almost unrecognizable as the woman who had walked about with Ambrose. Her face was alert and happy. She had a conversation with the conductor of the bus she boarded and got off feeling he was a nice man. When she collided with people on the pavement, which she frequently did from trying to look at everything at once, she smiled in such a friendly fashion as she apologized that they were constrained to smile back.

She had a lovely time buying the frock for Rachel, a patent pen for Dick, a game each for the twins, a scarf for her mother and for herself a pair of folding slippers for future travels. Letty was always looking forward to going away.

Then she went into a tea-shop. It was not a very smart place ; it was frequented by women whose noses went red when they drank hot tea ; they sipped pensively and wore grey, brown and black clothes. Letty reflected that she probably looked like that too.

' Never mind,' she said, smiling to herself, as she wrapped her handkerchief round the metal handle before pouring out from the tea-pot.

At eight o'clock she accompanied Ambrose to the restaurant designated by Rose for the meeting. Rose said you were always sure of some fun at this place. The music was loud, the lights were strong, the decorations unbelievable and the food vivid. Letty sat happily down in the lounge to wait for her sisters. They came at last ; Rose looking self-satisfied as usual, Laura lovely in a new little folded hat talking

with great animation to a prosperous-looking man
with a florid complexion.

'Has she forgotten Cecil Bradfield already?' Letty
wondered as she hurried towards them. 'Well, Rose
. . . well, Laura . . . !

Kisses were exchanged under the shadow of a giant
palm, Rose a little ashamed of kissing in public,
Letty unaware that there was anything to be ashamed
of, Laura hoping Letty's embrace had not disarranged
her face.

The prosperous-looking man was introduced as Mr.
George Boyd. His plump hand enveloped Letty's like
a soft, warm bun. But she could see he was very good-
natured and admired Laura extremely. Ambrose took
to him at once.

'When are you coming home, Laura?' Letty
inquired when they were seated in the crowded
dining-room.

'Oh, I don't know,' said Laura indifferently.
'There's nothing to come home for, is there? Mother
is all right, I suppose.'

Letty said she was.

'You must be having a good time here,' she said
half enviously to Laura.

'We go about a lot,' admitted Laura. 'George
has a car and he believes in a good time.'

Letty noticed that she called him 'George'. So
did Rose and Perry; they flattered him, too, and
gave him most of their attention. He seemed to be
paying for the dinner and Letty was relieved, because
she thought it was going to be expensive.

Mr. Boyd lived in Nottingham, it appeared, but
came a great deal to London on business. He was
a very amiable man, Letty could tell, because he

listened to Ambrose's conversation when she knew he would rather have been paying attention to Laura.

They had a hearty evening, with plenty of food, wine, noise, light and colour.

'You must let me dine you better than this,' said George, 'when we are all here together again.'

He looked significantly at Laura, who smiled in a way that might have meant anything.

'But this is a good place, George,' said Rose. 'They do you very well, I always think.'

'We know better places, don't we, Laura?' he said, turning on her his adoring, but rather congested, blue eyes.

They had evidently been going about together. Letty looked closely at her sister to see if she could gather anything from her face, but she could not.

'I hope to improve our acquaintance,' said Mr. Boyd, pressing Letty's hand on parting.

'What shall I say to mother about your coming home?' Letty asked Laura.

Rose nudged her warningly.

'Don't hurry her,' she whispered. 'Leave her alone.'

Ambrose was so pleased with the evening that, after seeing the others go away in George's car, he actually took a taxi back to the hotel.

CHAPTER FOUR

I

RACHEL was at Greenbanks 'keeping grandma company' as Louisa put it, when Laura came home at last from her long visit to Rose. She arrived unannounced one June afternoon, and made Rachel as shy as if she were a stranger. Even when she had taken off her fashionable hat, Rachel did not feel any more comfortable, and all during tea, she noticed that her aunt was different, that she looked round at everything as if it were not worth looking at. Rachel kept quiet because she realized that Auntie Laura was now more apt than ever to be cross.

' Has she been here long ? ' inquired Laura in her new voice.

' Two days,' replied Louisa with a smile to Rachel.

' I suppose there's nothing to prevent her going home to-morrow,' remarked Laura.

Rachel gulped a little into her weak tea. A very heavy feeling came over her ; she took a long breath to support it and smiled quickly at her grandmother.

' Please may I leave the table ? ' she asked.

' No more ? ' asked Louisa.

Rachel shook her head vigorously. She tore off her bib and ran out of the room. She went into the drawing-room and grimaced violently at the empty chairs. She always made faces when she tried not to cry.

'Rachel,' called her grandmother. 'Rachel, come and see what I've got.'

Drawing down her lower jaw and looking over the tears that stood in her eyes, Rachel went. In the hall, her grandmother held aloft a box and a pair of scissors. Laura was going up the stairs to unpack.

'What do you think of this?' asked Louisa in her comfortable voice, taking Rachel back into the drawing-room to reveal to her a cardboard doll, a double doll that could stand with its back and front wide apart and be dressed in layers of paper clothes that hung over its shoulders like sandwich boards. The clothes were all to be cut out with scissors.

Rachel shrieked with joy.

'Oh, Grandma, she's called Susie.' She always named her dolls abruptly. 'I must cut out her petticoat straight away. Oh, no—her vest. Her vest goes on first, doesn't it?'

She sat down at once on the floor and began to cut, the tip of her tongue curling round her lips as the scissors curled round the paper vest. She stopped to contemplate Susie with her thick-looking brown hair and pink cheeks, waiting to be dressed. She looked into the box and saw there was a crimson coat and a hat with a blue feather. A deep, rich delight filled her, and she returned to the cutting out of the vest.

Louisa sat with her hands folded across her waist, looking now at the child, now at the garden. The windows were wide open to the summer air. The beech-trees reached upwards with grey limbs to support their great canopies of leaves; on the borders of the lawn Darwin tulips, with lovely curves of stem and leaf, bloomed rose and saffron, heliotrope and dusky red. A thrush tried out his song; a few notes, then a pause, as if he waited for an answer in between.

Charles came in, kissed his mother and went to the piano. He had lately added the first movement of the 'Moonlight Sonata' to his repertory, and the first thing he did on entering the house these days was to go at once to try it over. He was very earnest, looking first at the music and then at the keys before he struck a note. Louisa smiled with tender amusement. He had silenced the thrush, but she would as soon listen to him.

Laura sauntered in from her unpacking, greeted Charles and sat on the end of the couch to gaze at the garden as if she did not see it.

Into this peaceful evening pool, she presently threw a stone.

'Well,' she said, with exaggerated nonchalance, 'I'm engaged.'

'Engaged!' exclaimed Louisa, snatching off her spectacles and staring open-mouthed at her daughter.

Charles turned round on the piano-stool.

'What?' he asked loudly.

Rachel suspended her scissors. To be engaged was evidently startling.

'Do you mean . . . you and Cecil . . .?' faltered Louisa with sudden hope.

'Oh, Mother, don't be absurd,' said Laura, plucking at a frill on her dress.

She would not go on. They remained looking at her. There was a silence in which the thrush was heard again.

'I'm engaged to George Boyd,' said Laura at last. 'I suppose Letty told you about him.'

Charles turned again to the piano and searched his score to find out where he had left off.

'Quick work,' he remarked.

'What do you mean?' asked Laura coldly.

But Charles was launched again on the 'Moonlight Sonata' and could only shrug his shoulders briefly in reply; even that threw him out and he struck several wrong notes.

'Tell me about it, love,' invited Louisa gently. She smoothed her face of all anxiety, in case anxiety should annoy Laura who was now so easily annoyed.

'There's nothing much to tell,' said Laura flatly. 'He'll come to see you when I tell him to.'

'You haven't known him very long, dear,' said Louisa gravely.

Laura was mute. Her face closed, her grey eyes— her father's eyes—looked coldly at her mother. Louisa moved restlessly under them.

'It's all very well,' she said to herself, 'but I've a right to question her about the man she proposes to marry. Of course I have.'

Thus bolstered, she pursued the subject.

'How old is he?'

'I didn't inquire.'

'What is he?'

'He has a hosiery mill.'

'In hosier-ee, in hosier-ee, we shall get socks and stockings free, vests, pants and other woven wear,' sang Charles, playing appropriate chords. Rachel laughed delightedly from the floor.

Laura reddened angrily, but she merely announced that she would probably be married in September and went out of the room.

'The amusing thing is,' said Charles to his mother,

'that she behaves as if it's *our* fault she's marrying this chap instead of Bradfield.'

' Oh,' said Louisa in a choked voice. 'It isn't amusing at all. I must go after her, but I don't know what I shall be able to do.'

She could do nothing with Laura, and was moved to do what was rare with her ; she sought the offices of her husband.

' I'm very worried about Laura, Robert,' she began in the bedroom.

' Why ? ' asked Robert from the adjoining dressing-room, taking off his shoes with his usual energy.

' I don't think she loves this Mr. Boyd,' said Louisa.

' Why has she engaged herself to him then ? ' Robert's voice was brisk and matter of fact.

' I don't know,' faltered Louisa. ' Unless it is to spite Cecil Bradfield.'

' Surely women have got past that,' said Robert, unclicking his collar. ' Personally, I should give her credit for more sense ; but if she hasn't, she deserves all she gets.'

' Couldn't you speak to her, Robert ? ' asked Louisa. ' I've tried, but it's no good. Perhaps if you . . . '

' Good Lord, no ! ' cried Robert. ' I've never talked to any of them about these things. Not in my line at all. I've never set myself up as an example and I can't begin now. But don't worry, Lou. Children will go their own ways. Parents are utterly useless after infancy. We feed and shelter them. That's our part. What theirs is, I have never been able to find out. Where's the girdle of my dressing-gown ? Oh, don't trouble. I've got it.'

With that, he went off to the bathroom, and there was nothing left but for Louisa to say her prayers.

In spite of prayers and arguments, however, George Boyd appeared in due time at Greenbanks. Pleasant, prosperous and ordinary, Louisa judged; forty or thereabouts. Very kind, she was sure, but not the husband for Laura who was so gay and sweet when she was happy and so cold and hard when she was not.

Louisa received George kindly, but with reserve. She held off in the hope that Laura would change her mind and let him go as suddenly as he had come. If the marriage were concluded, Louisa would make the best of George Boyd, but in the meantime she would not make quite the best of him.

George complimented Louisa on the house, the housekeeping, the garden, smoked Robert's best cigars with appreciation, listened without protest to Charles's performance on the piano and did not get in anybody's way. But the only people who welcomed him whole-heartedly into the family were Aunt Alice and Ambrose.

To Aunt Alice, any betrothal was a good one, any husband would do. She gushed and simmered, and had George and Laura into rice biscuits and ginger wine on Sunday morning after church. The ginger wine, which, she assured them, was quite harmless, proved to be nothing of the sort. It had gathered potency in the depths of the dining-room cupboard for years and now that it was out, it worked swiftly, and made Aunt Alice, for what was probably the first time in her life, considerably amusing.

To Ambrose, his prospective brother-in-law was a man after his own heart; he listened. Ambrose's talk was new and sounded very well to George, as they paced the garden together or sat in the rooms where, subtly, the Ashtons now felt excluded and

Ambrose completely at home. Ambrose was somehow reinforced by George, and in the house where hitherto he had hardly been able to get a footing, he was now happy and at ease.

'Laura has done very well for herself,' he said to Letty. 'Boyd is worth fifty of that Bradfield chap. He's a very sound man ; very sound and worth a lot of money, three thousand a year as far as I can make out and the prospects of making more. Laura's a very lucky girl.'

When George's visit came to an end, Ambrose went with Letty to the station to be with his new friend to the last.

'Well, good-bye, old man,' he said in warm farewell. 'September will soon be here.'

September was soon there, and Rachel, in a pink frock with a basket of rosebuds, assisted as bridesmaid at the ceremony of marrying the wrong man. It was just as exciting for her as if it had been the right one.

II

'Another one gone,' wrote Louisa to Kate Barlow in Bradford. 'Another room empty.'

Many letters had passed between the two since the meeting in King's Place. Louisa had expected no reply to her first letter. It had been like sending a message off into the void. She wrote down the Greenbanks news, inquired after Kate, sent her love, posted the letter and turned away. She was determined to keep on sending such letters, even though Kate should never acknowledge them. The girl should not persist in her friendlessness if Louisa could help it.

The determined assaults she planned were, however, unnecessary. Kate replied, proving more responsive by correspondence than she had shown herself in person. Louisa was delighted and wrote again. Kate again replied and the interchange went on. Kate's letters were sympathetic, even friendly. Louisa was highly gratified the first time Kate signed herself ' yours affectionately '.

Every week now, Louisa wrote to Kate, sitting at the leather-topped table that stood between the two west windows in the drawing-room. Inside the old shagreen blotter, members of the family had blotted addresses and tried out spellings from childhood upwards. There were old scribblings by Rose and Letty ; ' C. Bradfield, Esq. ', in Laura's hand and again ' niece, neice ', in Laura's hand ; in Charles's ' profess, proffess, profess ' ; a recent address which, when looked at through the mirror hanging on the wall proved to be : ' Miss Mabel Dawson, Springfield, Elton.'

' Ah,' thought Louisa, deciphering it. When her family did not tell her things, she found them out in these ways.

She wrote to Kate on this blotter, giving the news in her fine, pointed hand, or apologizing when there was no news to give : ' I have no news, dear, or else my brain is a bit quiet.'

Usually, however, her family provided her with plenty of news. There was Laura with her wedding, and her big house in Nottingham where George had lived before his marriage.

' Getting married isn't what it used to be,' wrote Louisa. ' Laura just bought what she wanted and moved in. When I think of all those hand-drawn sheets and pillow-cases we did, and those nightgowns all tucks and fancy stitchings—(I have mine still, they were so substantial) I feel times have changed very much.'

Louisa bemoaned the fact that her children were getting married one by one.

'I fancy Jim is bothering with Mabel Dawson.' ('Bothering with' was a Lancashire term for courtship that would have made Ambrose shudder.) 'Do you remember her? A smart girl with red hair and rather a lot of teeth. Prominent teeth are sometimes rather smart, though I do not know why they should be, do you?'

'Lizzy is engaged to the milkman; a nice match. Even Bella is walking out with the boy who drives Gibbs's van. Everybody seems to be going from this house. I am glad Rachel will be a little girl for a long time yet.'

CHAPTER FIVE

I

RACHEL sat in her place at the table in the front room of the Misses Wilsons' school and waited with impatience. She had a little crooked sum of long division on her slate, but the November morning was as full of sunlight as a glass of golden wine and she felt that her grandfather must surely be going out into the country on such a day and would take her with him.

She looked at the sum on her slate. It diminished like the mouse's tale in *Alice in Wonderland*, but unfortunately it would not dwindle right away ; it would not come out and Rachel was sick of it. She disliked arithmetic at any time, but more than ever on this lovely morning when she longed fiercely to drive into the country. She looked out of the window and sighed. If only Grandma would come now, before she had to bother any further with this sum !

'Rachel, attend to your work, dear,' said gentle Miss Patty from her place at the head of the table.

Rachel bent her head obediently, but lifted it again at once. Was that Tom clattering up the street ? She was sure it was. She knew the smart, light fall of his hooves. Oh, how lovely, how lovely ! She was so excited that she began to hum aloud. The industrious little girls looked up in astonishment and giggled.

'Rachel, Rachel !' admonished Miss Patty.

Rachel blushed, but smiled happily as she bent again over the slate.

'I don't need to mind about this now,' she thought. 'I can put anything down. I don't need to get it out now.'

She made squiggles on her slate; then she put down grotesquely 5 into 17 goes k times and carry j. She laughed into the palm of her hand at this, shrugging up her shoulders delightedly. Grandma would be coming any minute now. Any minute now, Fanny, the maid, would look in at the door to say: 'Please, Miss Patty, Mrs. Ashton for Miss Rachel.'

'Rachel, you must get on with your work,' said Miss Patty in a slightly firmer tone.

Rachel bent again. Oh, bother this sum! She didn't know what else to put on to it. She scrawled 'X.Y.Z.' at the bottom and drew a line. Where was Grandma? She should be here.

Suddenly she sat upright. That was Tom going away again! Yes, it was Tom going away again! They were going without her. They were gone. She went on listening long after the sound of Tom's hooves had died away in Elm Street, her eyes slowly filling with tears. Then disappointment bowed her back and the tears fell on the grotesque sum. After a moment's struggle, she used them to clean the slate, and started, with a heavy heart, all over again.

The morning dragged. Even the prospect of making a real ball to play with from winding wool on to a circle of cardboard did not cheer her. With unusual pessimism, she did not believe Miss Patty when she said it would turn out to be a ball sometime during the lesson in needlework the following week.

When school was at last over, she rushed to get her hat and coat to run to tell Grandma how terribly she had wanted to go driving this morning. But before she could reach the gate, Bella from Greenbanks, looking very queer, stopped her and said she was to go home for dinner to-day, not to Greenbanks.

'Why?' asked Rachel, standing on the path with her red coat crushed under her arm. 'Why have I to go home? I don't want to. Where's Grandma? Did they go driving without me? Haven't they come back?'

'Now, you must let me take you home and be a good girl and don't ask questions,' said Bella, speaking breathlessly. 'Come along quickly. Your grandma didn't go driving to-day, more's the mercy.'

Bella caught sight of Miss Patty's Fanny at the door, and leaving the mystified Rachel on the path, went towards her.

'Eh, the master's been thrown out of his trap this morning—at Wellford. 'E's dead. They're bringing 'im 'ome now. I've got to get 'er out of the way. Isn't it awful?'

Fanny was struck speechless, but Rachel pushed her aside. She had heard.

'What's the matter with Grandpa, Bella? How could he be thrown out of the trap? Tom would never throw him out of the trap. Why, he goes so smoothly—like this.' She moved her hand carefully in a straight line to demonstrate the smoothness of Tom's going.

'Eh, dear . . .' said Bella with a deep look at Fanny.

The maids stood together.

'Eh, and Mrs. Ashton's such a nice lady, isn't she?'

asked Fanny lugubriously. 'She always speaks so nice and affable to me when she comes for 'er.' She nodded towards Rachel who was searching the maids' faces for some inkling as to what had happened. 'And 'im such a 'andsome well-set-up gentleman— although you do 'ear some funny tales, don't you? I mean to say . . .'

Bella nodded her head and moved away.

'Well, we'll 'ear no more tales about 'im now, poor master,' she said. 'I must take 'er 'ome. Eh, isn't it a mess?'

She took a firm hold of Rachel's hand and hurried her to the gate.

'You're pinching my hand,' complained Rachel. All sorts of horrid things were happening this morning. 'Can't I go in and speak to Grandma a minute? Just one minute, Bella?'

'No, you can't. You've to go straight home, and do be a good girl, for goodness' sake. Nobody's got time to bother with you to-day.'

So Rachel, for the first time in her life, had to pass Greenbanks without going in.

II

Louisa went into the bedroom down the three steps where Laura used to sleep to look for the last time at her husband. His body had lain in a ditch, on a bed at the Three Fishes at Wellford, in an ambulance, in a mortuary, but now they had finished with him and he was at peace.

A shot from a spinney bordering the road—it was a lovely day and someone had gone out as usual to kill something—had frightened Tom. The trusty cob had tossed his master and the woman out of the high cart like dolls. Robert was killed outright, but the woman would live.

Downstairs in the shrouded drawing-room, Robert's children were gathered : Thomas, Rose, Letty, Jim, Charles and Laura, and the husbands Ambrose, Perry and George ; all silent, all ashamed because Robert had been killed in the company of the woman from the Three Fishes.

Louisa stood at the foot of the bed, her hand slackly on the cold brass rail. The blind moved slightly in the draught from the open window and sent long slats of sunlight over the dead man. Sparrows twittered cheerfully in the garden, a man pushing a hand-cart along Elm Street called out : ' Any rags, bones ? Any rags, bones, bottles, old jam jars . . . ? '

Louisa looked at Robert. His beard poked even in death as if he still smiled under it. He had smiled like that when he set off to go to Italy, or Spain, or even when he was only going to Wellford. Louisa felt no resentment. In his life he had humiliated her, and the manner of his death was a final humiliation. But she looked at him as if he had been outside her life, as if he had never hurt her, but had been someone charming, gay, happy in his own way and who was now dead before his time.

' My poor boy . . . ' she said, and went to lay her hand briefly on his hair in farewell. It felt thick, living and faintly warm from the sun. She held her breath . . . perhaps he was not dead ? She bent over him. But he was dead. He who loved to be alive was dead. She went away, her face working, to compose herself before going down to the others.

CHAPTER SIX

I

THE funeral was over. Rose went back to London,
and Laura—who dazzled Rachel by her habit
of wearing lilies-of-the-valley pinned into her coat,
their tender leaves bruised by a diamond brooch—
Laura returned to Nottingham with her kind, but
florid, George. All the time she stayed at Greenbanks, Laura had the fantastic idea that Cecil Bradfield would come to the house to say how sorry he was
for the death of her father. But the idea came to
nothing, and Laura went away without a sight of
him.

Tom, the cob, was sold. Rachel wept when she
went to say good-bye to him at the timber-yard. He
stood just as usual, patient in his harness, shaking his
head now and again, and pawing the sets of the yard
as if he were ready to take her for a drive at any
minute. But he had killed his master ; nobody could
forget that, and Jim said a horse-and-trap was no good
to him ; he must have a motor-car.

Robert Ashton's will was the one he had made on
his marriage ; he had not altered it. He left everything to his wife for her lifetime, the capital afterwards
to be divided among her children. There was no
mention of the timber business. Jim was bitter about
that and called Thomas, Ambrose and Charles to a
meeting in the dining-room.

There was a yellow fog outside the windows, the

lights were on in the room. Jim's nostrils were white as he pointed out that the prosperity of the business had for years been due to him.

'Who built the new mill? I did. Who put the band-saw in? I did. Who got the railway contract? I did.'

Who this, who that, and the answer always the same. Charles, at the end of the table, waited for an opportunity to ask who contrived the new conveyor and a few other things, but Jim allowed no opportunity. When Charles realized that Jim was intent on driving one nail home, he sat back in his chair and fiddled with a match-box, turning it over and over, rattling the matches and annoying Ambrose, who tried, by furious glances, to remind Charles that this was business.

Charles saw that there was not going to be a square deal, but he would do nothing about it. He would not expose Jim's little game, but let Jim not imagine that Charles did not know of it.

Thomas was restive; his centre of interest had moved long ago from Greenbanks to Birmingham. If Jim went on much longer, he would miss his train. Ambrose, who loved law and argument, would have deviated, but Jim kept him ruthlessly to the point.

'Who is going to manage this business? That's what has to be settled. I'm not going to waste my time and energy on it unless it's made worth my while. Charles should be the first to admit that he can't manage the place himself.'

'Admitted, admitted,' said Charles from the fire, having deserted both the table and the meeting.

Finally, Jim proposed, and the others agreed, that Jim should manage the business and pay Charles a salary. Jim should also be allowed to buy his mother out by instalments. Thomas managed to carry as his sole point that the whole position should be reconsidered in a year's time, when it could be seen how both Jim and Charles had gone on.

This being agreed upon, Jim's nostrils resumed their normal hue, and Charles, with a strange smile at his brother, went to play the piano in the drawing-room. Thomas rushed for his train to Birmingham.

Left to herself, Louisa wandered about Greenbanks, lost and thrown sadly out of gear. For thirty-seven years, her life had revolved round Robert's needs, Robert's hours of going out and coming in, and although she knew she had never come near the real Robert, any more than he had come near the real Louisa, she greatly missed what she had known of him. Night after night, she woke to listen for his breathing in the dark and lay down again trembling and desolate because she could not hear it ; day after day, at noon and in the evening, she listened for his coming and had nothing to do when he did not come. Because he had met his end in disreputable company, his children did not want to speak about him ; at any rate for the present. There was only Kate Barlow to whom Louisa could tell things in her letters.

Louisa was more than a little bewildered by her situation as sole legatee. She had never had any more to do with money than the receiving of a lump sum weekly from Robert for housekeeping. She had bought her own clothes and the children's, when they were at home, and the bills went in to Robert, who rarely asked questions and as rarely complained.

Letty had also hoped to keep house on this method, or lack of method, but Ambrose would have none of it. From the beginning, he allotted a fixed sum for housekeeping, increasing it as the children grew older, but always insistent that Letty should keep within its limits. When Letty wanted anything that could not come under the head of housekeeping, she saved money for it by pinching her family mildly in several places ; she gave them cheaper meals, made their socks do a little longer, and even, although her husband would have been furious if he had known, sold old clothes to an enormously fat woman who came round once a month. She found all sorts of ways of saving money, and the extra hat, the half-day in Liverpool, the chocolates hidden in the corner of a drawer, the surprise for Rachel, gained in value by being got in the teeth, as it were, of Ambrose. Letty liked to indulge in a little resentment towards Ambrose and at times ventured on caustic remarks about not having a penny of her own in the world.

'But I might have some day,' she said darkly. She knew she was Aunt Alice's favourite niece.

Money had value for Letty, but not for Louisa. Robert had always given her all she wanted ; she spent shrewdly, and to the best advantage, the money that came into her hands. Her face was set firmly against waste and extravagance, but she was vague, even stupid, about the source of her money. The very names of investments, shares, bonds, consols bewildered her. Up to the time of Robert's death, she had never signed a cheque or crossed the threshold of a bank.

It was Ambrose who showed her how to sign a cheque, and explained about passbooks, balances and overdrafts. It was Ambrose who took her on her first visit to the bank. Jim was too busy for her affairs and Charles treated her ignorance as a huge joke. She knew he would tease her at the bank and make her look ridiculous. But she felt she could rely on Ambrose to carry the matter off with due seriousness, and she was right. The visit went off very well, was even pleasurable. She found the interior of the bank very impressive and thought she had never seen such neat young men in her life before.

The municipal offices intimidated her and she was glad when Ambrose undertook to pay the rates. He made out her income tax return as a matter of course.

'You *do* know all about that, I'm sure, Ambrose,' remarked Louisa with ambiguity.

Louisa began to rely on Ambrose and to look to him to answer her questions and solve her problems. Ambrose was pleased. He had a real wish to help her, but he also had a passion for managing other people's affairs. He managed the affairs of the clerks in his office. For instance, when he discovered that Barton had a bedridden mother, Ambrose decided that something must be done.

'You should get your mother into the Workhouse Infirmary, Barton. No use paying for her to be looked after when you could get her looked after for nothing —and looked after much better, too. Pride? You must put pride in your pocket. Pride is too expensive for you, Barton.'

Poor Barton's life became a misery of anticipation of the recurrent question :

'Got your mother into the Workhouse Infirmary yet, Barton ? '

'She doesn't want to go, sir.'

'Doesn't want to go ? But she'd soon get used to

it. Don't you be put off by that, Barton. You get
her in.'

Almost every morning as Barton handed him the
letters he remembered to ask: 'Got your mother
into the Workhouse Infirmary yet?'

At last, Barton, out of flurry and desperation, lied.

'Have you got your mother . . .' began Ambrose
again.

'Yes, sir, yes, sir,' said Barton hurriedly, walking
away. Ambrose walked after him.

'Oh, good,' he said warmly. 'I'm glad to hear
that. When did she go?'

'Oh, a few days ago . . . Tuesday, sir. . . .'

'Good,' said Ambrose again. 'Have you been to
see her yet?'

'No, sir.'

'Not yet? Humph, I'm surprised. Well, you go
up and see that she's comfortable, and if she's not,
tell me. I'll see to it. I'm thinking of going on the
Board of Guardians myself, but in the meantime, I
have influence, Barton. You let me know if there's
anything wrong. In fact,' said Ambrose, thinking it
was a good chance to look over a public institution,
'I might go up and see your mother myself.'

Barton groaned inwardly.

'I should wait a bit, sir. I mean, she'll feel strange
there yet. She'd be put out . . . an important gentleman like you, sir . . . she's not used . . .'

'That's all right, Barton,' said Ambrose genially.
'I'm quite an ordinary chap, really. I'll call round
and see the old lady one of these days.'

The clerks in the outer office wondered why Barton
buried his head under the lid of the correspondence
desk for such a time, and emerged at last with wild

eyes and tight lips. He took his greenish bowler hat from the peg and, without asking permission, went out in the middle of the morning to see about getting his mother into the Workhouse Infirmary.

And now Ambrose had all Robert Ashton's affairs in hand. He pointed out to Louisa that it was unnecessary to continue to employ lawyers when there was a barrister in the family who would do everything free of charge. Robert Ashton's papers were therefore transferred from Messrs. Budd, Watson & Budd to Ambrose, who went into them very thoroughly. He sat in his private office, undoing bundle after bundle of papers, doing them up again, docketing, numbering, making lists, making notes, writing letters to debtors and creditors, and whistling silently through his teeth from pleasure in the work.

His father-in-law's investments were, in Ambrose's opinion, old-fashioned. They could be bettered. Ambrose had always studied the financial columns of his newspaper. He himself had no money to play with. His salary was a good one, but he had three sons to educate. Dick was now ready for a public school, and Ambrose was considering one in the south, where Dick should rid himself of the accent he had acquired, in spite of his father, at the King's School, Elton. Letty said she could not hear the accent and wished her sons to go to hardy, north-country schools, or even to Edinburgh, but Ambrose would not hear of it. They must go south and speak like gentlemen.

But it would cost money and Ambrose knew it. He had a pension to look forward to ; he planned to take it at sixty and settle somewhere south himself, probably Bournemouth. In the meantime he was

stern about expenditure and never allowed himself to
indulge in speculation on the Stock Exchange.

But he had always worked out what he would do
if he had the money and had made considerable fortunes on the backs of envelopes in the evenings.
Here was a chance to use his knowledge and inciden-
tally improve his mother-in-law's income. He suggested one or two things to Louisa, who did not
understand, but told him to do whatever he thought
best. They turned out quite well, and Ambrose was
vastly pleased. He talked finance in the tram in the
mornings, and offered and accepted good tips.

II

Christmas came round again, but Greenbanks was
very quiet. Rose said it was too long and expensive a
journey to take again so soon after October. Thomas's
Margery had measles and they had to stay in Birmingham. Laura wrote to say that as there was evidently
not to be the usual family gathering, she and George
would take the opportunity to go to Switzerland for
the Winter Sports.

The table had hardly to be expanded at all to
accommodate Letty, Ambrose, Dick, David, Roger
and Rachel, and Louisa's heart was sad at the thought
of her scattered children.

'But I can't expect things not to change,' she told
herself. 'And I mustn't make a nuisance of myself.
I mustn't let them think they are obliged to come here.'

She consoled herself by turning Robert's old
dressing-room into a little bedroom for Rachel and
begging her company for the whole of the holidays.

The room had been papered afresh, with a paper
that had small sprigs of flowers on a white ground.

There was a great air of virtue about the mahogany
furniture as if it had belonged to Queen Victoria or
a church, but the curtains were of frilled muslin and
there was a cheerful floral eiderdown over the white
honeycombed quilt, which squeaked slightly when
Rachel crushed it up in her hand as she did several
times before going to sleep. The bed-valances were
edged with pointed crochet-work and the dressing-
table mats had white fringes which Rachel liked to
comb out, although it was hard work and broke
several teeth in the comb. The toilet set was of green
china moss encrusted with tiny glossy rose-buds; there
was a tray for Rachel's brush, a pair of candlesticks
without candles, lidded pots and tidies, and a little
tree—or rather twig—with two abortive branches for
Rachel to hang her rings on if she had possessed any.

Rachel was charmed with everything. This room
established her claim to Greenbanks; she no longer
merely visited but half-lived there. Auntie Laura
would no longer be able to dismiss her by saying she
must go home. Greenbanks was as much her home
as the house in Beech Crescent. She had a bedroom
in both places, and of the two she much preferred the
one at Greenbanks.

Her grandmother found a doll that had belonged
to one of the girls; it had hair done up like a lady
and a purple taffeta dress. You could not play with
it; it was too strange in the face. But Rachel liked
to hold it on her knee and look at it for short periods.
There were also some thin, small books with royal
blue and magenta backs and pictures of children to
match those on the drain-pipe in the drawing-room.
The books had double titles: *Selina's Mistake or Con-
science Knows Best; A Basket of Roses or Always Tell*

The Truth. Rachel could not quite read them, which was a pity because they were improving. But she liked to have them arranged on the bed-table as if she could.

She loved being at Greenbanks, and cried when she had to leave her room for the one in Beech Crescent, whereupon her father said sternly that if that was the result she must not stay there again. Rachel decided not to cry next time she had to go home.

It was some time in February that Louisa began to notice South Africa. She had hardly heard of it since the Boer War, and if ever in the course of years its name happened to occur in conversation she thought vaguely of a picture of a man like a lay-preacher, perhaps Kruger, with a fringe of whiskers round his face, and a tie drawn through a ring over what was probably a dickie ; a man who looked respectable and was dangerous. South Africa had for years been washed, for Louisa, by an ocean of indifference, together with the North Pole and Politics and similar remote places and subjects. But now she began to be aware of South Africa.

Ambrose suddenly spoke of it with enthusiasm ; a colony for gentlemen, he said. Neither Louisa nor Letty paid much attention to him. Then Louisa overheard him say to Jim that he would call at the South African bureau when he was in London the following week.

' Whatever for ? ' wondered Louisa. Ambrose was very kind, but he seemed to have a finger in every possible sort of pie. She wondered what he was fiddling with now.

It was strange how out of what had hitherto been blank, a subject, a name, a word you hadn't heard of for years began to form, to recur, to draw references, developments to itself. Louisa was amused to find this applied to South Africa. When she went to Mrs. Crossley's to tea, Mrs. Crossley read out a letter from a cousin whose daughter had gone out there to be married, and the very next day when Louisa went into town, she saw in Thomas Cook's window a large pear-shaped chart bearing a name in red.

'There's that South Africa again,' remarked Louisa.

One evening in March, South Africa ceased to flutter playfully before her notice and struck at Louisa in grim earnest.

Charles, playing the piano, said suddenly :

'D'you know, I'm thinking of going to South Africa ? '

Louisa's knitting fell with her hands into her lap.

'South Africa ! ' she exclaimed, with the blood rushing in her ears. 'South Africa ! '

'Darling,' laughed Charles, turning round on the piano-stool, 'you speak as if it were hell ! '

Louisa's head trembled, her hands trembled ; she gazed at him with startled eyes.

'Mother ! Mother ! ' protested Charles gently, as if he were trying to waken her from a bad dream.

'South Africa . . .' repeated Louisa. 'Charles, what do you mean ? You shouldn't frighten me with these jokes.'

'It's not a joke, darling. Jim, supported by Ambrose, suggests that I should go to South Africa. He doesn't want me down at the yard, you know. And I'm not sure that I want myself there.'

'Oh, Charles. . . .'

'But why worry, darling ? South Africa is quite a good spot. I don't think I object to going there at all.'

'Oh, Charles, don't speak of it! Don't think of such a thing!' Louisa besought him piteously. She got up and went to him at the piano. 'Why should you go to South Africa when you've got a good home here and a share in the business, whatever Jim may say? I don't know how Jim can think of such a thing—pushing out his own brother. . .! It's that Mabel Dawson, little red-haired thing, turning him against his own people like this. . . .'

'Now, Mother,' laughed Charles, clasping her round the waist with both arms. 'Don't upset yourself like this. I'll have another go at the business, if you like. But don't blame me if it doesn't come off. Jim's determined to get rid of me. But I'll have another go at it, darling.'

She clasped his head close, keeping back her tears.

'Oh, Charles, if you ever left me . . . the others have gone . . . but you . . .'

'All right now, all right,' said Charles. 'Where's that knitting? And you just listen to me play this.'

She returned to her chair and took up her needles. But she was not reassured. South Africa had loomed up to darken all her horizon.

CHAPTER SEVEN

JIM got his way. Charles was to go to South Africa. Louisa's protests, arguments, tears were useless, because Charles himself had no objection to going. Again, as often before in her life, there was nothing to be done.

She set about getting his things ready. Charles ordered his clothes, chose his socks and ties, but his mother collected everything else, making endless journeys to shops and coming in fatigued and heavy-hearted. She filled the trunks with everything she could devise for his comfort, putting in surprises that he would come across months later when he was far away.

She walked about endlessly in his room, opening and shutting drawers absently, or gazing out of the window into the sodden garden where a coal-black Flora bent to look, it seemed, at one snowdrop blooming with miraculous purity among the damp worm-casts.

All her children had left her, she thought; died, married, gone to other places. All but one, now. It was one of life's ironies that the only one left to her should be Jim, the one, she admitted, she could have best done without. They had all gone, but nothing in her life had been like this; this was a rending hole that nothing could fill again.

'I'm an old woman, I shall never get over this,' she thought, pressing her aching side. When she was alone, everything ached ; her side, her throat, her eyes.

She stood by the bed and her fingers arranged the green eiderdown as if he were sleeping under it.

Where would he sleep in South Africa ? What sort of a place would he get into ? Her imagination provided nothing when she called upon it ; it made it so much worse not to be able to imagine where he would lie, where he would live.

She was bitter against Jim and Ambrose. They had put it into Charles's head to go to South Africa ; he would never have thought of it himself. Jim wanted the business, and Ambrose interfered for the sake of interfering ; between them they were pushing Charles out into the wilderness. They had got the family on their side by saying that Charles wouldn't work. All this fuss about work, thought Louisa scornfully. What was work for ? To provide food and shelter, she supposed. But she did that for Charles.

' You can't afford to do it,' said Ambrose. ' There's enough money for you to live quietly at Greenbanks, but no more. Although I hope to improve your income considerably in time. I do my best, although now and again we get a setback. Those Northern Kalgool Silver Mines, for instance, haven't done as well as I expected.'

Louisa was not interested in Silver Mines ; she wanted to know why Charles couldn't stay at home and keep his place in the business.

' Because it isn't fair to the others that he should be carried as a dead-weight. He must be made to earn his living like other people,' said Ambrose.

' Either he gets out or I do,' Jim had said.

Sounds of Charles at the piano generally roused

Louisa from these painful broodings and brought her hurrying to be with him while she could. The time was all too short.

'There'll be no piano there, dear,' she said, hoping that this consideration would make him change his mind ; but Charles had only said cheerfully that he thought he would buy a banjo.

Although he was being sent away because he would not work at home, Charles was to be handsomely treated. His first-class passage was booked, and three hundred pounds paid into the Union of South Africa Bank. Relations and friends hurried forward with parting gifts. Perhaps it was because Charles's plans were so vague that these were various enough to meet every emergency ; a fountain pen, a revolver, a writing-case, a ground-sheet, a patent foot-rule, a shooting-stick, sleeve-links, a folding-stool, binoculars, books and other implements of war and peace.

Charles professed himself highly gratified.

'I didn't realize people were so fond of me,' he said to Jim. 'Or perhaps I shouldn't have been able to tear myself away.'

On the eve of his departure for London, there was a family gathering at Greenbanks. Rose was in Paris with her husband, but sent her best love with a pair of enamelled sleeve-links from the Rue de Castiglione. Laura came from Nottingham, without George. Aunt Alice, inclined to tears, came from Park Row. Letty and Ambrose brought their children.

The boys envied their uncle enormously and begged him to remember them in the matter of stamps and elephants' tusks. They were dumb with delight at the sight of the revolver which, although unloaded, their mother would not allow them to touch.

Everybody was being very nice to Charles ; Aunt Alice smiled whenever she caught his eye. He stood about amiably, longing to play the piano but feeling obliged to give his family his full attention for the last time. Only when Ambrose began a homily of the advantages of a fresh start in a new country did Charles break out into chords until he had finished.

Rachel was engaged in leaning against the Chester-field with her legs pushed out against the carpet, seeing how far she could slip without actually falling, when she became aware of a conversation about herself.

' I'm going to London with Charles,' Louisa announced suddenly.

' Oh, *Mother* ! ' cried Letty.

It had all been settled ; Louisa was to say good-bye to Charles at Elton station with the others. No use harrowing herself by going as far as London, they said.

' I've changed my mind,' said Louisa. ' I shall go to London.'

She would see him as long as she could.

They all looked at her as she sat with her fists on her knees, her mouth set, her foot tapping the floor. She looked back at them, refusing their consideration. This anguish of parting—what did they know of it ! They couldn't help ; they mustn't interfere then.

' I shall go to London,' she repeated.

' You are most unwise,' said Ambrose.

' Mother, don't,' begged Charles.

' I'm going to London,' said Louisa.

' Then someone will have to go with you,' said Laura. ' Shall I ? '

' No, you go back to your husband, Laura. I don't need anyone. Unless—' her eyes lightened suddenly

'—unless Ambrose would let me take Rachel with me ? '

Here Rachel stopped her experimental falling to listen.

Louisa looked hopefully at Ambrose.

She did not need anyone to look after her to-morrow, she needed someone to look after. Charles understood.

' Let Rachel go, Ambrose, there's a good chap.'

Ambrose looked worried. He knew Louisa blamed him for Charles's departure ; he would have liked to oblige her, and re-instate himself.

' But the journey . . .' he objected.

Rachel waited with bated breath, her eyes darting from one to another as they argued. London ! that place low down on the map ; the biggest, blackest dot of all. It was a very important thing to do, to go to London. It would be good to say in school every time the stick pointed to London : ' I've been there, Miss Patty, haven't I ? '

She made her way to her grandmother's knee, but she knew better than to plead or beg while her father was there.

Ambrose, having argued at length, suddenly gave in.

' Very well. She may go.'

Rachel began to skip and hop about the room.

' I'm going to London. Dick, I'm going to London ! You've never been to London ! '

' Come along, Rachel,' said Letty. ' I must take you home. You must have your hair washed.'

Before every event, great or small, Rachel had her hair washed. She did not like having it washed, but she liked the after-part. She liked sitting in her pink dressing-gown on a little stool before the fire, having a piece of parkin and a glass of milk, while her hair changed itself from wet bootlaces to shining rings, both big and little.

Her father, laying aside his newspaper and his paternal dignity, often helped to dry her hair. He brushed it with a little brush and curled it round his fingers, amused by the way it clung and was obedient to his whims. Rachel kept very still for him to do this, and munched her parkin under his elbows.

When Letty watched Ambrose drying Rachel's hair, a sort of warmth stole into her. After all, he was really very good, very kind. . . .

On this occasion, Rachel asked her father about London. He gave her a great deal of information; so much, indeed, that she went to bed in a muddle, not sure whether London stood on the Tower or the Thames, or if Big Ben lived in the Houses of Parliament, or why the King sat on a scone to be crowned, or why London had a tube in its inside like Dennis Thompson when he had appendicitis; but sure, all the same, that London was a place full of strange and marvellous things.

It was all very exciting the next day at the station saying good-bye to the people who had come to say good-bye to Uncle Charles; even the journey was exciting in parts, eating the tempestuous soup and searching for sweet biscuits among the plain.

'When are we coming to London,' she kept asking.

'Soon,' they replied.

And after they had arrived at a dark station and got into a cab, she went on asking : 'When are we coming to London, Grandma ?'

'This is London,' said Louisa.

'No, I mean real proper London,' insisted Rachel. 'This is just streets. I mean London.'

'But this is London, love.'

This went on for some time, but at last Rachel gave it up. It was hopeless to explain to grandma what she meant by London. She gazed out of the cab window with wide eyes and forgot to be disappointed.

'All those lights make a picture ! Do you see ? A baby drinking out of a bottle. Oh, Grandma ! See, wait ! he's going to wink his eye ! Oh, we've gone past ! Couldn't we go back a little way? Oh, look at that man standing up there ? Why is he standing up there ? Is he a dunce? A statue? What is a statue, Grandma ? '

Her chatter never ceased, and Louisa was glad of it. At an hour that would have horrified her father, Rachel went up in a lift to bed. She was bathed in a hotel bathroom by Louisa, who, when someone tried the door, called out from force of habit : 'I won't be a moment.'

Rachel fell asleep within five minutes, and Louisa went down again to Charles. They sat together in the lounge ; their conversation was like the conversation of people on railway stations ; it was as if he were already in the train and she standing by, waiting to see him go.

'You'll remember you've got warm pyjamas if the weather should turn cold.'

'Yes, Mother, I will.'

'You'll post a letter to me at the first opportunity, won't you, love ? '

'Oh, of course.'

'I'll send you the *Elton Times* every week. You'll like to keep up with the news, I daresay.'

'Yes, yes, I shall.'

At last, Louisa said she would go to bed, and Charles gave a sigh of relief and went out.

' Poor mother,' he thought. ' Why does she distress herself so ? '

But the next morning when he actually stood in the train and she on the platform waiting to see him go, he himself felt strange and hollow with pain. He remembered his childhood and how she had always loved him the best. He began to wonder if he would ever see her again ; she was getting old, she might die before he could get back. His casual bearing left him and he clung to her hand over the door, his face as pale and twisted as her own.

Rachel hopped about at their feet, interested in the wheels of the train, in the porters, in the people who were crying, in the great glass roof—but most of all in the splendid packets of chocolate that were being wheeled about.

The agony was long. The train did not move. Louisa's lips ached intolerably. She was determined not to cry, not to upset him. When the train went out, she could give way, but not before. She began to long for the train to go, to get it over, to let her heart break this iron oppression, and yet when the train began to move, she hurried along with it, and Charles had forcibly to tear his hand from hers.

' Oh, Mother, take care . . . let go, darling ! Now, now . . . be brave. I'll soon be home. I'll work hard and get home in five years with a fortune. Or three, perhaps. I'll try for three. Good-bye, Mother darling. Good-bye, Rachel. Take care of Grandma. You'll be a big girl when I come back. Good-bye. . . .'

They waved to him until the train wound its great length away, until nothing was seen but the back of the end carriage, and then not even that.

Rachel took her grandmother's hand to go out of the station. Louisa's face was grey, her lips trembling and awry. Rachel was awed. She did not wail aloud as she had done when Laura cried in the Italian garden. She was older now; the shadow of grief touched her. She walked along beside her grandmother, looking up now and then, but saying nothing.

'Oh, never have any children . . .' said Louisa in a strangled voice, not knowing what she was saying. 'It's better not. You won't suffer then. When they leave you, when your son leaves you . . . well, never mind, love, never mind . . . you don't understand . . .'

CHAPTER EIGHT

A T Greenbanks, where before there was Charles, there was now only Jim. Louisa sat alone with Jim at the shrunken table, whereon the cloth touched the floor all the way round, and her eyes darted about to see that there was nothing to offend Jim's fastidious taste. He had a cold habit of removing anything that displeased him to the sideboard, ringing the bell and leaving the flustered Bella to find out what it was without any help from him. On these occasions, mistress and maid exchanged deep looks that meant : 'We're caught again.'

Jim did not like coloured table-centres, not even the prettiest ones worked by Laura as a girl ; he didn't like flowers in tall vases ; he didn't like old-fashioned high tea, and Louisa had to change her lifelong habits and eat vegetables at night, which did not agree with her. There was, in fact, little that Jim did like ; and Louisa found it more difficult to keep house for this one son than she had done for the whole of her family together.

Louisa was ill at ease alone at Greenbanks with Jim. She felt bitter towards him because he had made Charles go to South Africa, but she also felt awkward in his company. She took herself to task about this. She reminded herself with what passion she had prayed for his life when he had scarlet fever, how she had sponged his burning limbs with vinegar and water ; sponging and praying, sponging and praying all through the night, until his delirium ceased, and he slept and she fainted. God had answered her prayers and saved his life, and now she felt awkward with him at meals.

' It's no good,' she said to herself, weighed upon by the silence of the house that had once been so full of life and movement. ' I must have somebody with me.'

She was sitting alone in the drawing-room on an evening in June. The air borne through the open windows was fragrant with night-scented stock. Louisa had always sown this under the windows in hidden places, and when on summer evenings, a sudden sweet scent drifted across the conversations, she said nothing, but she smiled. This was what she had worked for ; what she had planned in April to come off in June.

But this year, this evening, she did not smile. The fragrance made her sad ; Charles could not smell how sweet it was. Her eyes wandered to the closed piano ; no one had played a note on it since he left four months ago. Louisa sighed. She had nothing now to do for anybody, and she did wish she had someone to take the awkwardness out of being alone with Jim.

Her mind cast about vaguely and then came to a sudden halt.

' Why,' she cried, leaning forward eagerly in her chair. ' I could have Kate ! '

She got up and stood in the middle of the empty room.

' I could have Kate ! if she'll come. Why ever didn't I think of it before ? Well, well . . .'

She hurried, talking to herself, to the writing-table. She took a piece of paper and began at once : ' My dear Kate.' Then she paused. How should she put it ? How persuade Kate to come ?

Should she refer with boldness to the past and say :
' It is probably all forgotten, and if it isn't, what does
it matter ? You and I ought to be able to live happily
at Greenbanks together. I, at any rate, am not an
invalid ! And I shall be so glad to have you . . .'

Something like that she would say, but how about
salary—money ? It was awkward. From that point,
her thoughts reached Ambrose. He had talked a good
deal about the expense of upkeep lately, and urged her
not to consume so much gas. He always said ' consume ' in relation to gas ; and Louisa smiled to
remember that Rachel had inquired if they ate gas at
Greenbanks. Perhaps it would be better to make a
show of asking Ambrose if she could afford a companion, although she was determined to have Kate
whatever Ambrose might say.

She put down her pen. The matter must be settled
at once. In spite of her sixty years, Louisa was as
impetuous as a girl in some things. This was one.
She wanted to consult Ambrose this evening. There
were two ways in which she might do it ; she could
climb the hills to Beech Crescent, or she could speak
to him on the telephone, lately installed on the insist-
ence of Jim. The telephone was quicker, but she
disliked it. When she had to answer it, she spoke in
a voice without expression and could not be beguiled
into giving any information other than that asked for.
Her conversation on the telephone, if she could manage
it, was all hail and farewell. But this evening, so
carried away was she by the idea of getting Kate to
Greenbanks, that she went to the telephone of her own
accord.

After gripping the receiver with blenched fingers for
what seemed to her an unaccountable time, she heard

Ambrose himself saying : ' Hello, hello ' over and over
again with great rapidity and cheerfulness. When she
could manage it, she got in her own ' Hello ' ; not a
very loud one, because she thought it a foolish mode
of address for a woman of her years.

' Who is that ? I said who is that ? ' said Ambrose.

' Silly man, he doesn't give a body time to answer,'
thought Louisa, but replied : ' Mother.'

' Are you there ? ' asked Ambrose, throwing cheerfulness aside and getting cross.

' Mother,' said Louisa again.

' Who ? ' bellowed Ambrose.

' It's Mrs. Ashton,' said Louisa more firmly.

' Oh ! ' said Ambrose, becoming natural. ' It's you,
Mother, is it ? Speak up, will you ? '

' I wanted to see you. Shall I come up ? '

' You want to see me ? No, don't come up. Letty
is just coming down with Rachel ; I'll come with
them. No trouble, I hope ? No trouble with Charles ?
What's he doing all this time in Cape Town ? Spending money . . .'

' Good-bye,' said Louisa, replacing the receiver.

The telephone had its merits, after all ; Ambrose
could be cut off.

It would be twenty minutes before they reached
Greenbanks. Louisa went into the kitchen to see
about something cooling to drink for them ; they would
be thirsty in this warm weather. As soon as she
pushed open the baize door, she knew Bella was talking
about her young man. She always talked about young
men in a loud, high voice with swoops of laughter.
Louisa had often paused apprehensively to wonder if
Bella was drunk ; but it was men, not alcohol, that
went to Bella's head.

When Louisa entered the kitchen, Bella lowered her voice, but she could not give up the conversation.

'I've just been telling Lizzy, 'm, that we broke the news to 'is mother yesterday that we was going to get married,' she said, all smiles and contortions.

'Dear me, Bella, are you going to leave me too?' asked Louisa.

'Oh, not yet, 'm. Not for ever such a long time, but we was just breaking it to 'is mother.'

'And how did she take it?' inquired Louisa.

'"Oh, well," she says : "It's 'is own look out," she says. "It's 'im getting married, not me. 'E's old enough to please 'imself," she says. "It's nothing to do with me." She was very sensible about it,' finished Bella.

Louisa hid a smile as she went into the larder.

'Sensible, but not very hearty,' she said to herself.

Lizzy was a quiet girl, she never got loud about her milkman ; but Louisa liked Bella best for all that.

By the time Louisa had returned to the drawing-room, Ambrose, Letty and Rachel were coming up the steps to the front door. Ambrose struck the steps smartly with his stick as he mounted them ; he wore a grey suit and a panama hat turned up at the back.

'Ambrose is getting stout,' thought Louisa.

Letty had an air of not attending to Ambrose's conversation, but she looked very nice in her saxe-blue dress, her mother thought. Rachel glowed like a wild rose under her best hat ; it was a Leghorn with a wide brim and buttercups round the crown. This hat gave her immense satisfaction, and she always tried not to chew the elastic. As this was rather a strain, she took the hat off and put it on a chair in the drawing-room before she dashed through the windows into the garden.

When she revisited the Greenbanks garden after an interval, no matter how short, she always behaved like a released pit-pony for the first five minutes. Before she had stopped her careering on the lawn, Louisa had broached her subject in the drawing-room.

'Kate Barlow!' cried Letty and Ambrose, unanimous for once in their amazement. Their rounded eyes stared at Louisa.

'Yes, I want Kate Barlow as a companion,' repeated Louisa firmly.

'But, Mother, she would never come,' began Letty.

'That's not the point, Letty,' interrupted Ambrose, from the rug before the empty hearth, on which he took up his position summer and winter alike. 'The point is that she ought not to be asked to come.'

'What do you mean, Ambrose?' inquired Louisa.

'Why should you bring such a woman into this house when there are plenty of deserving, entirely respectable women who would be glad of a home?'

'Kate is my friend,' explained Louisa with the politeness she would have used to a stranger.

'That may be,' conceded Ambrose, 'but is she a fit person to bring into the midst of your family?' He sank his chin into his collar, which was a winged one and could therefore receive it comfortably, and looked gravely at his mother-in-law.

Louisa's face flushed and her thumbs twitched with indignation.

'What harm can poor Kate do to anybody?' she asked. 'What are you making such a to-do about, Ambrose?'

'My dear Mother, I am simply stating a fact. Kate Barlow has put herself outside the pale ; public opinion will keep her there, in spite of your kind, but misguided, efforts to restore her. I think it is a great mistake to bring her here.'

'But if she were a man, I suppose you'd consent to receive her?' asked Letty.

Ambrose frowned. How trying women were when they got on to this subject!

'He would have to cut half his acquaintance if he didn't,' put in Louisa.

Now there were two of them at it! Ambrose looked at Louisa in surprise. She was usually so mild.

'You don't suppose, do you, Ambrose,' went on the goaded Louisa, 'that because women keep quiet they don't know what men do?'

Ambrose almost tottered on the hearthrug. Such plain-speaking on the part of his mother-in-law was astounding, and it was in very bad taste. After all, her husband . . . And he was dead too! He recovered himself and made a slight bow in her direction.

'I hope you will understand, Mother, that I cannot discuss the subject with you. You must say what you like, both of you.'

A puff of fragrance blew in from the night-scented stock, but no one noticed it.

'There is no need to say any more,' said Louisa. 'I wanted to know about the expense of having a companion, that's all.'

'In my opinion, you can't afford a companion as well as two maids,' said Ambrose, folding his lips.

'Very well,' said Louisa. 'When Lizzy gets married next month, I shall not replace her. In the meantime I shall ask Kate Barlow to come as soon as she can.'

Rachel had returned unnoticed to the drawing-room and was listening with interest.

'Is somebody coming, Grandma?' she inquired.

'There now,' cried Ambrose, outraged. 'What will you do when the child finds out? You see, the awkwardness begins at once.'

Rachel scanned her father's face with heightened interest. Letty frowned. How foolish to rouse the child's curiosity!

'Is that all you wanted to consult me about?' asked Ambrose of Louisa.

'Yes,' admitted Louisa, with a shade of apology in her voice.

'In that case, I will now go,' said Ambrose, picking up his hat and stick. 'Put on your hat, Rachel. Letty, are you ready?'

'I haven't told Mother about Laura's invitation for next week,' said Letty, hoping he would not make a fuss about her remaining behind a little longer.

'Will it take long?'

'Well, it will rather. . . .'

'Very well, I won't wait. Come along, Rachel.'

'Can't I stay till Mummy comes?' ventured Rachel.

'No,' said her father.

He liked company, especially when he was annoyed, and Louisa had annoyed him considerably.

CHAPTER NINE

LAURA'S invitation had come at an awkward time for Letty. Her private funds were low, and she had not, she declared, a rag to wear.

'I'm sure you always look very nice, love,' said Louisa soothingly.

'Laura has such grand friends and dinner at night,' said Letty anxiously. But nobody seemed to mind about this as much as she did.

Aunt Alice offered her amethyst pendant and earrings, which was kind, but not such a solution of Letty's difficulties as a small cheque would have been.

She counted her secret hoard, and looked about to see if she could possibly contrive something out of the housekeeping money. If she could keep out of Gibbs', the grocers, she needn't pay the bills until she got back. She usually paid every week, and Gibbs would think it strange if she went in and did not pay ; but Jenny should go in with the orders.

And between now and going away, she would provide cheap suppers : grilled herrings, eggs, stewed tripe —the doctor said people didn't eat enough tripe. And she could make brawn with cowheel and shin of beef ; she could even leave the hard-boiled egg out of that ; it only improved the appearance, it didn't really make the brawn any better. That disposed of suppers, then. For dinners : hot-pot ; although it was rather warm weather for hot-pot and Ambrose might complain ;

well, he must complain for once, she could always apologize ; besides, he should give her some money for herself ; it was his own fault if he got hot-pot in June. Hot-pot, then, and ox-tail, mutton and rice—all those nice cheap things and she might manage.

She managed. And the visit was delayed until Miss Poole had time to make up a piece of white satin into a blouse.

'Rather more elaborate than usual,' said Letty happily to her mother. 'A pointed yoke of double net and a net frill round the top of the boned collar, and full sleeves down to there with a long tight cuff.' Letty's hands flew about demonstrating. 'And little blue bows set alternately with tiny crystal buttons all down the front and down the sleeves.'

'Oh, Mummy,' breathed Rachel. White satin and blue bows and crystal buttons ! The blouse sounded like the creation of a fairy instead of Miss Poole who was shaped like an egg-timer and had a black serge heart, stuck with pins, attached to her person.

'It sounds as if it should be a very nice blouse,' said Louisa.

'Yes, doesn't it ?' said Letty with satisfaction. 'Just for very best. And I've got Rachel a muslin frock and a new pink sash. I think we shall do.'

'I'm sure you will,' said Louisa warmly.

At last, after fittings and discussions, the blouse was sent home. Letty allowed Rachel to peep into the box where it lay in all the glory of its shining satin, blue bows, crystal buttons and net frilling, and put the lid on again with care.

'It is so beautifully packed. I shan't disturb it. I shall carry it in the box just like that,' she said.

And with the box in one hand and Rachel by the

other, she travelled to Nottingham to stay with her sister.

Even as her mother and aunt kissed affectionately in the gloom of Victoria Station, Rachel realized that Auntie Laura must now be very rich. She actually wore two gold chain bracelets on each wrist over her fine, soft gloves. Four gold chain bracelets altogether. Rachel herself had only one of very small chain with a heart-shaped padlock, which she was allowed to wear for parties and special occasions. It lay in its case with the pink sash and muslin dress in the trunk the porter was now deftly bowling along the platform. Rachel gave a sudden skip at the thought of it ; perhaps, seeing that Auntie Laura wore four bracelets all at once, she would be allowed to wear hers every day in Nottingham. Nottingham seemed to be that kind of place.

' I'm longing to see your house, Laura,' said Letty, looking eagerly out of the cab window to take in the new place. She loved new places.

But when they arrived at the house in the Park, she was awed by the size ; four storeys behind and seven in front ; and the grandeur : a cupola, towers, a great front door under a Gothic arch and all sorts of windows —bay, oriel, sash, lattice, stained and plain ; and when she entered she was awed by the hall which reminded her somehow of a church, a dental waiting-room and a museum.

Speech left her. She could only say :

' Not here, dear,' when Rachel prepared to throw off her hat and coat on entering as she did at home.

The bedroom, to which they were conducted by a maid with the queer name of Twilley, was a bower of climbing roses ; crimson roses climbed up the white wall-paper and fell back in cascades from the frieze.

The mahogany furniture was inlaid with lovers' knots in yellow ; the dressing-table had three mirrors in it in which Rachel saw herself for the first time in profile and was considerably surprised thereat. The carpet was soft and rosy, and when Rachel stood in the white skin rug on the hearth, she felt she was not going to be able to get out again, so deep and entangling was it.

' Oh, Mummy, isn't it a rich house ? ' she whispered when they were left to themselves.

' It is indeed,' said Letty. ' She's a very lucky girl.'

' Who is ? ' asked Rachel.

' Auntie Laura.'

' But she's not a girl,' protested Rachel.

' Isn't she ? ' inquired Letty absently, hanging up her clothes in the wardrobe. ' I'm glad I had this new blouse made. I think they're going to be rather grand here, darling.'

' Yes,' said Rachel happily. ' I think they are.'

She loved to be talked to in this way by grown-up people.

' I think they are. I think they are,' she repeated in her little pipe. She hopped about until she fell over the skin rug and was sobered.

' Are you going to wear the blouse with the blue bows on, Mummy ? ' she inquired.

' Dear me, no,' said Letty. ' I shall keep that for best occasions. Come along now and wash your hands for tea.'

Laura was waiting for them in the yellow drawing-room. She had changed into a lace dress.

' You are thin, Laura,' remarked Letty. ' Do you think Nottingham agrees with you ? '

' Oh, yes,' said Laura indifferently.

'Is that a tea-gown?' inquired Letty, when Twilley had left the room.

'This? Yes, I suppose so. I put it on so that I shouldn't have to change again. George won't dress when we're alone.'

'It's very pretty,' said Letty admiringly. 'I've heard of a tea-gown, but I've never seen one before. I don't suppose anybody wears them in Elton.'

'Oh, Elton,' said Laura with a laugh. 'No, I suppose not. Well, tell me some news.'

Letty noticed a sudden flush in Laura's cheek and wondered what it meant. She could not know that Laura was hoping her sister would say something about Cecil Bradfield.

'What do you think about Mother asking Kate Barlow to come to Greenbanks?'

Laura's flush faded.

'I suppose Mother needs someone. It might as well be Kate as anyone else.'

'Ambrose doesn't think so,' said Letty with a short laugh.

'Oh, Ambrose,' thought Laura. 'After all, I'm luckier than Letty,' she thought. And as happiness is often comparative, she cheered up and put the thought of Cecil out of her mind with resolution.

Her husband came in, pink in pale grey. He greeted the visitors cheerily, and sank into a deep chair.

'Come and sit on my knee, little 'un,' he grunted, extending a plump hand.

Rachel looked at her mother. Letty smiled, but Rachel understood that she must comply. She went to perch herself on the extreme end of the knee. But this would not do for kind Uncle George. He pulled her down to his shoulder and began to stroke her cheek. She lay very still, looking sideways at her mother.

It was dark in the shadow of the deep chair and Uncle George's chin. There was a smell of the dining-room cupboard at Greenbanks, of decanters and cigars, with an addition of hair-lotion.

Rachel made an attempt to sit up, but Uncle George pressed her head back into place and went on stroking her cheek. He talked to Letty.

' How's your husband ? Nice chap, your husband. I get on very well with him.'

Letty was gratified. She thought it was nice of George to say that. She was inclined to think it was nice of people to do what they did. She had been gratified by Ambrose himself at the beginning. Letty was, by first intention, rather naïve. But by second nature, or experience, she was a little hard.

' Ambrose gets on very well with *you*,' she said happily.

A great sigh rose from the depths of the big chair.

' Mummy.'

' And the old lady is all right ? ' inquired George.

Letty looked blank.

' The old lady at Greenbanks,' amended George.

' Oh,' cried Letty, who had not recognized this description of her mother. ' Oh, yes, she's very well, thank you. She misses Charles terribly, of course.'

' Good thing he went all the same,' said George. ' Never do any good in this country. If you can't make your way in this country, you've got to get out that's all.'

' Mummy,' Rachel tried again to rise, and was again resisted by kind Uncle George.

' How's the other one ? Jim, is it ? Keen eye to

the main chance, hasn't he ? Well, he's none the worse for that.'

' Mummy ! ' Rachel broke away from the shoulder and sat upright with her hair on end and one cheek encrimsoned from contact with Uncle George's prickly coat. ' What time do I go to bed here ? '

' Good gracious, child ! ' cried Letty. ' Are you ill ? '

' No,' said Rachel desperately.

' I've never heard her ask to go to bed in her life before,' said Letty in alarm to Laura.

' Perhaps she's tired,' said Laura.

' Yes, I are tired,' nodded Rachel, relapsing from stress into a diction beneath her seven years.

' Kiss Uncle George good night then,' said her mother.

Rachel plunged hastily in the direction of the dark rich smell and scrambled with relief from Uncle George's knee.

II

Laura managed to talk about Cecil Bradfield after all. The sisters were walking through the Park on their way to town.

' This is a queer place,' Letty said, looking round. ' You feel as if those great front doors ought to open and let out papas in side-whiskers and mammas in pork-pie hats with large families behind them, always on the way to church. It feels as if it has always been Sunday morning in the Park, doesn't it ? The Sunday morning atmosphere is still here but the side-whiskers and pork-pie hats and large families and church-goings have all gone. Poor place ! ' said Letty, amusing herself. ' It's like a large. very imposing frame with

no picture in it! See, the pavements are greenish as
if nobody ever walked on them, and we haven't met a
soul since we came out.'

'I don't particularly want to,' said Laura, faintly
resenting this criticism of the Park.

'Couldn't you have found somewhere a bit gayer
to live?' asked Letty, who privately thought Laura
needed cheering up.

'You have to live in the Park in Nottingham,' said
Laura briefly.

'Oh,' said Letty, admitting the mysterious obligation,
and added, 'Rachel, don't make such a noise.'

'Anyway, it's much better than Elton,' said Laura.

'Oh, it's quite different. But I love Greenbanks
and Elm Street, don't you? You used to anyway,
Laura.'

'I do still,' said Laura, softening, and then said
suddenly, 'Do you ever see Cecil Bradfield these
days?'

'Not often. But sometimes I do. He speaks to
Rachel now and again.'

'Funny,' said Laura with a short laugh. 'I was so
keen on him once, wasn't I?'

'Well, we thought so,' said her sister.

'Oh, I was.'

'I always wondered what happened,' ventured Letty,
and covered her nervousness at this approach to
Laura's secrets by calling out to Rachel not to kick
the toes of her shoes.

'Oh, we quarrelled about that green velvet hat of
mine,' said Laura lightly.

'Laura!' Letty stopped still in the road.

'We did,' laughed Laura, looking into her sister's
face.

'Not about a hat ! Laura, you couldn't break everything off about a hat ! '

'We did,' insisted Laura. 'He said he didn't like
it, and I said he'd get used to it, and he said he wouldn't
try. It was a joke at first, but it got serious. We both
said terrible things,' Laura rolled her gold mesh bag
between her hands. 'I was worse than he was ; you
know what I am. When he tried to make it up, I
wouldn't. But he didn't try often enough. I suppose
I should have given in in the end. . . . Oh, well '—
she turned away suddenly—'it's all over long ago.
Come along. Come along, Letty,' she repeated with
irritation, seeing that Letty stood where she was, her
eyes filling with tears.

What fools women were, Letty was thinking. What
fools, what fools. . . . For pride, for vanity, to be
taken notice of, to escape . . . they marry. She, and
then Laura. *She* could manage, but Laura—younger,
prettier, rasher—how would she . . . ?

'Come along, Letty,' urged Laura. 'You'd better
call Rachel in. We're getting into the traffic now.'

'Rachel,' called Letty, darting forward.

They came to the shops, and Letty's eyes dried.
But it seemed to Laura that they had left Cecil standing
in the Park where they had spoken of him, and that
when she passed that way again, he might be there.
Strange the illusions of love that beset the imagination,
only to dissolve again, leaving the heart sick.

Laura did not mention Cecil's name again to Letty,
and Letty was half glad, because she wanted to enjoy
this visit to the full ; she wanted to make the most of
this delicious holiday. Holidays were rare to Letty.
She did not count as holidays the weeks she spent at
the sea with Ambrose and the children in August.

Those were only what the boarding-houses designated as 'home from home'. She counted as holidays the visits she made, at long intervals, to Rose, and to her sister-in-law, May. She enjoyed those visits immensely, but this was incomparably the best visit she had yet made. The house was so large and fine, there was no noise in it, the food was wonderful—all the things they never had at Beech Crescent, salmon, things in aspic, marvellous spun sugar confections, wines and salted almonds. Letty, who hardly ate at home, speculated with excitement as to what would come to table next.

And George was out most of the time. Letty was glad. It made her uncomfortable when George touched Laura, which he did whenever he passed her ; laid his hand on her neck or clasped her arm with his plump fingers. Letty turned her head quickly so that she should not see the shadow of distaste in Laura's eyes.

But as the days went on, Letty, responding like a cat to the softness of life in Laura's house, began to persuade herself that everything was all right, really. She ventured to express this one day when they were having tea alone in the drawing-room, Rachel having gone with Twilley to look at Mortimer's Hole at the Castle.

' So Madeline Brewster is going to leave her husband ? ' inquired Laura, adjusting the blue bud of flame under the silver kettle. She liked talking about unhappy marriages, she liked to think that there was no happiness to be got out of marriage, that she was really no worse off than anyone else.

' Yes, she's leaving him,' said Letty. ' She says she's not happy with him.' She passed her cup for more tea and added : ' All this talk about happiness ! As long as you get your keep . . .'

To her surprise, Laura burst out laughing. She laughed till she almost cried, while Letty gazed blankly.

'Oh, Letty,' said Laura, wiping her eyes. 'You've got it boiled down to that, have you?'

Letty still looked blank.

'What's the matter?' she said.

'Nothing . . . nothing! Have some more keep— I mean cake. Let's plaster our souls with chocolate cream, darling. It will perhaps hold them together as well as anything else. Shall we go to the pictures to-night?'

'It would be nice,' said Letty demurely. Let them go anywhere, everywhere, Letty was always ready.

She enjoyed the pictures, she enjoyed coming home in a cab, she enjoyed going to bed in the large, soft bed where Rachel slept with her hand on a new doll bought by Laura. She turned off the light, and a faint wash of moonshine illumined the dark. The trees in the Park kept up a slumbrous whisper. Letty lay happily between the cool sheets. She felt renewed, refreshed and hopeful about she didn't know what. This was certainly a wonderful visit.

The next morning, when she went down to breakfast, there was a letter from her mother beside her plate.

'Good gracious,' she exclaimed at the first few lines. 'Kate Barlow is coming to Greenbanks after all! Can you understand it, Laura? Now, would *you*?'

'I'm beginning to think I might do anything,' remarked Laura.

'Well, I wouldn't come back and have everybody digging up my past. Like a lot of dogs they'll be in Elton; all after an old buried bone. Goodness knows

what they'll bring up. Do you want the letter,
Laura ? '

' Yes, pass it over. You remember I'm having a
few people in to dinner to-night, don't you ? I asked
them before I knew you would be here. Just the
Davises and Miss Lindley Pratt and Gerald Hythe.
Very quiet. You won't mind, will you ? '

Letty didn't mind at all. She was delighted. She
enjoyed company when Ambrose was not there.

After breakfast, Laura interviewed her cook and
Letty looked at them both with respect. How she
wished Jenny would address her like this, how she
wished she could speak thus to Jenny ! Ice-pudding !
Rachel heard that too, and had visions of frozen rice
or frosted bread-and-butter pudding, and thought how
delicious !

The sisters went into the town and Letty stood by,
dazzled, while Laura ordered vast quantities of flowers.
Afterwards Letty had her hair waved by Laura's
hairdresser, and then they went home to rest in the
garden for the afternoon.

Towards six, Letty went up to dress, taking Rachel
with her to keep the house quiet. In the bedroom,
Rachel talked incessantly, but Letty was absorbed in
her toilet. She washed in the nice hot water provided
by Twilley, and when she was in the middle of drying
on the soft towels, Twilley reappeared suddenly and
had to be told to wait a moment until Letty could
snatch her dressing-gown.

' You can come in now, Twilley,' she called. ' What
is it ? '

' Can I help you, madam ? '

' Er—no, thank you,' said Letty. ' But I may need
help later. I'll ring, shall I ? '

'Very good, madam.'

'What did she want to help you with, Mummy?'
inquired Rachel.

'Goodness knows,' said Letty. 'I don't.'

She put on her best needlework camisole and the
moiré silk petticoat with the little pleated frill, that
made a charming sound when she walked. She put
on her open-work stockings and her best glacé kid
slippers. She put on the black silk-voile skirt with the
ribbon belt and a rosette at the back, which she hooked
merely temporarily, while she took the white satin
blouse from its box.

'Ooh, Mummy,' gasped Rachel, 'isn't it *beautiful*?'

Letty picked the large rolls of tissue paper out of
the sleeves and let them fall in all their lovely limpness.
She straightened the two dozen bows with careful
fingers, and put the blouse on.

As she gazed admiringly at herself in the mirror, she
thought, suddenly, that here was an opportunity to ask
Twilley for help. It would oblige the girl: besides,
she longed for the glorious blouse to be seen by somebody as quickly as possible. If it hadn't been that she
was afraid she might meet George, she would have run
along to Laura's bedroom at once. Instead, she rang
for Twilley.

'Will you do me up at the back, Twilley, please,'
she said, looking through the mirror to see the effect
of the blouse on Twilley's face. But she could not see;
Twilley bent so low behind her back; and Letty was
obliged to mirror her own satisfaction only.

When the back was hooked, Twilley asked if there
was anything else, and on being told that there was
not, she went away without a word. Letty thought
perhaps she would not like to have such a well-trained

maid ; Jenny was warmer. Jenny would have been as enraptured as her mistress.

'Now dear,' said Letty, talking to Rachel in an absent way.

'Now what?' asked Rachel, who loved to be in at these grown-up performances.

'Now my handkerchief,' said Letty, taking the one with drawn thread corners and scenting it with lavender water. She put it in a fold of her belt. She put a little violet powder on her nose, rubbing it in with what she called a 'shammy leather'. She put on her engagement ring over her wedding ring and stood smiling at her reflection in the triple mirrors. It wasn't often she had the time to dress herself so carefully, but really it was worth it.

'Letty,' said Laura at the door. 'Are you ready?'

Letty turned, with the smile still on her lips, to confront her sister whom she did not immediately recognize. Laura was a miracle of elegance in black chiffon, her lovely shoulders and arms bared. She was, in fact, in evening dress, such as Letty thought you only put on for balls.

The sisters stared at each other, and Rachel stared from one to the other.

'Is that all you have to wear?' asked Laura blankly.

Letty looked down at her satin blouse. Her face gave Rachel a queer bursting feeling that she could hardly bear.

'I thought . . . Miss Poole made it specially,' said Letty, turning away. 'I thought it was nice,' she went on, plucking at the bow on her cuff. 'But I see now. I see it won't do. I'll not come down, dear, don't worry.'

'Oh, don't be absurd,' said Laura crossly. It was

too silly of Letty not to bring an evening dress. She herself had got so far from Elton standards, even in her short married life, that she had not realized she must expressly state that an evening dress was necessary.

'You see I haven't got an evening dress now,' said Letty. 'I don't go to dances any more, and we live quietly, as you know.'

She felt herself explaining to her sister as if she were a stranger.

Rachel had been edging towards her mother, and now reached her. She took her hand, and over it she looked at her aunt. She hated her passionately for hurting her mother, for not liking this beautiful blouse with all these blue bows on. Auntie Laura was a cruel woman, she'd been cruel to Uncle Cecil and now she was cruel to mummy. She hated Auntie Laura and her rich house and longed to get away from them now, this minute, to go home, or to Greenbanks, where everything was comfortable.

'I'll have my dinner on a tray here with Rachel, won't I, Rachel?' said Letty, smiling at her daughter.

'Don't be so tiresome, Letty?' said Laura. 'As if I mind about your blouse really. It was only that it gave me a shock. We always dress when we have people. It never occurred to me to tell you. I didn't mean to be horrid, Letty. It's a very nice blouse.'

'No, it isn't suitable,' said Letty. 'I don't want to disgrace you before your friends. I shall stop up here.'

'Of course you won't. Don't be ridiculous. I must go. Somebody's arriving. Now, Letty, you've to come down at once, or I shall never forgive you.'

Laura hurried out of the room, leaving Rachel

gazing up at her mother. Letty smiled down at her, a funny little smile that Rachel could not understand, but which hurt her. Letty loosed herself from the child's hands and put a little more powder on her nose.

'I suppose I shall have to go down,' she said nervously. 'But I don't want to.'

'Let's go home, Mummy,' urged Rachel. 'Let's run away now this minute.'

'I wish we could,' said Letty, half smiling. 'But you must let Twilley put you to bed, and I must go downstairs.'

'Can we go home to-morrow?' begged Rachel. She was tired of the big house where there was no one to play with.

'We'll see,' said Letty, and went downstairs.

It was a terrible evening. The flowers were exquisite, the wine and the food all that could be wished for, the ice-pudding a miracle of architecture and gastronomy, but Letty felt that her blouse brought all to ruin. Her cheeks burned, and when she lowered her eyes to her plate, she could hardly get them up again. She could find hardly anything to say, and when she said it, it sounded very Lancashire and plain. She got through the hours somehow and when at last the door closed on the guests, Letty escaped up the staircase with a hurried good night to Laura. The only relief she could find for her pent-up feelings was in packing her things there and then and in rehearsing excuses for a sudden termination to the visit.

CHAPTER TEN

I

AFTER her postprandial nap, which she took sitting bolt upright on a chair in the drawing-room because she did not want to sleep too long, Louisa went into the garden to pick flowers for Kate's room. She made a posy, the sort of posy she loved: nasturtiums, candytuft, marigolds, a white anemone here and there, pink larkspur and blue love-in-a-mist, sprigs of cat-mint and blue veronica; pink against blue, white between gold and crimson, the whole fringed with the feathery leaves of bleeding-heart. When it was made, she put it in a short cream-lustre jug and set it on the table by the bed where Laura used to sleep, but which was now for Kate.

She gave a last look round the room; everything was polished, fresh, inviting. Surely Kate would be happy here. She smiled at the glowing posy.

' *You* would take a prize,' she said to it, and went away to get ready to go to the station.

She put on her summer mantle with the silk fringe, and her new chip bonnet with two white roses at one side, and white ribbons as well as black to tie under her chin. Her friend and contemporary, Mrs. Brewster, had lately taken to a hat, but Louisa could not bring herself to follow that example. She had worn a bonnet since she was thirty years of age, and it would be a strange thing, she thought, to go back to a hat at sixty-one.

She smiled with satisfaction as she tied her two bows, the black under the white. She was so glad to have got Kate to come. They were going to live very happily together ; Kate would be like a daughter at Greenbanks, and Louisa would replace, if she could, the mother Kate could barely remember. It was a most happy arrangement. Louisa glowed ; she had not felt so hopeful since the day Charles turned round from the piano and said he was going to South Africa.

She was so glad to get the opportunity to make it up to Kate in some way for what she had suffered. She must have suffered. It was bad enough to be deserted, or denied, by her lover, to be turned out by her father, to be parted from her baby ; bad enough ; but how much worse the slow years, poor and lonely, in other people's houses !

'Poor Kate, poor Kate . . .' said Louisa. 'But now it's all over. All over. She shall see ! '

The moon-faced clock in the hall struck half-past three and Louisa hurried down the stairs. She crossed Bella in the hall.

'Now, Bella, be sure to bring in tea as soon as we get back,' she reminded.

'Yes, 'm,' said Bella.

Bella was glum lately. Her young man was slipping through her fingers. He kept saying his mother came first.

When Bella wanted to be taken to Blackpool on her afternoon off, he said he had to take his mother to the cemetery. All he could say to Bella's indignant protests was : 'Well, my mother comes first.'

Bella wanted to be married in one year, but his mother said he must wait three, and all he could say

again, when Bella upbraided him, was : ' Well, but
my mother comes first.'

' The great soft thing ! ' burst out Bella to Louisa
over the bed-making.

And here was Lizzy, getting married at the month-
end with a white silk dress and all. Bella thought it
was very hard lines.

Louisa reminded her that there was as good fish in
the sea as ever came out of it, but Bella said it wasn't
so easy as it sounded, and refused to be comforted.

' Poor Bella,' said Louisa, as she went down the
steps to the gate. But she smiled ; Kate would be
tickled by Bella.

But would she ? She began to wonder as she went
down Elm Street, under the leafy canopies of trees
hanging over garden walls. She could not remember
that Kate had ever been much tickled by anything.
She had got more excitement than fun out of parties.

Here Louisa saw the tramcar approaching and
hurried to reach it.

She arrived too soon at the station and walked up
and down the platform looking round. It was a
dreary place, with its dirty glass roof laid over white-
tiled walls ; half-way up the white tiles a brown tile
had been set to make a border ; all that labour, thought
Louisa, for such a miserable effect. Mr. Coates, the
station-master, was walking about in a top-hat and
black tail coat ; he looked as if he was waiting for a
funeral, but it was, Louisa knew, his customary garb.
Porters leaned their black-sateened elbows against
trucks and indicators, waiting. It was all waiting on
a station, punctuated by moments of feverish activity.

A signal fell down the line ; the porters moved to
the edge of the platform to be ready for luggage and

discarded newspapers. Louisa began to smile in anticipation of seeing Kate. The train appeared round the curve and, shooting upright its great plume of smoke as it came under the glass roof, drew to a standstill. Doors flew open ; people burst from the train like peas from a full pod. Louisa, her head up like a sea-lion looking for the keeper at the Zoo, scanned the crowd.

She was not tall enough to see over it, and began to hurry about, jostled on all sides. Suppose Kate had not come ! She had been hard enough to persuade and might have changed her mind at the last minute. Louisa's face lost its smile and sharpened with anxiety. The crowd filtered off and Kate was revealed superintending the removal of a small, worn trunk from the luggage-van.

Louisa hurried towards her.

' Well, Kate ! Well, my dear . . .'

Kate turned round from the trunk and Louisa approached to kiss her, but Kate thrust out a cotton-gloved hand and said :

' You shouldn't have troubled to meet me, Mrs. Ashton.'

' Not meet you ! ' cried Louisa, taking the hand. ' What an idea ! I've been looking forward to this for days.'

Kate smiled slightly and turned again to the trunk.

' Now where's that porter ? ' asked Louisa.

' I've arranged for the out-porter to send up my trunk,' said Kate, taking a cardboard suit-case in one hand.

' But we must have a porter for that,' said Louisa.

' Oh, no, I always carry this,' said Kate.

' But I was going to take a cab,' faltered Louisa.

'There's no need for a cab, Mrs. Ashton. You came on the car, didn't you? We can go back on one. This case is no weight at all.'

Kate put herself at once in the position of an employed person saving her employer's money.

Louisa's heart sank a little as they turned to walk down the platform. There had been none of those pleasant exchanges she had planned. Kate had not said she was glad to come : Louisa had not said how glad she was to have her, how she hoped they would be happy together. But perhaps Kate was right to be silent on these points ; perhaps these remarks, though pleasant, would have been premature, thought Louisa. She stole a glance at Kate ; she was just as pale, just as distant as she had been that day in King's Place. And Louisa had expected her to be quite different ; after those letters signed ' Yours affectionately '. There had been warmth, she was sure, in the letters, but there was none apparent in Kate herself.

Then she upbraided herself sharply for her lack of insight. It was an ordeal for Kate to return to Elton ; she was steeling herself to face it. That was it. Louisa hurried to keep abreast of Kate and asked warmly how the journey had been, and if Kate had got away nicely.

Then they sat side by side in the tram, with Kate's case protruding at the entrance so that they could keep an eye upon it. The familiar landmarks of the town hurt Louisa, as they passed, for the memories they must awaken in Kate ; the windows of the Assembly Rooms, unused since the new Town Hall was built, where Kate went to meet Philip Symonds at the Infirmary Ball ; the gates of Philip Symonds's house, empty now since his wife had left the town.

'Oh, dear,' thought Louisa, 'why didn't I insist on a cab?'

She had just realized that the tram would pass the Sycamores itself.

She tried to hurry into conversation, but it was too late. The house was upon them; as dark, as shadowed by the tree as ever. Without looking, Louisa knew that Kate drew in her shoulders at the sight of it.

It was a relief to reach Greenbanks and show Kate to her room.

'Here you are!' she cried, throwing open the door and revealing the posy in all its glowing beauty.

Kate followed her into the room and stood in the middle of it in silence. Louisa gave the counterpane a tug to keep herself in countenance. She had expected Kate to be pleased, and was as disappointed as a child.

Kate laid her bandbag and mackintosh on the bed, then took them up again as if there might be some offence in laying them there.

'Some people don't like you to put things on the counterpane, do they?' she asked with a short laugh.

Louisa realized suddenly that Kate must have been shown into many strange bedrooms in the years she had been employed in other people's houses; a paid companion, she supposed, was probably not expected to praise or criticize the room she was given. Louisa took a step out of herself.

'You must put your things where you like, my dear. This is your room, and I hope you'll be comfortable in it. You must tell me if there's anything missing. See—there's plenty of hanging room in the wardrobe, and these drawers . . .'

She opened and shut them rapidly to show their hospitality to Kate.

'You can arrange your things later this evening, can't you? Come downstairs now.'

'Just as you like, Mrs. Ashton,' said Kate. 'I shan't be a moment taking off my hat.'

'Tea will be ready, you see,' Louisa was worried by Kate's determination to do her duty. 'I'm sure you're ready for a cup. Perhaps you would like to wash your hands while I'm taking off my bonnet.'

As she untied her black and white bows she did not smile as she had smiled when she tied them. Her eyebrows were up; she looked worried.

When she went to take Kate down to tea, she noticed that the posy had been moved from the bed-table and put among the pots on the wash-stand. A book with a red cover had taken its place; Louisa thought at first it might be a Bible, and said to herself that of course she couldn't object to the posy being replaced by a Bible; but on looking closer, she saw that the book was called *Marcus Aurelius*, and then she did feel a little hurt. She thought perhaps she had heard of *Marcus Aurelius* before but wondered if she might be confusing it with *Ben Hur*.

On the dressing-table was a small brush with a silver back and bristles worn almost to the wood. This brush again cancelled out the book; Louisa was touched. All the girls of Kate's age had collected silver for their dressing-tables: Kate had never got any further than the brush. Louisa took Kate's arm in spite of her as they went down the shallow stairs to tea.

'Eh, 'ave you seen 'er?' asked Bella of Lizzy as she returned to the kitchen. 'Well, she's like something brought in by the cat on a wet night! That thin and shabby-looking! And she looks at you so funny; 'er

eyes go right through to your back-bone. I can't see
that the Missus is going to get much fun out of ''er.
She looks as if sitting in the cemetery with 'er tea, or
'aving a bit of gam among t' graves 'ull be all the fun
she can think of. Have you mashed our tea yet?
When the bell rings you can go into the room if you
like and 'ave a look at 'er.'

In the drawing-room among the silver-greens and
muted terra-cottas, Kate in her black frock sat on the
edge of a low chair.

Louisa would have liked to say : ' Won't you lean
back, dear ? ' but it seemed an impertinence to tell
Kate how to sit.

The long windows were open to the garden airs ;
the cakes and scones had been made by Louisa specially for Kate. It should have been very pleasant and
yet, Louisa, her face crumpled, searched for topics of
conversation in vain.

' What are my duties, Mrs. Ashton ? ' asked Kate,
stirring her tea.

Louisa looked guilty. She had not thought of
duties.

' Well, to tell the truth . . .' she stammered. ' Until
Lizzy goes, there won't be much to do. After that we
can arrange the work between us. But there's no
need to worry about that yet ; you must have a good
rest.'

' I don't need a rest. I am very strong ; very strong
indeed,' said Kate, with a peculiar vibration in her
voice.

Louisa drank hastily of her tea. This was most
awkward. It wasn't at all as she had meant it to be.

The door opened and she turned towards it eagerly,
hoping for Letty or Rachel. But Ambrose entered,

looking in, he explained at once, on his way home from the office. He had come, Louisa well knew, to have a look at Kate Barlow.

'How d'you do?' he said very gravely on introduction.

He took tea from Louisa's hand and sat down.

'A beautiful day, is it not?' he said to Kate, looking at her intently.

Why, she was a poor thing, he thought. Not at all what he had expected. Who would have thought she had ever had a passionate affair? Could she ever have been worth a second glance? Her eyes were rather fine certainly; but they had a strange expression, significant, conscious. This woman would not let anyone forget she had a past; she carried it about with her.

He was still observing her, under cover of conversation when she rose abruptly.

'If you will excuse me, Mrs. Ashton, I will go and unpack,' she said.

'Certainly, dear,' said Louisa, secretly tickled that Ambrose should be done out of further observation.

'She seems quiet enough now,' remarked Ambrose when they were alone.

'Of course she's quiet,' said Louisa rather sharply. 'I told you you were wrong in your idea of her. And now you've seen her, perhaps you'll withdraw what you said about Rachel not coming in while Kate is here.'

'Well, now I've seen her . . .' admitted Ambrose rather shamefacedly. He had not meant to go as far as that. 'I don't think she'll do the child any harm. She doesn't look the kind to do harm, does she? Not now, at any rate.'

Five minutes after Ambrose had left Greenbanks, Letty arrived.

'You've just missed Ambrose,' cried Louisa.

'Good,' said Letty absently. 'I mean, it doesn't matter. I've come to see Kate. Where is she?'

'She's unpacking.'

'Shall I go up?'

'No, no, I don't think so. There are all sorts of awkwardnesses we hadn't thought of, love. She seems to want to be treated as a companion here, just as she has been elsewhere. It wouldn't do for you to go rushing up to her bedroom. She might think you were doing it because you thought you'd a right to, or something dreadful like that.'

'Goodness!' said Letty.

'Mmm,' said Louisa dubiously. 'We must go very carefully. I'll go up and tell her you're here.'

Kate came down with Louisa to meet Letty again after a dozen years. They smiled and shook hands and found little to say. In a short time Letty went away.

And then there was Jim. Louisa had hoped that Kate would take off the awkwardness of being with Jim at meals, but she increased it; at any rate, on that first evening. She sat pale and remote, resisting Louisa's efforts to draw her into conversation. Jim spoke little as usual, but Louisa noticed his frequent movements of suppressed irritation.

'They're very slow in the kitchen to-night, aren't they?' he asked frowningly.

'I don't think so,' said Louisa troubled. But she whispered to Bella to hurry. Bella nodded reassuringly and Louisa felt a little supported.

Afterwards in the hall, Jim said in a low annoyed voice:

' I don't know why on earth you brought that woman here, Mother ; making everybody uncomfortable.'

Louisa was upset. She went into the drawing-room and sat opposite Kate, wondering if she had made a mistake after all. Kate seemed as uncomfortable as any of them ; perhaps she hadn't wanted to come, perhaps she had been over-persuaded. . . .

' Have you any sewing you would like to be getting on with ? ' suggested Louisa, after they had made conversation for some time.

' Is there any I can do for you ? ' asked Kate.

' No, thank you ; not yet. But I'll just get my knitting. I knit all Charles's socks. I don't think the socks in South Africa can be very good, you know.'

' I'll get my work then,' said Kate.

She returned to the drawing-room with a piece of embroidery at which Louisa exclaimed aloud.

' Kate, how beautiful ! Did you really do that? Why, it's lovely, dear. I've never seen such work.'

' It's for the Poor Gentlewomen's Guild. I sell it through them,' said Kate.

' Well, it is lovely.' Louisa pored over it through her spectacles. As she did so, it occurred to her that Philip Symonds couldn't have left Kate any money after all.

The evening went better when their hands were employed. Louisa had begun to recover her spirits a little, when the door opened, this time to admit Aunt Alice, in a glittering jet mantle.

' Good evening, Louisa,' said Aunt Alice in a high, put-on voice. ' I just thought I'd walk round. Betsey brought me. And is this Miss Barlow? I don't remember ever to have seen her before ; although I suppose I must have done. How do you do? What lovely work!'

Louisa looked at her sister-in-law without warmth. All these people coming to look at Kate! She was ashamed. Letty might have come out of kindness, but Ambrose and Aunt Alice had come out of sheer curiosity. They should have waited. It was indecent of them.

But Kate had her own way of dealing with them, it seemed.

'If you don't mind, Mrs. Ashton, I think I will go to bed,' she said, receiving her work from Aunt Alice's sallow hands.

'Yes, I should. No doubt you have had a tiring day,' said Louisa. 'Good night, dear.'

'Good night. Good night, Mrs. Taylor,' Kate bowed slightly in the direction of Aunt Alice and went away.

In her own room, she took up the book beside her bed. She had found Marcus Aurelius a good buckler against the slings and arrows of outrageous fortune; she fortified herself with his philosophies when places were difficult, people unpleasant, or she herself more than usually lonely and unhopeful. But strangely enough she sought help also when places were comfortable and people kind. She read a page or two now, and, reinforced, firmly locked up again in herself, she turned out the light and with a long sigh, composed herself to sleep in Laura's bed.

The next morning, while Rachel had her hand in the glass barrel on the sideboard feeling for a ginger biscuit, she turned to find a stranger in the room behind her. She released the biscuits abruptly, her heart leaping among her ribs like a captured fish. It was not only the silent entry of the stranger, there was something in her aspect that startled Rachel.

'It's Mistress Nutter,' she thought wildly, remembering a picture in the Lancashire Witches.

With her eyes fixed on the stranger, she began to edge towards the door, rubbing along the sideboard like a little cat.

'Who are you?' asked the stranger in a low, flat voice.

Rachel came to a standstill.

'Rachel,' she said.

'Rachel Harding?'

Rachel nodded, beginning to move again.

'Then I've seen you before.'

'Oh?' said Rachel, backing precipitately through the door.

'Grandma,' she whispered urgently at the foot of the stairs. 'Grandma!'

'Your grandmother is out.' The stranger had followed her into the hall; her face gleamed palely in the gloom.

'Oh,' said Rachel and fled out of the front door, down the steps out of the gate, down the street, keeping her loose slippers on with an effort.

She pushed through the little girls hopping and skipping on Miss Wilson's back lawn until she reached her special friend, Judy Spence.

'Oh, Judy,' she cried breathlessly. 'I've seen a witch. A witch came into my grandma's dining-room just now when I was getting a biscuit.'

'A witch!' cried Judy.

'Yes, a witch,' said Rachel, panting heavily.

'A witch? A witch?' The little girls gathered round, tossing the word about as if it were a spiked ball no one dared to hold.

'Yes, a witch just like that picture of Mistress Nutter in your book, Judy. You know—the one with the black cloud and the twisted-up tree. Oh, dear, it was awful, and I've got to go back for dinner. Suppose she's still there!'

The little girls shuddered deliciously, but the bell rang and they had to go back into school. Most of them forgot the witch very quickly, but one or two remembered to make awestruck faces at Rachel when they caught her eye, biting a tender underlip or rounding a mouth to make an 'Oooh' of horror. Rachel almost forgot the apparition herself in the excitement of John Gilpin's ride to Edmonton. But when school was over, she prevailed upon Judy Spence to go with her to the door of Greenbanks so that she could make sure her grandmother was there before she ventured in.

Louisa met her on the threshold and led her by the hand into the dining-room. Rachel drew back at the sight of the stranger at the table, but her grandmother urged her forward.

'This is Letty's little girl again. Hasn't she grown? Say how d'you do to Miss Barlow, Rachel.'

Rachel's mouth fell open in amazement. The witch was Miss Barlow, and no witch at all. But when she had to admit it at school, unless they had forgotten all about it, which she hoped they had, she would never be able to make the girls understand that Miss Barlow was just as important as a witch; there was something secret about her; you could tell from the queer voice people put on to speak about her.

So Rachel, in her turn, stared at Kate Barlow.

CHAPTER ELEVEN

KATE continued to be quite unlike her letters. When Lizzy was gone she made herself very busy in the house, going about her work swiftly and quietly, but without heart.

One evening when she was sitting with Louisa in the drawing-room, she let slip that she had never liked being a companion.

'I tried selling cutlery from door to door. I went out sewing by the day, and took sewing in. I bought a knitting machine. But I couldn't keep myself,' said Kate, looking at Louisa with her dark, discomforting eyes. 'This is the only way I can keep myself.'

'Oh,' murmured Louisa, fumbling in embarrassment with her knitting. 'I am very sorry, dear.'

She was very sorry, and also considerably dashed. She had known there would be some preliminary unpleasantnesses; there was, for instance, a great staring the first Sunday morning Kate had accompanied her to St. Anne's Church; in the streets too, many people now came across the road to speak to Louisa about the weather and ended up by speaking about Kate Barlow. Louisa had also heard the washerwoman shouting out Kate's tale above the noise of the running taps to an interested and highly exclamatory Bella. She knew there would be this kind of thing, but she knew it would die down and she hoped then that Kate would be happier at Greenbanks than she could be anywhere else. But she was

afraid now that Kate herself looked at it in a very
different light ; Kate seemed to think she might as
well be unhappy at Greenbanks as anywhere else.

' I think I'll go and write my letter to Charles,'
said Louisa to cheer herself, after this disclosure on
Kate's part.

She rolled up her knitting.

' I've finished the mending,' said Kate. ' Would
you mind if I read for a while, Mrs. Ashton ? '

' Of course not,' said Louisa. ' Why ever do you
think I should mind ? '

' Mrs. Barstow didn't like me to read—unless it
was to her,' said Kate.

' Then please don't compare me with Mrs. Barstow,'
said Louisa firmly. ' I want you to do just as you
like. I've told you so many a time. I shall begin
to get cross if I have to keep saying it.'

Kate smiled faintly and went to get a book from
the dining-room shelves.

Other people's books rarely offered surprises. They
were mostly the same everywhere : standard editions
of Shakespeare, Dickens, Wordsworth, Tennyson,
Scott, Thackeray. Kate would have welcomed a
change, but she did not find it among the Ashtons'
books. Their reading had left no trace on the shelves.
They must have borrowed novels from the Circulating
Library, changing them every three or four days,
thought Kate, taking down *Vanity Fair*, and returning
to the drawing-room.

Louisa was already seated at the writing-table
finishing her letter to Charles. She had received one
from him that morning. The Postmaster General, she
felt, was most kind ; he allowed letters from sons to
arrive on Tuesday, so that mothers could acknow-

ledge, ask and answer questions before despatching their own letters by the mail on Wednesday. This was really, in Louisa's opinion, the only satisfaction at all to be got out of Charles's being in South Africa.

Charles had left Cape Town where he had been for some time in a bank; he did not like banking he said. He was now in Johannesburg, looking round. He thought he might take work on an orange farm.

'The possibility of being able to send you lots of oranges is an inducement. You could put one in the sucking-pig's mouth when it comes to table at Christmas, give all the sour ones to Jim, and throw the rest at the electioneering candidates when next they put up to be shied at in Elton.'

Louisa smiled again at this; she would have liked to read it out to someone and glanced over her spectacles at Kate. But Kate was absorbed in her book and Louisa would not disturb her.

A few minutes later, Letty came into the room.

'I'm not staying, Mother. I'm just on my way to see Aunt Alice. Good evening, Kate.'

'Good evening,' said Kate, laying down her book as if it would not be becoming in her to go on with it while Letty was in the room.

Letty did not like Kate being there, so after listening to the piece about the oranges, she kissed her mother and went on to Aunt Alice's house in Park Row.

Letty knew that Aunt Alice would one day leave her some money and she tried to earn it. She often went to sit in the stuffy little parlour where the incandescent gases hissed softly on each side of the mantelpiece.

'Why don't you have electric light put in, Aunt Alice?' she asked.

' Goodness me,' cried Aunt Alice, ' I wouldn't spend the money on it.'

Letty thought that was very nice of her.

Betsey brought in evening tea and a few small cakes which should have been light and soft, but which were always heavy and hard. Aunt Alice asked Letty every time : ' How much sugar, dear ? ' and when Letty said : ' One piece, please,' put in two to make it better ; so that Letty could hardly drink it. Aunt Alice's intentions were kind, but misguided.

Kate's presence at Greenbanks afforded Aunt Alice a never-failing topic of conversation. She retailed to Letty at length what Mrs. Parsons had said to her ' only yesterday '—as if that made it significant—and what she in return had said to Mrs. Parsons.

' I don't much mind what people say,' said Letty. ' But Greenbanks is spoilt for all of us. Kate is like a death's head at a feast, and it's not as if life is much of a feast even without a death's head, is it ? '

She was feeling low. Ambrose was angry because she had claimed compensation for the hole he had burned by dropping cigarette ash on his trousers.

' D'you mean to say you actually took my trousers down to the Insurance Office ? A woman in your position ? You make me ashamed, Letty. I don't know what you will do next to disgrace me. Have a little dignity, I beg.'

He had gone on for a long time about dignity and the trousers. He made such mountains out of mole-hills, thought Letty. Everyday life with Ambrose had become a succession of mountain ranges.

' And what about Rachel ? ' inquired Aunt Alice. ' How does she like Kate Barlow at Greenbanks ? '

' Oh, she's only a child,' said Letty. ' She goes as much as ever.'

But to Rachel, had they known, it seemed that unpleasant events crowded upon each other. Miss Barlow arrived at Greenbanks, and almost at the same time she herself began ' music '. She had thought it would be very satisfying to play the ' Blue Bells of Scotland ' on the piano and carry her music about in a pig-skin case as Judy Spence did, but nothing in the least like satisfaction resulted from her lessons with Mr. Sellars.

Every Saturday morning, at half-past ten, she presented herself with a thudding heart and hot hands in the front room of Mr. Sellars's house in Pelham Street. Mr. Sellars smelled of beard and tweed and all his ways were sudden and disconcerting, so that nervous pupils shied and started on the piano-stool.

' Is that B Flat ? Is it ? Is it ? Is it ? ' he would shout, prodding the limp sheet with an angry forefinger. ' No ? Did you say no ? Speak up, can't you ? Is it B Flat ? Let's have this much clear at any rate.'

It was not B Flat. Rachel admitted it in a whisper.

The lesson worked up by stages to a crescendo of torture. First there were exercises which were bad enough ; then there were scales which were worse, and then, worst of all, came the ear-tests. Rachel had to get up from the piano stool to give place to Mr. Sellars, who sat himself down and with great violence played ' Do ' and then another note, which Rachel, her back turned, had to guess. She thought this was a game at first, and laughed when she got it wrong. She actually, for the first two or three times, turned round to look what the note was.

' Oh, was it " fa " ? it didn't sound like " fa " at all.'

' Good heavens ! ' cried Mr. Sellars, crashing his
hands down on the keys. ' Do you think I can waste
my time like this ? Turn your back and keep it
turned. These are ear-tests, not eye-tests. I'm not
an optician, I'd have you know, but a musician. Yes,
I teach stupid little girls and train idiots to sing in
choirs and play accompaniments at concerts. I'm a
musician. Go on,' he finished in a flat, bitter voice.
' What's this ? '

' Do ' again and another note after it ; but Rachel
could not often think what it was. Her ears couldn't
hear the notes ; they were waiting for another outburst from Mr. Sellars and never had to wait long.

After what seemed a dreadfully long time, she was
permitted to return to the stool. Her legs trembled
so that she had to take care not to kick the front of
the piano. The storm, she knew, was over, and she
set out, weak with relief, on the voyage of two lines
of ' piece ' which she could always negotiate safely.
Mr. Sellars calmed down and became quite mild
towards the end. But it was no good ; Rachel knew
all would have to be gone through again next Saturday
morning.

She escaped from Mr. Sellars with immense relief
and ran, leaping and skipping, to Greenbanks. Six
days before she had another lesson ! And she need
not begin even to think about it until Wednesday or
Thursday ! The biscuit out of the barrel never tasted
so good as it did on Saturday morning, the garden
never seemed so pleasant, or her grandmother so
comfortable.

But unfortunately Miss Barlow was always there ;
coming into the dining-room when Rachel was getting

the biscuit, or walking round the garden in an old purple velvet hat, or sitting in the same room with her grandmother. Miss Barlow did not speak much to Rachel but sometimes she sent her a dark look as if she did not approve of her.

The summer holiday was drawing near, although Rachel thought it would never come. The prospect of bidding good-bye to Mr. Sellars for eight long weeks and of going to the seaside in Wales was almost unbearably delicious ; Rachel's heart bounded every time she thought of it.

At last, the great trunk was brought down from the attic and the boys and Rachel brought their special treasures and laid them hopefully down beside it. Some were accepted by Letty and some were not ; the boys stuffed the rejects into corners unseen, but Rachel, being without guile, wept.

The twenty-seventh arrived at last.

The bread was stopped, the milk was stopped, the papers too. The blinds were drawn and Jenny was sent off with her basket hamper. Belcher, the out-porter, came with his lorry for their trunks and boxes. The front door was banged and tried again by Ambrose. They were off.

'Do we go the Whittle way or the Bargrave way?' Rachel asked her mother, as they went up the subway.

'What? Oh, the Whittle way,' answered Letty, who was harassed by the getting off.

'The Whittle way,' mused Rachel. 'That way,' she demonstrated to herself, shooting out her right hand and knocking into her mother's hat-box.

'Oh, child, what *are* you doing?' cried Letty. 'Run on in front with the boys, for goodness' sake.'

Rachel speeded up her trot obediently. Scutter,

scutter, scutter, diving round other people, coming up against your family and keeping close. You never realized how necessary a family was until you went out with it in a crowd—and then, if you were separated from it for a moment, what a panic fell on you until your eyes lit on their familiar hats and faces and how you fought until you regained them !

At last, they reached the platform. Letty stood surrounded by bags and boxes, Ambrose walked about with his hands behind his back, the boys congregated round the penny-in-the-slot machines, but without laying anything out, because experience had taught that they were not good value. Rachel edged nearer and nearer to the bookstall. Hundreds of picture books making a little house and in the house, where Rachel felt she would very much like to live, a man with glasses and a bowler hat looking out. He was something rather like a rabbit only in a different sort of hole, thought Rachel, before giving her entranced attention to the books. When Auntie Laura travelled by train she bought an armful of these books, but her mother never bought any at all. It was a great pity.

In a small blue purse at the end of a long blue thong, which she wore as if it had been racing-glasses, Rachel had her holiday money ; sevenpence half-penny in coppers. It occurred to her suddenly that she, like Auntie Laura, could buy a book. She cast an anxious glance to see if the train was coming and began to move hastily backwards and forwards along the front of the stall, looking, craning, considering. Then she halted ; there was a book with a boy on the back, he wore a tam-o'-shanter and was biting into an apple. He looked bad ; and Rachel liked bad heroes. She leaned over and spelled out the name of the book, *The Fortunes of Wee* . . . something. Rachel loved ' Fortunes of ' . . . This was the book ! But under the title were the depressing words ' One shilling net '. Rachel fell from her tiptoes to her heels ; but brightening, she rose again and addressed the man in the hole.

' This book isn't a shilling, is it ? ' she asked, putting her forefinger on the bad boy.

' What's that ? Yes, it is,' said the man. ' See, it's marked : " One shilling." '

' I know,' said Rachel. ' But it says a shilling net and this is only paper.'

The man stared at her, then burst out laughing.

Rachel shrank away, blushing deeply. She regained her mother and the trunks, and, although the man leaned out of the hole and was anxious to explain, she would not look at him again, but kept her head turned away until the train came, which, fortunately, was almost at once. She did not know what she had done, but it was evidently something silly.

She was very relieved to get into the train, but when it started, she cried out in alarm. ' We're going the wrong way ! Mother ! We're going the wrong way.'

Her family sat stolidly on the seats, indifferent to disaster.

' Mother ! ' shrieked Rachel. ' We're going the wrong way. You said the Whittle way—*that* way ! " she shot out her right hand.

' It's all right,' said Letty dismissingly. ' We're going the Whittle way.'

' But how can we be ? ' protested Rachel. ' It's to this hand. When you go on the tram . . .'

'Oh, Rachel, do be quiet, until I see if we've got everything,' implored Letty.

'You silly, we turned round as we came up the subway,' scoffed Roger.

Rachel turned to him. Although he almost always began everything he said to her by 'you silly', there was often something to be got out of him.

'Turned round?' she inquired, with wide eyes.

'Yes, you silly, can't you grasp that? See, I'll draw it for you.'

Rachel squeezed in between her father and brother. Roger, who liked to draw everything, drew and demonstrated. But she could not understand.

'She can't see it,' groaned Roger, flinging himself back in disgust. 'Can't see it! Would you believe it? A simple thing like that. She *is* going to be a duffer.'

'Ah, but it may be fault of the teacher and not of the pupil,' said Ambrose, laying down his paper. 'Look here, Rachel.'

He, in his turn, drew and demonstrated, and in the middle of his explanation, Roger called out to Rachel to look out of the window at Whittle.

'You see, we *are* going through it, you silly! You'll have to admit that, I suppose.'

Ambrose, mustering his patience, continued his explanation, but Rachel still could not understand, and he gave it up and said he would go and have a smoke in another carriage. He left Letty with the children, and she noted it with resentment.

Rachel leaned against the plush with her hands spread out on the seat and her legs dangling. She was red with embarrassment and smiled to keep the tears back. That mistake about the net book and now not being able to understand about the Whittle way—it was rather much !

Letty had closed her eyes, and the boys were deep in their papers, which they read folded into quarters and as if secretly, almost hidden in their hands. Sexton Blake papers they were, and when each had finished his own, he would exchange it for another's. As they read, they brought things out of their pockets and conveyed them to their mouths. But these were secrets too, and Rachel could not make out what they were. She thought David's must be ' Cure 'em quick ' because his teeth were getting black.

The boys were lucky ; they were old and had a lot of spending money. Dick had gone up to sixpence a week. Nobody could cope adequately with them and they did pretty much as they liked. They had papers and sweets for the journey, too ; although Rachel had to admit that she could have bought a paper herself if she had been a bit cleverer.

Then like a flash of light, or a sudden sweet pain, she remembered they were on their way to the sea. The untoward incidents of the start were forgotten. Rachel drew up her legs in ecstasy and began to sing softly to herself, her eyes on the dipping fields and woods outside the windows.

CHAPTER TWELVE

I

AFTER midsummer, Dick went to Romstead
School and Rachel, leaving the pleasant shallows
of Miss Wilson's in Elm Street, entered the deeper
waters of Elton High School.

Ambrose intended to send his three sons to public
schools ; but it would be a severe strain on his re-
sources and he was glad to be able to save on Rachel.
She need not go away to school ; nobody asked where
a girl had been educated. And he did not believe
in all this education for women ; in fact, he considered
knowledge definitely unbecoming to them. It destroyed their charm ; they did not listen so well if
they knew too much.

Take Letty, for instance. There had not been a
sweeter girl anywhere, reflected Ambrose, than Letty
when he married her. He could see her now in those
little sprigged dresses she used to wear, with her blue
eyes lifted to his face, drinking in his words. She
looked up to him in those days ; she brought him her
little problems and it had made him very happy to
point out how unimportant they were and how easily
solved by him. He remembered how, when Dick
was born, Letty was a little rebellious about leaving
him to go to church on Sunday mornings, and said
she couldn't see that it mattered when you went to
church so long as you went. But Ambrose pointed
out that Sunday morning was the recognized time

for going to church by people of a certain class, that there was a sort of *noblesse oblige* about showing yourself in your pew on Sunday morning. If you didn't go in the morning, people only too readily jumped to the conclusion that you didn't go at all ; or if it did happen to get out that you went in the evening, they concluded that you couldn't afford maids and had to stop at home to do the work yourself. Either way it was too complicated, explained Ambrose ; it was much simpler to do as everyone else did.

' But *God* doesn't mind whether you go in the morning or the evening, does He ? ' asked Letty.

Letty, at nineteen, had talked like that ; she was very child-like and sweet. He explained that one had a duty towards man as well as towards God, and she had seen it in the end and accompanied him to church in the mornings.

But look at Letty now. Now that she knew more she had hardly any charm at all ; not what you could call charm. She never asked him anything, and when he talked, she listened absently or with an expression he found difficult to put a name to. She had even begun, of late, to contradict him, and before the children, too ; she contradicted, but she would not argue, and that made her contradictions more than ever annoying and inexcusable.

No, Rachel should not go away to school. She should remain within the sphere of his influence. He would see to it that she grew up into a womanly woman ; that was what he admired most, a nice, refined, womanly woman. He looked forward with pleasure to forming Rachel according to his ideal.

So Rachel went to the High School. In a navy-blue hat with the owl of Minerva embroidered on the

riband, a gym slip and a white blouse, she joined three
hundred and fifty other girls, both large and small,
and was, to outward appearances, submerged. It was
all, to one fresh from Miss Wilson's school, extremely
confusing : ' mensa ' being a table ; and compasses ;
and mixing sulphur and copper shavings together and
noting that, after you had mixed them, they were
still sulphur and copper shavings ; which was not
strange, Rachel thought, since she had not expected
them to be anything else ; climbing the rope at gym,
which she could never do, but swung backwards and
forwards on the knot at the end, make feeble efforts
upwards like a fly trying to struggle out of the treacle ;
and worst of all, having to sing alone at the singing
class, if singing alone it could be called, since, although
she opened her mouth wide enough, no sound emerged
therefrom. It had been a dreadful ordeal, worse than
any ear-testing by Mr. Sellars on Saturday morning.
Miss Poulton-Baynes, the singing mistress, had called
out encouragingly from her place at the grand piano,
and all the class had obligingly waited, with interest,
for her to sing ; and still she had not been able to
manage it. At last, Miss Poulton-Baynes to make a
joke of it, got up from the piano and came to put
her ear to Rachel's mouth. Even then Rachel had
not been able to sing enough to flutter, ever so slightly,
the little tuft of reddish hairs that grew in Miss
Poulton-Baynes's listening ear.

It was after this singing lesson that Rachel, returning
weak, but convalescent to her form room, discovered
that the lid of her desk contained several small holes
which could be filled with blotting-paper soaked in ink,
and prodded well home with the pointed end of her
new compasses. She did this during the Geography

lesson ; it must be fun filling teeth, she thought, and decided, working busily, to be a dentist when she grew up. She paid full attention to the English lesson that followed, because it was about the Round Table. But during arithmetic, she returned to the desk-holes and found with delight that the fillings had set quite hard and could all be picked out again. The High School did not seem so bad after that.

II

Ambrose had instructed Louisa how to visit the bank ; she now visited it on her own account and cabled two hundred pounds to Charles. She then informed Ambrose, who was extremely annoyed and at once told Jim. Together they descended upon her in deep displeasure, but she took no notice of them.

Charles wanted the money. He had found a farmer, he wrote, who would take him into partnership if he would buy a plough, a harrow, a few other implements and a car to get about in. It is a splendid chance, Charles said, if he could only take it. His mother was determined that he should.

'It isn't fair to the rest of us,' said Jim angrily. 'You seem to care precious little what happens to us.'

'I know that you, Jim, will always be able to look after yourself,' said Louisa. 'And what is the use of all these grand investments Ambrose keeps talking about if they won't bring in a few hundred pounds to cover what I sent my son?'

'What investments?' asked Jim.

'Oh, just a few little things I have been trying to improve for her,' said Ambrose. 'Converting some old Industrials and so on. I advised her to buy Hope

Venture Mines and that kind of thing, and they've
done quite well.'

'Those have, I admit,' said Jim.

Ambrose felt suddenly happy and began to enlarge
on the subject of investment ; what an art it was,
how much study it involved . . .

Louisa slipped from the room. Let them talk.
Charles had his money.

She was glad to think he would settle on a farm.
It was a good, open-air life and would be splendid for
his chest ; as a boy, every cold had gone to his chest.
He would really settle this time, she felt sure, and the
others would not be able to carp and cavil at him
any more. At *her* really ; because she received all the
sharp things they said about him into her own heart.

He was always in her thoughts. She did not disturb
Letty by showing how she yearned for her son, or
annoy Jim by referring to him ; neither did she speak
much of him to Kate Barlow, who was to have been
such a comfort. But to Rachel, she sometimes revealed her heart. Sometimes as they walked along
Elm Street, Rachel with her arm through her grandmother's, Louisa would say : ' I was just thinking,
love, how I wish I could see my boy coming out of
the gate.'

' Which boy ? ' asked Rachel, puzzled.

' Why, your Uncle Charles, of course. I was just
thinking what it would be like. I'm rather silly,
aren't I ? ' She would squeeze Rachel's arm and turn
away her head momentarily.

She decided now that she must at once knit him
some good, stout stockings to get about his lands in.
He had mentioned snakes lately, which disturbed her
a great deal, especially in the night-time. She won-

dered if there was some special snake-proof wool to
be had at the wool shop. There could be no harm
in asking anyway.

Summer passed. In the early morning now, there
was a smell of frost and chrysanthemums in the air.
In spring, the trees were shapely, in summer they lost
their figures, thought Louisa, in autumn they found
them again. The beech trees backing the house were
still dark summer-green, but the silver birch by the
gate was hung all over with dangling gold hearts
and the bird-cherry had not a pink leaf left. One
morning Louisa looked out of her bedroom window
and saw the dahlias standing like black gallows all
round the lawn.

'How dreadful they look! They must come up
at once.'

There was a great deal to do in the garden. Sam
was getting old ; when he was bending over the beds
he did not straighten his back but went bent-up ready,
from one bed to another. Rachel thought this was
very funny, but Louisa, who had twinges of lumbago
herself, sympathized and talked of getting someone
to help him. Ambrose, however, said she could not
afford two gardeners and proposed that Sam should
be dismissed. Louisa would not hear of that. She
herself, as her children grew out of her care, had come
to a love of gardening late in life. She gardened with
passion, but her back would not allow her to work long.

'I'll help you, Mrs. Ashton,' volunteered Kate.

'Will you, dear? That is kind of you.'

'I don't know anything about gardening, of course,'
said Kate.

'You'll soon learn. Though I wish it was a more
interesting time of the year for you to begin.'

Kate began to dig, to hoe, to rake, to roll with the same indifferent efficiency that she brought to the housework; but gradually she showed signs of a dawning interest in what she was doing.

She sought out Louisa with a root of Michaelmas daisies she had lifted.

'Just look at this slug, Mrs. Ashton. The size. . . ! And see the wife and family! All those rather pretty little glassy balls are eggs, I suppose? What damage they would have done to this plant if I hadn't spotted them, wouldn't they?'

'The sea-thrift simply asks to be divided, doesn't it?' she called out. 'It falls into bunches of three!'

Kate talked quite a good deal in the garden, but in the house she was as silent as ever. Letty said she did not enjoy sharing her mother's company with Kate, and Louisa was driven to pay visits to Letty. She fell into the habit of calling for Rachel after school and going with her to Beech Crescent.

One afternoon at the end of October, Rachel found her grandmother waiting outside the iron gates.

'Your mother telephoned to say she was going out, my pet, so I thought we might have a walk round by the cannons and then go back to Greenbanks for tea.'

'Ooh, yes,' agreed Rachel with enthusiasm.

She loved to go round by the cannons; a pair of ancient guns which had once dealt death in the Crimea, but which now stood at the top of Elton Park and were scrambled over by successive generations of children at play.

Rachel climbed on to the worn wooden carriage and, bestriding the cold, dark, shiny gun, shuffled herself over the Russian eagles to the very mouth of the cannon, where she sat, dangling high in the air, looking over the tops of the trees at the town below and the hills beyond. She always had strange thoughts when she sat at the mouth of the cannon; she felt removed from her everyday life into a world where she was quite alone; it was rather frightening, but exciting. After a time, the cold of the iron she sat on becoming more insistent than was comfortable, she shuffled herself backwards and descended by the gun-carriage to rejoin her grandmother, who had been tranquilly sitting on a seat, thinking her own thoughts.

Outside the gates behind the cannons there was a little old-fashioned shop where flat cakes, covered with red sugar, were sold at two for a penny. The shop-door was always open, summer and winter alike, and from a long way off you could see the red cakes standing one on top of the other in piles on a cloth spread over the low counter. The shop was a kitchen really, and an old woman was generally sitting in a rocking-chair by the fire; she got up very cheerfully to serve you. It must be a nice place to live, thought Rachel, with the fire and the red cakes, and the cannons so near.

This afternoon, Louisa and Rachel visited the shop and came away with two red cakes in a bag. They returned to the Park and Rachel took one cake in her hand like a winter sun, and ate it while walking precariously over the peaked stones edging the descending paths. Louisa carried the paper bag until Rachel was ready for the second cake. She loved bringing Rachel where she could enjoy herself. She wondered if she had taken the same deep pleasure in her own girls, and could not remember that she had.

'Perhaps I hadn't the time,' she excused herself.

They left the Park, but the streets were almost as pleasant, hung over by trees in their last fragile beauty. They turned into Elm Street, which, gilded over by the setting sun, stretched quiet and empty to the gates of Greenbanks. Louisa walked slowly, a little tired now, but Rachel went along with a peculiar gait of her own, one foot on the pavement and one in the gutter. Someone was playing a piano somewhere. Louisa walked on and Rachel continued to hop.

Suddenly Louisa came to an abrupt halt.

'Can you hear someone playing a piano, love?' she asked sharply.

Rachel ceased hopping.

'Yes,' she said and went on again.

The intent expression faded from Louisa's face.

'It was only my fancy, I suppose . . .'

She moved on again. But before she had gone a dozen yards she pulled up again.

'Rachel,' she called, 'what are they playing on that piano?'

Rachel listened obligingly.

'I don't know, Grandma.'

They stood stock still in Elm Street, straining their ears.

'It's not a piece, is it?' asked Rachel. 'It's all up and down anyhow . . .'

''Sh,' commanded Louisa abruptly. 'Listen!'

Rachel thought her grandmother was behaving very strangely, because they were already listening.

'It's chords, isn't it,' asked Louisa, putting her hand rather heavily on Rachel's shoulder. 'Isn't it chords?'

'Yes, it's like chords . . .' agreed Rachel, startled by the colour of her grandmother's face.

'But it can't be. Of course it can't be,' said Louisa, beginning to hurry along Elm Street so fast that Rachel had to break into a trot. 'No, it's absurd,' said Louisa, coming to a dead halt and breathing heavily. 'It's all fancy. That's what it is—fancy . . .'

On the silence of Elm Street, major and minor chords, ascending and descending, broke out anew.

'But it comes from our house, doesn't it? Does it, think you?' asked Louisa sharply.

'Yes,' cried Rachel. 'But Grandma . . .'

But Louisa darted forward. In her flat shoes, her bonnet slipping backwards, her mantle flying open, she ran along Elm Street, with Rachel running too.

'Run on and open the gate,' gasped Louisa.

Hardly had Rachel got the gate unlatched before her grandmother pushed through the inadequate opening and made for the steps. Rachel rushed after her, extremely excited about she didn't know what. Together they got up the steps and came into view of something that had not been there when Louisa had left the house an hour ago—a collection of trunks and boxes with a parrot in a cage beside them.

Louisa took no notice of these things, but burst through the front door and made straight for the drawing-room. There, at the piano, with a monkey on his shoulder, was Charles, playing chords. They crashed into silence as Louisa caught his head in her arms and pressed it to her breast.

'Oh, Charles . . . oh, my boy . . . Charles!'

'Now, Mother—Mother darling—don't upset yourself like that. Mother—hi! What's the good of my coming home if you're going to choke me the minute

I get here ? ' Charles extricated himself and put his
mother, in spite of herself, into a chair. ' Now, darling, keep calm, keep calm ! '

He knelt down by the chair and let her hold his
face in her hands and bring it home to herself that
this was really Charles and that he was really restored
to her.

Rachel was not so amazed by the return of Charles
as she was by the sight of the monkey. A monkey in
the drawing-room at Greenbanks ! Such a thing to
happen to *her* to find a monkey in the drawing-room !

' Well . . .' she exclaimed softly, advancing by
inches to where the monkey perched in mournful
contemplation on the back of a chair. ' Well . . .'

She reached it at last and very cautiously put out a
finger to touch it, if it would let her. To her immense
delight, the monkey—far from being afraid—put a
small cold hand into her palm and left it there con-
fidingly, while it continued to gaze out of the windows
with sad eyes. Rachel was entranced. She hardly
dared to breathe ; a warm flood of love for the monkey
filled her. But why was it so sad ? If only she could
make it understand that she would be its friend.

' Grandma ! ' she whispered, turning her head very
carefully so as not to startle the monkey into taking
its hand out of hers. ' Grandma ! Look ! '

She smiled ecstatically and turned her head very
carefully back again.

Louisa managed to take her eyes from Charles.

' Oh, what is it ? A monkey ! Dear me, Charles,
what about fleas, love ? You don't mean to say you
brought a monkey all the way from Africa ! Poor
little thing. Well . . .'

' Come here, Pongo,' called Charles, thereby end-

ing Rachel's ecstatic moment, for Pongo went by way
of the green chair, the plant stand, the stool and
floor, to his master's shoulder, where he sat with one
paw on Charles's head and looked wistfully disillusioned.

'Well, well . . .' said Louisa, regarding this strange
visitant to her drawing-room.

'Hello, Rachel,' called Charles, 'I haven't had a
look at you yet. How you've grown!'

People were always surprised at this, it seemed;
but perhaps they would have been more surprised if
you never grew at all.

Rachel came shyly near and kissed Uncle Charles's
prickly cheek.

'I daresay I've got a string of beads in one of those
boxes for you,' said Charles. 'What d'you think of
my monkey?'

'Oh, I think he's lovely,' said Rachel with fervour.
'But he looks so sad. Is he homesick?'

'Oh, he'll be all right when he's settled down.'
Charles turned back to his mother. 'I do hope I
haven't upset you turning up like this, darling.'

'Nay,' said Louisa, wiping her eyes. 'Too much
happiness never upset anybody that I ever heard of.
But what made you come, love, so suddenly?'

'Well, as a matter of fact,' said Charles, 'that
farmer chap turned out an absolute rotter. He got
hold of that car I bought—second-hand, you know—
and simply cleared out.'

'Dear, dear, how disgraceful!' said Louisa mildly.
'There are some terrible people in the world.' She
didn't care what sort of people there were in the world
so long as they were the means of restoring Charles
to her.

'Happily I hadn't bought the plough and things as I was just on the point of doing, so I had enough money for my passage home.'

'Well,' said Louisa. 'Wasn't it providential?'

'I decided to come back all in a minute—I'll tell you why later—and just managed to get a berth. After all, there's nothing doing in South Africa.'

'Isn't there, love?' asked Louisa.

'No, nothing, and I went all over, didn't I?'

'You did,' agreed Louisa. 'No one can say you didn't go all over,' she said, thinking, for the first time, of Ambrose and Jim.

Bella came in with tea, her broad face abeam.

'Well, Bella, you see who's here,' said Louisa, lying back exhausted but happy in her chair.

'Yes, 'm, I see. I was the first to set eyes on 'im, and I daresay I behaved a bit daft in consequence. But I've never 'ad a monkey 'anging on to my back 'air before, Mr. Charles, so you'll 'ave to excuse me.'

'It was a lively welcome anyway, Bella,' said Charles.

'What d'you want doing to the bird?' inquired Bella from the door. 'It's still on the front, squawking.'

'You can have it in the kitchen for company.'

'Oh . . . well . . . thank you,' said Bella doubtfully. 'But it's got a funny way of looking at you. It seems as if it's itchin' to nip at something. I 'ope it won't be me.'

'You'd better carry it into the kitchen for Bella, Charles,' said Louisa, beginning to pour out tea.

Charles went, the monkey still on his shoulder.

'Oooh, Grandma,' breathed Rachel, clapping her hands together. 'A monkey and a parrot! Just think!'

'Yes, love,' said Louisa, turning her face towards Charles coming in at the door. How well he looked, how bonny! The trip had done him a world of good!

It was not until half-way through tea that she remembered to send Rachel to bring Kate Barlow to tea. Kate would not come until bidden. Louisa reproached herself for forgetting her; but she could not reproach herself for long. She was too absorbed in Charles.

Kate came, looking at Charles to see if he knew about her. And when from his manner it was obvious that, if he had ever heard of her, he had completely forgotten, she sat down in a corner, consciously effacing herself.

News travelled fast in Elton. Before Louisa could take a drink of tea, the telephone bell rang and Bella came to say Mr. Jim wanted to speak to her.

'Mother, Jack Foster says he saw Charles on the station this afternoon. Of course, he's wrong, isn't he? The thing's absurd—but he swears he saw him.'

'Yes, Jim,' said Louisa, fumbling with the receiver. 'Charles has come home. He's in the drawing-room now,' she added happily, 'having his tea.'

'What in the name of God has he come back for?' burst out Jim.

'Jim!'

'If he thinks he's getting in down here again, he's wrong, that's all. I suppose he's broke now . . . the waster . . .'

'Oh, Jim!' cried Louisa.

'Oh, he makes me sick!' shouted Jim, and crashed down the receiver.

Louisa went back to the drawing-room. She took up her cup again, but her lips trembled so that she could not drink. She put down the cup and smiled at Charles.

'Well, love, go on about that terrible journey . . . five days in the train, did you say?'

Hardly had the trembling left her limbs and she was able to drink her tea, than looking out of the window, she saw Ambrose hurrying up the steps to the front door. Louisa put her cup down again. Jim upset her, but Ambrose annoyed her.

'By Jove, it's true then!' cried Ambrose, coming into the room. 'Mrs. Pratt told me she'd seen him driving up Elm Street in a cab and I wouldn't believe her. She was so sure, though, that I thought I'd come up and see. Well, Charles, you've fairly taken us by surprise. What's the matter? What brought you home?'

'The *Antonia*, to be exact,' replied Charles, with a pleasant smile.

Ambrose shot an angry glance at him and all but snorted. Here he was with his idiotic remarks again! They had always upset Ambrose, and now they upset him again.

'Have a cup of tea, Ambrose,' said Louisa, who wished he would go.

He took a cup from her and sat down, trying not to seethe too visibly. How Charles had the nerve to come home full of cheek like this, he couldn't think! He ought to explain, to apologize . . . anyhow, he ought to be different, he ought to be humble . . . . He had a great wish to bring Charles to his proper attitude.

'I suppose you used the money sent you for farm

implements to come home with ? ' he inquired in a cold voice.

'Yes, wasn't it lucky he had it ? ' interposed Louisa, while Charles lit another cigarette. 'The man was quite a bad lot and went off with the car they had bought together. Wasn't that awful, Ambrose ? '

'And what do you propose to do now ? ' persisted Ambrose.

But before he could get an answer to what he felt to be a thoroughly awkward question, he was terrified to feel a nightmarish clutch on his neck from behind. He poured tea over his legs and remained for a second or two with his eyes fixed, while Charles roared with laughter, and Rachel piped out :

'It's only the monkey, Daddy ! It's only the dear little monkey ! '

Abruptly, Ambrose recovered himself.

'Take it away ! Get it off my chair ! Charles, can't you keep your outlandish pets somewhere else ? As if it isn't bad enough coming home yourself in this way without bringing silly things like this to startle people. Take that animal away, Rachel, and don't let it come near me again.'

He breathed heavily. He was furious because he had been frightened out of his dignity and made to look a fool at the very moment he was about to make a fool of Charles.

'My new trousers too,' he said pettishly. 'They're ruined ! '

'You'd better go and sponge the stain with cold water in the cloak-room,' advised Louisa. 'I don't think it will be much,' she finished with irritating mildness.

Ambrose went out of the room. But while he was

in the cloakroom, he heard Jim arrive and his face cleared at once. Here was an ally! Let them see what Charles would look like now! He rushed out to join Jim in the hall and saw at once that Jim was angry enough to please even him.

'What the devil do you think of this?' asked Jim, his nostrils white.

'I think it requires some explanation,' replied Ambrose, following him hopefully into the drawing-room.

'Hello, Jim,' said Charles.

'What have you come back for?' began Jim at once.

'Jim . . .' Louisa besought him. She saw by his face that her new happiness would be ruined.

'What have you come back for? That's what I want to know?' persisted Jim.

'Oh, Jim, the poor boy's only been home a few hours. Do leave him alone.'

'Now, Mother, leave this to us. What's happened to that money, Charles?'

'All gone away with the Ewigkeit, or whatever it is,' said Charles airily. 'I used it to come home with. You don't understand the conditions in South Africa . . .!'

'I understand *you*,' broke in Jim angrily.

'That's all right, then,' said Charles. 'To understand is to forgive. Not that I feel in any particular need of pardon from you, Jim. The money was Mother's. I'll account for it to her.'

'Yes, dear,' said Louisa staunchly, glaring at Ambrose because she dared not glare at Jim.

'You've got a damned fine cheek,' said Jim, 'that's all I can say.'

'Let it be all, then,' advised Charles.

'Oh, don't be such a damned fool,' said Jim. Anger made him inarticulate. He stood with his fists on his hips, looking furiously at his brother, while Ambrose rose and fell on his toes, and Louisa wiped her forehead with her handkerchief. They made her feel ill, baiting her boy like this.

Into the family scene burst Letty.

'Charles!' she cried, running to him and throwing her arms round him. 'I couldn't believe my ears when Bella telephoned! My dear, dear old boy! How lovely to see you again! Let me look at you!' She held him off, then hugged him again.

Bah! thought Jim, women will welcome anything —wasters, mongrels, stray cats—anything.

'Come on, Ambrose, let's leave them to it,' he said in disgust, making for the door.

CHAPTER THIRTEEN

I

'AS a matter of fact,' said Charles, when he was alone with his mother in the drawing-room, Ambrose having taken Letty and Rachel away long before they wanted to go, and Jim having gone in search of Mabel Dawson's company. 'As a matter of fact, although I wasn't going to give those two the satisfaction of knowing it, I really came home to make a billiard-marker.'

'A billiard-marker!' echoed Louisa in astonishment.

'A billiard-marker,' repeated Charles. 'The most marvellous billiard-marker ever imagined. Honestly, Mother, it's like something out of one of those books by that chap Wells. It's revolutionary, it's incredible —and the surprising thing is that nobody's ever thought of it before! Of course, you always feel like that about the best inventions. It should—although it doesn't do to be too sanguine, I know—but it should make our fortunes, darling. Yours and mine. Because, of course, you'll be in on whatever I make.'

He patted her hand, and she leaned forward to kiss him again, only too glad of the excuse.

'The idea hit me bang in the eye in the middle of Johannesburg, and d'you know I wasn't a bit cut up when that farmer chap let me down, because I was dying to get home to try the thing out. I couldn't have done it out there; I couldn't get the parts. I shall have to go to Birmingham for those, and get

clocks specially made and all that, and of course I
want to be on the spot to place the thing, and go round
to interview the billiard-hall proprietors. By Jove,
won't they jump at it ! '

' Will they ? ' asked Louisa with no doubt in her
voice.

' Rather ! It will save them hundreds of pounds a
year. You know they're absolutely at the mercy of
the men who keep time and take the money. These
men can and do swindle the proprietors out of pounds
a week.'

' Do they ? ' asked Louisa feelingly. ' Dear me,
fancy that ! '

' I don't suppose you understand how they do it,
darling, but I'll explain to you properly later. I'll
just show you the drawings now. Wait a minute, I'll
sit on this stool and we can have the drawings on your
lap.' He arranged himself at her knee. ' By Jove,'
he said, with a wag of his head. ' This will make Jim
and that ass Ambrose look sick, I can tell you.'

' Will it, love ? ' asked Louisa delightedly.

She was so happy to have him near her, to watch
his hands arranging the drawings he took from his
pocket-book, to look down on the crisp spring of his
hair, so occupied in being intensely happy that she
could hardly follow what he said.

' Well now, look at this,' he began. ' Of course
they're small, these sketches. I must get them drafted
out in large to-morrow. I can have the old nursery
again, can't I ? '

' Of course,' said Louisa, keeping her knees very still
to accommodate the drawings.

' Well now, say a man comes in and wants the table
for an hour,' resumed Charles.

'Mmm,' nodded Louisa. She understood that at any rate.

'He goes to the desk, pays his money and receives two heavy counters, like big pennies ; one counter one half-hour, you see, or maybe one quarter-hour, I don't know. I haven't worked things like that out yet. He puts these counters into this slot and that sets this clock going. When the clock has gone one hour, the counters fall, the weight stops the clock, rings a bell telling everybody time's up, and if it's night, it puts the lights out over the table.'

'Charles !' cried Louisa. 'Can it do all that ? '

'It can,' said Charles with another wag of the head. 'And what's more, it registers the number of games played and the money taken. It does away with all possibility of cheating.'

'Well, I never heard of anything like it,' said his mother. 'It's almost human. Fancy you thinking of all that !'

'Of course there's an awful lot to be done,' said Charles, gathering up the drawings and putting them carefully into his pocket-book. 'I must begin work on it at once.'

'It's wonderful, love,' reiterated Louisa. 'And you shall have the nursery all cleared out for you to-morrow. In fact, I think we can get it ready to-night, so that you can begin first thing in the morning.'

'I'd like to do that if possible. I knew you'd understand about my having to come home for this, Mother.'

Louisa's smile was proud, confident, loving.

'Well, I'll go and begin on that room straight away. Kate Barlow will help me.'

'I must say, I should have thought you'd have chosen

someone a little more cheerful to replace me,' remarked Charles, pulling Pongo to his shoulder. 'What on earth's the matter with her?'

'She's had a very sad life,' said Louisa.

'Oh, she's the one who had a child or something, is she?' asked Charles cheerfully.

'Hush, love, don't mention it,' begged Louisa in alarm. 'She never does.'

'But where is it?' persisted Charles.

'I don't know, and I don't think she does either.'

'Queer sort of mother, isn't she? Still, I suppose I can't expect all mothers to be like you.'

Louisa beamed. These were her dearest rewards, these half-tender, half-teasing tributes from Charles.

'D'you think you could make Pongo a jacket, Mother? He feels the cold, I think.'

'I daresay I can manage a little jacket for him,' said Louisa, going away full of happy bustle. When Charles was about there was always so much to do and that was what she loved.

She told Jim about the billiard-marker when they were at breakfast together, Kate having left the room and Charles being already at work in the old nursery. Jim listened to her with an expression that flustered her and prevented her from presenting the billiard-marker in the most favourable light.

'Of all the idiotic schemes,' he began.

'It isn't, Jim, really; it's wonderful. It's because I'm not telling you about it properly. It's all very intricate, but I'm sure Charles will explain to you, if you will just give him a word of encouragement,' she pleaded.

'I encourage him? No fear. I'll leave that to you, Mother. You do quite enough damage by encouraging Charles without help from me.' He folded his napkin and got up, pale with anger.

'Of course, he's unique,' he said from the door. 'He'll come all the way from South Africa to make a thing anyone could make with a bit of wood and a few weights and a clock. It was bad enough to come back for no reason at all, but it's fifty times worse to come home for such damfoolery. Don't tell anyone about it, Mother, for God's sake. They'll think he's mad. I'm ashamed of him. And Mabel actually asked me if there was insanity in the family. That's a nice question to be asked, isn't it?'

'I daresay you brought it on yourself,' remarked Louisa caustically. 'Whatever you may say about your brother, Jim, I think we shall come to be very proud of him.'

'Bah,' said Jim. 'He's a waster. He'll never be anything else, never!'

He went out and left Louisa sitting on at the table. She smoothed the salt with the salt-spoon, waiting until the trembling left her limbs. Jim always made her tremble when he was angry.

II

For the first time Rachel consciously loved; she loved the monkey. She did not think about loving her grandmother, but she thought about loving Pongo. In the middle of the arithmetic lesson, her heart would dissolve with love for him. She waited eagerly for the Christmas holidays when she could be with him all day. In the meantime, she begged to occupy her little room at Greenbanks.

He was so funny in his ways; so funny when he bit the middle out of Mrs. Brewster's glove—the part

stretched tightly across the plump palm Mrs. Brewster
extended to pat him; so funny when he ran up the
form of the tray-bearing Bella and threw potatoes-in-
their-jackets about the dining-room; so funny when
he daubed the washing on the lines with blacking from
the pot Sam had left about. Rachel wished very much
they would allow him to be funny always, because when
he wasn't funny he was so sad.

'What is it?' she would ask him when they sat
together in one chair. 'Don't be home-sick. It's
very nice at Greenbanks with Grandma; you'll see by
and by. Is it because you're cold, darling?'

The droop of Pongo's hand over his knee was so
disconsolate that she almost wept. But when he was
lively, her heart lifted with joy and relief, and she
brought her special friends from the High School to
look at him.

With Rachel and her friends trooping in and out,
and Charles banging and sawing in the old nursery,
Greenbanks recovered something of its former bustle.
Louisa felt the tide of life flowing through herself as
well as through the house and was renewed.

In a series of attacks by Ambrose and Jim, she placed
herself firmly between them and Charles, and finally
routed Jim by pointing out to him that he himself
lived at Greenbanks at her expense.

'You pay nothing here,' she said, while he stared at
her aghast. 'If Charles pays nothing either, I see
no difference between you.'

It cost her a great deal to say this, but when she was
hard pressed about Charles, she would say anything.

'How was I to know you wanted paying?' asked
Jim, with scornful emphasis on the last word.

'I don't,' said Louisa hastily. What a dreadful

conversation between mother and son ! She looked
imploringly at him, but he said furiously that he would
relieve her of his presence as soon as he could make
enough out of the business to get married. At present,
he said, it took all he could make to buy her out. He
said no more about Charles after that. He kept out
of the house as much as possible, and showed his
displeasure by silence when he was in it.

Louisa was astonished by the energy with which
Charles threw himself into the making of the billiard-
marker. He would not leave it, even to play the piano,
and sat at meals with an abstracted frown such as she
had never seen on his face before. He made innumerable journeys to the timber yard for pieces of wood,
enraging Jim because he took them without asking
permission. He went backwards and forwards to
Birmingham and had great difficulty in getting satisfactory clocks, weights, bolts, bars, nuts and screws.
When the first marker was assembled, it would not
work at all and Charles was in despair for two days.
He actually asked Ambrose to go up to the nursery
and have a look at it to see what he thought. Louisa
put the billiard-marker into her prayers and felt she
was answered when Charles startled the household
in the middle of the night by the sound of rending wood
and ringing bells.

Louisa got up herself and went to the nursery to
tell him she would go down and make him some nice
hot cocoa to keep him warm while he was working.

' No, no, Mother—I haven't time. Don't bother me,
darling. I've got a brain-wave about this thing. Go
back to bed.'

She went away, very proud. In the middle of the
next afternoon as she and Kate Barlow were busy on

the last of their repairs to his neglected wardrobe, he
burst in to tell them that the marker was working.

' Come and see it, Mother !   Come on, Miss Barlow.
By Jove, it's marvellous ! '

Louisa arrived in the nursery very short of breath
from haste and excitement.

' Go on, Mother, work it yourself.   Put your counters
in here.   See, you've set that clock going.   Now I'll
move the fingers on an hour and this other clock rings.
Yes, I've two clocks now ;   that's what held me up.
Now see !   It turns this switch if it's electric light, or
pulls this wire if it's gas over the table.   What do you
think of that ? '

Louisa was so overcome by the ingenuity of the
billiard-marker that she wept a little and could not
speak for a moment.

' Well, fancy . . . fancy you working all that out
—making it all yourself.   You're so clever, love.   Isn't
it wonderful, Kate ?   Have you ever seen anything
like it ? '

Kate murmured obediently.   She was always inadequate at rejoicing.

Charles was beside himself with the release, the
elation of creating something and finding it a success.
After demonstration and re-demonstration to his
mother, he went down to the telephone and rang up
all his friends ;   he even rang up Ambrose and asked
him to call in on his way home.

When Jim came in, Charles shouted over the
banisters :

' I say, Jim, come up and look at my marker.   It's
working ! '

Jim glanced up coldly and went on into the dining-
room.

'I'm not interested, thanks,' he said.

'Come on and don't be such an ass,' cried Charles. 'The thing's a marvel!'

Jim closed the dining-room door without speaking again. Charles straightened himself up from the banisters with a black face.

'Ah . . . the devil, the devil, the devil . . .' he muttered between his teeth.

But the sight of his marker standing in the nursery, with its bland, secretive front and its ingenious, complicated behind, restored his good-humour.

'Now I must take out a patent at once,' said Charles. 'You'll lend me the money, won't you, Mother? I shall be able to pay you back three times over very soon.'

'Of course you shall have the money,' said Louisa. 'I'll give you a blank cheque at once.'

She was so glad Ambrose had instructed her in the giving of cheques, blank and otherwise.

Louisa felt herself swept into a vortex of excitement. Things began to happen very quickly. Charles's friends, Jack Crewe, Stanley Brewster and the rest, whom she had known as boys but who were now grown men, several with wives and families, answered the summons and came to give their opinion of the billiard-marker. They came to laugh; she could tell from their approach that they looked upon this as another amusing imbecility on the part of Charles; but their faces changed as he put the marker through its paces for them. They took on the expression of intent small boys.

'Let's see how that lever acts. Like that? And what's this? I see. Let's have it again. By Jove, it's a jolly good idea, this, Charles! But suppose . . . by Jove, you've thought of that too. . . .'

They could hardly tear themselves away from the new toy.

Charles had the marker photographed and a booklet printed. He worked hard on this booklet, and the blotter in the drawing-room was heavily scored with efforts at composition.

' Now, Mother,' he announced at last. ' All is ready. I'm going to hire a car to-morrow and take the whole thing to Hartley's.'

' Who are Hartley's ? ' asked Louisa.

' You don't mean to say you don't know Hartley's of Manchester ? They're the biggest billiard-hall pro- prietors in the country. Practically all the halls in Lancashire are owned by Hartley's. If they take me up, my fortune's made.'

' Is it really, love ? ' asked Louisa, impressed. ' And you are going to take it to them to-morrow ? '

' To-morrow I put my fate and fortune to the test ! ' cried Charles, going to the piano and breaking out into chaos on the keys. ' Oh, damn, I wish I could express myself on this thing.'

Louisa prayed earnestly that night for the billiard- marker. Her faith would have puzzled a theologian ; it would have puzzled her if she had looked into it, which she did not. Her prayers were all petitions for her children and thanks for blessings received. She went regularly to St. Anne's Church and followed the Book of Common Prayer with her lips and eyes, but her heart was never engaged by it. The clergy came to Greenbanks to weddings and funerals and sometimes in between they made an afternoon call. Louisa talked comfortably with them about the parish, the bazaar, the funds for this and that, the choir and the ' Field Day ', but let them make the least reference to the state of her soul and she immediately became so impossibly polite and formal that they had to change the conversation or go.

She had never mentioned the misdeeds of her husband to God, but she prayed for Charles's success with the billiard-marker ; and when he set off in the hired car with the great awkward thing in three pieces beside him, she prayed again : ' Oh God, let Hartley's take the billiard-marker, I beseech Thee.'

She waved the car out of sight and went back to the house to occupy her time as best she might until he should return. She tried to keep her anxiety to herself, but could not help remarking at table that she wondered how Charles was going on at Hartley's.

' Really, Mother,' said Jim in exasperation. ' You seem to have no sense at all where Charles is concerned. You either can't or won't see that he is completely incapable of producing anything marketable. This is simply another wild-goose chase he's on. The whole thing is ludicrous ; and what's worse, it's expensive. I suppose it never occurs to you that it is extremely unfair to the rest of your family to throw money away like this on Charles.'

' It does occur to me, Jim, because you are always saying so,' sighed Louisa, pushing Rachel's plate a little closer to give herself countenance.

Rachel went red and took a drink of water. She did not know what her uncle meant, but was sure it was something unpleasant to her grandmother.

Louisa would not go out in the afternoon in case Charles should get back sooner than he had expected. She drew up her chair to the drawing-room windows and sat there with a three-cornered shawl round her

shoulders to keep warm.   In spite of herself she went
to sleep.

She awoke to see Charles and the taxi-driver carrying
a bulky shape up the steps and knew at once that
Hartley's had not jumped at the billiard-marker.   She
went out into the hall.

' Well, Mother,' said Charles, paying off the man.

' Well, dear . . .' she replied, waiting.

The man went.

' No luck,' said Charles.

' Oh, Charles . . .' faltered Louisa.   ' Why?   What
did they say?'

' They said it would cost too much to install, but I'll
tell you about it later.   I must go and wash.'

He went upstairs, but he did not come down again.
She guessed he was sitting with his disappointment in
his bedroom.   She sat in the drawing-room with hers.

Charles was bitterly disappointed.   He spent the
following day almost in silence ; but the day after that,
his hopes began to rise again, and he set out to see
what Sorrel's in Liverpool would do for him.   Louisa's
hopes rose again, but were again dashed by Charles's
despondent return in the evening.

' Same tale,' he said.   ' They won't risk the outlay.'

He went to London, to Birmingham, to Leicester,
to Nottingham ; he carted the marker half round
England, but although many professed themselves
interested, none would take it up.

' Well, they can send me where they like now,' said
Charles.

And Ambrose and Jim began to talk about Malay,
and Louisa's happiness ebbed again.

' Anyway,' said Charles, buttoning Pongo inside his
own jacket for warmth.   ' You'll be glad to get back

to the sun, won't you, old chap? It wasn't fair to
bring you, was it?'

Pongo looked out from his master's coat with eyes
that were sadder and brighter than ever. The weather
was very cold. In the mornings every leaf on the
privet hedge was a tiny three-cornered hat braided with
white; the laurel leaves were stamped out of black
iron, and you could hear a ball push its way over the
rimy grass. Rachel, who had loved frost and snow,
now hated them for Pongo's sake.

The parrot, Perkins, flourished in the kitchen, echoing Bella, scattering his flat white seed over the floor
and watching visitors with a wicked, wary eye. Rachel
could not think it fair that the parrot should be so well,
when Pongo was so ill in England.

One day when she came flying in from school at
midday, the basket by the drawing-room fire was
empty. She went into the kitchen, but there was only
the parrot; into the dining-room, but there was only
Miss Barlow; upstairs, but there was only her grandmother.

'Where's Pongo? I can't find him,' said Rachel
apprehensively.

Louisa stood with a crumpled face, anticipating the
child's sorrow. She had been dreading this question.

'Love,' she said reluctantly, 'Pongo's dead.'

Rachel stared, the colour draining out of her face.
Tears came suddenly into her eyes and stood there.
She turned and felt for the stairs with her feet.

Louisa leaned over the banisters.

'It was the cold, love,' she offered.

Rachel nodded and hurried on.

She got behind the couch in the drawing-room and
wept there. When the gong went, she had to come out

and go to table to convey meat and potatoes to her swollen lips under the eyes of Uncle Jim and Miss Barlow. She escaped as soon as she could and put on her hat and coat to go back to school. She did not kiss her grandmother as usual, but went off with a husky good-bye. Louisa understood ; you had to bear things in your own way, she knew.

CHAPTER FOURTEEN

I

IN February, Charles, with less money and fewer presents, sailed for Malay. He was to go to a rubber-planting friend of Jim's, to a definite job this time. And let him stick to it, warned Ambrose and Jim, because it was his last chance. The family was sick of him, and would see to it that no more money reached him from his mother.

' I'm by no means certain that we've seen the last of him,' said Ambrose, turning in his collar to Jim when Charles had been got off.

' By Jove, if he dares to show his face here again . . .' exploded Jim. But he didn't finish the sentence, because he didn't know how to. Speech is so useful ; you can leave off anywhere.

Rachel was not allowed to make absences from the High School, so Louisa travelled alone with Charles to London. Rose appeared at Waterloo with the worthy, but defeated, object of keeping up her mother's spirits by cheerful and incessant conversation.

When the train had taken Charles away from her once more, Louisa had to accompany Rose to Sydenham Hill on a visit. She travelled so rarely that, when she did, she had to travel everywhere at once. When she had stayed with Rose, she would have to go and stay with Laura in Nottingham.

She was quite lost in Rose's house. She supposed it was because she had never seen much of Perry

and the boys, or even of Rose since her marriage.
They were a lively family, full of jokes which Louisa
couldn't grasp. She had no knitting, nothing to do
but sit by the fire and smile uneasily. She felt Rose
and Perry called her 'the poor old thing' in their
bedroom at night. When the visit was over, she
thanked them sincerely but was glad to get away.

Laura's house was much quieter. It was too quiet,
she was sure. Before a day was gone, she knew that
Laura was not happy with George, although George
seemed to be quite happy with Laura. He was now
very fat and ate and drank enormously, sitting at the
head of the table in a throne-like chair with a great
letter 'B' in gold on the blue leather, and looking
continuously for Twilley to come with more.

'A little more of that turbot, please. The sauce is
excellent. You must tell Cook I said so.'

Louisa caught a glance Laura directed to a smear
of the excellent sauce on George's plump chin and her
eyebrows lifted with anxiety. The poor child . . .
but she shouldn't look at him like that ; no, she should
not ; it was a dreadful look. George had gone to
pieces ; but Laura seemed to wish him to go to pieces
so that she could despise him the more. Louisa did
not like that.

Laura had given up dinner-parties, racing, dancing.
She seemed to spend a great deal of time alone, reading, or even, her mother surmised, doing nothing at
all. Solitude and unhappiness had worked on Laura.
She was driven in on herself and had grown quiet.
Things meant no more to her ; possessions, position,
all that she had once thought so enviable—nothing.
It seemed to Louisa that Laura could hardly bring
herself to answer people's greetings in the streets or

shops, could not be bothered to say good morning or good-bye. Louisa was alarmed.

'I wish you had some children,' she said.

'I don't want any,' replied Laura. 'Why bring anyone else into a world you are tired of yourself?'

'Laura, how can you talk like that? You are young and strong, with a good husband and plenty of money. Most people would consider that you had everything.'

'It seems like nothing to me,' said Laura.

'Oh, love . . .' faltered Louisa.

'Don't worry, I'm getting used to it.'

'Getting used to what? George seems so good.'

'Oh, very good,' agreed Laura, and would go no further. She had always been able to put a stop to inquiry.

Louisa returned sadly to Greenbanks. Charles was gone, Laura unhappy; Letty was 'getting through' matrimony, she wasn't enjoying it; Kate Barlow would never, Louisa felt, be happy at Greenbanks or anywhere else. She was as quiet, as steadily hopeless as ever. The only thing she allowed herself to hope for was next year's garden; she did look forward to and plan for that; but no more.

'Eh, dear,' sighed Louisa to herself in the drawing-room. So much unhappiness. . . .

And then Rachel came in, and an invisible breeze blew Louisa's cloudy troubles away.

'You said I could come back to tea, didn't you, Grandma?' asked Rachel.

'Of course I did, love.'

'Can I stay the night?'

'Well, we shall have to ring up and ask your father.'

'Perhaps he'll say yes,' said Rachel hopefully.

Rachel was proud of her long winter stockings, but, as a matter of fact, she looked rather a sight in them. She had grown out of her gym-slip; her hair, which had been cut short, straggled happily over her cheeks, pink with the cold; her light-and-dark eyes were alert and interested; she sniffled cheerfully until driven at last to produce a handkerchief from the elastic of her gym-knickers.

This costume, this hair, these habits annoyed her father intensely, but Louisa smiled on them all.

'I'm glad to see you've been looking after Miss Barlow while I was away,' she remarked.

Rachel had been coming in to dinner as usual, and on her return Louisa noticed a change in the child's behaviour to Kate Barlow. Kate had no way with children; she was stiff, awkward and took all they did and said too seriously. Rachel had hitherto observed her with inconvenient interest, but made no attempt to be friendly with her. She now seemed bent on improving Miss Barlow's acquaintance.

'Will you have some water, Miss Barlow?' she had inquired solicitously at dinner, lifting the jug with an unsteady hand and pouring water with liberal impartiality both in and out of Kate's glass.

'Now see what you've done,' remonstrated her grandmother. 'The jug is too heavy for you.'

But Rachel was not to be deterred from kindness.

'Shall I carry your work-basket into the drawing-room for you before I go to school, Miss Barlow?' she inquired.

Louisa was puzzled, but Rachel now explained.

'Well, you see,' she said. 'We've made up a league at school, and one of the rules is that you have to do one good deed every day and one brave one. You know—it's like the Knights of the Round Table. I've chosen Miss Barlow for my good deed, because she's always here, isn't she? and I don't have to keep thinking every day what to do for it. Look, this is my badge,' she fished in a minute pocket on the shoulder of her tunic and brought out a yellow painted disc. 'G.L., you see; that means "Golden League". We're going to right wrongs. Yesterday we hit a coalman with our school-bags to make him stop whipping his horse. He stopped all right and tried to catch us, but of course he couldn't. And the horse looked so pleased; sort of pleased and surprised. But don't tell anyone about the League, will you, Grandma? Because you have to keep good deeds secret, haven't you? It says enter ye into the lavatory to say your prayers, doesn't it?'

'Nay, nay,' protested Louisa, hastily suppressing a smile. 'I never heard of that before.'

'It's in the Bible,' said Rachel, her eyes flying wide at her grandmother's ignorance. 'Only it says "closet" there, and that's rather a rude sort of old word, isn't it? Can I have *What Katy Did*, please?'

'I think Bella put it back in the book-case. I'll just go and see about your staying the night, while I bethink me,' said Louisa, hurrying off with her fingers pressed to her lips. She must tell Bella about prayer in the lavatory; she must tell somebody, and Kate wouldn't do.

Rachel arranged herself on the hearthrug with her book. It had been Laura's and Rachel couldn't think how she could have left such a splendid book behind. She sighed with pleasure as she looked for her place. You could read in peace at Greenbanks. At home the twins were always fighting round you. They fought

with loud breathings, but never a word. Locked
together, they rolled all over the floor, under the
table, sometimes under the sideboard. Rachel, reading on with a frown, would exclaim with exasperation
from time to time : ' Oh, keep out of the way ! Don't
get on me.'

When the fight was over, the twins, hair stubble on
end, collars worked out of jackets, ties wrung into
wisps, would sit down to their homework at the table.

' You do smell hot,' Rachel would remark, wrink-
ling her nose with distaste.

The twins, bowed over their inky labours, would
try to control their breathing in case one or the other
should inquire contemptuously :

' Puffed ? '

And yet the twins belonged to each other and to
home. Rachel felt that she really belonged to Greenbanks.

Her grandmother came back to say that she could
stay the night and Rachel rolled over face upwards
to say ' Hurray ! ' Then she rolled back again and
went on with Katy.

The next day was Saturday, and when Louisa and
Rachel went into town they bought two dolls at the
penny bazaar : one for Rachel and one for Judy Spence
who had been bidden to tea at Greenbanks in the
afternoon. The dolls were very satisfying, with pot
heads, very glossy, painted with coal-black hair, red
cheeks, blue eyes, and button mouths ; they had pot
hands and feet, too, on which last were painted minute
black boots. Rachel had thought they were both
equally pretty in the face, but when she unwrapped
them in Mr. Gibbs's shop she found one had a crooked
eye. It was a great deception. She wrapped them

up again with haste. She would give Crooked Eye
to Judy, and the other was called Muriel and belonged
to her.

At Miss Siddle's she took the dolls out again.
Was the eye very crooked and would Judy notice it?
Not much, she decided, and wrapped the dolls up
again. Besides, Judy wasn't entitled to a doll really;
she ought to be glad to get one at all, even with a
crooked eye. Rachel hopped determinedly in and
out of the gutter, and began to sing aloud to dispel
uncomfortable thoughts.

'Can we look in the ottoman for something to
dress them in?' she asked her grandmother.

Louisa, her arms full of Saturday parcels, said they
would look in the ottoman immediately after dinner.

The ottoman stood at the foot of Louisa's bed.
It was long and stiff, with a high rolled end; no one
dreamed of accepting its invitation to recline. It was
upholstered in green embossed plush and lined with
striped print, freckled, in places, with iron mould.
When Louisa opened it, it let out a smell of time, a
faded, shut-up smell of prints and silks and flannels
that had been there for years. Rachel leaned into
it, drumming her toes on the side, entirely unaware
that the ottoman contained an almost complete record
of her grandmother's life.

'Where's your little box?' she inquired.

'It's down the side somewhere, love.'

'May I look at it?'

Louisa felt down the printed sides here and there, and
finally brought up a little glazed box shaped like a
doll's trunk with gilded edges and a tiny picture in
medallion on the lid. Rachel took it in both hands
and went to the fireplace where, by the bell-pull,

there hung a little water-colour drawing of Louisa as a child in short black boots and a royal blue frock, clasping the very box Rachel now held in her hands.

It gave Rachel a queer feeling to hold the box and look at it in the picture. She felt the little girl with a round face and curls so fair that you could hardly see them on the paper could not possibly be her grandmother, but the box was the very same box still. She looked from the box in her hands to the box in the picture for several minutes. Then she handed it back to her grandmother and leaned into the ottoman once more.

Louisa dived low in search of the rolls of cuttings left over from years of dressmakings. Her fingers felt and recognized the boned bodice on the floor of the ottoman; she saw, without looking at it, the silk and lace of her own wedding-dress, fretted into holes now by the years. The skirt, she remembered, had been used for christening-cloaks for the children.

Her groping hand brought out a roll of sprigged muslin. She straightened up and stood looking at it.

'What's that, Grandma?' asked Rachel.

It was a piece of the dress Louisa, a young married woman, had had made to go to that great picnic in Pelham Woods. She remembered, in a flash, the cheerful voices, the green gloom, the blaze of king-cups by the pond, and Robert kissing Mrs. Bellingham in the thicket to which Louisa had inadvertently strayed. It was her first experience of the kind. She thrust the roll of sprigged muslin back into the ottoman.

'That won't do, love,' she murmured.

She drew out some baby-clothes, the bodices very yellow.

' Oh, whose are those ? ' cried Rachel.

' I daresay they all wore them,' remarked Louisa, folding them up again and remembering that Jane, the tiny red-haired one, had died in the nightgown with the featherstitching on the hem.

She felt something hard and brought it out ; a pair of ankle strap slippers. She was vague about them.

' I expect I thought they would come in, and they never did,' she said, putting them back.

' Here's your mother's wedding veil,' she cried to Rachel. ' I keep forgetting to give it to her.'

' Was I a bridesmaid at Mummy's wedding too ? ' asked Rachel, remembering the pleasant time she had in that capacity at Auntie Laura's.

' No, love,' said Louisa.

She found a piece of red bombazine at last, and Rachel said it would do splendidly for Muriel and Crooked Eye.

Louisa replaced an embroidered linen sheet, a beautifully stitched night-gown and a night-cap with a frilled edge. These were her death clothes ; there was a note in her drawer to say where they were to be found. When they grew yellow from being put away so long, she took them out and had them laundered. She smoothed these over now with her hand and closed the ottoman lid.

Rachel went downstairs with the red bombazine and had another close look at Muriel and Crooked Eye. When Judy Spence arrived she thrust Crooked Eye into her hand and said : ' See, isn't that a nice doll for you ? ' Then she snatched it back and cried : ' Oh, I've given you the wrong one ! That's yours ' ; and gave her Muriel.

II

Spring ripened into summer and Rachel grew
excited once more about going to the sea. Louisa
was disinclined to go anywhere, but thought she
would take Kate for a fortnight to Lytham ' later
on '.

The weather was fine, and in the afternoons Louisa
sat in the garden, warmed through by the sun, smiling
frequently at the Dresden China daisies set in groups
above the stone edging of the border. They were so
pink, so neat and sweet, and the name was just right.
Some flowers made you smile ; winter aconites for
instance, when you bent down and turned up the
green ruffs to see their yellow heads. A very perfect
rose made you grave ; and you felt you had to be very
careful with primroses.

As she was thinking this one July afternoon, Kate
came out of the drawing-room windows.

' Would you like to look at the paper, Mrs. Ashton ? '

' Well, I don't know . . .' said Louisa in a depre-
catory voice. ' Is there anything in it ? '

This was her attitude to newspapers. She had never
had time for reading in her youth and middle age,
and now when she was old she could not begin to
find pleasure in it. As Kate had dispelled her pleasant
lazy mood, she bent to take her knitting from the
work-bag on the grass.

' Austria has issued an ultimatum to Serbia,' said
Kate.

' Oh,' said Louisa mildly. It meant nothing to
her. If Austria had sent a what-ever-it-was to Malay,
she would have been alert at once.

' The trouble in the Balkans seems to be worsening,'

remarked Kate. 'It started with that assassination, of course.'

'Mmm?' inquired Louisa. 'I'm just going to turn this heel, dear, so I shan't be able to speak for a moment or two.'

She was therefore extremely surprised when everybody began to talk about war.

'War,' she cried. 'What are we going to war for? Who with? What's it all about?'

Mr. Gibbs, the grocer, explained at great length, but she did not believe it would come to anything until she passed the Town Hall on the tramcar and saw the Mayor reading the Declaration of War from the steps.

'Good gracious me!' said Louisa. 'I never heard of such a thing!'

Events began to move with startling rapidity; Letty and her children came home from the sea; Jack Crewe, Stanley Brewster and most of Charles's friends went off in uniform and high spirits to Salisbury Plain; a family of Belgians arrived in the town and were put into Mrs. Parson's empty house in Elm Street. The little girl was brought to tea at Greenbanks by Rachel, who could hardly take her eyes off the unusual guest. To meet anyone who actually said 'Bonjour' outside a French exercise, and to be called 'Mademoiselle' by a child of her own age was an experience of which Rachel could not have enough.

To add to the general confusion, Jim announced that he was going to marry Mabel Dawson in October, and Louisa, with misgiving, was obliged to take the prospective daughter to her bosom in grim earnest. She had put it off as long as she could, but now she asked Mabel to tea. She received her uneasily, wondering what she could find to say to her, but Mabel, smart, hard, thin, did all the talking, her lips shooting backwards and forwards over her shining, prominent teeth.

And suddenly, in the middle of her visit, Kate came in with a cable from Charles to say he had sailed for England. A deep flush dyed Louisa's cheek as she read it; the paper crackled in her trembling hands.

'Well, he's coming home again!' she murmured. 'He's coming home.'

She looked up from the cable to Mabel with eyes that said unmistakably: 'You'll go now, of course.' So Mabel went, skittering down the front steps on her high heels, leaving Louisa free to wipe her eyes over the cable, and go to tell Bella the wonderful news. After that she went upstairs to look at the bedroom where he would soon sleep again, but no sooner had she reached it than she realized why he was coming home. He was coming to enlist. She sat down on his bed, chilled to the heart. That was it, of course. He would go to the war. The war, hitherto remote, loomed up very dark. It would have been better if he had stopped in Malay.

'I don't know how I shall break it to Jim that Charles is coming home again,' she said apprehensively to Kate Barlow when she went downstairs to escape from her foreboding thoughts.

But when she told Jim, he did not fly into the rage she had expected, but merely looked black and rather embarrassed.

The days dragged; Louisa could not settle anywhere in the house, she was always looking out of windows, going to doors to see if any news was coming of Charles's arrival. At last he wired, and she put on the new bonnet she had had made for this day and went to meet him at the station. She clasped him in her arms again and brought him home with triumph and damp bonnet-ribbons. He looked better than ever. These sea trips did him a world of good. The billiard-marker and his ruined hopes seemed all forgotten.

'Wait till I get to this war,' he cried in the cab. 'I'll make 'em run!'

'Oh, Charles,' faltered Louisa, her hand on his. 'Must you go?'

'By Jove, I wouldn't miss it for anything.'

'Don't talk like that, love. It isn't a game. And if anything should happen to you . . .'

'Oh, I bear a charmed life!' cried Charles. 'Ask Jim. I'm the bad penny; I always turn up. Have you noticed?'

'Silly boy,' said Louisa, all smiles. He always talked such pleasant nonsense and made her feel gay in spite of herself.

Letty and Rachel were waiting to welcome him, and Ambrose called in from the office, with no reproaches or awkward inquiries this time. This home-coming had none of the unpleasantness of the last, but a shadow hung over it for all that.

'Well, Jim,' said Charles, offering his hand which Jim accepted. 'I'm trying my luck with the North Lancashires to-morrow. What are you going to join?'

'I'm not a free-agent,' murmured Jim, on his way out of the room. 'I'm in a one-man business and I'm getting married in a fortnight.'

'Oh,' said Charles. 'Well, good luck, anyway.'

His smile proclaimed that he would rather be going
to the war than getting married.

'Specially to Mabel Dawson,' he said to his mother
afterwards. 'Heaven keep such a rat-faced little
thing from my bed and board. You have to pray
about such things, Mother. You don't seem to be
able to help yourself when it comes to women. Look
at Jim. He's made himself damned unpleasant in
this house all his life. You're afraid of him; no good
denying it, darling! And even I—I don't mind
admitting now I'm going to the front—am not as
comfortable as I might be when he's about. And yet
he's completely under the thumb of that little——
But I won't startle you, darling. My language has
taken on a sudden breadth. I myself have taken on
a sudden breadth, because I'm off to the war! And
everything has suddenly become very clear and easy
to me. Have you ever had that feeling, Mother?'

'No, love,' said Louisa humbly.

'No, I suppose it's different for women,' said Charles,
dismissing them.

Yes, thought Louisa, it's different for women. They
don't do; they bear what others do; they watch
them come and go, they are torn and healed and
torn again . . . but it was no use saying this to
Charles.

The next day he enlisted as a private.

'Well, you are a fool,' said Jim. 'Why didn't you
try for a commission?'

'Because I'd have to wait,' said Charles, his bright,
scornful eyes on his brother. 'And because I'd like
to earn my commission.'

'Ass,' said Jim. 'Better men than you have
accepted commissions.'

'Better men,' said Charles, 'at any rate in their own opinion, have not joined up at all.'

Jim sent a furious glance at him, but Charles received it on the buckler of another smile and went to the piano.

'I wish I could play the Marseillaise,' he said. 'Grand rousing tune, isn't it?'

'Come and say good-bye to Charles,' Louisa had written to her daughters, but only Laura came.

She came, and they all went to the station to see Charles off with his strange companions : the man from the bacon counter in Pollitt's, the postman who used to come round with the half-past-two delivery ; all sorts of men, tall, short, lively, quiet, with bags like short bolsters, stuffed with their things, and groups of relations seeing them off. Louisa's face was wet with tears, but Charles assured her they were premature.

'I'm only going to Whitchurch,' he reminded her. 'It's not befitting for a hero's mother to cry when he's only going to Whitchurch.'

'No, love,' agreed Louisa, continuing to cry.

The train bore him away, leaning out of the window over the head of the ex-postman. He was gone again.

Louisa, with Rachel hanging on her arm, and Letty and Laura coming along behind, walked out of the station. It occurred to her, in the midst of her heaviness, that she could go at once to the wool shop and get some khaki wool for socks ; socks and scarves and gloves and all kinds of things.

Letty said she would go with her.

'You can go on to Greenbanks with Auntie Laura, can't you, Rachel?' she asked her daughter.

'Oh, yes,' said Rachel, rather shyly.

Her silent and elegant aunt intimidated her a little.

They went together down Station Street, two navy-blue figures, Laura in a coat and skirt, Rachel in a gym-slip with the ends of the girdle dangling round her lengthening legs.

They turned the corner of Station Street and almost collided with a tall man in officer's uniform, who saluted and would have passed on but that Laura, very white, put out a hand and caught him by the arm.

'Cecil!'

'Oh—Laura . . . !'

Rachel stood between them, her memory stirring. They both looked very strange, she thought. The tenseness of the moment communicated itself to her. Laura spoke first.

'You're not going away, Cecil?'

'Not to-day, no.'

There was another pause, while they looked at each other as if they could never look enough.

'I must see you, Cecil,' said Laura breathlessly.

'But . . . I . . .' He looked round in a strange way and looked again at her.

Her eyes implored him desperately.

He turned abruptly to walk with them.

'Rachel, can you go back to Greenbanks alone?' asked Laura, when they had gone a little way in silence.

'Yes, if you could give me a penny for the car,' said Rachel.

Laura gave her a penny from a gold bag and Rachel boarded the car. She paused on the platform to wave, but they were not looking at her : they were walking with bent heads as if they did not know where they were going. When the car was about to turn the

corner, Rachel, craning her neck, saw them go into
the Park.

When her grandmother returned with a soft bulky
parcel of wool, Rachel was sitting on the square block
of stone at the top of the steps.

' I've begged you for the night,' said Louisa.
' Where's Auntie Laura ? '

' She went into the Park with Uncle Cecil,' said
Rachel.

Louisa looked at her sharply.

' With Uncle Cecil ?   With Cecil Bradfield, do you
mean ? '

Rachel nodded.

' Where did you meet him ? '

' When we were coming away from the station.
We ran right into him.'

' Oh ! ' Louisa looked very disturbed, and sat down
on the hall chair.   ' Dear me, I am tired,' she remarked
after a moment.

' Shall I take your bonnet upstairs ? ' suggested
Rachel.   It was a granddaughterly office she often
performed.   Louisa gave the little erection of straw
and tulle into her hands and having climbed the
stairs, and tried on the bonnet before the looking-
glass, Rachel laid it on the bed and went down
again.

Louisa had gone into the drawing-room where Kate
Barlow sat with her sewing.

' Well, we might as well be winding some wool,'
said Louisa, turning from the window.

Habit was strong.   In the old days, she never had
time to stand and wait for anxiety to materialize ;
there was always something that had to be done.
Now, when she could have waited, she looked for

something to do. She sat down where she could see the gate and asked Rachel to hold the wool for her.

Rachel sat on a low stool and propped her elbows on her knees. She sighed now and then, as the wool-winding proceeded, but her grandmother did not seem to hear her, and Rachel did not like to complain more openly, because Uncle Charles had just gone away.

The light faded and still Laura did not come. When Louisa could not see the gate any more, she allowed Kate to put on the lights and draw the curtains.

'That will do, love, thank you,' Louisa said at last, releasing Rachel, who immediately made a bound to the sofa and drew *Little Women* from behind a cushion.

She seemed to be doomed not to be able to read this evening, however, for no sooner had she found her place in the book than the door opened and Laura came into the room.

She took off her hat as she advanced, and her face showed calm and lovely under the lights.

'Well, Mother,' she said, standing before Louisa, 'I'm going away with Cecil to-night. And don't be hurt or shocked, darling, because it would spoil my happiness and nothing must do that.'

Louisa leaned forward as if trying to grasp what it was that Laura had said. Whatever she had expected from the meeting with Cecil Bradfield, it was certainly not this.

'Don't look like that, darling,' said Laura, half smiling, and touching her mother's cheeks lightly with two fingers. 'There's nothing to worry about. I know it must startle you, but you must be happy for me, because I'm going to be happy myself, at last.'

' Laura, what are you saying ? ' Louisa besought her.
' What are you saying, child? You can't go away
with Cecil Bradfield. Laura ! '

She spoke the name sharply as if Laura was asleep
and she was trying to wake her.

But Laura only smiled as if a child had spoken.
' I can, Mother. I shall.'

A spell seemed to hold the room. Louisa stared ;
Kate, her sewing fallen, stared ; Rachel, whom they
had forgotten, stared at Laura ; and Laura smiled
in some radiant trance of her own. The clock ticked
swiftly under its glass case, and at last, Laura glanced
at it and moved towards the door. The spell broke
then, and Kate Barlow jumped from her chair and
ran, with a swirl of black skirts, to seize Laura by the
arm.

' You fool,' she said, her voice cracking. ' If you
stake everything on one man you're mad ! He'll
leave you ! He'll deny he ever loved you. He'll say
he never had anything to do with you. Whatever
pleasure there is, he'll share it with you—but all
the rest he'll leave you to bear yourself. I know ;
no one knows better than I do. Look at me ! Aren't
I warning enough ? Look at me ! Do you want to
be like me ? '

She thrust her pale, distorted face into Laura's as
if the very sight of it was enough, and would tell all
her tale.

Laura smiled, half with pity, half with contempt.

' I shan't be like you, Kate,' she said, removing
Kate's grasp from her arm. ' Cecil may be killed in
the war. We know that ; that's why we're going
at once. But nothing but his death or mine shall
part us.'

Kate in her turn smiled and her smile was almost a reflection of Laura's.

' I thought like that. I was just as sure as you are. Don't you suppose every woman is? I tell you, if you go, you'll pay for it until the day you die and get out of this cruel, stupid world.'

' These warnings are no good to me, Kate,' said Laura. ' Because you and I are different. I don't know what your particular hell is; I suppose it is public opinion. But it doesn't matter what people think about you if you don't mind about it; and I don't. Not at all.'

Kate suddenly pushed past her and went out of the room. They heard her running, running up the stairs.

Louisa, whose breath came short from distress, began to plead with Laura to wait, to think it over, only to wait a little.

' No, Mother,' said Laura, ' I've waited too long. I'm going with Cecil to-night. When his leave is up, I shall get into some hospital or women's corps and try to get out to France myself. But I'll write and keep you posted. And you're not going to cast me off, darling, are you? Just because I'm going to be happy at last? I've been wretched, Mother. I couldn't have gone on.'

' And what about your husband?' asked Louisa, trying not to be moved by Laura's face and her voice. ' What about him?'

' I'm sorry about George,' said Laura gravely. ' But after all, he'll hardly miss me. There'll still be food and sleep and the club.'

She said this without resentment of any kind.

' You should never have married him, the poor

man,' said Louisa sternly. 'You should have left him alone. You married him out of selfishness, and now you leave him out of selfishness. And he has to pay. I don't know that he has ever done you any harm, except to give you a lot of money and let you do as you like. It's very mean to treat him like this, Laura.'

'Mmmm,' said Laura, hanging her head over the hat in her hand. Then she looked up again :

'But I'm going all the same,' she said, and went out of the room.

Louisa followed her, and Rachel was left alone. She stood in the silence they had left behind and was bewildered. The room felt very strange after what had happened in it ; they had all been so strange —but Miss Barlow was the strangest. What did she mean when she said : 'Do you want to be like me ? ' What was it to be like Miss Barlow ? Rachel tried to put two and two together and failed as lamentably as she frequently did with more concrete sums in the arithmetic lessons she detested.

CHAPTER FIFTEEN

I

LAURA left her pearls on the dressing-table, with a request that her mother should send them back to George.

'You don't mind doing that for me, do you, darling? I haven't time to see to them,' she said while she was packing.

Louisa stood half in and half out of the room, utterly at a loss. Her instinct was to help her daughter to pack, but she didn't know whether it was right to assist her in any way to leave her husband. Leaving a husband was a thing none of Louisa's generation had ever contemplated. She was filled with apprehension as to what would happen now. Her imagination surged with people coming with angry or anxious faces to ask: 'Where is Laura?'

There had already been quite enough talk in Louisa's life, but now there would be more. People had always talked about Robert, and now they would talk about Laura and says she was a chip off the old block.

Louisa winced at the prospect of more talk; she blamed Laura and was angry with her; then she became apprehensive for her because she was leaving the 'safe' life; then, watching Laura flying about her packing with a happy face, she marvelled that nothing was ever as you expected it to be. Leaving a husband should surely be a momentous, dramatic affair, yet here was Laura behaving as if she did it every day.

Louisa's thoughts and sympathies ran all one way one minute, and all the other the next ; and before she could do anything with them, the taxi was at the door and Laura was going down the stairs.

Rachel came out into the hall with *Little Women* in her hand. She had not yet grasped what was going on. When they had kissed Laura, her grandmother took Rachel by the hand, and the old hand twitched and worked over the young one. The taxi-driver carried Laura's cases away ; Laura followed him and was engulfed by the October night.

'Good-bye, darling. I'll write very quickly,' she called out from the darkness.

'Well . . . well . . .' murmured Louisa. '*I* don't know. . . .'

She had never thought she would let a daughter of hers go away like this. But what could she do ? Children grew up ; they pleased themselves ; they grew in power to go their own ways as you diminished in power to prevent them.

Feeling old and tired, she turned from the door with Rachel's hand still in hers. Soon this little one would be growing up and going her own way in her turn.

'Dear me, I am tired,' remarked Louisa as they went into the drawing-room. She bent wearily to poke the fire into a blaze, then sank into her chair with relief.

'Will you have your footstool ? ' inquired Rachel, rooting under the sofa for it.

'Thank you, love.' Louisa closed her eyes, not because she wanted to sleep but because she wanted to think.

Rachel turned to *Little Women*. The excitement was

ebbing out of the house ; soon all would be as before, Rachel felt.

But Louisa, resting her body, kept her mind active on the problem of what she was going to say to George when she returned the pearls. And what she was going to say to Jim when he came home ; to Letty and Ambrose, Rose and Perry, Thomas and May, Mrs. Brewster when she called and Aunt Alice and the rest. She must think of something that would protect Laura. Always there was this need of defending your children ; no matter how old you got, you had to keep on with that. . . .

Jim was the first to hear. Louisa waited until he had finished dinner, and then, standing behind his chair, said nervously :

' Well, Jim, I suppose you will have to know some time. Laura has gone away with Cecil Bradfield.'

Jim twisted round in his place as if he couldn't believe his ears.

' What ? ' he asked sharply.

Louisa repeated it a little more firmly.

' She's gone away with Cecil Bradfield ! ' echoed Jim. He took this in for a moment in astounded silence.

' By heaven ! ' he burst out alarmingly. ' Here's another scandal ! There's no end to them in this family, Mother.'

' Well, I can't help it,' said Louisa, withdrawing into a flat obstinacy as she did when attacked. ' You children are grown up now, you go your own ways.'

' It's like Laura to spring this on the family just when I'm going to be married,' said Jim, throwing down his napkin with such a furious hand that he knocked over the salt-cellar. ' She always was as selfish as they're made.'

He threw another angry glance at his mother, who blinked and kept her lips tightly shut.

'Mabel is sick enough about our family as it is—all the talk there's been in the past. She's hard enough to convince that I'm not like my father, without another behaving in this disgusting way. Suppose she won't marry me now?'

'She'll marry you,' said Louisa. 'She's got her head screwed on properly, has Mabel.'

'You don't need to make it sound like that,' said Jim. 'Having her head screwed on properly, as you call it, is one of the things I admire most in Mabel.'

'Yes, of course,' said Louisa, soothing but ambiguous; 'but we mustn't quarrel about Mabel. We must arrange what we are going to tell people about Laura.'

'Nothing,' said Jim furiously. 'Nothing at all. Certainly nothing until after my wedding. Why on earth couldn't Laura have gone off from her own house instead of causing all this scandal here? Selfish little beast! It's just like her. Have you told Ambrose?'

'No,' faltered Louisa.

Jim went out of the room, and Louisa, standing with lifted eyebrows in the hall, heard him telephoning to Ambrose in the cloakroom.

Within twenty minutes Ambrose and Letty hurried in at the front door.

'Mother—what's happened?' cried Letty.

'Into the drawing-room! Into the drawing-room . . .' said Ambrose, fearing any disclosures in the hall, which might be overheard by Bella in the kitchen or Rachel in bed upstairs.

'Mother, why on earth didn't you send for me?'

began Ambrose weightily, closing the drawing-room door. 'Why did you let her go off like that? I would have stopped her.'

'Laura wouldn't have taken any notice of *you*, Ambrose,' said Louisa, quite surprised at his attitude.

'Mother, did she go all in a minute like that?' broke in Letty. 'It seems incredible. I saw her at half-past three . . .'

'Letty, one moment, please,' said Ambrose, raising a hand. 'There is no time to be lost. I must go after them. Where have they gone, Mother?'

'I don't know,' said Louisa blankly.

'You don't know,' repeated Ambrose, astounded. 'You mean to say you don't know?'

'I didn't ask,' said Louisa.

'You didn't ask?' repeated Ambrose. 'You mean to say your own daughter has gone away with a man not her husband and you didn't ask where she was going?'

Louisa shook her head. 'It never occurred to me,' she said.

Ambrose stared at her in amazement. They were all alike in this family; Letty too. You could not make them realize the seriousness of things.

'Do you realize what has happened, Mother?' asked Ambrose gravely. 'Do you realize the significance of the step Laura has taken to-night? Here I come prepared to go and fetch her back, save her, save poor Boyd's name and honour, and you tell me it never occurred to you to ask where they were going?'

'No,' said Louisa.

'And yet she is your daughter and only my sister-in-law,' remarked Ambrose sternly. 'And I brought my pyjamas and everything,' he added, throwing a little case on to the sofa. Letty knew he was disappointed to be cheated of pursuit of Laura and her lover. How he would have enjoyed the situation, she reflected.

'I'm sorry, Ambrose,' Louisa said. 'It's very good of you, but even if you had gone after them, Laura wouldn't have listened to you, why should she ? '

She had said that before and Ambrose picked up the newspaper with ostentation. Let them do as they could now. He washed his hands of the affair.

Letty wanted to know every detail of Laura's going. As she asked and listened, her heart beat uncomfortably fast and she felt that, if she did not take care, she would burst into tears. Laura had gone ; she had broken away.

'It's not fair ! It's not fair ! ' Letty cried to herself.

Laura had got what she wanted ; whatever happened to her afterwards she had got, once, what she wanted. She had had the courage to take it.

'Not that I ever wanted to go off with a man,' Letty had thought on the way to Greenbanks with Ambrose.

No, she had never seen anyone she wanted to go off with. When she thought of going, it was never with a man. Once she had indulged in wild dreams. For years after she was married she felt that someone would one day come, someone she could love with all her heart, with that high, free elation and that deep satisfaction she could imagine. She would be able to share everything with him ; her fears in the night about loneliness, death, the end of things. He would understand, she felt, but he would not explain, for after all there is no explanation. He would laugh, too, at what she laughed at ; he would enjoy shop incidents, tram incidents, street incidents—all the queer, funny things that go to make up every day. Letty felt, for years, that someone like this would come before it was too late.

' It's not really me, having the children and living with Ambrose,' she would think in bewilderment. ' This isn't my life really ; it will all be different soon. I shall begin to live as I want to—soon.'

But the years went on and now she was over forty and looked for nobody to rescue her as if she were a damsel in distress. She no longer expected to be loved by any man. Men wanted youth and beauty ; no matter how old and ugly they were themselves, they felt entitled to youth and beauty in women. She had missed the great love she had dreamed of as a girl, but she thought about it no more. Her wishes had changed as she grew older ; she now only wanted to get away by herself, to enjoy life in her own way.

' It's as though I have grit in my wheels,' said Letty to herself.

Ambrose was the grit ; the wheels of Letty's life rasped, ground, stopped when they shouldn't, set her teeth on edge ; and as the years of matrimony lengthened behind her, the wheels ran less and less smoothly ; they were worn now and the slightest thing sent them wrong.

Her mother, although Letty never complained openly, often reminded her in obscure and diffident ways that she had her children ; set them before her, as if to point out that here was the be-all and end-all of her existence. But Letty could not feel that.

While the children were very young, it had been one

long scramble to look after them ; to get them up,
put them to bed, feed them, see to their clothes, take
them out, amuse them ; and now that they were
growing up they were growing away from her. Dick
in his last term at Romstead seemed like a stranger,
and David and Roger had now gone away to school
and would return for the holidays entirely changed.
How was she to fill her life with them when they were
not there ? Rachel was still available, and Letty had
a faint hope that things might be different at Beech
Crescent when Rachel left school. But Rachel would
probably marry ; it was no use building on her. It
was no use building on anyone, Letty felt.

She knew what she wanted, but could not have ;
it was freedom. Laura knew what she wanted and
she had got it.

When she had asked all her questions and heard all
the tale, Letty relapsed into silence in her turn, and
Ambrose, at the mention of Laura's pearls, put down
the newspaper to offer to send them back to George
himself. He felt no one would be able to break the
news to the poor chap as kindly and as adequately as
he himself.

It was late when they left Greenbanks, but Letty
knew that Aunt Alice would never forgive her if she
did not go round to Park Row and tell her what had
happened. Aunt Alice was already in bed, but sat
up to receive the news with due astonishment and
chagrin. She usually liked women to go off with men
not their husbands, but not in her own family.
Letty could not bring herself to enlarge much on
Laura's departure. Life seemed suddenly to have
taken on a dreadful aspect, with old women sitting
up in bed without teeth, and Ambrose waiting down

below, and Laura going away while Letty herself had to stay behind. She kissed Aunt Alice's withered cheek and left her still exclaiming.

II

Laura had gone and everybody was upset, but the plums had been ordered, had arrived, and must be made into jam or be ruined. Louisa, on the second morning after Laura's departure, was standing over the great pan in the kitchen when such a furious peal came at the bell that it continued to dance on its wire long after Bella had gone to the door and ushered a visitor into the drawing-room.

Louisa sighed. She hated to be called away when the crucial moment of setting was approaching.

Bella came back into the kitchen, looking startled.

'It's Miss Laura's husband, 'm. It's Mr. Boyd.'

Louisa dropped the wooden spoon into the jam.

'Oh . . .' she faltered, staring at Bella who was not supposed to know anything about Laura's flight. 'Whatever shall I do ? '

'Eh, I don't know, 'm. Isn't it awkward ? '

Mistress and maid continued to gaze at each other helplessly and would have continued indefinitely so to do had not the drawing-room door opened and impatient footsteps begun to sound all over the hall and seemed about to approach the kitchen.

Louisa, galvanized into energy, tore off her apron, smoothed her hair on each side of her brow and hurried through the baize door.

'Well, George, well,' she cried, putting a heartiness she did not feel into her voice.

George thrust a sheet of paper covered with Laura's handwriting at Louisa.

'What's the meaning of this? That's what I want to know.'

His face was so suffused with blood that Louisa was alarmed.

'Come into the drawing-room, come and sit down. . . .'

'Not I. I haven't come here to sit down. What's this in this letter?'

'You know as much about it as I do,' said Louisa, getting him into the drawing-room by the simple expedient of going there herself.

'Where is she? Where has she gone?'

'I don't know,' said Louisa.

'You don't know! You, her own mother, don't know where your daughter has gone?'

'Why should her mother know more than her husband?' asked Louisa.

'Who is that man? Is it somebody she's picked up? By God, this war is sending everybody off their heads. Who is he? Some chap tricked out in officer's uniform I suppose?'

'We've known him all our lives. Laura was engaged to him. She has always loved him, George,' pleaded Louisa.

'Why did she marry me then? Answer me that. She's treated me nicely, hasn't she? Why didn't she stick to him, and not get me into this mess?'

'Oh, George, I wish she had. . . .'

'Why didn't you send for me at once? I'd have stopped her.'

'She gave me no time. But nothing would have stopped her.'

'She always was a headstrong little fool. I don't know why you didn't bring her up better. The whole thing's abominable. Me with that great house on my hands . . . I was just going to sell it—had a splendid offer—when I got engaged to her, curse the day ! It's cost me a fortune, that house, and so has she. I thought it would be a splendid family house, and now she's left me alone in it. What'll they think at the club ? What'll all my friends think ? As nice a lot of people as you could meet ; Laura had done very well for herself to get in with them. She had a lovely time with me and my friends, a generous, open-handed lot. Look at the races and the parties—why, she didn't know what parties were,' spluttered George, ' until I showed her. Those people thought no end of Laura. I gave her everything I could think of to make her happy. What more did she want that I hadn't given her ? What did she want ? She'd only to tell me . . . if she'd mentioned a thing, she'd have got it. . . .'

George suddenly put his fat hands over his face and began to cry. He stood in the middle of the drawing-room and blubbered, bowing his head over his great stomach.

Louisa was helpless. She could only say over and over again : ' Don't, George. George, don't . . . I'm so sorry. . . .'

She searched vainly for words to comfort him. She wrung her hands and thought of brandy and soda and tea and finally of Ambrose. Ambrose would know what to say to George. She ran to tell Bella to telephone for him. When she returned George was drying his eyes on a silk handkerchief, and they sat opposite each other in silence until Ambrose arrived.

Ambrose was equal to the occasion. Louisa could tell that as soon as he greeted George. His manner was just right. She escaped gratefully and left him to it. She sent Bella in with coffee, but she herself did not return until Ambrose summoned her to say Good-bye to George.

' I shall take the poor chap out to lunch,' whispered Ambrose. ' He'd be uncomfortable here. He's going back to Nottingham this afternoon. He's no more anxious to spread this abroad than we are. I've advised him to wipe his hands of the whole affair as quickly as possible, but he doesn't seem to be able to make up his mind to it.'

Louisa said good-bye to George. He had come briefly into her family and now he was going out of it. She had never thought much of him, but she was sorry for him. Laura had treated him very badly, and in his limited fashion he loved her.

He only took Louisa's hand in his large soft one and dropped it again limply. He was shamefaced because he had wept before her, because his eyes were still red and swollen, and because he imagined his position was the most ignominious a man could ever be in.

Louisa could not bring herself to watch him go away. She returned to the kitchen and began to write on the jam covers ' Plum : October 10th, 1914 '.

III

A week later Jim's marriage to his Mabel was accomplished. Mabel's red hair was in a special frizz and her teeth were more than ever prominent from joy, but no tulle, orange-blossom, or organ music could make her into a bride to be wept over by the congregation. No one felt emotionally apprehensive as to how life would deal with this bride, but many reflected that love was a queer thing since it could move Jim Ashton to lead Mabel Dawson to the altar.

At the reception afterwards, the bridegroom's family were as segregated as they had been in the right-hand pews at the church. They felt better able to parry inquiries about Laura in a body. Ambrose hummed and hawed a good deal behind his wing collar ; Rose took the offensive and asked a great many questions before she could be asked any ; Aunt Alice clung to Louisa, in case, if left to herself, someone should get the truth out of her. Louisa behaved with the most composure ; she had acquired the art, in Robert's time, of making no explanation.

' I should have thought Laura would have stayed for her brother's wedding,' remarked Mrs. Brewster reproachfully.

' No,' smiled Louisa.

' Has Laura gone home ? ' asked Mrs. Parsons of Aunt Alice, who fluttered and looked trapped.

' Laura is looking for war work,' said Louisa, coming to the rescue.

When Jim had gone away at last with Mabel, his relations escaped with relief to Greenbanks.

' It's too bad,' said Rose indignantly. ' Laura's putting us into this wretched situation. I never felt so uncomfortable in my life ; I shall be glad to get away from Elton, Mother.'

Rose was very angry with Laura. Not only had she made the match with George, and considered it a very good one, but Perry was accountant for George's firm, and would now, in all probability, lose George's business. Laura should have thought of this, Rose felt, before she went off with Cecil Bradfield.

Louisa made no reply to Rose. Since they had all

joined together to condemn Laura, she herself had gone over to Laura's side, defending her silently and blaming her no longer. Indeed, although it would hardly do to say so, she thought it was better for Laura to be happy with Cecil than to wither in bitterness and hatred with George.

Rose, Thomas and May left Elton that same afternoon. Rose wanted to get back to her husband, Thomas to his engineering works, which had just been taken over for Munitions.

Louisa and Kate Barlow sat down alone to high tea. They had not dared to have high tea when Jim was at home, but now he was gone and they had it ; moreover, Bella put a table-centre under the tall vase of flowers.

' Another one gone,' said Louisa. ' Another room empty.'

And then remembering that she need no longer keep the best of everything for Jim, she added :

' And now we can eat the hearts of the celery. Help yourself, Kate.'

CHAPTER SIXTEEN

ELTON seethed with war-time activities, and women
discovered new values. Delicate daughters
who had hitherto done nothing but follow their
mothers from drawing-room to drawing-room,
now stood daily in hospital sculleries, steeping their
thin white arms in greasy dish-water, in the hope
of reaching the wards when all the examinations
should be passed. At these examinations, girls
from shops and offices might be seen scribbling
competently through their papers, while young
Miss from the Manor, the Hall and the Grange,
bit her pen and wondered how on earth to spell
' diarrhœa '.

In the Y.W.C.A. huts it was discovered that though
no one had heard before of little Mrs. Potts of some
street or other, she rapidly came to the head of affairs,
displacing many grander ladies on her way. And
Mrs. Simmons, who had been a hospital-nurse before
her marriage and had no aspirations to the society of
the Webberleys, the Sysons and the Withingtons, now
found herself invited by them to discuss the principles
of Nursing and First Aid over luncheon, tea or dinner
almost every day ; until she was appointed Matron
of the Park Hospital, and Webberleys, Sysons and
Withingtons flocked to serve under her to the best
of their ability.

The spoon of war stirred the contents of the
provincial pan very thoroughly, and Mrs. Spence

called at Greenbanks one Saturday afternoon to ask
Kate Barlow to join the Bandage Class.

Louisa was immensely gratified, and sat with a
delighted smile throughout the visit. Here at last
was an opportunity for Kate to return to social life !
It was splendid ; it would do her all the good in the
world ! Louisa herself had despaired of making Kate
happy ; to do that it would take, she felt, something
more than she had to offer. But here was an invitation from outside, and Kate must see now that
people were ready to accept her. And if they were
ready to bury the past, why shouldn't Kate bury it
too ? Bygones would be bygones at last, thought
Louisa, and beginning with the Bandage Class, Kate
would be drawn back into a normal life.

Kate did not receive the invitation very graciously,
but Louisa intimated to Mrs. Spence by nods and
signs that it was just her way. When Kate seemed
about to refuse the invitation outright, Louisa bustled
Mrs. Spence out of the house.

' She will let you know, Mrs. Spence. She will
just think it over and let you know,' she said, con-
ducting Mrs. Spence to the door.

' She doesn't need to do that,' said Mrs. Spence.
' If she decides to come, let her turn up at the Town
Hall, Room F, at three o'clock on Tuesday. I'll look
out for her.'

' There,' said Louisa, returning to Kate in the
drawing-room. ' Wasn't that kind ? '

' Kind ? ' said Kate, with her inflection.

Louisa was a little flustered.

' Well, I mean, wasn't it nice to seek you and say
she would be looking out for you ? You must go,
Kate dear. You really must. It's too dull for you

being here with nobody but me. You're a young woman, you know. It would do you good to get out and see people.'

'I don't want to go,' said Kate.

'Oh, but please do, dear. Just to please me. Besides, we must all do our bit,' said Louisa, delighted to have thought of this. 'We must all do our bit for the war.'

Kate was silent for a moment, then she said :

'I can knit at home—I mean, here,' she amended.

'You can knit here, and you can make bandages there,' said Louisa firmly. 'You are so clever with your fingers, dear ; you will be a great help to them. Do please go once and see how you like it.'

'I don't know what I shall do,' said Kate, dismissing the subject.

Louisa dared not approach it again, but she watched eagerly. She knew Kate was thinking about the Bandage Class when she looked away from her sewing or her book at times to consider ; sometimes her face hardened and closed, and Louisa was afraid she was deciding not to go ; but sometimes a faint eagerness and hope showed for an instant before she looked down again, and Louisa hoped then that she was deciding to go.

Kate left Louisa in suspense all Sunday, Monday and Tuesday morning and then she said she would go to the Bandage Class, if Louisa liked.

'Oh, Kate, I am so glad, dear. I'm sure you'll enjoy it,' cried Louisa. 'I would like you to get out a little more. Three o'clock Mrs. Spence said, didn't she ? Perhaps you'd better get ready.'

Kate went to get ready. Every Christmas Louisa gave Kate among other presents a cheque, and with it Kate bought material for dresses. But the dresses were always black and very plain ; she dressed like a companion out of perversity, Louisa felt in moments of irritation. Life had made her a paid companion and a paid companion she would be, in spite of Louisa and everybody else.

Kate came down now in her black dress, her black coat and hat.

'Well, now, good-bye, dear,' said Louisa, seeing her off.

'Good-bye,' said Kate. Her cheeks were faintly pink and her lips trembled a little, softening her face. She went down the steps, but at the gate she paused, and Louisa was afraid she was going to change her mind and not go after all.

'Good-bye,' she called, invisibly pushing Kate through the gate.

Kate went through. Louisa turned back into the house with a sigh. Kate had taken the plunge.

Kate reached the Town Hall, almost in spite of herself. She kept thinking she wouldn't go, but her legs kept on taking her there. She went into the dim, echoing corridors and was directed to Room F, where most of the others were already assembled.

As soon as she entered Room F, Kate felt in a panic to get out again. But Mrs. Spence, true to her word, was looking out for her, and showed her where to hang up her hat and coat. Kate looked round the room. She was a crow among doves ; she was harsh and black among pink-and-white softness, crêpe-de-Chine blouses, pearls, waved hair, easy laughter, piles of snowy lint, gamgee tissue, cotton-wool.

At the far end of the room there were a few dowds huddled together and Kate would have gone to take her place among them, but Mrs. Spence, determined to be kind, led her to her own table and presented her to the company.

There were many who had been school-friends of Kate's but were now established matrons; they greeted her kindly from their security, but she saw in their eyes that they recognized the difference between themselves and her; and she hated them as she sat down. They tried to draw her into their pleasant, common-place conversation.

'How is Laura Ashton? Someone said she was in Dieppe?'

Kate gave a cold non-committal answer. Did they think she had come there to be pumped?

'How is Mrs. Ashton? She is such a sweet old thing, isn't she? So kind.'

'Kind to have me to live with her, I suppose you mean?' thought Kate.

They talked about their children, until someone frowned meaningly. They talked about other people, but it was hard to talk about other people without gossiping a little. Kate wondered if they thought she hadn't enough sense to know they would talk about her when she was gone. A glance from her dark eyes asked them this, and the talk was stilled again.

But it went on, and Kate, making a splint with skilful fingers, listened and thought: 'Not a spark, not a spark!' Not a spark of intelligence, or *difference*; all babble. Was this the society that had rejected her? What stuff it was made up of! She despised it, she resented it, and yet her heart swelled with childish grief to be so barred out.

Her lowered eyelids were like drawn blinds shutting her away from them. It was painful to raise them when tea was served, painful to eat in their company. They were telling low stories now. She did not know it was their habit; she thought they were poking them at her. Philip Symonds and his elderly wife and she herself were fit subjects for music-hall jokes, she admitted in anguish. Oh, let her get away, let her get away!

When the clock showed half-past five, she escaped. She rose abruptly, said good afternoon, put on her black things and hurried back to Greenbanks.

'Never again,' she said savagely to herself.

'Never again,' she said to the sadly disappointed Louisa. 'Never ask me to go among those people again, Mrs. Ashton, please.'

Her tone threw the blame for the wretched afternoon on Louisa, who accepted it with a sigh. There was nothing to be done for Kate, it seemed.

The war offered chances to Kate Barlow which she did not take; the war offered chances to Ambrose Harding, and he took them all.

Committees multiplied in Elton and Ambrose fell naturally into place as chairman of most of them. It seemed to be municipally recognized that a committee-room was the proper place for him. In a Board Room, with its close, respectable atmosphere, chaste bottle of water, portraits of local worthies on the walls, the dusty litter of Ambrose's mind could blow freely over the company without causing them any annoyance; it was what was expected at committees.

Ambrose, with his solid good looks and a diction that fell pleasantly on Lancashire ears, made an excellent figure-head; and a figure-head was all that he was required to be. The work was being done by somebody in the background as usual. Ambrose did not know he was a figure-head. He was immensely in earnest, and meant to devote his whole heart and intelligence to the work of the War Relief, Soldiers' & Sailors' Families Association, War Pensions, but he was so taken up with the fuss and formality attached thereto that neither his heart or his intelligence had much of a chance. He worked very hard ; he sat for hours in committee, he went without meals, pored over papers far into the night, stood at the telephone in the hall at Beech Crescent until his hands shook and his feet froze to the tiled floor ; he attended every meeting, every function, and had his finger in almost every possible pie. He had glimpses of life that he had never had before ; and many of them were startling.

'Who is the father of this child ? ' he asked a woman brought before him in committee.

'Well, I couldn't just say,' the woman answered as casually as if he had asked what sort of a day it had been last Tuesday.

Ambrose fell back. He reached for his handkerchief and blew his nose unnecessarily. He was acutely conscious of the presence of ladies at the table, Miss Barton, Mrs. Simpson. . . . He looked as embarrassed, for a moment, as if he were the unknown guilty party.

'Preposterous . . . preposterous . . .' he murmured, recovering himself and taking refuge in speech. 'We ought to do something about this, Brownhill. We ought to send a memorandum to the War Office.'

'Nothing can be done, sir, I'm afraid. The woman is entitled to the allowance her husband assigned to her,' said the clerk in charge, stifling a yawn. This was his third committee that afternoon, and the close air of the Board Room was beginning to tell on him.

'But it's appalling to encourage women in immorality in this way,' began Ambrose, desirous of dealing worthily with the situation.

'Edna !' shouted the woman. 'Stop pulling at me. I've told you we're going as soon as this 'ere gentleman can make up 'is mind about my money. You can't 'ave yer tea until yer get it. And that's that.'

Ambrose had to give in.

In his desire to do his work properly, he often went round visiting himself, but he rarely got any pleasure out of it.

'Oh, ye're 'ere, are yer?' shouted a woman from a door-post. 'I was just going to write to t' War Office about yer if y'adn't come to-day.'

'My good woman,' explained Ambrose. 'You don't seem to understand that this is purely voluntary work on my part. I give my services to the nation in these matters without monetary remuneration whatever. In other words, I do it for nothing.'

'I don't care what you do it for,' said the woman. 'But I'd like to know what yer mean by being late with my money. 'And it over. I'm waiting to go out.'

'Savages,' muttered Ambrose, going away very red in the face. 'That's what these people are . . . savages ! This work would have been pleasant in the south. I should have met with nothing but courtesy and gratitude. But here . . . bah !'

When he was put on the Tribunal, he inspected hundreds of attestation papers, and when the reasons given were not satisfactory, he sent for the attestor in person.

' I 'ave bad feet with bunions, besides I don't hold with war,' he read over to a great navvy smelling of clay and shag.

' This won't do, my man. I'm afraid you'll have to provide a better reason for non-enlistment than this. The nation needs every man it can get.'

' Why don't you go yerself, then ? ' asked the man.

Ambrose looked steadily and coldly at the impertinent inquirer.

' Because I am over age.'

' Get off—you're better fit to go than me, with the soft life you've led. I'm a navvy ; I've been out in all weathers all me life, mostly wet, and stead of doin' me good, it's nearly rotted the bones off me. Besides, I've told you I don't 'old with war. What should I go killing them Germans for ? They're nobbut chaps like meself. I'd as soon kill you,' said the navvy, with a glint of humour in his eye.

' You'll be finding yourself in jail, my man, if you air those opinions,' warned Ambrose.

' I'll go to jail sooner than to any bloody war,' said the man from the door. ' And you can do as you damn well like about that paper. And don't let anybody send for me again to be questioned by such as you, you bloomin' Cissy.'

Such incidents were painful ; but Ambrose kept on.

Charles was now at the Front and Louisa lived with sharp fears day after day.

' What are they doing now ? ' she would ask Kate, and would listen while Kate read from the newspaper, her hand beating her knee from time to time.

' It's terrible, it's terrible. I wish they'd let all those poor boys go home.'

She had a nightmare feeling that she was cowering

very low, very small and without protection, waiting for the giant hand of war to crush her.

Then Charles came home on leave and Louisa forgot the nightmare in her efforts to cure his chapped hands and frost-bitten ears. He had got into a terrible state, she told him, but he said it was nothing and fell asleep under her ministrations. He was always falling asleep. When Ambrose held forth about war, Charles murmured : ' Funny ; it's not a bit like that really,' and fell asleep before Ambrose could convince him that onlookers often saw most of the game.

Charles observed life and his family with a new detachment.

' I'm glad Laura left Boyd,' he said, sitting with his mother in the drawing-room as of old. ' I wish Letty would leave Ambrose. She used to be such fun, but she gets flatter and flatter as the years go on. It's all the effect of Ambrose. Poor chap, he means well, but he's so damned dull. He blights Letty. Have you seen Jim lately, Mother? Pity he's so mean, isn't it? He used to be quite decent to me when I was a kid, although he never could bear you to touch his things, d'you remember? The rows there were when I used his knife or anything else of his! I suppose that possessiveness has grown on him. You know, he daren't join up, not because he's afraid of war, but because he's afraid something will happen to that business and his chance of making money. He must be having a rotten time, knowing everybody thinks he ought to fight, and yet sticking on to make a fortune while competition's slack.

' Aren't people queer?' he asked his mother, dangling his hands swathed in Louisa's bandages.

'Aren't people queer? Look at your Miss Barlow, creeping about the place, all buttoned up in herself. She's only done one big thing in her life, and that's giving birth to a child, and she's mortally ashamed of it and has gone about mourning ever since. I must try to make her change her point of view. She'd be a lot happier.'

'Charles!' cried Louisa. 'Don't speak to her about it! Don't, I beg, Charles. She can't bear it. You don't know what she's suffered about it. I don't. She's never told me. But if she wants to keep silence, she ought to be allowed to. No one should poke and pry into other people's dark places. I can't allow it, Charles.'

'All right, all right,' said Charles soothingly.

'You know,' he remarked later. 'The only person I find completely satisfying, Mother, is you.'

'Me?' asked Louisa, going quite pink.

'Mmmm,' said Charles. 'The French have an expression "Bon comme le pain." When I heard it, I thought of you. You're good, like bread; you're essential, you know, Mother. The world couldn't get on without people like you.'

'Nay, nay,' protested Louisa. 'I'm not half clever enough. Not clever enough for your father, not half clever enough for you children. I've always felt that drawback.'

'It's better to be wise than clever, and that's what you are, darling. But don't look so bothered. I won't praise you any more. Lord, you do make me laugh when you look like that! When I think of you sometimes at the Front, I roar with laughter. Just remembering how you look over your knitting, or those priceless sort of flat remarks you take people down with. When Mrs. Brewster asked if Mrs. What's-her-name lived with her husband and you said : " Oh, no, she has her own money, you know." And when Miss Barnes had that motor-accident and you said : " She talks as if that accident had disfigured her and spoiled her chances. She forgets she always had a face like that." Oh, darling, you're devastating at times.' Charles threw back his head and showed all his beautiful teeth in a long laugh.

Louisa smiled demurely over her knitting. She hadn't meant to be funny, but she was glad she was, for all that.

Then Charles went to Salisbury Plain on a course and later returned to the Front with a commission.

Laura was attached to a hospital in Dieppe ; she wrote that she had seen Cecil twice. George still refused to divorce her. ' But when the war is over, perhaps he will see reason,' she wrote.

Rachel knew the war only as a plasticene relief map on which the form moved flags backwards or forwards. When forwards, the form was jubilant for five minutes or so in the morning ; when backwards, they were despondent for the same length of time.

When Ambrose sent his daughter to the High School to receive, within the sphere of his influence, a suit-ably feminine education, he had reckoned without Miss Cope.

Nature had been both kind and unkind to the Headmistress of Elton High School in that she had a fine brain—she was a Wrangler—but no looks. Miss Cope was one of those people with fat cheeks and a thin nose ; she wore her black hair parted down the middle and pulled into a little knot at the back of her head, thereby heightening her resemblance to a

Dutch doll. She had a large figure, completely shape-
less, because since she did not approve of stays for
her pupils, she did not wear them herself. Miss Cope
was like that ; she practised what she preached.

Ambrose saw Miss Cope only on her platform
during speech-day and other ceremonies.

'Not attractive,' he remarked when they returned
home from one such occasion.

Letty was stung. She admired Miss Cope and
resented this male attitude.

'Are you ? ' she asked abruptly.

Ambrose was very taken aback.

'What did you say ? '

'I said, "Are you ? "' repeated Letty and hurried
out of the room.

Outside in the hall, she clapped her hand to her
mouth and stared aghast at the tiled floor. What an
awful thing to say to Ambrose ! How awful she was
becoming !

Ambrose, however, continued to dismiss the Headmistress as unattractive and to be entirely unaware that
she was undermining his plans for his daughter.

Rachel came into contact with Miss Cope during
her fourth-form year when her depredations on the
lid of her desk were discovered and the damage was
considered so extensive that she was sent to the Head.

She blushed and stammered in the presence and finally
admitted that she had been playing at filling teeth.

Miss Cope hastily suppressed a smile. This was a
funny little creature ! An attractive little thing !
Miss Cope had to fight against attraction. Having
no beauty herself, she loved beauty in others. But
she assumed a sternness she did not feel and pursued
her inquiries. Rachel's head sank lower and lower.

'And when do you pursue these dental practices?' asked Miss Cope.

'Mostly during Geography,' admitted Rachel.

'Ah—during Geography.'

Rachel nodded, being almost beyond words. Then fearing that there might be disrespect in a nod, she whispered hoarsely: 'Yes, Miss Cope.'

'Don't you like Geography?'

'Not very much.'

'Why?'

Rachel raised her eyes and looked desperately at the green-curtained door. She didn't know why she didn't like Geography. She just didn't like it.

'I think Geography is great fun,' said Miss Cope.

Rachel's eyes turned for the first time to Miss Cope. Fun! What a strange description of Geography!

'Just look at this book for a moment,' invited Miss Cope, reaching to a shelf behind her.

Rachel approached the awful desk. She tiptoed and leaned forward to look at the book from upside-down, which was all she dared venture.

'No, come round here,' said Miss Cope, restraining an impulse to put out a hand and draw the timid little creature nearer. Miss Cope resisted these impulses, because she thought they were not befitting to the dignity of a headmistress.

'What do you think of that,' continued Miss Cope.

Rachel bent, full of polite desire to think something. There was nothing on the page but a few lines drawn, but Rachel saw at once a vast expanse of snow, mountains, the tips of fringed pines—a whole world bound in iron.

'What is it?' she asked.

'It's the Ice Age,' said Miss Cope, turning the

fascinating page and revealing another drawing of strange houses and temples covering a little hill ; and the hill was as it were sliced through, exposing another city inside.

'What is it ? ' asked Rachel, too interested now to wonder whether it was polite to keep on asking.

'It's three ancient cities built one on top of the other—that's the way they used to build them.'

'Oh, what's this ? ' cried Rachel. 'Is it the Flood ? '

'Yes, it's the Flood.'

'The Flood wasn't just in the Bible land then ? Was the Flood all over the world ? Was it over here —where we're standing—*here ?* '

'Yes, Elton was included in the Flood,' smiled Miss Cope.

Rachel's eyes were wide. She felt herself under water with Miss Cope. But Miss Cope broke the illusion ; she turned the page and Rachel leaned forward eagerly.

'Oh, look at those little fleets setting out from those maps ! Where are they going ? '

'They're the Angles and Saxons coming to Britain I think—— Yes, they are.'

'Does it tell you all about everything in the reading ? ' asked Rachel.

'Yes,' said Miss Cope.

The drawings were so deceptively simple and child-like and Rachel burst out :

'I think I could draw like that.'

'You could certainly try,' said Miss Cope.

'But this is history,' said Rachel. 'I like History. It's Geography I don't like.'

'Geography makes history. But I'll lend you the book, shall I, and then you can see that for yourself ? '

' Oh,' breathed Rachel, taking the entrancing book
from Miss Cope's hands. ' Thank you very much.'

' You'd better run along home now. You're going
to be late.'

Rachel made for the door. They had both forgotten what she had come for, but Miss Cope remembered just in time.

' By the way, no more dentistry on desks, Rachel!
I shall have to send a bill to your father and recom-
mend that you pay for it yourself out of your pocket-
money.'

' Yes, Miss Cope.' Rachel was momentarily
abashed. But Miss Cope smiled in a warm, friendly
way and she knew it was all right really.

She read the book, and while she read it, she lived
in an enchanted world. She did not understand all,
but it is not necessary to understand to marvel. She
listened eagerly to the Geography lessons in the hope
of hearing more of the wonders related in the book,
but though Miss Tattersall, prompted by Miss Cope,
altered her methods of teaching, she was far from
equalling the book in interest. When Rachel moved
into a higher form, however, Miss Harris could often
make magic in her lessons, and when Rachel won
the Geography and History prizes, she received a
copy of Miss Cope's book for her own.

Rachel had a passion for reading, shared by no
member of her family. None of the Ashtons read
much ; Ambrose read the papers ; London and local
papers, morning and evening papers took up all his
spare time. The boys progressed from Sexton Blake
to Sherlock Holmes and historical romances, and
seemed to stop there. But Rachel, surreptitiously
visiting the book-cases where her father had all the

best books on show, extracted volume after volume of
Shakespeare, Sterne, Fielding, Goldsmith, Dickens,
Scott, Jane Austen, bound Cornhills, bound Punches.
. . . She skimmed over what she did not understand
and got what she wanted from the rest. The illus-
trations of Doré in Dante's *Inferno* terrified and fascinated her ; they gave her nightmares, but she went
on poring over them. When she wanted to impress
Judy Spence with some horror seen or imagined, she
would say : ' You know—like in Dante's *Inferno.*'

She read the classics with avidity, not knowing them
to be classics, but she read with equal avidity *St.
Hilda's, Brenda Shows the Way, The Hockey Heroine* and
other school tales lent to her by Judy, who always
had books of this kind given to her at Christmas. She
read, too, the penny novelettes she found in the kitchen
at Greenbanks and at Beech Crescent. She made no
discrimination between these literatures ; she read
and enjoyed them all.

She also had a passion for declamation—in private.
She was too shy for the school stage. But she would
recite from the open page of Tennyson as she brushed
her hair, and take Shakespeare into the bathroom to
shout from it as the bath was running ; the covering
noise gave her a splendid opportunity to let herself go.

At Greenbanks Louisa once came knocking at the
door in alarm.

' Rachel ! Rachel ! '

Rachel turned off the flood of eloquence and the
taps simultaneously.

' Yes ? '

' Whatever is the matter, love ? Why are you
calling out ? '

' Oh, it's only Richard the Third. I was just

doing : " A horse, a horse ! My kingdom for a horse ! " So sorry I disturbed you, darling,' said Rachel, opening the door to reveal herself surprisingly, after all that desperation and passion, as a little girl in her petticoat waiting for the bath to fill.

CHAPTER SEVENTEEN

I

TOWARDS the end of the March afternoon, Rachel, her school-bag sagging from her shoulder, progressed in her jerky fashion up the Greenbanks garden on her way to tea within. She stopped and then went on, she loitered and then ran. By the gate, under the laurel bushes there were snowdrops like little congregations of White Nuns at prayer. Higher up on the banks, the yellow crocuses lay in tatters.

'Oh . . .' said Rachel, making a growl. She shared her grandmother's disgust of sparrows. They ignored the crusts and pieces of fat that were allowed to lie so untidily on the bird-table for them, food that would have done them good, said Louisa, and that she would be glad to be rid of, and they destroyed the yellow crocuses, the winter aconites, the mauve bulbocodium, from pure wantonness. Louisa disliked them for it, but when Ambrose suggested that their nests should be pulled from under the eaves in spring, she said it was unthinkable.

Higher still under the windows, Glories of the Snow spilled their loose, heavenly blue, and Rachel saw that her grandmother was trying to save these from the sparrows, for she had planted a forest of little twigs and on the path lay a reel of black cotton. She must have been interrupted at her work, or forgotten it, thought Rachel, because the reel was still there, and soon it would be dark and no one would be able to find it. She picked it up to take into the house.

On the wide, shallow step at the door, she turned to look back at the garden. It was very still under the clear, quiet sky. Rachel felt she could stand there a long time and be still like the trees. But she was hungry, and turned the door-handle briskly. She threw her school-bag down on the hall chair, her hat and coat after it. She was about to call out for her grandmother as usual, when the green baize door from the kitchen opened, and Bella, pressing an apron to her face, beckoned silently.

Rachel stared in amazement.

' What's the matter ? ' she called out. Then as she advanced through the gloom of the hall she added : ' Are you—are you crying, Bella ? '

Bella drew her through the door.

' What's the matter ? ' repeated Rachel, her eyes wide with apprehension. ' There's nothing the matter with Grandma, is there ? '

Bella shook her head.

' It's Mr. Charles . . .' she began, but could not go on for weeping.

' Charles ? ' said the parrot from his cage in the window. ' Now, now, now. Cheer up, ducky.'

' What's the matter with Uncle Charles ? ' asked Rachel.

' He's dead,' sobbed Bella. ' He's killed . . . poor missus.'

Rachel moved her hand up and down the kitchen table which had its afternoon red cloth on. She tried to take in the fact that Uncle Charles was dead, would never come home again, never see this kitchen with the pictures of ' Cherry Ripe ' and the little girl in the white satin bonnet, or the parrot he had brought home from Africa. She moved to Bella and put her arms round Bella's stiff print waist. She was ashamed that Bella should weep while she, a relation, could not shed a tear.

She was still standing with her arms round Bella's waist, looking bewildered, when Kate Barlow came into the kitchen.

Kate's face was white and hard. Here was another of the vile tricks life played ; she was disgusted with life ; sick of it, sick of it.

' Your grandmother is in the drawing-room, Rachel,' she said. ' Will you go in to her ? I'm not going to let anyone know yet,' she said to Bella. ' It's best to let her be quiet for a time.'

Rachel went reluctantly. She felt that grief must have changed her grandmother into a stranger. She tiptoed out into the hall, going as quietly as if Charles lay dead in the house instead of in a field in France. She listened at the drawing-room door ; there was not a sound. Gulping a little, she slowly turned the handle and went in.

Her grandmother was sitting just as usual in the low chair by the windows. She turned her head as Rachel came falteringly across the carpet.

' Well, love ? ' she said, with her smile.

Rachel could not bear that. She burst into tears and threw herself down at her grandmother's knee.

Louisa bowed herself over the child's head.

' Hush, love. Hush, now . . .' she said, stroking Rachel's hair.

But Rachel wept ; she wept for her grandmother, not for poor Charles.

' Hush, love,' said Louisa. ' I don't feel he's dead.

I feel he has come very near. Never to leave me any more. I've seen him go away so often, but I shan't again. He'll stay with me now, until I go to him. Don't cry, love. Dry your eyes. Don't disturb him by crying. Let's sit here quietly with him.'

Gradually, Rachel made herself quiet ; she leaned against her grandmother, her hand in hers. A strange peace filled the room. The dusk deepened ; darkness fell and no one disturbed them. Rachel, worn out after her tears, had fallen asleep, but Louisa kept communion with her son.

II

' She's taken it very well,' said some with relief.
' Does she feel it, do you think ? ' asked others.
' How wonderful she is. . . .'
' How queer. . . .'
They passed their opinions on Louisa. She did not know what they said, and would not have heeded if she had. The first exaltation did not last, but it returned. When Charles's things came home, Louisa broke down. She locked herself away with his clothes, creased by his living body, his bed, his pocket-book with an unfinished letter to her. No one knew what she suffered in Charles's room, but when she came out of it, there was a worn radiance in her face that silenced well-meant condolences.

Through Charles, living, Louisa had known her greatest happiness. Through Charles, dead, she began to know some ineffable life of the spirit. Love and sorrow took the scales from her eyes ; she experienced something she could not express, she felt something she could not understand. God was ; and there was a life of the spirit lived still by Charles, and lived, at

moments, by herself. During these next months
Louisa was only half in the world. When people spoke
of her loss, they dragged her back to it; she was
stricken, desperate because she would never hear his
voice again, never touch him with her hands; but
when they left her alone, her spirit struggled upwards
again towards its new vision.

When Mr. Boulton, the Vicar of St. Anne's, came to
offer her what consolation he could, she almost cried
out : ' Don't confuse me ! Don't disturb me ! Don't
make words of it. . . .'

Mr. Boulton was confused himself; he stammered
before her face, strangely bright, and went away,
humble and sad, feeling he had accomplished nothing
in the way of comfort.

The war dragged to its close.

Laura wrote to say that she was discharged from
hospital and would go, as soon as it could be managed,
to Kenya with Cecil Bradfield, who had come through
the war with no more injury than a bullet through his
shoulder and a tendency to come to a dead halt in
the middle of London traffic. George still refused
a divorce ; they would just have to wait until he was
tired, Laura said.

' I am not coming home before I go to Kenya,
Mother,' wrote Laura. ' It would only make a lot oi
talk, and good-byes are so harrowing. I cannot bear
them. I shall just slip away, and when George has
come to his senses, Cecil and I will come home and
spend a real Christmas with you at Greenbanks.'

But in spite of the fact that she did not come home,
it got about that she had gone away with Cecil Bradfield. There was not the sensation in Elton there
would once have been. The war had blown most

people's ideas sky-high, and the pieces had not yet
come down. When they did come down, they would
never fit together again as they had done before the
war. But there were still a few people, such as Mrs.
Scholes and Miss Gunnerby, who made a point of
visiting Louisa to put seemingly innocent questions
in their purring voices. To these Louisa briefly told
the truth. She was beyond caring what people
thought. Mrs. Scholes and Miss Gunnerby went away
outwardly astonished at her attitude, but inwardly
rather shamed by it.

One by one, in Elton, the war committees were
disbanded. Ambrose was awarded an O.B.E. He
was immensely gratified. It looked so well on letters,
'Ambrose Harding, Esq., O.B.E.' He tried it out
himself as many times as any youthful bride, and
wondered whether he could possibly have it on his
dispatch-case : 'A.H., O.B.E.' But he remembered
what fun these rough North Country people had made
of Sir Joseph Briggs when he had 'Sir J.B.' printed on
his case after knighthood, and he came to the reluctant
conclusion that it would not quite do.

Ambrose was having trouble with his eldest son.
Dick, released from the O.T.C., refused to become a
doctor, and insisted on going into his Uncle Thomas's
engineering works in Birmingham. They warred for
some time, but Dick won. Ambrose was hurt and
disappointed, but the O.B.E. did a good deal to restore
him. He threw out his chest and slapped the pavement heartily with his stick as he walked down to
the office in the mornings to keep his weight down.

CHAPTER EIGHTEEN

IT was summer, but the tent of the sky had sagged with rain and hung low and sodden over Lytham; land and sea looked as if a roller had gone over them, flattening them, merging one into the other. A few gulls wheeled over the leaden water, flashing white as they turned. Under the sea wall there was a little huddle of donkeys waiting to be ridden; they looked so patient that Rachel's heart ached every time she looked at them. She therefore tried not to look often.

'Because it's no use being so sorry,' she told herself sternly. 'I can't do anything for them. If I could buy them, now, and turn them on to the grass by the Windmill. . . .'

It was six years since the war had ended and Rachel was now seventeen and a half. She had come out with her father after the rain to walk on the sands. Ambrose walked steadily along at the edge of the sea, but Rachel kept falling behind to give free rein to her elation. She was extremely elated because the results of the Higher Certificate Examination were out and she had passed with distinction.

'Oh, joy, oh, joy!' she sang to herself ecstatically. She would have her name in black letters on the great oak board in the Hall. She had done much better than anyone else. Miss Cope would be so pleased.

'He-he!' Rachel threw her arms round herself, then dropped them hurriedly in case her father should see and ask why she behaved thus in public. It was awkward being elated in the company of her father, but she felt it was time she caught him up for a little while. He seemed to be upset about something to-day.

Ambrose Harding walked at the edge of the sea, clasping his stick behind his back; his head poked from the collar of his overcoat like the head of a tortoise from its shell, and he turned it from side to side to survey the flat, featureless, treeless Lancashire coast with gloom.

All his thoughts were gloomy to-day. Rubber and cotton seemed, from the paper, to be going from bad to worse, and he had invested Louisa's money heavily in both. After the war, his activities released from committees, Ambrose had turned again to speculation on the Stock Exchange, and in consequence Louisa's income had shrunk. She hardly noticed it, because her wants were few, but Ambrose felt that if the shrinkage continued he would have to make the deficiency good out of his own pocket. That was an uncomfortable prospect.

True, he had more money to spare in these days, now that the boys' education was over. Although it had cost a good deal to set the twins up in Natal. At the thought of his sons, Ambrose sank deeper into depression. They had, all three of them, obstinately gone against his wishes. He wanted Dick to be a doctor, but Dick was an engineer. He had secured excellent places for the twins in cotton, but the twins, ineradicably impressed in childhood by Charles's departure for South Africa, had joined two school-friends in Natal.

What was the good of having children? Ambrose asked bitterly. You denied yourself all the amenities of life; you lived in a small way in a small house, you had no car, you never travelled, you smoked inferior cigars, drank inferior wine, made your overcoat do three winters, did without what you wanted for years to pay for their education, and as soon as they were of an age to make some return, either in companionship or in money, they went off and left you, and you hardly ever saw them again before you died. Ambrose had looked forward to being proud in the company of his well-grown sons, but they had removed themselves. He felt cheated and sore.

There were only three of them left at home now. And Letty was no companion to him. She never tried to be, he thought dismally, trailing his stick behind him on the sand. Letty was strange; he didn't know what was the matter with her. She simply stood off. When he tried to tell her of his worries, she usually sighed and said: 'Oh, well . . . it can't be helped, I suppose.' It was as if she blamed him. Blamed him for *what*? Ambrose was bewildered and indignant.

The house had been very dull since the boys went away, but perhaps now that Rachel had left school things would be better. She would be company for Letty and have time to spare for him now that she had finished with her books. That is, if she were not always running off to Greenbanks. She was so often at Greenbanks, and Ambrose resented it. But he could not object openly; it would sound foolish to complain that the child was always with her grandmother. They must make life at home more attractive to her, he decided. This winter they would all go out together; Rachel and Letty and himself. He supposed they would have to take Rachel to dances, and he did not like the prospect; but it should be done. They would go once a week to the Cinema;

and that Ambrose would enjoy. He had a secret affection for the cinema, but thought it was beneath his dignity to be seen there. However, people would know that he was accompanying his wife and daughter. They would go to the theatre, to the football matches, and the Rugby and hockey matches on Saturday afternoons, where the young people were to be found. And Rachel must be taught to play Bridge. She should have as good a time as possible ; he would see to it. He cheered up suddenly and called out :

' Come along, child, come along ! '

Rachel bounded obediently to his side, and he thought with pride that she had recovered her looks. She had been pale from taking that unnecessary examination, but now she had colour in her cheeks and her eyes were clear and lovely.

' Shouldn't be surprised if she makes a very good match,' thought Ambrose complacently.

He began to cast about among the young men of Elton, the Withingtons, the Selbys, the Webberleys ; none of them, however, appeared to be quite good enough. But there was time enough, he told himself ; she was not yet eighteen years old. He took his stick from behind his back and used it to walk briskly along the hard, firm sand. They could say what they liked about the Lancashire coast, he said to himself, but the sands were good.

Rachel was still engaged on the result of the Higher Certificate Examination. She was thinking that she had almost left school last July and might have missed all the glory. It had been a very near thing.

Ambrose had instructed Letty to call on Miss Cope and give Rachel's notice. Letty had called, but returned with the notice ungiven. In the room behind the green-curtained door, Miss Cope had convinced Letty of the value of education.

'But it isn't as if Rachel will have to earn her own living,' Letty had begun.

'That has nothing to do with it,' said Miss Cope briskly. 'My argument is that Rachel is storing up now something that will increase her happiness and efficiency, no matter what she does in later life. She will probably marry; I hope she does.'

'Do you?' asked Letty in surprise. She thought it was strange for a spinster to say this; she expected a sour-grapes attitude.

'Yes, I hope Rachel will marry,' continued Miss Cope. 'But I hope she won't marry because she can't do anything else to keep herself, or because she is bored at home, or because she wants to acquire money and position.'

Letty kept her eyes on Miss Cope, as if Miss Cope was getting to the root of her matter.

'Why did I marry?' she asked herself. 'Because I thought it would be fun. Fun! I thought it would be fun.'

'However,' went on Miss Cope, 'marriage or no marriage, children or no children, life—the real life— is lived in the spirit, and I hold that the right education helps the spirit to maintain its own life, makes it independent of material prosperity or adversity. That is the ideal we strive for. To enrich the spirit, to enrich the personality.'

'Perhaps that's what is the matter with me?' thought Letty. 'Perhaps if I had been more educated . . .'

She looked back to blame Miss Bertram's school and the Belgian convent.

'Education frees the spirit. Love, faith, mother-
hood, art, may free the spirit, but we can't wait for
them ; they may not come. So we must educate.'

Miss Cope felt as if she might be thought to be
making a speech, and hurriedly returned to the
subject in hand.

'Rachel is very young ; sixteen and a half. Too
young to be turned loose yet. Too young to be given
over to feeling, emotion. Women have so much of
that in their lives, haven't they ? Let her stay another
year in this comparatively clear and simple life. Give
her another year, Mrs. Harding, I beg.'

And in the end, Letty had promised ; without
sanction from Ambrose, she had taken it upon herself
to promise that Rachel should stay at the High School
for another year.

She might have been hard put to it to redeem her
promise if Rachel had not opportunely wept in the
middle of her parents' argument. She sat on the
edge of a chair with her knees together and her toes
slightly turned in and wept into her hands. She
looked awkward and touching and Ambrose gave in
as he sometimes did when least expected to. Rachel
with a streaked face kissed him gratefully and went
back for another year. Now it was over. She had
definitely left, but her thoughts remained at school.
They were busy with the familiar rooms ; with the
Hall where her success would be read out on the first
morning of term after prayers, although she herself
would not hear it, with the notice board in the corridor
where it would be posted up, the Sixth Form room,
the Mistresses' Room where it would be discussed.

Under Rachel's elation there lurked an immense
regret to have finished with all that. But she would

not acknowledge it ; she kept the result of Higher Certificate held high like a shining light to look at.

Ambrose turned at the edge of the sea. He was getting too far up the estuary for his liking ; the chemical factory, hurriedly erected in the war and since fallen into ruin, offended his eye. Rachel, following his example, turned her face towards little Lytham with its quiet air, its grassy front, its windmill, its rows of prim houses, like old maids looking out to sea, not expecting anything, but contented nevertheless.

A figure disengaged itself from the promenaders and came towards them.

' There's Mother ! ' cried Rachel, and flew off, glad of the excuse to fly anywhere.

Ambrose, watching, saw Letty hand something to her daughter and turn away again to the front. She was not coming to join them after all. It was just like her, thought Ambrose with a return of gloom. She was always going off somewhere by herself.

Rachel flew up with letters in her hand.

' Mother brought the letters. And there's one from Miss Cope for you. Do open it, Father ! I'm dying to see what she says about the exam.'

' You may open it yourself,' said Ambrose, running his finger under the flap of an envelope bearing the name of an unsatisfactory rubber company.

' Tch,' he exclaimed in exasperation as he read. They wanted him to take up the shares. Another worry. He foresaw a torturing time ahead. Would it be throwing good money after bad ? Or might the losses be retrieved in this way ? He was interrupted in the mental see-saw that had already begun by an exclamation from Rachel.

' Oh, Father ! '

Her voice was louder than he liked, and he frowned more deeply.

' What is it ? ' he asked testily.

' Oh, Father ! '

She crushed Miss Cope's letter against the front of her yellow jersey.

' For Heaven's sake don't make such a noise,' said Ambrose. ' What is it ? '

' I've been offered a State Scholarship ! ' She made her voice as quiet as it would go at the moment. ' A State Scholarship ! '

' What ? '

' A State Scholarship. That means I can go to Oxford or Cambridge without costing you anything— or at least, not much. Oh, I can't believe it ! I can't believe it ! Is it true ? ' She smoothed out the letter and looked at it again. Excitement had got into her eyes and she could hardly see. ' Yes, it is ! It's true, all right.'

' Give me the letter. What do you say it is ? A State Scholarship. I've never heard of it,' said Ambrose peevishly. He didn't want to be bothered with the thing. He wanted to give his mind to rubber shares.

' Oh, Father, it's the most wonderful thing,' said Rachel, trying to speak calmly. ' It's the highest compliment a girl can be paid ! Oh, I say—Oxford ! Those old libraries where you can actually go and read in the books, and those old gardens where you can go any time ; they say they're lovely. They call their chambermaids " scouts " and Sunday supper " Nondy "—it all sounds rather silly to an outsider, doesn't it ? But I daresay it won't when you are *in*.

Oh, Father, fancy being able to go to Oxford ! My life isn't over,' said the seventeen-year-old Rachel. 'And I thought it was ! My life has only just begun. Oh, Oxford ! '

'Will you be quiet, please ? ' asked Ambrose. 'How can I read this letter when you are whooping in my ear.'

'I'm sorry,' whispered Rachel. She trembled like a young horse waiting to be off. In a minute, in a minute she would run, run, run—all the way to Blackpool and back.

She was thick with honours ! Distinction in Higher Certificate, Miss Cope's praise, the offer of a State Scholarship !

'Well ? ' she asked eagerly, seeing that her father had finished the letter at last.

He handed it back to her.

'I don't know what Miss Cope is thinking about,' he remarked. 'She knew very well that I gave in to her about your staying at School another year, and now she expects me to give in again and let you go for three years to a University. I don't know what she takes me for. A man who can be overridden at any time, I suppose ; made to change his mind by a headmistress, or your mother. She is quite mistaken.'

The bright colour ebbed out of Rachel's face.

'Father ! You don't mean . . .' Apprehension widened her eyes. 'You wouldn't refuse it for me, would you ? You don't mean that ? '

'I most certainly do,' said Ambrose, beginning to walk along the sands again, with his chin jutting forward.

'Father, you couldn't ! You couldn't do that,'

cried Rachel, following him. 'You don't know what it means to me. It's the most wonderful chance . . .'

'You must leave it to me to know what is best for you,' said Ambrose dismissingly.

'But you don't know what's best for me,' cried Rachel. 'How can you? You don't know anything about me.'

Ambrose flushed.

'Now, Rachel,' he admonished warningly, 'don't speak to me like that. You know very well I do not approve of all this education for women. There is nothing more objectionable on this earth than a blue-stocking. I won't have you made into a blue-stocking. I'll keep you from that in spite of yourself and later you'll thank me.'

'Oh, heavens!' cried Rachel, in disgust. 'There aren't any blue-stockings now. They've gone out. There might have been some in your time, but there aren't any now.'

Ambrose's irritation increased at this consignment of himself to the past.

'Now, now,' he admonished warningly again.

'It's all very well your having principles, but why should you drag me into them? Why should you sacrifice me to them?' Rachel's cheeks were bright with anger now.

'Rachel, how dare you speak to your father like that?'

'Sorry, sorry,' said Rachel hurriedly, making an effort.

'Oh, Father, listen,' she broke out again, catching at his arm. 'Let me take this scholarship! Please, please! It's what I've never dreamed of—such a chance! I've always longed to go to Oxford, but I knew you couldn't afford it, with the boys costing so much. But now it won't cost hardly anything, and I'll teach or something when it's over and pay you back every penny.'

'Ah,' said Ambrose. 'Now you've given yourself away. I have no wish for you to teach or something. That is not the kind of life I wish you to lead. In fact, I will not allow it. Understand that. I will not allow it.'

Ambrose struck Lytham sands with his stick.

'Oh, Father, you couldn't make me miss Oxford,' quavered Rachel, her eyes smarting with tears.

'Oxford—bah! Do you think the men want you there? Poking in, trying to ape men. I've no patience with these women intellectuals—lot of frumps!'

'Good Lord, do you think I'm going to bother about whether the men want me there or not?' cried Rachel. 'And when have you seen any women intellectuals, Father? And aren't men intellectuals ever frumps? These reasons for refusing a State Scholarship are all silly—positively silly.'

Her voice broke, and she felt wildly up the sleeves of her jersey for a handkerchief. She had come without one. She brushed her eyes with her sleeve.

'Look here,' said Ambrose. 'I'll have no more of this. I cannot accept State aid for a child of mine. The thing is impossible for a man in my position. Impossible. And let that be the end of it.'

Rachel halted abruptly.

'Oh, God,' she groaned.

'What did you say?' asked Ambrose, turning sharply.

Rachel closed her eyes to blot him out. She stood

stock-still with her eyes closed. After looking at her sternly Ambrose continued along the sands. He was annoyed to find himself so upset. His hands positively trembled on his stick ; he thought it might look ridiculous shaking in the rear, so he brought it round to the front.

How dared she speak to him like that ? He would not have thought it of her. She used to have such polite, pretty ways, and now she shouted abuse at him on the sands, and said ' Oh God,' at the age of seventeen. Very bad form that, in women. That's what this modern education did for them. These modern girls, smoking, riding motor-bicycles, flying airplanes, breaking speed records ; they would do anything for notice. Every time he read in the papers about women flying round the world, or exploring strange countries, accomplishing astonishing feats—he knew it was just for notice. What else could it be for ? Men did these things for the love of them, to try them out, or to advance knowledge, experience, but women did them for notice, just to get into the papers, to be made a fuss of. And now his own daughter wanted to be Senior Wrangler, or win the Newdigate Prize. What for ? That's what he'd asked her. What for ? And she had not been able to answer. Because there was no answer. That's why. Ambrose seethed with anger, and a flat, grey wave crept over his unheeding feet and soaked them through ; but it did not cool him.

He walked on until he found himself getting too far up the estuary again ; there were stretches of black mud and Southport looked no distance at all across the water. Really Lancashire was too horrible. As soon as he could—and it wouldn't really be long now before he could claim his pension—as soon as he could, he would go back to the South where the landscape was charming and people knew how to speak and behave decently. The thought of the New Forest villages made him ache. He turned abruptly to survey Lytham. The whole place, thought Ambrose in disgust, was so damned flat. And in the foreground of the flatness, like a small, isolated skittle, stood his daughter where he had left her.

Ambrose left the sands and went heavily back to Miss Simpson's upper sitting-room on the front. Tea was almost ready ; it had to be a hybrid meal, because Miss Simpson would not cook anything after six o'clock in the evening. The tea-cups were, therefore, flanked by Miss Simpson's large, tarnished cruet ; Ambrose looked at it with disgust tempered by hunger.

Letty greeted him mildly, soothed by her long afternoon alone, and went on getting raspberry jam, seed cake and iced buns out of the cupboard. In a few moments, the cheerful maid bore in a dish of fried plaice (which did Miss Simpson credit), and the large tea-pot.

Ambrose sat down with a sigh. He would have liked to enjoy these things, but the long envelope poking out of his pocket reminded him that he had still the rubber-share question to settle, and Rachel was still on the sands.

' Where's Rachel ? ' inquired Letty.

' I dunno,' murmured Ambrose, seeking refuge in a piece of bread-and-butter.

Letty got up to look out of the window.

' I wish she'd come, before the fish gets cold,' she said, scanning the emptying front.

'I wish I could have my tea, before the tea goes cold,' remarked Ambrose crossly.

Letty returned to the table.

Ambrose had reached seed cake, before Rachel came in.

She said : 'Hullo, Mother,' and with bright cheeks and eyes sat down to eat fish without a word.

'You're very late,' remarked Letty.

Rachel nodded. Letty noticed, for the first time, that Rachel was like Laura. These family resemblances were so tricky ; they kept cropping up. Rachel was looking exactly like Laura just now ; some sort of concentrated passion under bright looks, her hands dealing swiftly with the things on the table. Laura was brilliant in anger ; Rachel was the same. Letty wondered what had made Rachel angry and looked at Ambrose. He too was angry, heavy, sulky, affronted.

'What can have happened ? ' wondered Letty, but she would not ask.

Ambrose entrenched himself behind the evening paper, which had just arrived. Rachel, having finished tea, jammed on her hat and went out again. Letty took her book into the bedroom ; she preferred even to read alone.

Ambrose sat on in the window with the paper. But there was nothing of any interest in it, and he was annoyed by the presence of Miss Simpson's large eunuch cat on the window-sill. It kept turning its great face on him in contemplation.

The summer dusk deepened and Ambrose lighted the incandescent gases in the chandelier. Letty came back and prepared to get biscuits and the seed cake out of the cupboard again. The maid, still cheerful

at the end of her long day, laid a three-cornered cloth
and brought in the hot milk.

Rachel returned ; she snatched off her hat and
stood with her hair on end before her father.

' You refuse this scholarship for me,' she said, thereby enlightening Letty. ' Very well. I'll get along
without it. But I think it's time someone told you
that you have always spoilt everything.'

Letty gasped from her chair to hear Rachel put
this into words. She was frightened to hear it at last
from other lips than her own.

' You spoilt everything when we were little,' went
on Rachel. ' You'd suddenly say we'd been to enough
parties just when the best was coming off, or stop us
from going out in a boat, or skating, or playing with
the Drummonds, when we'd got to like them so much.
The only reason you ever gave was : " Because I say
so." How could you expect us to accept that, once
we started thinking for ourselves ? The boys have
gone where you can't spoil things for them. I suppose,
because I'm a girl, I've got to stay on and put up
with your spoiling things for me.'

' Rachel ! ' cried the outraged Ambrose. ' How
dare you speak to me like this ? '

' You've driven me to it,' said Rachel.

' That's enough,' said Ambrose sternly, and even
Letty felt that it was. ' I might have reconsidered
the matter ; but now my decision is final. The letter
goes to Miss Cope to-night. Go to your room.'

Rachel went. She whistled, as she felt her way
down the four steps from the sitting-room, and fumbled
her way along the cold, shiny wall-paper to her room.
She sat in the obscurity on the quilt that had covered
other lodgers. Gradually the heat left her cheeks, her

neck drooped, her hair fell over her face. The exhilaration of anger was gone and only disappointment was left. Rachel wept.

The holiday was ruined. The sun shone again at Lytham, but in the upstairs sitting-room at Miss Simpson's there was gloom and constrained silence whenever Ambrose, Letty and Rachel were together. At meals, Ambrose treated beef, mutton, puddings, cheese and his daughter with aloof dignity. Letty could bear it no longer.

'Rachel, you must apologize to your father. We can't go on like this,' she said in exasperation.

'Why should I apologize? I only told him the truth.'

'You were rude and unkind,' hedged Letty. 'No daughter should speak to her father in such a way.'

'You can't expect me to have a State Scholarship taken away from me without a word.'

'Well, I can't help it,' Letty said, as she frequently did. 'You must apologize to your father. It's all so stupid as it is. I can't stand it.'

'Oh, bother . . .' said Rachel desperately. Life looked as flat as Lytham now to Rachel, and she was sick of both.

'I'm sorry I spoke to you like that, Father,' she said abruptly before supper on the second day of Ambrose's heavy displeasure.

Ambrose bowed his head gravely. He could not forget what she had said, but went to the table more cheerfully and began a conversation on the weather forecast to show that he had accepted her apology.

But Rachel soon showed that, although she had apologized, she had not forgiven. She remained aloof and uninterested. Children make parents as wretched

as parents make children ; but children do not really
believe that. They can't understand how it is that
those whom they take for tyrants can be hurt by the
victims of the tyranny.

Ambrose bore the tacit antagonism of his daughter
for a few days longer and then announced that they
would return to Elton. This, a silent trio, they did.

CHAPTER NINETEEN

I

THEY returned to number 5, Beech Crescent. Rachel, alighting from the taxi, looked at the house as if she had never seen it before ; it was a dreadful substitute for Oxford, she told herself.

All the houses in the Crescent were alike ; semi-detached, with a bay-window and a front door on the ground floor, a bay window and a small window on the first floor, and an attic window set in the peak of the gable ; they all had privet hedges and flights of steps in front, and at the side, pieces of trellis with a door in it leading to the back premises. Rachel noticed for the first time that the houses were built of black paving-stones. They actually matched the sets of the street, she thought, comparing one with the other.

' How absurd ! ' she said to herself, and yet was delighted to have discovered it. Her face lightened as it had not done for many days, and Ambrose carrying in the smaller bags, saw it and thought with relief : ' She'll get over it. She'll soon settle down.'

But once inside the house, gloom fell again upon Rachel. It was all so depressing. Letty had not much taste, but she defended herself about the house by saying that Ambrose had chosen everything in it. In the dining-room, the carpet was red and blue, the furniture heavy, the oil-paintings so dark that you might peer into them almost for ever without knowing what they were about. The drawing-room was light, with yellow satin upholstery embossed with velvet, hand-painted Worcester vases and innumerable water-colours on the walls. Ambrose considered it a sign of culture to have as many pictures as possible in a house. There were a few straggling ferns in pots dotted about the rooms, and one on the hall table. Letty could not arrange flowers when she had them, but she mostly did without them to save out of the housekeeping money for something she would enjoy more.

Rachel did not take any notice of her bedroom at Beech Crescent. It had a faded flowery wall-paper and white-painted furniture, now very chipped. When she turned on her spring mattress in the night, it sounded as if several dust-bin lids had fallen off in Beech Crescent.

There was a temporary, make-shift air about the housekeeping, as if Letty were just keeping it going from day to day until something better should turn up. Rachel unconsciously added now to this atmo-sphere. She escaped to Greenbanks whenever she could, and in the little room set aside for her there she kept her treasures : her books, her silver toilet set, her best nightgowns, the little blue clock, and a copy of *La Chocolatière* by Loitard. She loved her room at Greenbanks, so prim, so pretty, so comfortable, and in it she practised the housewifely arts she neglected at Beech Crescent. When she could not spend the night in this room, she left a bunch of flowers there, and thought of it with a smile when she went back to her bedroom at Beech Crescent.

Restless, resentful, bored though she was and increas-ingly became, Rachel was happy at Greenbanks. She loved being with her grandmother. One day when they sat together in the drawing-room, Rachel came across a poem in the paper she was reading. It was called ' The Old Woman '.

> ' As a white candle
> In a holy place,
> So is the beauty
> Of an aged face.
>
> As the spent radiance
> Of the winter sun,
> So is a woman
> With her travail done.
>
> Her brood gone from her,
> And her thoughts as still
> As the waters
> Under a ruined mill.'

Rachel bent over the poem ; it was as if someone had beautifully explained her grandmother. She looked up from the page to her grandmother sitting in the window, her hands empty now that she had no one to knit for.

' Darling,' thought Rachel.

Some dim comprehension of the courage, the isolation of each human soul, the inevitable loneliness in spite of love, reached Rachel. The room was quiet, the ticking of the clock the only sound. Rachel was aware, for a moment, of the mystery of herself, her grandmother, eternity before and behind them both. Then she jumped up. Youth will glance at these things, but hates to look long. She went to the piano ; but on the way she put a kiss on the soft, wrinkled brow of her grandmother.

' That's right, love,' said Louisa, coming back from far away, years away, where she had been with Charles when he was a little boy. ' Play something. That little song.'

' Schubert's " Serenade " ? '

' It's plaintive,' said Louisa, when Rachel's hands fell from the keys. ' It's sad somehow, but I love to hear it.'

' Why are all the best things sad ? ' asked Rachel in exasperation. ' All the best plays, novels, pictures, music, sad ? You enjoy the cheerful ones, but you never remember them. Why ? '

' Nay,' said Louisa, shaking her head. She could not answer that.

Bella came in with tea. She brought in a cheerful, bustling atmosphere with her broad person.

' Here you are,' she announced. ' The cake's come out a treat, hasn't it, 'm ? '

Bella liked making people comfortable ; she liked to think of them enjoying a cake that had come out a treat. It showed in her face.

Bella was at present ' walking out ' with a widower, a half-hearted little chap, who said he didn't think he would get married because times were bad and might be worse. Soon, Louisa knew, Bella would come to the conclusion that he was waste of time and turn her attentions elsewhere. Louisa did not quite know why Bella could not secure a man ; but she thought it might be that she frightened them all. There was nothing coy about Bella ; honest marriage was her purpose, and she probably made it too clear on early acquaintance.

' I expect you'll be married before me, Miss Rachel,' remarked Bella once with a sigh.

' No, I don't think so,' Rachel reassured her. ' I don't think marriage is going to be anything in my line.'

It wasn't that she had not entertained the idea.

Life seemed to be hanging back ; she was eager to get on with the living of it, and had considered the young men she now met at dances and tennis. Some of these were attracted by her and followed her about. Rachel was flattered, but hardly responsive. Alan Syson patrolled the town in his car to take her home whenever he could find her ; he arranged parties to dance, to go to the pictures ; but he was a thick, white young man with red hair and what Rachel called cow's eyelashes, and after the first pleasure of being sought wore off, she found herself indifferent, and was relieved when he transferred his affections to Sybil Crowther.

She felt quite a powerful attraction later to good-looking Jack Hunter ; but when he kissed her with violence one night at a dance, she decided he wouldn't do either. Because two men had not pleased her, she thought none ever would. She withdrew from young men and refused to go to any more dances. She did not enjoy them, she said, so why go? They bored her. Everything bored her in this purposeless, stay-at-home life and she took no trouble to disguise her boredom. She yawned about in chairs until the tears came. She was listless and pale. She followed her mother about the town, standing on one hip at counters while bacon was being cut, or the merits of one material were weighed against another.

' Is this what you've been doing ever since you were married ? ' she asked her mother.

' It is, my dear,' said Letty.

' I don't know how you've stood it,' said Rachel.

' I sometimes wonder myself.' Letty, now that she saw Rachel bored by her life, felt it to be more boring than ever.

' And yet Grandma makes it seem different somehow, doesn't she ? '

' She's different herself. We can't all be the same,' said Letty defensively.

' No. I wish Father could see that,' said Rachel, taking up the basket indifferently and going on to the next shop.

When Judy Spence came home for the Christmas holidays, Rachel revived considerably. Judy was at Westfield College, and Rachel was wrung with envy at the accounts of the bed-sitters, the cocoa-parties, the debates, the plays, the excursions into London. It was too bad, she felt, that Judy, who had not done half so well as she had in the Higher Certificate, should be allowed these experiences by her enlightened father, while her own father kept her kicking her heels in idleness at home. But she did not grudge it to Judy, who was a darling and her great friend.

Judy's legs were like rolling-pins, the same thickness all the way down ; her cheeks were too red for beauty ; her teeth were crooked, but they were young and sound and always shining in laughter. Judy was full of life, and when she was there the matrons' tea-parties she and Rachel were called upon to attend were not only tolerable but enjoyable.

In their mothers' drawing-rooms, they moved about demurely, replacing embroidered napkins on large slippery laps, or assisting bony knees to balance plates when the tables ran out. They handed tea and toast, sandwiches and cake with gravity, but their eyes gleamed when they met, and sometimes, when they stood together, their shoulders shook ; their faces, however, remained so guileless that the matrons, forgetful of their own youth, suspected nothing.

The conversation of the matrons was a source of bewilderment to them.

'They're so cautious, have you noticed?' asked Rachel. 'They never say straight out what they think. They behave like a lot of cats on hot bricks. My dear, Miss Cope has brought us up wrongly; we shall never fit in here.'

'I don't intend to try,' said Judy firmly.

Rachel sighed for herself in secret.

The matrons loved illness, it appeared, and it was a great day for them when Mrs. Webberley appeared at tea at Mrs. Spence's; Rachel and Judy were glad not to miss it.

Mrs. Webberley had had a serious operation and this was her first time out to tea. The hostess was highly gratified by her presence and sat close to her distinguished guest, associating herself with her by saying to the others from time to time: 'Yes, isn't it dreadful?' as if it had been her operation too.

'All my inside has gone,' said Mrs. Webberley, plaintive but proud.

'Dear, dear . . .' said the matrons with sympathy.

'So you must never,' said Rachel, taking Judy by the scruff of the neck when at last they escaped into the garden, 'you must never, in a moment of temper, accuse Mrs. Webberley of having no guts. Because, you see, it would be *true*.'

The heartless creatures clasped each other and rocked with laughter in the drive.

'Just look at those girls,' said a matron at a window. 'Don't they enjoy life?'

'They're so sweet and young,' said another. 'They're touching, aren't they?'

But the holidays came to an end, and Judy went

back to Westfield. Elton seemed more than ever boring when she had gone. Rachel wandered between Greenbanks and Beech Crescent complaining that she had nothing to do.

Ambrose did his best to secure entertainment for his daughter. He carried out his intention of taking Letty and Rachel to the cinema once a week, but it was not a great success. The pictures so often made Ambrose very uncomfortable; but he was determined to be a modern father and sat them out without a sign of disapproval. Letty and Rachel were, nevertheless, on tenterhooks the whole time; bedroom scenes and too-realistic love-makings made them squirm.

'Why does Father come with us?' asked Rachel of Letty. 'He means well, I know, but none of us can enjoy the pictures. I'm altogether too nervous, and I know you are, and probably he is.'

It was a wretched state of affairs. To mend it, Rachel made a preliminary inspection of the photographed scenes outside the cinemas, and asked to be taken to the most innocuous.

Ambrose tried in other ways to interest his daughter. He presented her to several of his Commissioners, mostly men of substance, who got their wives to ask her to tea as a preliminary. But Rachel liked going to tea in a large house no better than in a small one, which was not at all. She was often ashamed of herself, but could not help it.

'These are the people to get in with,' said Ambrose confidentially. 'They're nice people and have a pleasant way of life. If they take you up, you'll have a very nice time.'

But his plans fell through. Rachel resisted being

taken up; it wasn't what she wanted. She kept saying she wanted to *do* something. She didn't want to sit about waiting to be done to, done for.

Ambrose was extremely irritated. He was irritated with himself because he had done the wrong thing about the rubber shares; he hadn't taken them up, he had sacrificed Louisa's money, and now the new company was doing well. He was irritated with his wife and daughter because they would not be happy.

' It's wicked not to be happy,' he told them repeatedly, during that winter, ' wicked. Here you are, both without worries of any kind, without responsibilities— I shoulder them all. You've nothing to do but to enjoy yourselves. Why can't you? It's wicked not to be happy in such circumstances. You must make yourselves happy.'

' Yes, but in his way,' said Rachel to Letty.

II

It was in February that Mr. Boulton announced in the Parish Magazine that, after prayer and consideration, he had accepted a call elsewhere and would be leaving St. Anne's Church with which he had been so long and so happily associated.

Vicar's and People's Wardens went about inspecting likely successors, and for several Sundays the pulpit of St. Anne's was occupied by clergy on trial. Then it was announced that the Reverend Cyril Northcote, M.A., had been offered the living and had accepted it.

Mr. Boulton, with his tired wife, paid a farewell visit to Greenbanks.

' I think you might see a few changes at St. Anne's,' he said. ' Northcote is by way of being High Church, you know.'

His eyes twinkled as he thought of the stubborn old
Mr. Brewster and a few more parish stones he was
leaving behind in the shoes his successor would shortly
step into.

Neither Louisa nor Kate had been in church when
Mr. Northcote was tried out in the pulpit, but Aunt
Alice remembered that he was a handsome man and
had preached a lovely sermon.

At one of Louisa's infrequent tea-parties, the ladies
spoke with pleasurable anticipation of their new Vicar.
He was unmarried ; they were glad of that. After all,
you can do so much for and with a man who has no
wife. And there is an appealing helplessness about
him ; you feel gentle about his socks, gloves and his
buttons in general, and you fear his housekeeper gives
him tinned fruit and cold boiled ham at every meal.

Kate, helping with tea, took no part in this talk.
She felt no interest in vicars. She went to church
with Louisa, but she read Marcus Aurelius.

' I am quite eager to see this Mr. Northcote,' said
Louisa when the ladies had gone.

Kate smiled ; there was a sort of twisted indulgence
in it for Louisa.

' Yes,' she said.

On Sunday morning, when the March wind was
very cold and the dust as sharp as needles, Kate and
Louisa went to St. Anne's Church. Louisa peered with
interest round the large obstruction of Mrs. Brewster
in the pew before her to watch the new Vicar enter
with the choir ; but Kate did not notice him.

Not until he went up into the pulpit did Kate pay
any attention to him ; then she raised her eyes and
indifference left them.

The Reverend Cyril Northcote was tall and spare ;

his face was lean, his eyes dark, deep set and earnest ;
he had a wide, mobile mouth and excellent teeth, and
his hair, greying after forty-eight years, was thick,
straight and untidy. It was this untidy hair that
endeared him from the start to so many of his women
parishioners, hardly one whose fingers did not itch
to get hold of a brush and tidy up that hair. When,
at parish functions later, the Vicar appeared with his
hair brushed, the news went round at once.

'Look, he's done himself up so nicely. He's brushed
his hair.'

But before the evening was over, his hair resumed
its native habit of straggling and sticking up behind,
and the ladies said 'Tch, Tch,' over him as if he were
a favourite son unable to look after himself.

'Well, I enjoyed that sermon,' said Louisa as they
left the sandstone porch of the church and went out
again into the stinging dust.

'Yes,' said Kate.

She was uncommunicative as usual, but Mrs.
Brewster joined Louisa.

'Yes, it was a good sermon,' admitted Mrs. Brewster,
'but he set us all at sixes and sevens by standing up and
saying : "In the name of the Father, the Son and the
Holy Ghost, Amen" in the pulpit instead of kneeling
down to a prayer as the old Vicar used to do. I
wonder what Joshua will have to say about that.
He's stayed behind.'

The old ladies found plenty to discuss as they walked
home ; Mrs. Brewster in a fur coat and a hat which
was very troublesome in the wind ; Louisa trim and
cosy in her bonnet and mantle, but both with the
same, flat, easy low shoes on their feet.

It was not long before the new Vicar paid his first

call at Greenbanks. Rachel was lying at full length
on the couch reading with rapture a story by Katherine
Mansfield, when Bella opened the drawing-room door
and announced : ' The Reverend Mr. Northcote.'

Rachel sprang off the couch, pulled down her
jumper and shook out her pleated skirt ; Kate laid
aside her embroidery and prepared to rise, with a
faint pink in her cheeks. Louisa looked expectantly
over her spectacles ; she was old and did not move
before she was obliged.

Mr. Northcote, having tactfully given them time,
came into the room briskly, giving an impression of
clerical tails lightly borne and flying out behind.

' How-d'you-do ?　How-d'you-do ?　How-d'you-
do ? ' he said, bowing to them in turn and in the right
order, then advanced to take the hand of his hostess.

' I'm glad to see you, Mr. Northcote,' said Louisa
with welcome in her voice. ' This is Miss Barlow,
and this is my granddaughter, Rachel Harding.'

They all sat down.

' Now what are we to talk about ? ' wondered
Rachel, who was still inadequate to social occasions,
and had already put a label on Mr. Northcote.
' Parson,' she labelled him, and sorted out suitable
conversation : bazaars, socials, model markets, sewing
meetings, girl guides, boy scouts. . . .

' I see somebody here knows a good deal about
gardening, Mrs. Ashton,' remarked the Vicar.

' Oh, yes, gardens,' added Rachel to herself.
' Gardens, too, of course.'

' Yes, yes,' smiled Louisa. ' Miss Barlow here is
very interested in gardening. I am too ; but Kate
does all the work, don't you, Kate ? '

Mr. Northcote's attention was drawn to Kate. She

sat very still, pale, dark-haired, dark-eyed, with full
but folded lips, and flaming on her black-clad knee
a piece of needlework, a square of birds and flowers,
as bright, as rich, as an illumination in a missal.

'Oh, excuse me . . .' said Mr. Northcote eagerly,
'but what wonderful embroidery!'

Kate smiled faintly down at it.

'May I look?' he asked, rising. He took it from
her hand and returned to his seat.

'It is beautiful, isn't it?' said Louisa.

'It's an incredible piece of work,' said the Reverend
Mr. Northcote, leaning farther back to the light from
the windows and looking with keen interest at the little
brilliant flowers Kate had put into the grass.

Rachel looked from Mr. Northcote to Kate.

'She's pleased about that,' she thought. 'She's
actually pleased about something at last.'

Kate seemed to be embarrassed by her own pleasure.
She blushed and got up to place the tea-table by
Louisa's chair.

'Where do you get such designs?' asked Mr. Northcote, still intent on the needlework.

'I do my own,' answered Kate.

He looked at her with lively interest.

'But this is the real thing,' he said, shaking the
square at her. 'Do you know, I've never seen a piece
of work like this outside a museum? What on earth
do you do with this work when you've finished it?'

'I sell it through the Poor Gentlewomen's Guild.'

'Oh, dear,' thought Louisa. 'It sounds so awful.'

'Er . . . oh,' said the Vicar, turning again to the
needlework. He wondered why she was a Poor
Gentlewoman; another parish tale that would come
out by and by, he supposed.

'Well,' he said heartily, as Bella, looking at the visitor with interest, brought in tea. 'I think it is marvellous work. I hope they give you a good price for it.'

'About ten shillings for a piece like that,' said Kate, unusually communicative.

'What?' cried Mr. Northcote in a loud voice. 'Ten shillings! It's scandalous. Ten guineas it should be! Oh, Miss Barlow,' he said, taking tea from Rachel's hand, 'this won't do, you know. Mrs. Ashton, it won't do.'

'Won't it really?' inquired Louisa, very pleased for Kate.

'You really must not part with these pieces of work at that price, Miss Barlow, if I may be permitted to say so,' said Mr. Northcote, eating Bella's excellent sandwiches very fast and with evident enjoyment. He looked round the room with approval; there was a serenity about it that pleased him. In fact, he thought, this was the pleasantest house he had found yet in the parish.

'What can I do with them?' asked Kate.

'Well, we must find out. We must find out,' said Mr. Northcote. 'I wish St. Anne's had a " *trésor* "; I wish the Church to-day laid up beautiful things as it did in the past. Why should God's house be so hideously furnished? There seems to be an idea that anything will do in a church, if it is drab enough; pitch-pine and serge, sage-green and puce. Have you noticed our altar-cloths, Miss Barlow? They're all green face-cloth embroidered in puce, or puce face-cloth embroidered in green. And fringe on them. How I hate fringe! And the dreadful banners we've got! They look as if they should be carried by Painters' and Decorators' Unions.'

He took a large bite of ginger cake and Rachel
laughed aloud. He wasn't at all like a parson, and it
was fun to hear him speak of altar-cloths and banners
as if they were altar-cloths and banners. He laughed
when Rachel laughed, and chewed his cake with
vigour. Louisa smiled and Kate seemed prepared to.

'And I haven't a stole fit to wear,' he told them,
taking his second cup of tea from Louisa's hand.

Louisa could not quite remember what a stole was,
but Kate knew, it seemed.

She said rather hurriedly :

'I could embroider a stole if you like. It wouldn't
take long.'

'Tch,' said Mr. Northcote with self-reproach, setting
down his cup and looking deeply at Kate. 'Now
I've put my foot in it, and you'll take me for a mendi-
cant priest, when really I am nothing of the sort. I
didn't mean to beg, or hint, really, Miss Barlow.
Please believe me.'

'Oh, I know,' said Kate, and Rachel observed with
surprise this unaccustomed liveliness. 'I know you
didn't think of such a thing, and perhaps I ought not
to have offered to do it so soon after your remark. But
I will do one with pleasure. I have never done a
stole ; it will be good practice.'

'Well,' said Mr. Northcote, with a frank air, 'I
accept with many, many thanks. I'll provide the
materials, of course. Can I have a blue watered-
silk ? I've always wanted a blue watered-silk,' he
confessed naïvely.

Rachel laughed again. Mr. Northcote laughed too,
and Kate smiled completely this time.

'Yes, a blue watered-silk,' she said. 'Would you
like a trail of bramble ? Berries and leaves and spiny

stems, do you think? The wine-colour would look well on the blue.'

'Beautiful,' agreed Mr. Northcote, with enthusiasm, 'beautiful, and Mr. Brewster won't like it at all.'

They all laughed at the mention of Mr. Brewster; the Vicar enjoyed their laughter and took another piece of cake.

'He came into the church the other day,' he told them, 'and took up his stand before that little print I have hung in the niche under the west window. I went down to him. "Good morning," I said. "What's this?" he said, pointing to the print with his stick, and glowering at me from under his eyebrows like this.' The Vicar glowered amusingly. '"That's the mother of the Virgin," I said. "The mother of the Virgin," he bellowed. "What in the name of the goodness is the mother of the Virgin doing in this church?" "Because she happens to be the patron of this church," I said. "If you call your church by the name of St. Anne, you surely have no objection to a picture of St. Anne hanging in the church, have you? You wouldn't object if St. Anne was represented in a stained-glass window, would you?" He glowered again speechlessly, both at me and at St. Anne, then he went away muttering darkly into his beard.'

'You see he hasn't been used to . . .' murmured Louisa rather vaguely.

'No, no,' said the Vicar, 'and I quite understand. I always go slowly. I don't want to offend anyone unduly; but for one who objects, there are literally dozens who starve for beauty, colour, music in the churches. Oh, I say,' he broke off, 'is that the time?' He compared the clock on the mantelpiece with his wrist-watch and rose. 'I have stayed a long time for a first call, I'm afraid. Do forgive me, Mrs. Ashton.'

' Please don't hurry away,' said Louisa.

' I must, I'm afraid. I have a little work to do before Evensong. I have reinstituted Evensong at St. Anne's. Reinstituted only—but some of my parishioners behave as if I had invented it. Good-bye, Mrs. Ashton. Thank you so much. Good-bye, Miss Barlow, and don't look upon me as one who begs at sight, will you? Good-bye, Miss Harding. Are you one of my parishioners too? '

Rachel shook her head.

' Ah, well . . . good-bye, good-bye.'

He followed Kate out of the drawing-room, and they heard his cheerful departure. Kate came back into the room.

' What a nice man ! ' exclaimed Louisa.

' Yes,' said Kate.

CHAPTER TWENTY

I

AMBROSE was forced to admit to himself that he had been a fool to invest his mother-in-law's money as he had, and no less a fool to keep Rachel at home against her will. These two worries, ducats and his daughter, pressed heavily on him.

Cotton was going from bad to worse ; two companies had paid no dividend to Louisa this year, and he expected to hear any day that one of them had been dissolved. He kept remarking to Louisa that Greenbanks was a large house for one old lady, but she had no idea that he was suggesting she should leave it, and did no more to help him than placidly agree.

Ambrose groaned at the thought of having to bear this load of worry for another two years. In two years' time, he would be sixty. He could take his pension then, hand over Louisa's affairs to Jim and shake the dust of Elton from his feet for ever. But he had to wait two years. He could not disclose the muddle Louisa's affairs had got into until he was ready to leave ; Jim might blame him, though Jim should remember that he had never done anything at all for his mother. Ambrose had at least tried. He would, however, prefer not to live in close proximity to Jim afterwards. He would go with his family to Bournemouth so blessedly far away ! Bournemouth meant peace and a return to his own kind. Bournemouth looked like Abraham's bosom to Ambrose ; but it was two long years away.

This worry must of necessity be borne in silence, but about Rachel, the other worry, something would have to be done. She had been at home almost a year, and a dismal year it had been for all of them. She was as far off as ever from settling down and becoming the light of the home. She never sang, thought Ambrose, as she went about her duties, dusting the sideboard or whatever light work she did ; she never helped him on with his overcoat, or came to meet him and hang on his arm as they went into the house together. She never wheedled to be taken out or given a new hat. She was a terrible disappointment to him ; but she was so listless and pale that he could bear it no longer. He laid aside his dignity as head of the family and asked Letty almost humbly what she thought could be done with the child.

' I don't know what can be done now,' said Letty. ' She should have gone to Oxford. Dances and young men are nothing to Rachel yet ; she likes to use her brains. Goodness knows where she gets it from, but that's what she is like and we can't help it. If you want to make her happy, you should let her go on somehow with her studies.'

Ambrose put this suggestion from him ; he did not like it. But it persisted in haunting him, and as July approached, he found he could not face the prospect of a holiday with Rachel as she was. He climbed down very abruptly in the end and spoke to the Director of Education in the tram one morning.

' Er . . . my daughter rather wishes to continue her studies,' he began.

' Ah, yes,' said Mr. Barr. ' She had a State Scholar-

ship offered to her, hadn't she? And didn't take it.
A great pity, that; she might have done well.'

Ambrose winced; everybody seemed to know about
his refusal of the scholarship, and no one seemed to
look at it in the right light.

'You can't get the scholarship back now, you know,'
said Barr, who was, Ambrose thought, a tactless man.

'Of course not,' said Ambrose with dignity. 'What
I wished to ask you was how my daughter could
continue her studies, without leaving home, and without putting me to great expense.'

'You could send her to Manchester University or
Liverpool two or three times a week and let her take
Intermediate if she hasn't got it—she probably has—
and after that read for a degree. But send her to see
me, if you like.'

That evening Ambrose laid down his paper and
addressed his daughter.

'Rachel, I hoped you would settle happily at home
and be a pleasure to your mother and me, but that
was evidently too much to expect. Children, it seems,
have no sense of gratitude in these days. However,
it is no use considering that now.' Ambrose waved
gratitude aside. 'I should like you to understand
that in spite of your stubborn attitude, I wish you to
be happy. If you can only be happy at your books,
you must go back to them. You are evidently younger
than I thought; you seem to want to go to school
indefinitely. I have made inquiries and I find you
can go to Manchester or Liverpool University two or
three days a week and read for a degree of some kind.
You can do this if you like.'

Rachel was amazed. As he spoke, her eyes widened,
her mouth opened, her cheeks went pink.

' Daddy ! ' she cried.

She hadn't called him that for years, Ambrose remembered.

' Well, I could eat my hat ! ' she cried, moved to an inelegance he would have deplored at any other time, but was strangely gratified to hear now. ' Liverpool University ! Oh, I shall like that ! May I go to Liverpool ? I'm exempt from Intermediate, and I'm not nineteen yet. I'll have my degree by the time I'm twenty-one. I've not wasted much time really. How can I find out about it ? Shall I go and see Miss Cope ? '

' No, no,' said Ambrose, who had not forgiven Miss Cope. ' I've spoken to Barr at the Education Office. Go and see him.'

' Oh, thank you, Father. Thank you most awfully for this.' Rachel kissed him with warmth.

' Ask for Barr when you go to the Education Office. Don't be fobbed off with clerks. I know Barr well ; he'll look after you,' said Ambrose, rather loftily.

Rachel nodded energetically and ran out of the room.

Left to himself, Ambrose lowered the newspaper he had picked up as a shield, and gazed over it into the fire. His cheek, not so firm as it used to be, still glowed from his daughter's kiss. It was a relief to have made the peace with her. Children were difficult, very difficult, he mused. You had sometimes to let your principles go to make them happy. It was not entirely consistent with parental dignity to climb down as he had done ; but it was very gratifying to be able to make Rachel happy. He sighed as he settled himself more deeply in his chair, his legs extended to the blaze ; he relaxed ; and by and by the newspaper slid softly to the floor and Ambrose slept.

II

In October, therefore, Rachel came out of dry-dock,
where she had been held up so long, and armed with
a new case, a new fountain-pen and a contract, made
her first trip to Liverpool.

She was shy and nervous on her journey from
Exchange Station to Brownlow Hill, and shyer and
more nervous when she entered the begrimed terra-
cotta buildings of the University. But happily she
soon fell in with Miss Witherspoon, a kind young
woman, who loved to show about, explain, introduce,
point out and generally put people in the way without
getting anywhere herself. Miss Witherspoon was
afflicted with short sight and spots ; she sputtered
when she spoke and said ' That's right' heartily to
every remark. Rachel followed her about with gratitude, but at the end of the afternoon was glad to say
good-bye. Miss Witherspoon, on the other hand, was
reluctant.

' I'm ever so sorry you're an external,' she said.
' We could 'uv had a lovely time together at the Hostel.
We could 'uv gone to the Rep. at nights and all those
kind of things.'

' It would have been nice,' said Rachel politely.

' That's right,' said Miss Witherspoon. ' It would.'

Rachel was quite surprised to find herself glad to
be going back to Elton at night. Her year at home
had changed her. An entirely scholastic atmosphere
no longer seemed to her the ideal. She was as glad
as she had expected to be to find herself again among
books, lectures, teachers, students, but she was un-
expectedly glad to get away from them when she had
finished her work.

She escaped with determination from Miss Witherspoon, who seemed inclined to accompany her to the
station, and took a tram to the docks. She felt elated
to be going about thus, emancipated, alone, after her
dismal year at home. Liverpool excited her. When
she reached the docks, there were great American liners
standing out in the river, Lascars lounging on the
quayside, and a great Biblical cloud in the sky that
looked as if God ought to be sitting on it. Liverpool
was a cosmopolitan kind of place, Rachel felt, and went,
much exhilarated, to the Exchange Station, where she
found an empty compartment in her train and sang,
with her feet up on the opposite seat and her new
books in her lap, all the way home to Elton.

'Well,' said Ambrose, 'how did you get on?'

She told him almost everything about the day,
because he had given it to her ; but she left out about
Miss Witherspoon saying 'That's right,' and about
expecting to see God sitting on a cloud over the Mersey.

Thereafter, Rachel went to Liverpool three times a
week. She pursued her studies faithfully at the University, but outside it she enjoyed herself.

She went to as many different places for lunch as
could be managed. She went to light, bright, new
cafés, where waitresses and food were turned out
exactly to pattern, where the orchestra played loudly
all the commonplace tunes, where people had coffee
and baked beans on toast, and sweets smothered in
whipped cream. These places hadn't much atmosphere, Rachel decided. And in search of atmosphere,
she penetrated to basement restaurants, where the
waiters were old and creased, with dim ties, shirt-fronts
and napkins, where women had stout and glasses of
Rachel didn't know what, and men's eyes glittered in

the perpetual electric light. Rachel looked very out of place, so young, candid, and happy; and everyone stared at her. But she did not know she was out of place and stared back, because she had not seen people like this before and was interested.

One day, at one of these places, a waiter spilt soup on her dress. Immediately a man from a neighbouring table jumped up. He was rude to the waiter, Rachel thought, but very polite to her, for he scrubbed her skirt with his napkin and was extremely concerned. Rachel thanked him and thought him most kind, although he had a thick nose and a thick lower lip. She reminded herself that people couldn't help their looks, and smiled on him. When she left the restaurant the man left too and said it was nice to get out of the smell of food, wasn't it? Rachel agreed and he walked along at her side. He said he'd seen her before at the restaurant, but she said no, she had not been before. He said he had seen her somewhere else, then, because he remembered her face. He could not forget a face like hers, because, he said, it was such a fetching one. Rachel blushed at the compliment, but seeing her tram approach, she held out her hand—she often shook hands in the wrong places—and said good-bye.

The man took her hand and said: 'Look here—what about . . .'

'My tram,' cried Rachel and leaped on it, leaving him dumbfounded.

Rachel, being her mother's daughter, wandered about Liverpool very happily; she took excursions on the ferry to New Brighton, to Liscard, to Wallasey; she visited the Cathedral, the Art Gallery, the Chinese and the Jewish quarters. The shops interested her immensely, and she was always bringing home small

strange presents for somebody ; a queer little foreign
melon for her grandmother ; boned herrings for her
mother because they looked so shining and neatly rolled
in the shop ; a persimmon for her father, because she
didn't know what it was. Sometimes, for her third
day in Liverpool, she had no money at all and would
beg sandwiches from Bella at Greenbanks and eat
them in the cloakroom at the University.

On Sunday and Thursday nights, by an arrangement
which delighted both herself and her grandmother,
Rachel slept at Greenbanks because she was thereby
twenty minutes nearer to the early train she had to
catch on Monday and Friday mornings.

At Greenbanks, as winter deepened, Rachel watched
week by week the progress of the blue stole under
Kate Barlow's skilful fingers. She had noticed before
that embroidery made Kate happy ; actually happy.
Embroidery, but not sewing. Over her books Rachel
observed Kate at her mending, or her plain sewing
for the house. Kate sewed with remarkable rapidity,
threading needles, snipping threads, ripping cottons,
with her brows drawn low over her eyes, her face
concentrated, severe. When it was done, her face
cleared, her brows lifted, she drew a long breath. She
brought out the little wooden frame, removed the linen
towel that covered it, and leaned with quiet joy over
the blue watered-silk mounted on canvas and drawn
taut by screws. She played for a while, arranging
her skeins, her needles, the fine blond silken thread
that bound with Lilliputian stitches the stiff gold into
place. Then she began to work, and in the quiet room
her needle made a delicate, regular click as she
fashioned fine thorns of gold.

Louisa, too, noticed her absorbed, happy face, and

thought that the Vicar's praise had worked wonders in Kate. Although she did not seem to go out of her way to get any more of it. Whenever he called, which he frequently did, the stole was hustled out of sight and never mentioned in the conversation. But Kate was secretive in all her ways, Louisa reminded herself.

One Sunday evening in November, soon after Rachel's arrival to spend her precious night at Greenbanks, Kate appeared at the drawing-room door and said :

'I think I'll go to church.'

It seemed to cost her an effort to say it, and she added :

'If you will allow me, Mrs. Ashton.'

Kate, when disturbed herself, always tried to disturb other people. Louisa responded instantly to the prick.

'Dear me, Kate, you know you are free to do as you like. Go to church, my dear, and welcome.'

'In fact, hurray ! ' said Rachel when the door closed. 'It's much nicer without her. But why was she in a state about going to church ? '

'Was she ? ' asked Louisa mildly.

'Oh, rather. Couldn't you tell ? '

'I didn't notice anything in particular. Perhaps she doesn't like us to see she's changing her ideas. She used not to think much of church ; she just went with me in the mornings. But I think Mr. Northcote is bringing her round to a different way of thinking. I heard them talking when he came to tea on Tuesday. He said that Mark somebody of hers was all very well, but it was simply Christianity with Christ left out. Something like that he said, and Kate seemed to listen to him.'

'So you think the thaw has set in, do you, darling ? '

said Rachel. 'About time too. How long has she
been here? Years and years, and she's just as unaccommodating as ever. She never fits in any better,
does she? How old is she, Grandma? I used to
think she was quite old, but lately I've thought I must
be wrong.'

'She's forty-one or two; something like that,' said
Louisa.

'Oh,' said Rachel. She was not wrong after all,
she thought. Forty was a done-for age, in her opinion.
'May I have another piece of Miss Siddle's toffee to
help me through my Middle English? Oh, dear,' she
sighed, 'there's a lot of desert to be gone through
before they'll give you a degree. I wish it was all
Pepys and Duchess of Malfi and Tom Jones. Am I
very dull for you, darling, working like this?' she
inquired, arranging herself on the couch.

'No, no, love, I'm quite comfortable,' said Louisa.
'I like sitting like this with you beside me. I'll get
the paper when I'm ready. You get on with your
work.'

Rachel bent to her book and Louisa pursued her
thoughts, which were not, in spite of what she said,
comfortable. She had a letter from Laura in the
hanging-pocket under her skirt. All Laura's indifference to social conventions had broken down.
She was going to have a child.

'Mother, what shall I do? I can't let my baby be
born like this. So far Cecil and I have been all right.
Things have been rather uncomfortable at times, but
we accepted them as the price we had to pay for
being together. We are two adult creatures; we
know what to expect, and we can more or less manage
life. But everything must be straightened out for this

baby. Parents have to be unassailable, or children suffer agonies. Somehow you might be able to bear people talking about your father, but not about your mother. You must be able to be proud of your mother. I want to be like you in my baby's eyes. What on earth can I do? I've written three times to George, but he hasn't answered. Oh, if we could only be married and move to Rhodesia or somewhere.'

Louisa blinked through repressed tears at the drawing-room fire. Poor Laura! And who would have thought that soft, fat George had such a hard heart? He never gave any reasons for refusing to divorce Laura, but kept on saying ' No ' curtly through his solicitors.

Louisa was still thinking of Laura when Kate came in from church. Instead of going straight upstairs as usual, Kate came into the drawing-room. She smiled at them as she warmed her hands at the fire.

' It's a very cold night,' she said.

But there was a glow about her for all that.

' Did the Vicar preach well? ' asked Louisa.

' Very. And he had his candles lighted and a procession round the church afterwards,' said Kate.

' So there will be more trouble at the Vestry meeting,' said Louisa.

' Isn't it absurd? ' said Kate. They did not know whether she referred to the Vicar or the Vestry meeting.

She withdrew her hands from the blaze and went out of the room.

' Is she singing? ' exclaimed Rachel. ' It may have been a hymn-tune, but she was actually singing.'

Louisa nodded, very pleased.

' She looked rather beautiful when she came in, didn't she? ' asked Rachel in surprise.

'She was lovely as a girl,' said Louisa.

Then she sighed. These girls were not any happier for their loveliness, she was afraid. Laura was lovely; and Rachel grew in beauty every day it seemed to her fond grandmother. She looked at Rachel with anxiety; but Rachel was reassuring to-night. Her hair stood on end and the middle finger of her right hand was extremely stained with ink.

She held up the finger for her grandmother's inspection.

'Fountain-pen is right,' she said in disgust. 'Mine is always playing. I can't turn it off.'

CHAPTER TWENTY-ONE

I

THE Vicarage garden was very dark; laurels clapped their cold leaves and the stark trees reached upwards, wanly illumined in their topmost branches by the lamplight from the streets. Kate Barlow stood at the door, without ringing the bell. She was bringing the blue stole to the Vicar. She had allowed him to think she had forgotten all about it so that his surprise and pleasure should be the greater when she gave it to him in time for the Christmas celebrations three days hence. But now that the giving was at hand, she shrank from it; she was nervous, and angry with herself.

'Why did I come? Miss Parks and Harriet Wilson and half the women of the parish come to this door on some pretext or another. Why should *I* come?'

She stepped down from the entrance, but paused again on the gravel path.

'I can't do any little normal thing without magnifying it out of all proportion.'

She mounted the two shallow steps again, and at that moment the square of stained glass in the inner door sprang into light. She rang the bell hastily, and the Vicar himself opened the door.

'I thought I heard someone,' he said. 'Who is it?'

He peered out.

'Miss Barlow! I'm so sorry. Have you been here long? Doesn't the bell ring?'

' Yes, yes, it does. I've only just tried it,' said Kate.

' Come in, come in,' invited Mr. Northcote.

Kate entered the cold, cavernous hall and followed the Vicar over the echoing tiles to his study. Here a fire blazed in the grate, a reading-lamp shone over the flat desk littered with books and papers. There were copies of holy pictures on the walls : a Van Dyck Crucifixion, Sassoferrato's Praying Madonna, and the tender and lovely ' Virgin and St. Anne ' of da Vinci.

' Do sit down, Miss Barlow. I've just finished for the day, and I'm very glad to see you.'

His voice, his welcome, was warm. He moved to place a chair, tall and graceful in his cassock, which he always wore in the house, and sometimes now in the street, to Mr. Brewster's disgust.

' Parson in petticoats,' growled Mr. Brewster. ' Apist ! '

' What ? ' people asked.

' You've heard of Papists, haven't you ? ' asked Mr. Brewster snappishly. ' Well, he apes 'em. He's an Apist.'

But Kate felt none of Mr. Brewster's irritation at the sight of Mr. Northcote in his cassock.

' I mustn't stay a moment,' she said, taking the chair he set before the fire. ' I've brought your stole.'

' My stole ? What stole ? '

Kate smiled with secret pleasure.

' Your blue watered-silk stole, don't you remember ? '

' Oh ! ' cried Mr. Northcote, comprehension and delight dawning together. ' My blue stole. I thought you'd forgotten all about it long ago. Have you really done it ? Is it in here ? I must open it at once. Where's my knife ? '

He snatched it from the table and cut the string of

the box. Kate watched his long hands fumbling mannishly with the enveloping tissue papers. She smiled nervously, her eyelids fluttering a little. Mr. Northcote bent over the revealed stole, pushing his lean face and untidy hair into the light from the reading-lamp.

'But it's exquisite ! It's exquisite ! ' he said.

He lifted up the stole on one finger and gazed at it in admiration. Kate relaxed ; he liked it ; he was pleased with it.

'What work ! What wonderful work ! What patience and skill. I'm proud to accept it,' he said, turning to her warmly. ' It's a most beautiful thing, and it gives me great joy to use beautiful things in the services of the church, as you know. As I have often said to you, haven't I ? Thank you very, very much, Miss Barlow,' he said earnestly, pressing her hand. ' Will you put it back into the box, because you'll do it much better than I can.'

Kate drew off her gloves, and he stood by her at the desk while she packed the stole. This woman, strange, remote, interested him. She was totally unlike the women with whom he mostly had to deal. It was a perpetual disappointment to the Reverend Cyril Northcote that the most interesting women did not occupy themselves with parochial affairs.

He knew Kate Barlow's story. Mrs. Scholes had soon told it to him. But it only deepened his interest. He looked at her now. The sight of her face, he thought, among the faces of the ladies of the parish, was as arresting, as pleasurable as the discovery of that small, beautiful, human head among the grotesques in the carving at Lincoln or Southwell, or somewhere else he had not time to search his memory for just then. This face was austerely moulded in cheek and temple and eye-socket, but the lips were full and the eyes sad and passionate. She was no longer young ; but Mr. Northcote did not think much of youth, as youth ; it was too callow for him.

He was so deep in his thoughts that he almost started when Kate turned from the box and said she must go.

' No, don't go,' he implored boyishly, ' do sit down. I've been working hard all day, and shall be glad of five minutes' conversation, even if you can't spare any more. How is Mrs. Ashton ? '

He threw crumbs of small talk until she was reassured.

' Have you read Strachey's *Life of Queen Victoria* ? ' he asked.

' No.'

' Oh, you must. I must lend it to you.' He took it from his shelves and laid it ready on the desk.

' I'm thinking of buying myself a set of Medici prints. Have you seen them? Here they are in little.'

They pored over the reproductions together.

They talked about Mr. Brewster and the parish. The Vicar found Kate's comments and views astringent and liked the taste of them. Kate's eyes fell at last on the small clock on his desk and she rose in dismay. She had been with him more than an hour. She was alarmed and angry to have broken her long reserve. She drew back into herself and said good night almost brusquely. She went away, refusing his offer of escort, down the dark garden, through the cold streets to Greenbanks, where Louisa was wondering what had become of her.

The Reverend Cyril Northcote was in no way

alarmed by her abrupt departure. He liked dealing with difficult people. It was invigorating, it sharpened the wits, it made him feel he was doing something worth while. Miss Barlow was certainly difficult. She must be drawn from that cold stoicism, he determined. No good shutting herself in a refrigerator to escape pain ; she would only suffer another kind of pain in its stead. She must let life flow warmly in her. He thought he would say this to her later when their acquaintance improved.

In the meantime, he might send her that spare copy of *The Imitation of Christ*. It was a good idea, he thought. He rummaged in a drawer until he found the small red leather book, and rummaged in another drawer until he found an envelope of the right size. Then he sat down and wrote a note in his rapid, flowing hand, to say he felt he had not thanked her half enough for the exquisite stole, and would she please accept the copy of the *Imitation* as a small return for the hours of work she had put in on his behalf, and also read it and weigh its merits against those of the *Meditations of Marcus Aurelius* of which she was so fond. He sent her his best wishes for a happy Christmastide and remained hers very sincerely in God, Cyril Northcote. He addressed the envelope, stamped it lavishly, and went in his slippers over the sharp pebbles of his drive, to post it in the pillar-box outside the gate. He was all ardour to get it off ; in the morning, perhaps, he would feel he had been a little impulsive, but to-night he was all ardour to get the book and the note off to this new, this interesting friend.

The envelope reached Greenbanks at half-past five the following afternoon. Bella, bulging with curiosity, carried it into the drawing-room.

'It's for you, Miss,' she said to Kate. No letter had come for Miss Barlow as long as Bella could remember.

'For me!' said Kate in surprise, taking the bulky envelope into her hand. Mysteriously, although she had never seen his writing, she knew it.

Louisa looked expectantly over her spectacles; she, too, was surprised by the arrival of a letter for Kate. But if Bella and her mistress hoped to be enlightened as to the contents of the envelope, they were disappointed, for Kate laid it face downwards on the chair beside her and went on with her mending. Bella returned to the kitchen, and Louisa continued to knit a shawl for Laura's baby. Illegitimate babies needed shawls as much as legitimate ones, but there was not the same happiness to be had in knitting for them. Louisa knitted with pity and apprehension for this child.

Kate finished the seam she was sewing, and murmuring something Louisa could not catch, she took the letter and went up to her room. She did not come down for some time, but when she did, Louisa, looking at her, thought there must have been good news in the letter, and perhaps a Christmas present. Louisa was innocently curious as to the sender of a Christmas present to Kate, but she knew it was too much to expect that Kate would show it to her, as anyone else might have done.

At Christmas it was Louisa's habit to give Kate, among other presents, a cheque, part of which Kate laid out at Cockbain's January Sale in material for a new dress. This year Louisa gave the cheque as usual, and as usual Kate bought material at Cockbain's Sale, but whereas she had always bought black before, this time she bought a supple deep-red cloth, which quite startled Louisa when the parcel was undone.

'I thought I'd have a change,' said Kate.

She threw a fold of the cloth over one shoulder and looked into the mirror; then she turned towards Louisa.

'Does it suit me?' she asked.

'Why, yes, dear, yes. Red always suited you,' said Louisa, gaping a little.

Kate noted her surprise.

'You've no objection to my wearing red, have you, Mrs. Ashton?' she asked.

Louisa recoiled. Why would Kate keep on saying these things?

'Of course I haven't,' she said rather sharply. 'You've been with me all these years, Kate; surely you know better than that by now.'

'Yes, I do—really,' admitted Kate, and Louisa was startled again. It was the first admission of the sort Kate had ever made. Kate smiled, too, at Louisa, without a twist or hidden meaning and took her red cloth upstairs.

For the next few days she busied herself in making the dress, and when it was done, she put it on and Ambrose did not know who it was sitting in the drawing-room. Surprise and indignation followed recognition. A red dress, and her hair looser about her face and an air of he didn't know what about her! Ah, *now* he could believe that she had had a passionate affair with Philip Symonds! He considered it most unseemly. When sinners repented, one treated them with kindness and tolerance as long as they observed a proper humility and kept themselves apart. But

when they cast off repentance and came prancing back
into social life as if they were entitled to the amenities
enjoyed by those who had not sinned at all, then it
was time to call a halt, said Ambrose to Letty, who
merely snorted slightly, although she discussed Kate's
red dress at length with Aunt Alice later.

Aunt Alice's heart was giving her a great deal of
trouble ; she had to keep very quiet and nowadays
hardly ever left her stuffy little house in Park Row.
Letty collected items of news as if they had been fresh
eggs and bore them to the invalid daily. Kate's red
dress was much enjoyed, but took a long time to digest,
and Letty grew a little weary of it.

When Louisa gave one of her tea-parties, the ladies
looked at Kate's red dress in surprise ; they modified
their manner towards her ; some were cooler, some
warmer.

But when Mr. Northcote came to tea, Louisa saw
that he had nothing but admiration for it.

Kate herself seemed indifferent to both admiration
and censure ; she had set about the design of a great
altar-cloth and let the world go by.

II

In the middle of one January afternoon, a cable
arrived from Kenya for Louisa.

'MOTHER. Please go to see George about me.
LAURA.'

Louisa read it over and over, and then let it flutter
to the floor. She stood over it, looking frightened.
'Go to see George.' What a task to set her ! It
was beyond her. She couldn't talk, couldn't plead.

She had never been able to plead for herself, let alone anyone else. She couldn't manage George. Why, last time she had to send for Ambrose. The suggestion of Ambrose came as a blessed relief, but she put it aside. Laura had asked her to go. ' Mother, please go to see George about me.' A cry from the other side of the world. She would have to go. She would have to do her best, although it would be no good.

' Oh, dear, I didn't want to have to face George Boyd again,' she said in distress.

She stood about in the rooms. She shuddered at the thought of travelling in this cold weather ; she disliked travelling at any time. And suppose George wouldn't see her when she got there ? Suppose he received her badly, and abused Laura ? What were the trains ? She could not ask Kate's help ; she couldn't talk about divorce and the illegitimacy of Laura's child to Kate. She couldn't ask Ambrose because he would insist on taking it out of her hands and going himself ; and Laura had said ' Mother, go to see George.' There was only Letty left. Louisa got Bella to telephone to Letty and ask her to come to Greenbanks as soon as possible.

Letty arrived, was told, and was angry.

' It's just like Laura,' she said. ' Always handing on the awkward situation to someone else. Cecil had to stand by and see her marry George because he hadn't liked her green hat. You had to send her pearls back and face George when she went away with Cecil ; we had to face the scandal she left behind ; poor Perry almost lost his job ; and now she wants you to go to Nottingham and get her divorce from George. Why couldn't she see George herself before she went to Kenya ? '

'Now, now,' said Louisa. 'Laura is very unhappy about her baby.'

'It's the first time she's been unhappy about anyone but herself then,' said Letty. 'It won't do her any harm.'

'But I must help her,' said Louisa. 'And so must you. We can't let a child suffer because we don't like awkward situations.'

'How can I help her?' asked Letty testily.

'You can come with me,' said Louisa. 'You'll be better at arguing than I shall.'

Letty demurred, but she saw her mother was in earnest, and gave way at last.

'When can you manage it?' asked Louisa.

'Ambrose is going to London the day after to-morrow, as it happens,' admitted Letty. 'We could get away as soon as he has gone. But you'll have to pay for me, Mother. I haven't a cent, and I can't ask Ambrose for money if you don't want him to know we are going.'

'I hope I can pay for my own child without being asked to,' said Louisa warmly.

'I'll ring up George's mill and inquire if he will be there on Wednesday,' said Letty.

She came back to report that George was confined to the house with gout and would not be at the mill for the rest of the week.

'So that's all right,' said Louisa inhumanly. 'We can see him at the house.'

On Wednesday, departing close on the heels of Ambrose, Louisa and Letty travelled to Nottingham and arrived unannounced at George's great, con-glomerate house.

He received them with astonishment and chagrin ;

but he was a simple person and did not know any more than they how to manage the situation. They sat awkwardly together in the drawing-room, which remained as it was in Laura's day. The fire was very hot and Louisa was obliged to take the liberty, as she felt it, of throwing back her sealskin mantle. George was wedged into a great easy chair, with one foot swathed in bandages and raised on a low stool. A fat dog panted on the hearthrug; both master and dog ate too much and took too little exercise.

Louisa pleaded Laura's cause as best she could, and George heard her to the end, his globular blue eyes fixed on her face. When other people blinked, thought Letty, they did it so quickly that you didn't notice it, but George's lids fell over his eyes and were slowly raised again. It gave him a particularly stupid expression.

'No,' thought Letty. 'Laura couldn't have stayed with this man.'

'Laura married me for her own convenience, and she left me for her own convenience,' remarked George, when Louisa had finished. 'I don't see why I should put myself out for her now.'

'It's for the child's sake,' urged Louisa. 'The child makes all the difference.'

'And you would hardly put yourself out at all,' said Letty, spurred to do her best to free her sister from this fat man. 'A little paragraph in some paper or other, or perhaps nothing but your name in a list of names that nobody reads now the details are left out. Yours wouldn't be a sensational divorce, Laura has been gone such a long time.'

George turned his many chins reflectively towards the fire. He was silent for some time, wheezing as he

breathed ; at his feet the dog wheezed too. Louisa
and Letty began to think he was going to sleep and
looked at him with anxiety. But he was thinking.
He was thinking that it was true that Laura had been
gone a long time. He tried to remember his grief and
fury, and could not. For several years after the war,
he had hoped and believed that she would come back ;
but now he was not sure that he wanted her. He was
settled in his ways ; he had a good housekeeper who
made him very comfortable, and there was always the
club and a game of bridge when he wanted it. . . .
George wheezed reflectively over his blessings. Then
a sudden severe twinge from his gouty foot stung his
mind into action. He opened his eyes as wide as they
would go and saw that to safeguard these blessings
a divorce was urgent. As long as Laura was his lawful
wife, she could probably claim his support. If Bradfield deserted her, she might fall back on her husband
and bring a squalling brat into this house. Women
thought nothing of doing that kind of thing. George
knew he was soft-hearted ; he might not be able to
turn them out, and it would all be damnable. He
must protect himself from that at all costs. The old
lady was right ; the child did make a difference. Let
Laura marry Bradfield and keep herself and her child
out of his way.

George turned his eyes and looked with mute alarm
at Louisa, and she, seeing that he had made up his
mind, leaned forward breathlessly.

' All right,' said George. ' She can have a divorce.
I'll see to it straight away. You can tell her. I'll
send for my lawyer to-day. Will you have anything
before you go ? Glass of sherry ? Well, excuse my
not getting up, won't you ? Good-bye, good-bye, so

glad you came and all that. Remember me to your husband,' he said to Letty, as he mopped his brow, bedewed with the perspiration of alarm.

Louisa and Letty hurried through the imposing hall to the door. They were afraid that if they did not get away quickly he might change his mind.

' Well, would you believe it ? ' asked Louisa in amazement, when they were outside. ' He gave in all at once, and that after saying no for all these years.'

' Something dawned on him when he was looking into the fire,' said Letty. ' I saw it. But I think if Laura and Cecil had tackled him in person themselves, he'd have given in long ago. He'd always take the line of least resistance.'

Louisa, trembling with excitement, insisted on going to the General Post Office to cable to Laura before taking the first train back to Elton.

' We shall be home quite early,' she said, with satisfaction.

' You see,' remarked Letty, ' everything has turned out right for Laura *again*.'

CHAPTER TWENTY-TWO

A FTER the visit to Nottingham, Louisa relaxed ;
she felt a peace created by absence of worry.
Laura would be happy about her baby now. Rachel
was happy, going backwards and forwards to Liverpool. And even Kate seemed in a fair way to being
happy at last. Certainly a change had come over
Kate. Whether it was a change of heart due to the
Vicar's counsels and the services at the church to
which Kate now went so frequently, or whether it
was the Vicar's admiration of her skill in needlework,
or whether it was his visits, congenial conversation
and the books he lent her, Louisa could not tell.
The Vicar had certainly done something for Kate
that Louisa herself had not been able to do. Louisa
thought she must have been very poor company for
Kate all these years. When she listened to the conversations of Kate and the Vicar, she realized that
Kate must be very clever indeed. No wonder the
life at Greenbanks had not satisfied her ; there was
no one for her to talk to. Louisa had not known
that Kate was clever when she left Greenbanks as a
girl, and she had never given a thought to her being
clever when she came back. Anyway, Louisa comforted herself, Kate had the Vicar now to talk to,
and she was certainly much happier for it.

Kate spent all her spare time on the altar-cloth,
which she did not keep hidden away when Mr. Northcote called, but brought out for his inspection and

advice. She did not sell anything to the Poor Gentle-women's Guild these days and Louisa would have liked to increase her salary to make up for it, but Ambrose refused to allow it. He said it was with great difficulty that Louisa's income was maintained at its present rate, and times were so bad that he didn't know how long it would be before it was very much reduced.

'I'm warning you,' said Ambrose solemnly. 'Don't say I haven't warned you.'

Louisa took the warning very mildly. Her wants were few and her children provided for ; so long as she could end her days at Greenbanks that was all she cared about.

February passed, with very cold weather without and warmth and peace within the house.

'I love Sundays and Thursdays,' said Rachel. 'Because I stay at Greenbanks. It seems so much warmer and homelier than any other house ; I suppose it's because you're in it, Grandma.'

The daffodils in the garden sent up their matt-green spears, the tulips their polished bores ; winter aconites bloomed and were promptly picked off by the sparrows. Forsythia shook out its yellow tangle on the back garden wall, and during a mild spell Kate hastened to plant an American Pillar rose at the end of the lawn facing the drawing-room side-windows. On her advice, the one-armed Flora was at last removed ; but Louisa would not part with the old stone eagle. He had brooded too long over her garden to be banished now.

Kate no longer took solitary exercise in the garden, but went into town with Louisa, who was glad of her arm when the streets were slippery. When Louisa

talked to her friends now in the shops, Kate no longer
stood off in silence, but joined in the conversations
and made Louisa happy in this and many other
small ways.

March came in ' back to front ', as Rachel said :
lamb first. They spring-cleaned at Greenbanks, and
Louisa had Kate's room re-decorated. She persuaded
Kate to choose the colours herself, and Kate chose
ivory white walls and black paint. Laura's old carpet
was dyed deep blue, and Kate hurriedly embroidered
little scattered rounds of flowers in green, magenta
and deep blue on a heavy old linen counterpane
Louisa brought out of the ottoman. The draw-
curtains at the window were dyed magenta and Kate
embroidered sprigs of the blue all over them in no
time at all. She asked Louisa if the washstand could
be moved out, and Louisa was not affronted, because
at long last Kate was making herself at home at
Greenbanks. When the room was finished, it was so
charming that all callers went upstairs to look at it,
and Louisa wondered how Kate, with her ideas, had
managed to live in a house like Greenbanks so long
without protest.

' It sounds positively hideous to me,' said Aunt
Alice when Letty described Kate's room to her. So
hideous that she thought of hiring a taxi to be taken
to see it, but gave up the idea because of the cost ;
no garage, it appeared, sent out a taxi under half a
crown.

Aunt Alice did not approve of Kate's colour scheme
on hearsay, but Jim's Mabel, on one of her infrequent
visits, made a note of it and determined to reproduce
it in her own house. She recognized it as unusual
and distinguished. Mabel was clever ; she had not

many ideas of her own, but she knew how to use
other people's. She was helping Jim upwards, ever
upwards as the years went on. He had an office in
Liverpool now, and it was Mabel's ambition to move
to Liverpool altogether by the time their one red-
headed, skin-and-bone baby—a girl—should be old
enough to play with the right sort of children.

March went out with wind and bitter dust, but
April brought her proverbial showers and sweetened
the garden.

On an afternoon of rain and shine in the second
week of April, Rachel stole to Greenbanks to tea.
It was neither Sunday nor Thursday, but Wednesday,
and she was not entitled to be there. She arrived
early with her books and opened the drawing-room
door softly, in case her grandmother should be still
at her afternoon nap, but Louisa, her hands folded,
her head against the cushion, opened her eyes and
smiled a welcome.

'Well, love. . . .'

'Well, darling,' said Rachel, going to lay her cool
cheek against her grandmother's. 'Don't disturb
yourself. I'll be very quiet. I'll just get an hour's
work done before tea.'

At the end of the room, before the long windows,
Kate Barlow was installed at her embroidery frame, a
large one, this time, on a stand of its own. She raised
her head and looked at Rachel, but no greeting passed
between them. Kate used to discourage greetings, and
Rachel had got into the habit of not expecting them.

Rachel arranged herself on two chairs by the
windows overlooking the banks and the steps. She
sat on one chair and put her feet on the rungs of the
other. On the floor she put Pepys' *Diary*, Everyman

edition, and took *Samson Agonistes* on her knee. She tapped her teeth with her pencil, preparatory to making notes. She could not get going, and kept looking out into the garden and thinking about irrelevant things. Funny all these ordinary little people picking Shakespeare, Milton—the great ones —to pieces for examination purposes. Pick, pick, pick with their perky question-and-answer beaks, like hens at a rose ; but after the rose was picked to pieces it all came together again and presented its lovely whole unimpaired. What queer coves there were at the University ! That so conceited young Pomfret ! He behaved like one of Wycherley's beaux ; and Miss Witherspoon said his room was draped in black sateen. Miss Witherspoon doted on him.

' She doesn't need to pretend to dote on me then,' said Rachel to herself, gazing out of the window. ' If she can't distinguish between me and that Pomfret. I am at least *real*. He isn't ; but still, perhaps he's happier like that. . . .'

She pulled herself together sternly and wrote in her notebook : ' I must get on.' Then she gabbled a few lines of *Samson Agonistes* as a self-starter. The device was successful ; she was off.

Louisa woke up altogether and reached for her knitting. The room was quiet. The fire fluttered softly in the grate, Kate's needle made its customary click. The sound of tea-spoons and china came faintly from the kitchen.

Rachel looked absently into the garden and saw a young man coming up the steps. Her thoughts immediately deserted Milton and Samson Agonistes.

' Who is he ? ' she wondered. ' I've never seen him before.'

There were not many young men in Elton that she had not seen before.

The young man seemed to be looking at the house with interest. He was tall and came up the steps with easy grace. The long, straight legs of young men were rather good, thought Rachel.

She could no longer keep the young man to herself, for he had reached the door. So she said :

' Someone is coming.'

Kate looked up from her frame ; her colour deepened. She took another strand of silk and threaded her needle with difficulty.

' Who is it ? ' asked Louisa tranquilly, turning her knitting.

' I don't know. A young man,' replied Rachel, flattening her nose against the window in an attempt to see the visitor standing at the door.

Kate bent to her work again, and the colour ebbed away from her cheek.

' Perhaps he's got to the wrong house,' said Louisa. Young men came no more to Greenbanks.

The bell made its high, flat, ancient clangour in the kitchen. The swing-doors buffled together as Bella responded. There was a subdued murmur of voices at the door ; then Bella appeared in the drawing-room.

Louisa and Rachel looked towards her with interest, but Kate took no notice.

' Please, 'm,' said Bella, looking surprised. ' It's a young gentleman asking for Miss Barlow.'

Kate raised her head.

' For me ? ' she said incredulously.

' He says he wants to see Miss Barlow, who lives with Mrs. Ashton, so, if it's not you, I don't know

who it is, I'm sure,' said Bella, entering as usual into
the spirit of the occasion.

'Who can it be?' asked Kate of Louisa.

'I should think it's some insurance young man or
someone like that. There are all sorts of young men
going about to doors since the war. You didn't ask
for his name, Bella?'

'No, 'm,' said Bella, and then added to excuse herself.
'Some people are so close with their names, aren't
they?'

Kate stuck her needle into the canvas of her frame
and prepared to rise.

'I suppose I'd better go and see what it is,' she
said.

'No, don't disturb yourself,' said Louisa. 'If he
insists on coming in, Bella, show him in here.'

Rachel shut her books and stretched her arms wide.
She hastily drew them in again as Bella ushered in
the young man.

'Good afternoon,' said Louisa, noting with faint
annoyance that Bella had again omitted to ask for
his name. 'How dark it is! There must be another
shower coming. Put on the lights please, Bella.'

A click of the switches flooded the room with light
and revealed the young man advanced no farther
than the threshold, but standing there, hesitant, intent, yet taken aback as if he had expected to face
one person only, instead of three. Bella closed the
door and a tenseness grew in the room. They all
looked at the young man now with sharp inquiry.

Louisa broke the silence.

'You wished to see Miss Barlow?'

'Yes,' said the young man gravely. 'But you
aren't Miss Barlow, are you?'

'No, no,' said Louisa smiling. 'This is Miss Barlow.'

The young man turned his intent look to Kate; a slow colour mounted to his cheek, some emotion they could not account for showed plainly in his face. He took a step towards her, a growing eagerness in his eyes.

Kate rose slowly, pressing herself upwards by her hands on the embroidery frame.

'Who are you?' she asked, as the young man advanced under the hanging lights.

'Who are you?' she cried again sharply, bringing him to a halt. 'What's your name?'

He looked at the others as if he hesitated to bring out his name before them. But Kate rapped out again:

'Who are you, I said?'

'My name is John Barlow,' he answered.

There was another silence. Kate's eyes remained fixed on the young man, but some invisible hand struck her, for she bowed herself over the frame and her face was deadly pale.

Rachel turned her head swiftly from one to the other. What was there in the young man to strike so at Miss Barlow? But Louisa knew. She knew that mother and son faced each other, consciously, for the first time, and under the tenseness of the moment pity filled her for both of them. The son had come to look for his mother, and the mother felt nothing but horror and repudiation at the sight of him.

'Why did you come?' asked Kate harshly from the window.

Her voice grated on Rachel's nerves and struck the eagerness from the young man's eyes.

'I can't do anything for you,' said Kate as if that could be all he had come for. Louisa knew that tone in Kate's voice and winced for Kate's son.

'I didn't want you to do anything for me,' he said gravely. 'I came to see if I could do anything for you. I've only just discovered that although I've had two hundred a year for more than sixteen years, you have been working for your living all that time. . . .'

A sharp cracking of wood silenced him. Kate had leaned too heavily on her frame. One side had given way, and now sagged slowly to the floor, bearing with it the satin and the little load of coloured silks. Kate, unsupported, still bent above it, looking at it as if it were some unspeakable disaster. She wrung her hands silently. They watched her from their places, the intent young man, Louisa full of pity, Rachel bewildered.

Then Louisa realized suddenly that Kate and her son should be alone together. She lifted her hand, but before she could make a sign to Rachel, Kate rushed between them, and fled from the room. The door fell to behind her with a loud noise, leaving the three of them aghast.

The young man lowered his eyes to the hat in his hands, hiding what he felt. He had a stricken look, but his mouth was set strongly against this hurt as if it had that habit.

Louisa recovered herself. She went across the room and took him warmly by the hand.

'Come to the fire and sit down, John.'

The young man partially recovered himself too.

'I must go. I ought not to have come, I'm afraid.'

His eyes were young, baffled, hurt as he looked at her.

'You can't go like this,' said Louisa. 'You must give her time. She's had a shock. Sit here with me. Ring for tea, Rachel. This is my granddaughter, Rachel Harding, John.'

They shook hands with unnecessary convention, avoiding each other's eyes.

'Shall I go, Grandma?' asked Rachel, in passing to the bell.

'No, love, no need to go now.' The damage was done, Louisa reflected. Rachel had assisted at a scene unsuited to her years ; there was nothing for it now but to bring the whole thing out into the light.

'Find the cigarettes for John, love,' said Louisa. 'May we call you John ? Because . . . we'd like to,' she finished, with her warm smile.

John Barlow murmured politely and took a cigarette. Rachel observed him as he lit it ; his hands shook a little. They were long and shapely, and something about them led her eyes in swift speculation to his face again. His eyes were grey, his hair was what might be called fair—a nondescript, English colour, but there was something in the line of cheek-bone and jaw that gave her a clue. His name, Miss Barlow's strange behaviour, the long secret—Rachel's heart beat thickly as she jumped to her conclusion : this was not merely some relation of Miss Barlow, this was her son. This was Miss Barlow's son.

Louisa saw that Rachel had grasped the truth and might not be able to hide her discovery.

'Go and see where the tea is, will you, love ? ' she said.

Rachel escaped from the room into the hall. She stood on the tiles, gazing at the door she had just closed. Behind it was Miss Barlow's son ! And he

didn't look at all illegitimate, thought Rachel. He
looked like Dick or the twins or any other young man.
He wore the same clothes, he had the same ways.
Where had he been all this time? Where had he
grown up? She thought of Dr. Barnardo's Homes, but
dismissed them. He didn't look as if he had been
anywhere like that.

Rachel took her eyes from the door and looked up
through the well of the staircase. There was silence
above. What was Miss Barlow doing? Why did she
rush away like that? Why didn't she welcome her
son? Rachel, at nineteen, expected behaviour to be
fitted to situation. She expected death to be followed
inevitably by grief, she expected marriage to be accompanied by love, she expected the appearance of a
son to awaken the appropriate mother-love in Kate
Barlow. She couldn't understand it at all. Rachel
had read a great deal; she was wise in theory, but
in practice she was as inexperienced, as callow, as
surprised by life as any other young creature.

She stood in the hall with her busy thoughts, her
eyes moving from the red, white and black tiles of
the floor to the bunch of grapes in clear glass on the
ground glass of the inner door of the porch, to the
old clock with time moving on over its engraved brass
face, to the sight of herself in the great mirror over
the half-moon table. By the time her eyes reached
this, she had only come to one conclusion.

'Life is very rum—very rum indeed.'

She remembered tea and went into the kitchen.

Bella was late with tea. When she had ushered in
the young man she had, as usual, listened at the door.
But when, after puzzling silences, the young man had
said his name, Bella, with a peculiar loyalty which

did not allow her to eavesdrop when there was anything really important going on within, tiptoed hastily to the kitchen to put two and two together as best she could. She had got a good deal further in her speculations than she had in preparation for tea when Rachel came into the kitchen to urge her to speed.

'What can I do to help?' asked Rachel.

'There's the toast to make yet. A nice little job for you. Will Miss Barlow come down to tea, think you?'

Rachel hid a smile. How did Bella know Miss Barlow had shut herself away upstairs?

In the drawing-room John Barlow had already told Louisa a good deal about himself. He had been adopted, when a few weeks old, by a couple named Sanders who despaired of having any children of their own. Eighteen months afterwards, a son was born to them, and later, three more children.

'They regretted having adopted me. They weren't well off. They had their own children. You can't blame them,' said the young man. 'You couldn't expect anything else.'

That was true of him, thought Louisa. He wouldn't blame, he wouldn't expect. In spite of his birth and upbringing as an unwanted, adopted child, John Barlow was not embittered; he had kept a sweetness of nature that showed plainly in his face when he let go his heavy thoughts for a moment.

'But when that two hundred a year was made over to me, it made a great difference. I didn't know what had happened at the time—I must have been about nine, I'm twenty-five now—but I know things were a lot easier in the house. Mrs. Sanders was good-hearted enough, but she had a temper and she couldn't help taking it out of me at times. But from this time, I was a help to them instead of a hindrance. Mr. Macdonald, the London lawyer who arranged my adoption for my grandfather, I understand—he managed everything for me. He was most awfully good to me ; you have no idea. He saw to it that I had my own name ; I didn't want to be a Sanders, and they didn't want it either. He sent me to Edinburgh to school with his own son, to Merchiston Castle. Then I went to the School of Architecture in Liverpool, and now I'm in Belton & Page's office. So you see, my mother gave me a good start. The money she made over to me has enabled me to do all this. Old Macdonald would never tell me where the money came from. But he died a month ago, and I got it out of Hamish, who is my friend, and traced my mother quite easily. I didn't mean to upset her or importune her in any way. I came because I couldn't bear to think she was earning her own living while I had that money, which I can well do without now. Could you explain that to her ? She might listen to you when she wouldn't listen to me.'

' I'll give her a little longer to herself,' said Louisa, ' and then I'll go up and talk to her. Here comes tea.'

He seemed, with touching confidence, to place his case in Louisa's hands, and his face cleared.

' You could love this boy,' thought Louisa.

Aloud she said to Rachel.

' Fancy, Rachel, John is in an architect's office in Liverpool.'

' Are you ? ' cried Rachel, her eyes flying wide.

It seemed very strange that Miss Barlow's son should be in Liverpool and she going three times a week and not knowing it.

'Do you live in Liverpool?' asked John Barlow, standing up to receive his tea.

'No, but I go to the University three times a week.'

'I finished there two years ago,' he said.

'Did you?' cried Rachel with more surprise. 'Were you at the School of Architecture then?'

'Yes.'

'Are you an A.R.I.B.A. now?'

He nodded; he was still rather pleased about that.

'Do you know "Prof": Reilly?' he asked.

'No,' admitted Rachel reluctantly, 'but I look at him.'

She looked at him because he wrote for the papers and had leaping tigers on his dining-room walls and went to the Sandon Club and had strange cosmopolitan friends whose artistic proclivities awoke awe in Rachel. Prowling about Liverpool to see what there was to be seen, Rachel often wished Professor Reilly would notice her and let her into the life he led, which seemed to be so much more interesting than the ordinary.

Louisa stole from the room and left them to discuss Liverpool and Professor Reilly together. Rachel forgot the cause of the young man's visit, and talked and laughed as if it were an ordinary occasion. She told him about the conceited Pomfret and his black sateen draperies, about the underground restaurants. She inquired about the docks and the Cathedral. Her eyes looked into his and he almost forgot what he was saying. He was wondering where he had seen this contrast of light and dark before, this very clear grey with a dark rim to the iris, and these dark lashes. He remembered suddenly that they were the eyes of a girl he had noticed on the Overhead Railway in New

York, whither he had gone for six months during his training at Liverpool. He had been enchanted by those eyes then, and here they were again.

Rachel saw him thinking about something that had nothing to do with what she was saying, and fell into abashed silence. She blushed and looked down at her hands and then out of the windows. He could not get the conversation going again and they were sitting awkwardly together when Louisa came back. They both rose, young and at a loss, to face Kate. She was white, her eyes were stained and under them were strange red marks as if bloody thumbs had pressed her cheekbones. She walked to the window and stood by the broken embroidery frame with her back to them. Louisa took Rachel away and left mother and son together.

They bore the closest possible human relationship one to the other and yet were strangers. The young man had no memories of his mother, but Kate's memories were a nightmare of fear and shame and bitter realization that there was no help to be had from anyone in the world—least of all her lover. The dreadful months had culminated in a night of terror and agony spent in the company of a vulgar woman got in by her father. That night she had screamed to die, while her father paced the corridor outside, waiting with cold fury for it all to be over, so that he could throw the child out of his respectable house into the world where it would be swallowed up and lost to view.

This son had cost Kate too much ; she could not associate him with anything but pain and horror. And to come now—now of all times in her life—when she felt herself to be on the threshold of a new hope, a new happiness, the only happiness she had ever known, since that other had been too brief, too shameful, her lover too unworthy, to count as happiness.

She could not bear to look at her son. Let him go, at once, and never come back into her life again.

Poor John was stammering about a house near Liverpool and life together and thanks for the money and some account of himself which he thought she might like to hear. But she scarcely heard him ; her blood beat in her ears. Let him go ; let him get out ! She felt caught in a trap from which, although she did not move, she was frenziedly tearing herself free, tearing his fingers from her in case he should try to hold her now—now—when for the first time she might get away.

' So you have nothing to say to me ? ' ventured John Barlow, when he had waited in vain for some response.

' No,' said Kate.

' I hoped you would come to live with me,' he said.

' It's impossible.' Her voice was cold and final, and left a silence behind it.

' Very well.' John Barlow accepted it, and turned away. But he did not go. He looked at the chairs and the carpet as if help could be got from them.

' I wish I hadn't come,' he said.

Kate, standing rigidly by her frame, laughed briefly. The laugh was bitter, there was a ' So do I ' so fervent in it that John Barlow was stung.

' I'll have that money made over to you,' he said in a business-like tone, and made for the door. But Kate halted him again. She turned on him in fury.

' I shan't touch it. Your father never helped me by a look or a sign when he was living. I swore never to touch his money when he was dead. If you don't

keep it, I shall give it to charity. Do you understand? I won't touch it.'

Her vehemence threw him back into bewilderment.
He stood completely at a loss.

Kate turned her back on him. She had finished.

He stood against the door for a moment, then opened
it quietly and went out. His one idea was to get away,
to relieve his mother of his presence. He was sore
and angry that he should have expected any other
result from this visit. He fumbled for the door-
handle to make his ignominious exit, but before he
could find it, Rachel had reached him.

'Don't go,' she whispered, remembering Miss
Barlow in the drawing-room, '—not like this.'

'I must. She doesn't want me here,' he said,
wrenching at the handle in spite of her.

It was dusk outside and the hall was almost dark.
Neither could see the other distinctly, but they warred.
He wanted to get out, she to prevent him. He couldn't
go like this; it was unthinkable.

'I'm going,' he repeated stubbornly.

'Well, I'm coming with you to the station then,'
whispered Rachel.

She snatched her hat and coat from the pegs in the
back hall and went out after him into the damp April
night. She pulled on her hat as she went down the
steps.

'You can't go yet,' she told him in a voice that
besought him to be reasonable. 'There's no train.
The next is 9.15 as far as I know.'

'Is it? Yes, perhaps it is,' he said, bringing himself
back with difficulty to such things.

'Let's walk up and down Elm Street,' suggested
Rachel.

They turned and began to pace the pavement side by side. The street was quiet and dim, lighted only by three lamps far apart; one at each end and one in the middle. In summer the trees leaned over the garden walls, but now they stood upright, burdened but lightly by young buds; near the lamps the up-standing silver buds showed on the service trees, and the tiny, down-dropping buds on the limes. The air was newly washed by rain and very sweet.

Rachel and John Barlow walked in silence. This was no time for scratching the surface of acquaintance. They were busy with their own thoughts. Rachel longed to remove the sting of his repudiation by his mother. She was indignant and horrified. Why couldn't Miss Barlow accept him, and love him, and go to live with him? It was so easy to do, thought Rachel impatiently. So easy, and it would have made him happy and let him have a background and a home like other people.

'Good heavens, she could have called herself "Mrs.",' she said impatiently to herself, thinking she had got to the root of the matter.

When they came to the lamp at the far end, they turned again.

'You know, you can't expect her to love you all at once,' began Rachel, although that was what she herself expected of Kate. 'Remember, she's never seen you since you were born. Grandma's been telling me all about it. She couldn't be glad you were born. It's impossible. She'll have to get used to you before she can feel anything for you. You do see that, don't you?'

'I was a fool to expect anything else,' he said bitterly. 'I don't know how I managed to persuade myself that she would be glad to see me. As you say, why should she ? '

' *I* should have thought she would,' said Rachel eagerly, trying to heal, to smooth, without really knowing how to disguise the fact that she considered Miss Barlow cruel and unnatural.

When they reached the far lamp, they turned again.

' I think the best thing to do,' counselled Rachel, ' is to leave her to get over the shock of you, and try again later.'

' No. I'm afraid it's hopeless,' said the young man.

' I don't,' said Rachel, because she didn't want it to be.

They walked on.

' You know, Miss Barlow is very queer ; very hard to understand,' she amended hurriedly, remembering she was speaking of his mother. ' She's been at Greenbanks all this time, and no one knows her any better yet. It's only just lately that she's begun to be more friendly with us. My poor little grandmother,' said Rachel with a laugh, ' has been hanging over the gate for years and years, holding out sugar, but Miss Barlow has never left the farthest corner of the field until now. She was just approaching, when you appeared.'

' Oh, damn,' said John. ' I wish I'd never come.'

' You mustn't wish that,' said Rachel. ' I'm telling you what she is like, so that you won't be hurt or surprised that she started away at first sight of you. She's like that. No one has to come near her. But I think she'll come round. That's why you mustn't disappear again. You must keep in touch with us somehow, so that we can let you know when to try again. I'm in Liverpool three times a week. . . .

Oh, keep back a minute ! There's Miss Barlow coming out of Greenbanks' gate.'

A figure passed hurriedly under the lamp.

' And I suppose I must hide from my mother,' remarked John, falling back against the wall.

' Yes. Oh, she's gone down the other way. She's probably going to church. She often goes in the evenings.'

' If she is religious, perhaps that's what keeps her from owning me,' said John.

' Well, it may be,' admitted Rachel. ' She certainly has got rather religious lately.'

' Then there's no hope,' said John.

' Don't say that,' said Rachel. ' I think there *is* hope. Anyway, you can have another shot, can't you ? You're not going to be beaten first time, are you ? '

' I don't know,' said John. ' I don't want to thrust myself on her.'

' But if it's for her happiness in the end ? ' urged Rachel. ' Anyway, let's go back to Grandma now. She'll be so worried to think you went away like that.'

' I don't think I will, thank you very much all the same,' said the young man. ' You see, it's no good getting you involved like this ; no good you and your grandmother being so kind and all that. Why begin ? It will probably come to nothing, and I'll have to disappear again.'

Rachel was hurt and indignant.

' What a horrid idea ! Don't say anything like that to Grandma. She isn't kind *for* anything. Do come back into the house for one minute, please.'

He followed her up the dark garden. Louisa was standing in the drawing-room, looking distressed. Her face brightened when they entered.

'Ah—that's right. I'm so glad you've brought
John back, love. I couldn't bear to think of him
going off like that. Rachel, run and tell Bella to take
supper in at once. I was upset to think of John taking
a train journey without a proper meal.'

'The journey is only an hour,' said John, smiling.

'Never mind,' said Louisa firmly. 'You need
your supper. You had no tea to speak of.'

She was relieved to be able to feed him, to draw his
chair up to the fire, to look after him ; her feelings
were expressed in these ways. She was upset that all
the good done to Kate should be undone by this visit,
but her sympathies lay with Kate's son. She could
not understand how Kate could let him go like this.

Rachel ran to the kitchen.

'Supper, Bella ! Supper, quickly, please ! We've
got to get it over while Miss Barlow's out.'

Rachel never tried to hide anything from Bella ;
she knew it was no good. Bella would know as much
about this incident as Rachel herself before the day
was out, if she didn't know already. Nobody knew
how Bella got her information, but get it she did.

'Right you are ! ' she cried heartily to Rachel now,
beginning to bustle at once. 'I wondered where
you'd got to with 'im. I didn't 'alf like the idea of
the poor young chap going off like that. Eh, dear
me, there's nowt so funny as folk, is there ? It's a
true saying, is that.'

'What's for supper ? ' inquired Rachel eagerly.
She wished it to be special for John.

'Tomato soup, fish cream—it's just done—and them
little tarts you're so fond of. There's a fruit trifle or
something, too ; something new the missus has been
trying.'

'Hurray. Shall I help you?' Rachel poised herself at the door, remembering to offer, but not wanting to really.

'Nay, get back to that young man,' said Bella, smiling to herself as she went into the larder.

But Rachel ran upstairs on the points of her toes so as not to be heard. She turned on the lights over her prim dressing-table and brushed her hair with such energy that she banged herself severely with the back of the brush twice in succession. Her hair sprang obediently into place, back from her forehead, turning forwards to curl over her ears, leaving the lobes to show beneath like pearls. She leaned into the mirror to scrutinize her face ; it would do, she decided. It was one of its good days. She gave sundry tugs to her frock, to her muslin collar and cuffs and ran down the stairs, arriving a little breathless in the drawing-room with a candid smile for John.

These two had, to all appearance, merely walked Elm Street, but they had in reality travelled much farther than that.

At supper, Louisa sat in her place at the head of the table, with Rachel on her left hand and John Barlow on her right. While they talked together, she turned her head from one to the other, admiring them. They were so young ; their eyes were so clear, their faces so smooth ; they were untouched, untried, and had so far to go. Louisa yearned over them and urged them to a little more fish cream.

They had finished, but were still at table when the door opened and Ambrose walked into the room. There was no one, unless it had been Kate herself, that Louisa and Rachel were more unwilling to see.

'Good evening, Mother,' said Ambrose. 'I called

for Rachel, because she hasn't been at home much lately. She mustn't desert us altogether, you know.'

Rachel smiled constrainedly, and Louisa introduced John with some misgiving.

'Barlow, did you say?' asked Ambrose, offering his hand to John, but looking at Louisa. 'Ah—indeed. How-d'you-do?'

He then subjected John to a close scrutiny, and Rachel's face took on an anxious expression. How would her father behave? That generation was so queer about these things. Ambrose turned to Louisa to see if his suspicions were true, but Louisa took no notice of him. She rose from the table and said:

'Now we will go back to the drawing-room.'

Rachel fell abruptly from the high, free place she had occupied for the last few hours as the friend and adviser of John, and became merely a daughter under authority. Parents were awkward; especially fathers. She wondered briefly why John was so anxious to saddle himself with a parent; Miss Barlow was an unaccommodating person if he only knew.

'Come along, Rachel,' said Ambrose, when he had had another good look at John in the drawing-room. 'Get on your things.'

'Bother,' said Rachel to herself, going out into the back hall. 'Drat it all, why can't I stay when I want to?'

She put her arms through the sleeves of her coat, clipped the belt round her waist, and pulled on her cap before the mirror. John Barlow would go away now, and she might never see him again. He might decide never to try again with his mother.

She pinched her lip between her finger and thumb, trying to think of some way to convey to John, under her father's eyes, that he must come back again. But she could think of nothing, and had to go into the drawing-room and give him her hand in formal farewell.

'Good-bye,' she said, and did not risk even a look at him.

She followed her father to the door and went home. Ambrose did not speak at all about the young man. He would not incur an indelicate explanation.

CHAPTER TWENTY-THREE

A MBROSE arrived at Greenbanks next morning before Louisa had left the breakfast-table. She had been worrying about Kate, whom she could hear moving about her duties overhead, and about Kate's son, but when she saw Ambrose, spruce, inquisitive, the worries fled and she stiffened with mulish resistance to the questions she knew he had come to ask. Ambrose roused this mood in many people.

' Who was the young man ? ' he asked, after greetings.

' Kate's son.'

' I thought so,' said Ambrose, as if he had followed up a difficult clue with success. ' And how did his mother receive him ? '

' Very badly,' said Louisa briefly, denying herself a second cup of coffee in case it should prolong Ambrose's visit.

' Very badly, did she ? I'm not surprised. It's rather hard luck to have a full-grown son turning up when she thought she'd lived down the scandal. And she evidently did think she'd lived it down at last, judging from those red dresses, new hats and so on. It's very hard luck indeed.'

' No one need worry. He won't come again,' said Louisa.

' It sounds as if you regret that,' observed Ambrose.

' I think it's a great pity Kate can't feel differently about him, and go and make a home for him as he wants her to.'

' Oh, he wants her to live with him, does he ?   Well, that would be the best for all concerned,' agreed Ambrose.   He would somehow have liked to make sure that the young man would not revisit Greenbanks. ' Can't you make Miss Barlow see that it is her duty to make some amends to him ? '

' I can't make Kate see anything.'

' If you gave her notice, she might be made to see,' suggested Ambrose.

Louisa was indignant.

' As if I could do such a thing ! '

She gathered her letters together and rose from the table, hoping that would be taken as a hint that the morning was getting on.

' Why not ? ' pursued Ambrose.   ' You can't afford her really, you know.'

Louisa did not reply.

' Where did the son come from ? ' asked Ambrose.

' Liverpool.'

' Liverpool ! ' he exclaimed, frowning heavily.   He felt it an outrage that Kate Barlow's illegitimate son should be in Liverpool where Rachel went three times a week.   ' Liverpool !   What on earth is he doing in Liverpool ? '

' He's an architect there.'

' An architect ?   How has he managed to make himself an architect ? '

The questions went on ; she had to answer them. She had to stand about while Ambrose turned over and over the subject of Kate and her son.   He would not let her get away, but at last Bella came to the door and said the greengrocer would like to speak to her, and Louisa escaped with alacrity.

' I'll say good-bye, Ambrose, because I might be

some time and I know you want to get to the office.'

' And if he doesn't, he ought to,' she said to herself, putting the baize-covered door between them.

Later in the morning, Letty called. In all her astonishment she was the most astonished to find that Kate could have had two hundred a year and had refused it.

' But she handed it over to her son,' said Louisa. ' He was able to have a good education and set himself up as an architect.'

' Yes, but it was the money she hated, because Philip Symonds had left it to her,' said Letty, to whom money was always money and acceptable no matter where it came from.

' Anyway, it's all been for the best,' said Louisa, who was tired and harassed.

' And Kate won't have anything to do with him ? ' asked Letty.

' I'm afraid not,' said Louisa with a sigh. ' She hasn't spoken about him since, and I don't suppose she ever will—not to me, at any rate.'

She wondered if Kate had gone to see the Vicar when she went out of the house last night. But Kate had only gone to the church. She fled to church, and knelt in the gloom at the back, hoping to lay the ghost of the past, risen so disastrously that afternoon, by the assurance of the present. Her friend was still there, that was his voice, that was his tall figure moving among the lights and the music.

As she knelt, her legs shook so that she had often to lean against the seat of the pew for support ; but she raised herself up again and again to lean forward to see him more clearly. She longed to go to him and pour out all that was dammed up in her heart. As a priest he would welcome that, but as a man he would be embarrassed ; it would change his idea of her. He knew her story, she was sure ; but it was a different matter to be confronted by living evidence of it.

As she knelt, watching him, she grew more and more wretched, until she could bear it no longer, but got up and stole from the church. Mr. Northcote saw a shadow moving in the obscurity and peered in vain to see who was leaving before the service was over.

Kate went out into the streets and wandered aimlessly about until she was too tired to walk any more. She went back to Greenbanks then to upset Louisa, who stood about waiting to say something comforting, but was given no chance. Kate, with the strange burning marks still high on her cheeks, locked up the house for the night and went to her room with no more than a brief ' Good night.'

The next day she went about her duties as usual, but her looks and manners were worse, thought poor Louisa, than in her first days at Greenbanks. They were the defences Kate put up, if Louisa had only known it. Kate hated to be looked at, hated to be speculated upon, hated being in a position to be pitied. Kate was so proud that she was the last person any humiliation should have happened to.

After several days of rigid behaviour on Kate's part, Louisa was driven to remonstrance.

' I admit I can't understand your attitude to that poor young man, Kate ; in fact, I hope you'll change it. But in the meantime, there's no need for us to go about in this stiff fashion. So let there be an end to it, my dear.'

Kate made an effort towards amiability after that, but without much success.

It was May now and the weather was fine and warm. Louisa persuaded Kate into the garden, drawing her attention to the tulips and the irises, the acrobatic blue-tits on their ropes of monkey-nuts, to the song of the thrush in the evening, to this and that, mutely reminding her that whatever happened there was always the garden and the sun, the trees and the birds. One's own spiritual consolations, she felt obscurely, were not much use to other people ; each soul had to find its own way. She was too diffident to proffer her own treasures, but she proffered the common treasures of life to Kate.

Mr. Northcote called one afternoon, but Kate did not come into the drawing-room. She kept upstairs, denying herself a sight of him. Louisa saw him watching the door expectantly and was obliged to make excuses for her in the end.

'She hasn't been very well lately,' she said. 'Perhaps it's the spring.'

She belonged to a generation that attributed many ills to this loveliest season ; spring brought buds, sunshine, songs of birds, but it also brought, or ought to bring, brimstone-and-treacle, sulphur tablets and strengthening tonics.

The Vicar was concerned and sent round a parcel of books and a note in sympathy. Kate was obliged to write a letter of thanks in reply. He called again, and this time Kate was in the drawing-room when he arrived and was obliged to stay there.

She greeted him with constraint and sat almost in silence until he asked how the altar-cloth was progressing. Then she blushed and said she had not been able to get on with it. The frame was broken, she said, and she could not work.

' Let me have a look at it,' said Mr. Northcote. ' I may be able to mend it. I'm rather good at that kind of thing.'

Kate looked at Louisa in distress, but Louisa thought it would be a good thing for Kate to have the frame mended so that she could return to the work she loved.

' It's in the old nursery, isn't it, dear ? ' she said. ' Perhaps if Mr. Northcote wouldn't mind stepping upstairs . . .'

The Vicar rose with alacrity, and followed Kate and Louisa to the old nursery, where Kate took the cover from the frame and stood pale and tormented while he examined the break.

' I'm sure I can mend this, if you find me the tools.'

Louisa brought out Charles's tools—the tools he had used to make the billiard-marker. When Mr. Northcote rummaged among them for what he wanted, it was as if he stirred up her heart, hurting her. She went away and left them together.

The atmosphere in the old nursery was strained. Kate withdrew to the window, and the Vicar busied himself with the frame, murmuring ' Ah, I thought so . . . Wait a bit . . . That's the way, I think . . .'

But his thoughts were on her. What was the matter with her ? What had happened since he last saw her ? She was as difficult, as remote as ever. The contact, carefully established between them, was broken and must be repaired as well as the embroidery frame.

There she stood, still, silent, not seeking his attention, not exerting herself to please in any way. He did not know any other woman who could stand like this. He glanced again at her, and thought swiftly that, in the high light from the window, she was an excellent subject for the artist who painted ' The Corridor '— Campbell-Taylor, was it? With her dark banded hair, clear-cut face and her hands folded over her red dress. And what a dress! With its close-fitting bodice and full skirt it belonged to no fashion he knew of, but how supremely it became her! The Reverend Cyril Northcote flushed a little as he bent over the frame. She must be brought round. He couldn't be treated like this by her. It disturbed him.

He understood her too well to make any direct reference to the change in her behaviour.

' I'm afraid this satin and canvas will have to come off,' he remarked.

' Oh,' said Kate, moving from the window.

He made her fingers fly, and by and by the remote look left her face and she gave him all her attention. He asked her to hold the frame steady, and she knelt down on the floor and grasped it with both hands.

' That's right,' he said with satisfaction. ' Now where are we? '

He kept up pleasant, reassuring murmurs, interspersed with more pertinent matter.

' I haven't seen you in church lately,' he remarked, choosing his screw.

' No.'

' I missed you. I haven't so large a congregation for Evensong that you could escape notice, you know. Did you read that St. Thomas Aquinas I sent? '

' Yes,' said Kate.

' What did you think of it? '

' Wonderful.'

'Isn't it?' he said enthusiastically. 'I've got another volume for you. If you could call round at the Vicarage any Tuesday or Thursday evening after Evensong, I could let you have it, and show you that set of Medici prints I was telling you about at the same time. I'm always in Tuesday and Thursday evenings; at home to the Parish, though not many avail themselves of the opportunity these summer nights.'

Kate made no reply to the invitation and Mr. Northcote asked if she knew where he had put the canvas and the glue.

'It's there, behind you,' she said in a livelier voice. He had nothing but the tone of her voice to tell him that she was recovering, but it was enough.

Kate Barlow kept clearer in her mind than he did the distinction between the Reverend Cyril Northcote as a man and as a priest. He took it for granted that he was a priest and forgot that he behaved and felt as a man. If anyone had challenged him, or if he had challenged himself, which he was not in the habit of doing, he would have said that it was his duty to win Kate's soul, to substitute reliance on God for Kate's reliance on self. And that he sincerely meant to do, but his behaviour was the behaviour of a man attracted by a woman.

'Now what d'you think of that?' he asked at last. 'Not a bad job, eh?'

'It's quite firm,' said Kate, smiling faintly and shaking the frame to prove her words.

'Of course it is,' said the Vicar with pride. 'I told you I was good at this kind of thing. Shall I help you to get the canvas on again?'

But Bella came to say that tea was ready, and they

went down to the drawing-room. Louisa saw at once
that the Vicar had done Kate even more good than
she had hoped.

As day succeeded day, Kate became less apprehensive at the ring of the bell and the announcement of a
visitor. Her son gave no sign of approaching her
again, and she tried to thrust him out of her mind.
She refused to think about him, she would not even
remember what he looked like. She concentrated all
her hopes and thoughts on the Reverend Cyril Northcote. Very gradually she began to be able to behave
as if her son had not crashed into the delicate new
structure of her life.

For some time she watched Rachel with suspicion.
The girl was in Liverpool a great deal ; the two might
be meeting. But by and by she gave up this watch ;
Rachel did not look as if she was harbouring a secret.
Part I of her examination was approaching and Rachel
was full of apprehension about it. She wilted from
close application to her books, and a little from another
cause.

She had looked up and down the streets of Liverpool
in vain for John Barlow. She was disappointed and
rather angry with herself for being disappointed. She
was afraid she was turning out to be the sort of girl
who frequently falls in love at first sight. She remembered that she had been violently attracted by Jack
Hunter at first sight, but the second or third she had
hated him. She wished now she could have another
sight of John Barlow and be cured of him. It would
be more comfortable, she thought, and she would be
better able to get on with her work.

But she was good at examinations, being just nervous
enough to be extremely alert. Unlike poor Miss

Witherspoon who came out in a rash, and had to lie down every afternoon with a headache. Two days got over and Rachel was not dissatisfied with herself. On the third morning, however, ten minutes before she was due to go in for her paper on ' Middle English Literature with Prescribed Texts ', she cast a preparatory glance over her fountain-pen and gave a cry of dismay.

' Whatever is it ? ' asked Miss Witherspoon.

' My nib's gone wrong. It's got crossed legs. Oh, I say,' she wailed, trying to write on the window-sill, ' I can't manage with this—and those beastly pens they provide they wear you to the bone ! What time is it ? Have I time to go to Philip, Son & Nephew ? Here, hold my things.'

She flew, hatless, out into the street and immediately ran full into John Barlow.

' You ! ' she cried, pulling up within an inch of him. ' What are you doing up here ? '

' I'm on my way to a job of ours,' he said.

' How funny, I've never met you before, and now I meet you here,' cried Rachel, too flurried to make much sense of what she was saying. ' Oh, I'm in such a hole. My pen's gone wrong. It always was a brute and now it's crossed its legs. I dropped it yesterday and forgot to look at it until now. I'm just going to Philip's to buy a penholder with a lifebelt on—you know, a rubber body-belt. . . .'

She was breathless, and the June breeze lifted her hair from her ears.

' Take my pen,' said John, snatching it from his waistcoat pocket. ' It's a nice one. It'll do very well for you.'

' No, no, I can't.'

'Yes, do, do. You can't keep dipping in the ink. Competition's too fierce these days. The next chap will get ahead of you. Take it.'

'Oh, thanks awfully,' said Rachel, blushing with gratitude. 'I know I oughtn't to, but I'm in such straits. I'll be very careful with it. How can I return it to you?'

'I'll be here any time you like,' offered John rashly.

'I'm out at one,' said Rachel.

'Right. One o'clock here. Good-bye—and good luck!' he called after her as she ran up the street. 'She can run,' he thought. He was proud of her for running like that.

Rachel snatched her things from Miss Witherspoon and went into the examination-room. She took her place and received her paper. It consisted almost solely of translation; it was concrete, concentrated, it made demands on what she had learnt; she hadn't to draw on other faculties, which might have been impaired by the strange thrill John Barlow's pen gave to her fingers. She kept her thoughts in their narrow appointed grooves, and worked doggedly through the three hours.

John Barlow arrived early at the meeting-place, and paced up and down the dusty street. He had not meant to meet Rachel Harding again, but Fate had taken it out of his hands and he was glad. He had no responsibility for this meeting, and felt free for the time being to indulge in excited pleasure.

He had bought a new tie in the interval, and hoped she would not notice that where he had worn a two-and-sixpenny foulard he now wore a seven-and-sixpenny Macclesfield silk. He was relieved to think that all the buttons were on his shirt-front. His shirts came back from the laundry with little red signals of distress to denote missing buttons, but Mrs. Fleming, his landlady, took no notice of signals. John stitched them on himself. He used to get the size wrong, but of late he had grown bold enough to go into haber-dashery shops and say to sympathetic young ladies behind the counters : ' Have you any buttons like this ? ' pointing to the buttons remaining on his shirt. The young ladies were always most helpful, but he could never feel any enjoyment about going into haberdashery shops.

But his blue-striped shirt and collar were brand new to-day, and bore no signs of his labours with needle and thread. He gave a surreptitious pull to the peak of his handkerchief visible in his breast pocket ; like most young men, he had a ' blower ' in his sleeve and a ' shower ' in his pocket. He pulled his coat down and hoped he would do.

He felt guilty, but tremendously elated.

' Any girl but this one,' he had said to himself after the visit to Greenbanks. He had kept out of her way and it had been difficult, because his heart recognized her at once.

But he was *nullius filius* in law ; he was nobody's son ; he was that outcast from the beginnings of social life, a bastard. Nobody would want such a match in the family. He was precluded from loving Rachel Harding. He had thought it all out, but he was glad that Fate had intervened to allow him, if only for a few moments, another meeting with her.

John Barlow was not without experience of girls. In New York he had a brief affair with a girl in the same house. She had pale gold hair and eyes as green as glass and as translucent. For a time she singled John out for her favours. He was bewildered by her beauty and no less by her mentality ; one was so great and the other so small. But it was she who discarded him as ' too dumb '. She took on an Armenian who was also in the same house, and John fought him on the landing in a jealous rage. He almost had his own nose broken, but after a time he discovered that his heart was completely intact.

Jean Macdonald, his friend's sister, had always been very friendly. He admired her ways with horses and dogs, and her frank speech and looks. And there was Miss Edwards at the office, who had a neat figure, an excellent permanent wave and great facility in getting out quantities. She was a comforting sort of girl, because whenever you couldn't find anything or wanted anything in haste, she always said : ' Leave it to me.' Gaskin was rather keen on her, and John had tried to cut him out in a half-hearted fashion ; but since the visit to Greenbanks, he hadn't been able to keep that up.

Jean Macdonald, Miss Edwards, the girls at the tennis club—they wouldn't do now. John Barlow had been rather desolate since the visit to Greenbanks.

His face before he saw Rachel approaching was both eager and apprehensive, but by the time she came up he had made a mask for himself.

' Here I am,' she said. ' And here's your pen. It behaved like a gentleman. Thank you so much for it.'

' How did you get on ? ' he asked.

' Oh, not too badly to-day,' said Rachel. ' But I'm so hungry and so thirsty. That room was so dry, and the invigilator too—like one of those little dried Japanese flowers ; he might have come out into something if he'd been steeped in water. Have you had lunch?'

'Er—no,' said John. 'Will you come to Reece's?'

'I'd love to, but I must pay for myself, because I want to eat a lot.'

They went down the street together. John thought there could be no harm in looking at her just for a while, in enjoying being with her just once. After all, as long as she kept clear of him. . . .

When they parted, they arranged to meet again.

'I say, will you keep my pen,' said John. 'I have another.'

He mentally dug out an ancient pen from the back of his office drawer as a justification for this offer.

'Oh, no,' said Rachel.

'Please do,' he besought, holding it out. He looked more desperate than the occasion warranted. 'Please, Miss Harding.'

'*Miss*,' mocked Rachel.

'Rachel, then. I don't want the thing. I'd be so glad if you'd take it. Well, take it and use it until your exam is over, if you won't have it for keeps. You can give it back when you've finished next week.'

'Well,' considered Rachel, blushing a little, 'I might do that, if you're sure you don't mind. It's most awfully kind of you. Shall we say the same place, same day, same time next week then? Will that do?' she asked briskly.

And John, by saying that it would do very well, stepped into the strong current and lost his foothold once and for all.

CHAPTER TWENTY-FOUR

THROUGH the long summer evenings Kate Barlow sat at her embroidery frame before the open windows in the drawing-room. The design of great twisted stems bearing masses of wistaria blossoms grew rapidly under her fingers. She hardly spoke as she worked, but often, as she felt for the exact spot with her needle on the under side of the satin, she looked out into the garden and smiled to herself.

Louisa noticed these smiles, and noticed too that there was a suppressed excitement, an expectancy about Kate in these days. And the bloom of a St. Martin's summer was on her, making her more beautiful than in her early youth. This beauty saddened Louisa ; she felt it had brought nothing to Kate, was now buried at Greenbanks and soon must fade for ever.

Kate was secretive. She did not give herself away. She let nobody know that she waited for the Vicar to speak the word that would release her. Release her from all the pent-up emotions of years, the loneliness, the bitterness, the emptiness. Oh, the relief of love ! Kate trembled as she waited. Surely he would speak soon. 'I love you,' he would say one night when they were alone together in his study at the Vicarage. 'I love you,' he would say. And that would be enough to make up for the misery of these long years. She did not go beyond those words. She looked no further ; she held herself back, waiting for them. But how she would pour herself out then !

How she would release her love for him, her devotion, her understanding—all, all she had, and she had much, she knew. She felt herself rich to bestow him. She wept into her hands in her bedroom, waiting for the blessed relief his first word of love would be.

He had restored her faith in God and man, he had filled her life where it had been empty. She loved him. She loved him for his kindness and delicacy with her, for having sought her out in the dark place where she had hidden herself; she loved him for his tall, thin body, his deep eyes and untidy hair, for his unaffected ways, for his love of beauty and colour, books and pictures, and his naïveté about his candles and processions; she loved him because he would understand about that first passion of hers and the havoc of her life and her repudiation of her son—all of which she would tell him, would explain when he had spoken that first word of love to her. She starved for that word; but he would speak soon. She must hold herself back, she told herself, and wait. So she waited, and Louisa and Rachel looked at her and wondered what she waited for.

Rachel often looked at Kate and said to herself: ' She's John's mother ! ' She metaphorically pinched herself into realizing it. It seemed incredible.

She felt uncomfortable about behaving to John's mother as usual, without disclosing the fact that she was meeting John in Liverpool. But it had to be done ; she was not going to be told not to see John.

She kept on meeting him, finding one excuse after another. Sometimes they were very happy together, but sometimes their meeting was clouded by heaviness on John's part ; he was worried, reluctant, ill at ease, and looked at her as if he had something on his mind.

But Rachel learnt how to dispel these moods ; she knew how to bring him round. She said to herself that she had to go more than half-way to meet him, because he did not expect that anyone would want to meet him at all. She bowled over his scruples like ninepins whenever he mutely set them up ; she made him deliriously happy and wretchedly unhappy ; and, though he fancied he did nothing, he did the same to her.

The last few weeks of term went by like this, and then the Summer Vacation tore them apart. Rachel was subdued in Elton and John wandered disconsolately about a dusty Liverpool. But soon Rachel was able to write to tell him she had got through Part I, and he wrote back ; writing letters was permissible, he argued with himself, and it was only polite to answer hers. But she wrote again to thank him for his congratulations, and after a struggle he wrote to thank her for her letter, and so it went on, and nobody knew. Rachel could be as secretive as Kate Barlow.

In the middle of August Aunt Alice died suddenly. Her last excitement had been the appearance of Kate's son at Greenbanks. It had kept her going a long time. She said over and over again to Letty : ' I wonder what the end of it will be. Eh, I would like to know how it will all turn out.'

But she was not to know the end of Kate Barlow's tale. She drifted out of life one hot night, soon after Letty's departure, after fanning her to sleep with an old-fashioned straw fan taken from behind the china urn on the bedroom mantelpiece.

Nobody wept much for Aunt Alice, except the faithful Betsey and Letty herself. During these last years, in her close attendance on the invalid, Letty had almost forgotten that she was trying to earn the legacy. But Aunt Alice had not forgotten, and when the will was read, it was found that she had left Letty fourteen thousand pounds.

Letty wept again with gratitude. Fourteen thousand pounds ! It was beyond her wildest dreams ; it was twice, three times, as much as she had expected. Remorsefully she thought too late of things she might have done for the old lady.

'But I didn't think of them at the time,' she consoled herself. 'I really did everything I could think of.'

She drew a cheque at once, bought expensive mourning, and decided to go to London to see Rose and have a little change.

She went, and in her absence Ambrose entertained himself with roseate plans for Bournemouth. He hailed Aunt Alice's legacy as the solution of all his problems. He would certainly be able to retire now on his sixtieth birthday next May. He could shuffle off the worries of his mother-in-law's affairs ; Kate Barlow would have to be dismissed, of course, and Greenbanks sold, but he would offer his mother-in-law a home with them in Bournemouth. He did owe that much to her, he admitted ; although it must be quite understood that he could not foresee that the investments would go wrong. Everybody's investments had gone wrong these last years. But his mother-in-law should be made very comfortable at Bournemouth ; there was really nothing for her to worry about. Rachel would finish at the University in June that year, and they could all be settled in Bournemouth before the winter. Everything had panned out beautifully, thought Ambrose.

He decided to broach the subject to Letty on her return from London, but when she came back, looking very well, she announced that she was going to Birmingham to see Dick. She asked Rachel to go with her.

'Because I can pay for us now, you see.'

But Rachel preferred to stay at Greenbanks; her Uncle Thomas's house had no attractions for her.

'Very well,' said Letty. 'We'll go for a few days to Southwold before you go back to Liverpool. I picked out Southwold from a holiday book. It looks a very nice place.'

Ambrose kept his plans to himself until one September evening when he and Letty were sitting together in the dining-room at Beech Crescent. The windows were wide open. Ambrose sat at one side of them with the evening paper, and Letty at the other turning over the pages of a paper book with a gay cover of palm trees and bright blue sky. Ambrose was afraid she was thinking of going off somewhere else and decided that he must lay his plans before her without delay.

'Letty, I've been thinking about your money,' he began, lowering his paper.

She looked sharply at him.

'Hadn't you better hand it over to me?' he suggested mildly.

'Thank you, Ambrose, but I prefer to look after it myself,' said Letty, turning over more pages.

'But you have no experience of handling money,' said Ambrose in a reasonable voice.

'That's true,' she said, with rather more significance than he liked. 'But I can learn.'

'Learning is expensive,' remarked Ambrose.

'I know.' He wondered if she was being significant again.

'I think you'd better let me manage it for you,' he said, after a pause.

' No, Ambrose. I shall look after it myself.'

Ambrose flushed, and raised the paper again. But he did not read it, and by and by, he put it down and said :

' I was rather looking to you to help me. I had some nice plans for us all.'

Letty did not encourage him by word or look.

Ambrose reached for his pipe. He felt vaguely uneasy. Surely Letty wasn't going to be unreasonable.

' You see I can retire next year,' he said between puffs as he lighted his pipe. ' I've been looking forward to getting away from Elton for years ; in fact, ever since I came to it, I've been looking forward to leaving it.'

He laughed with some embarrassment, and threw the dead match into the grate.

' I thought, now that you have this money, we might clear out next May.'

' And go to Bournemouth, I suppose ? ' finished Letty in a strange voice.

' Yes,' said Ambrose.

' Well,' said Letty, drawing a long breath as if she were about to take a plunge. ' You must do as you like, of course, but I may as well tell you now as later, Ambrose, that I shall not go to Bournemouth.'

Ambrose stared fixedly at her.

' I've always made it clear that I should go to Bournemouth when I retired,' he said.

' I know. And there's nothing to stop you from going ; but I shan't go.'

' You won't go ! ' He was astounded. ' You calmly suggest that I should go and that you should not go ? '

Letty nodded her head.

' What on earth do you mean ? ' asked Ambrose.

'Simply that I shall not go to Bournemouth.'

'You mean you want to stop here?'

'No.'

'What on earth do you mean then?' asked Ambrose again, his anger growing.

'Do you realize,' said Letty, 'that I am almost fifty? For thirty years I've done what you wanted; I've hardly done one thing I wanted to do, but I'm going to do it now. I've done my duty, I've had four children, I've looked after them and you and the house. The boys have gone. Rachel will go—oh, yes! You'll never get Rachel to stop here. There'll only be you left. Well, I've looked after you for thirty years; you must look after yourself now for a bit. I don't say I'm never going to see you again, but I'm never going to keep house for you again when Rachel has finished at Liverpool. No, never!'

This was frightful. Ambrose perspired with horror. He could only stare at her and try to believe his ears. She was going to leave him—after thirty years of married life! But it was impossible! It couldn't happen. No one ever did that kind of thing. Giddy young wives went off with other men; but women of fifty didn't leave their husbands after thirty years. She was mad. But that was the worst of it; she wasn't mad. There was a dreadful sanity about her; she meant what she said. It was this money.

'So you've only lived with me,' he said with slow fury, 'for what you could get out of me.'

'Nonsense,' said Letty. 'You've got more out of me than I have out of you. But it's no good talking about that now. It's over.'

'And your home, your husband, your children are nothing to you?'

'The children have gone, this house is only a shell,' said Letty.

'And what about me?' asked Ambrose heavily.

'Well, I've done my duty to you,' said Letty pettishly. 'Anyway, I'm going.'

'And where are you going, pray?'

'I'm going to Africa for one thing.'

'Africa!' cried Ambrose.

'Yes, to Natal to see the twins, and Kenya to see Laura,' said Letty, unable to hide the gleam of excitement in her eye.

'Good heavens, you can't go to Africa alone!'

'Oh, yes, I can.'

There was a pause.

'You're not like a woman,' said Ambrose bitterly.

'Now what exactly do you mean by that? What is it to be like *a* woman? Take the women you know : me, mother, Kate Barlow, Rachel—all different. Which is like a woman? You've got some pattern of a woman in your mind, and if women don't fit it, it is they who are wrong, I suppose, not you. Oh, Ambrose, if you'd ever thought a moment before you spoke, I might have been able to stand it. But all these hollow opinions you've kept bringing out . . .'

She did not finish, but shook her head impatiently.

Ambrose sat collapsed, with his hands hanging over each arm of the chair. He wasn't thinking ; he couldn't. Painful sensations assailed his mind. Then the mist cleared and he turned to Letty.

'You can't go,' he said almost in triumph. 'Your mother will have to leave Greenbanks. She can't afford to stay there. You'll have to make a home for *her*, if you don't make one for me.'

Letty was alert at once at this threat to her new freedom.

'What do you mean ? What's happened to mother's money ? '

'Her income has diminished considerably lately.'

'You mean since you took it in hand ? '

'I wish you'd be careful what you say,' said Ambrose.

'Mother's investments were very sound ; corporation stock and old-established trading concerns. I know that. What have you done with them ? '

Ambrose's mouth narrowed. He did not relish this catechism.

'Come along,' said Letty in a hard voice. 'You've gone so far ; you must go farther. What have you done with mother's money ? '

'Letty, I will not be spoken to like this . . .'

'Don't be absurd, Ambrose. What has happened to mother's money ? '

'It has suffered the same fate as most other people's money. The same fate as mine would have suffered if I'd had any to invest. I put your mother's money into rubber and cotton—and—er—a silver-mine or two. I took sound advice. I went into the business very thoroughly. I dealt with your mother's affairs as carefully as if they were my own.'

'But that's just it,' cried Letty. 'They weren't your own. That's what you should have remembered. You should have left them alone. That's what you have never been able to do—leave things alone.'

'Letty, I won't stand this ! '

'Yes, you will. You'll hear the truth for once. I'm ashamed of you. You're a meddler. You've meddled to the point of fraud this time.'

'Letty ! ' Ambrose looked curiously sick.

'A nice hole you've got yourself into ! And making Mother leave Greenbanks at her age ! '

Letty drummed on the table with agitated fingers, breathing rapidly, reviewing the situation.

' But she shan't leave it,' she went on angrily. ' I'll see to that. I shall have to make Greenbanks my headquarters and help her to keep it up. And so will you. You'll never get to Bournemouth. You'll have to keep that house up. It serves you right, Ambrose. You've no one to blame but yourself. As for the rest, you can explain yourself to Jim and Thomas.'

She got up as if she washed her hands of the matter, and left him abruptly.

She left him in his chair by the window, his pipe gone out and fallen down his waistcoat, leaving a trail of ash he would have been scrupulous to remove at any other time, but was now unaware of.

His mind moved about uneasily like a dog chased from the fire on a cold day. There was nowhere he could settle in comfort ; bitter draughts blew on him from all sides. Letty would only make Greenbanks her ' headquarters '. What a word ! What a substitute for ' home ' ! She ought to be ashamed of herself ; but she was not, and he could not make her ashamed. And those investments ! He would have to face Jim and remain behind after all ! It was an awful prospect.

In his thought-shiftings, he suddenly had a fantastic vision of himself living with George Boyd. Fat George Boyd, also discarded by an Ashton. He dismissed the vision angrily. There was still Rachel. Letty said Rachel would not stay with him, but she must be made to. The daughter must take on the mother's duty. That was only right.

Ambrose sufficiently revived to wish for a whisky-and-soda. He discovered that it was quite dark. He turned on the lights but forgot to draw the curtains,

and the mosquitoes came in from the Crescent and
added to his discomfort by biting him severely in
several places. Rachel returned from Greenbanks.
He looked at her to try to make out if there was any
truth in what Letty said about her wanting to break
away. But she was pale and quiet, and went off to
bed, when told, with a docility that reassured him.

He sat on in the dining-room with no company but
his thoughts, which were not pleasant. He decided
to go to bed at last, and on the way upstairs he told
himself that he wouldn't be surprised to find that Letty,
having determined to go her own way, had removed
to the boys' old room. But he found her already in
bed in her accustomed place, with her face turned to
the wall. He undressed in silence, turned out the
lights and lay down beside her.

' Good night,' he said as if to a stranger who was
not much to his taste.

' Good night,' murmured Letty, pretending to be
sleepy.

Ambrose lay staring into the dark. They had slept
side by side for thirty years, and now she was going
to take herself off to Africa. Under the anger, resentment, self-pity that seethed within him, something
stirred ; he didn't know what it was ; it was terribly
uncomfortable, a sort of ache. It would not let him
go to sleep. Distant town clocks struck the hours at
interminable intervals. He counted them despair-
ingly ; he was not used to sleeping badly and the night
seemed endless. At last he could restrain himself no
longer, but said in the darkness :

' Will you be long in Africa ? '

He held his breath, waiting for the answer ; but none
came, for Letty was asleep.

CHAPTER TWENTY-FIVE

I

IT was Bella who opened Louisa's eyes to the possibility of Kate's being in love with the Reverend Cyril Northcote. One evening when Louisa was sitting alone in the drawing-room she heard Bella wandering about in the hall and called to her to come in. Bella was sometimes at a loose end now that she had no young man to ' run out at the back ' to when her working hours were over. With every advance of time and fashion, Bella's chances of a young man grew less. She was not built on modern lines ; she was made for wear and tear, and could not hide her hips. No shingle, bingle or bob suited her square head, and when waists came in again she was lost indeed. She suffered agonies from tight stays on her nights out, but could not make any impression on her middle or cut a fashionable figure on the Victoria Boulevard.

' I shall 'ave to give up,' she said to Louisa. ' I shall 'ave to resign meself to stopping with you. I wouldn't mind if I thought you'd last my lifetime, but it stands to nature you won't, doesn't it, and then what shall I do with meself ? '

Louisa hid a smile.

' You mustn't despair, Bella. Mr. Right will turn up yet.'

' Turn up ? Nay, you've to go out rooting and scraping for 'em these days. They're that backward.

They're that milk-and-watery, they 'aven't the strength to trickle to the church,' said Bella scornfully.

She came into the drawing-room now, grateful for the summons. She poked the fire and swept the hearth, then stood with her arms folded beside her mistress's chair.

'Miss Barlow's gone to church, I suppose?' she remarked.

'Yes,' said Louisa, knitting a soft jacket for Laura's little daughter, who had considerately put off her arrival until her mother could welcome her without regrets.

'It's getting late,' went on Bella. 'Happen she's gone to call on the Vicar.'

Louisa smiled as she wondered again where Bella got all her information.

'Let's see, Vicar's single, isn't he?' asked Bella.

'Yes, he's single,' admitted Louisa.

'Mph,' said Bella significantly. 'And he thinks a lot of Miss Barlow, doesn't he? Always praising her fancy-work, and lending her books and that. Well, I daresay it would be a good thing if she could get him to marry her. She could forget all her troubles and settle down with the best then.'

'Bella, Bella,' protested Louisa, 'you mustn't run on so fast.'

'Nay, 'm, I'm not saying there's anything in it,' explained Bella. 'I'm only saying it would be a good thing.'

Louisa let her knitting fall into her lap. She had never thought of this. She must be stupid, she told herself. She had been stupid before about Kate, and now she was stupid again. Why should she take it for granted that Kate's life was over, that she had finished with love? She reproached herself for being old, with not being alert enough to see what was happening round her. Kate was in love with the Vicar, and for him she had rejected her son. She thought John would come between her and the Vicar. Louisa saw it all now.

'Well, well,' she murmured. 'I have been blind. . . .'

She glanced round Bella at the clock. It was long after nine. She tried to chase away her misgivings. 'Of course, if he marries her it will be splendid. . . .'

The sound of the front door being opened and closed put Bella to flight.

'Here she is now,' she said in a stage whisper, as she went. She never paused for conversation with Miss Barlow.

Kate came into the room. Her cheeks were carnation pink and her eyes shone.

'Have you been all right, Mrs. Ashton?' she inquired, looking at Louisa without seeming to see her.

'Quite, thank you, dear.'

'And how is the jacket getting along?'

She bent down to look, but she did not seem to see that either. Louisa heard her breathing fast as if from haste or excitement. Her eyes followed Kate inquiringly as she drifted about the room. Had the Vicar asked her to be his wife? Was that it? She looked very keyed up about something. Would she tell anyone if he had asked her, Louisa wondered. 'I don't believe she would,' she sighed.

Kate removed herself from Louisa's speculations and went upstairs. She closed the door of her room and sank down on the floor by the bed; she crouched there with her arms thrown out over the counterpane, and gave herself up to the warm precious memory of the hour she had just spent with the Vicar.

But the hour that filled her with elation, in retro-
spect, had filled the Reverend Cyril Northcote with
alarm. He was having a very uncomfortable time in
his study at this moment. This friendship with Kate
Barlow was taking him further than he wanted to go.
He had rather lost his feet in the sweep of emotion
that beset him to-night ; he must find them again.
She was dangerous to him ; he had realized that when
she stood before him, tall, dark, glowing, her sad
passionate eyes beseeching him—for his love. Yes,
there was no getting away from it. That was what
she wanted. And he had held her hand warmly,
closely, without thinking what he was doing. He had
gone too far ; he had to admit it. He had pulled
himself up just in time. He remembered himself and
walked her firmly to the door. He shut her out into
the night, without accompanying her to the gate as
usual ; and now it must stop. Sad, difficult though
it would be—it must stop. He must put an end to
it. He moved restlessly about his study, hating his
task, and not knowing in the least how to set about
it. He couldn't say anything to her—now. He
should have said it long ago. He walked up and
down, his wide mobile mouth drawn down into lines
that revealed a certain weakness usually hidden by the
animation of his expression. He decided to call at
Greenbanks the day after to-morrow ; to-morrow
there was a ruridecanal conference in the town but
Friday he was free and must go then.

II

The next day, the third of October, Rachel returned
to Liverpool and met John by appointment. They
were feverish after their long separation from each

other. John's scruples were momentarily swamped ; he could not take his eyes from her face. The tones of their voices would have betrayed them to anybody but each other ; but they remained bewildered, uncertain, apprehensive. They wandered about the docks, frequently colliding with each other, as they walked, as if they were intoxicated, as indeed they were. Whenever there was a loose cable, a plank, a stanchion, or other obstacle to be stepped over, John took Rachel's little elbow in his hand to assist her. He had never done that before, and every time he did it they were both filled with trembling happiness.

'I say,' he burst out suddenly, 'd'you think my mother would see me again ? D'you think there's any hope of my being able to straighten things out ? I must do *something* about it,' he finished desperately.

'Oh, I feel that too,' cried Rachel. 'Can't we try again ? '

'I sometimes feel it's hopeless, but I must have another shot. I don't know why, but I must. I'll just try once more, and if it doesn't come to anything —I'll have to give up, that's all.'

He looked white and wretched. Rachel wondered, foolishly, if this anguish was all for his mother, or if some of it was because of her. She did hope so.

'Look, I have to come back here on Saturday morning. I'm not coming on Friday this week,' she said. 'Will you come back with me to Greenbanks on Saturday afternoon ? It won't be so bad if you go in with me. I'll warn Grandma and get her to prepare Miss Barlow just before we arrive. Oh, let's get it over, John. It's got to come.'

'Right. I'll come on Saturday,' said John, setting

his jaw. 'But oh Lord, I do hope she won't be so upset as she was last time.'

'She won't, I'm sure. She seems to have got over the shock of you altogether. She seems to have settled down again and been quite happy lately. Grandma was saying so only the other day. I say, I must be getting to the station.'

He took her to the train. He stood on the begrimed platform, and she stood at the carriage window. Both looked as if they did not know why they were leaving each other. They did not speak, but as the train went out he raised his eyes with such a look of longing and despair that she sank back into her corner and wept.

III

The next afternoon Rachel, installed in the drawing-room windows at Greenbanks with her books, looked up and announced inelegantly: 'Oh, Lord, the Vicar!'

Kate immediately rose from her frame and went swiftly out of the room, murmuring something about not having changed her dress.

'Oh, Grandma,' cried Rachel, scrabbling at her books, 'do you mind if I disappear? I want to get some work done, and he's nothing in my line really. Will you excuse me?'

'Yes, yes, run along. But don't let him see you. It looks so rude, everybody rushing out of the room like this,' said Louisa, watching Rachel's exit mildly over her spectacles.

'The Reverend Mr. Northcote,' announced Bella, watching his entry with speculative eyes. She expected him to pop the question at any visit now.

Louisa apologized for being the only one to receive him, but said that Kate would be down soon.

'Ah, but I am glad to see something of *you*, Mrs. Ashton,' said Mr. Northcote as he sat down.

She noticed that his hair had been brushed determinedly into place. There was a severity of appearance and manner she had not observed in him before ; he seemed to have thrown off his pleasant, careless ways.

It struck her, all at once, that he might have come to propose to Kate. Oh, if only he had ! He certainly seemed nervous enough ; he kept looking at the door to see if she was coming, and he compressed his lips from time to time until they were almost white.

He made some hurried remarks about the garden, to which Louisa replied.

She said she would go on with her knitting if he didn't mind.

'This is for my newest granddaughter,' she told him happily. It was so lovely to be able to speak openly of Laura's baby ; to bring her into conversations and make security all about her, when she might have had none at all.

'Ah,' said the Vicar, watching the wrinkled hands dealing deftly with the tender pink wool.

Then he saw his opening and rushed into it ; it was clumsy and not in very good taste, but no matter, he must take it. Kate Barlow might come into the room at any moment and his chance, so good, so wonderfully opportune, might be gone for ever

'Ah,' said the Vicar again. 'Although I am a celibate priest, I feel very strongly the beauty of a home life such as yours, Mrs. Ashton.'

Louisa stopped knitting. What did he say? Celibate priest?

'Your ordered house, your garden, the tranquillity of your presence, your love for your children and theirs for you,' went on the Vicar as if he were in the pulpit. 'They are great blessings, Mrs. Ashton, and blessings I renounced when I took the vows of celibacy. My church comes first; I have other blessings, I know; but sometimes these warm happinesses tug at the heart.'

Louisa looked at him with undisguised blankness.

'Are you surprised to hear I am a celibate?' he asked, with a smile. 'But many, in fact most Anglo-Catholic clergy, take vows of celibacy, you know.'

'Do they?' murmured Louisa with embarrassment. She blinked a little and moved uneasily in her chair.

A celibate priest, he called himself. And yet she had heard nothing of it before.

'I suppose this is the "going slowly" he spoke of the first time he called,' she thought caustically. 'He didn't want to frighten his congregation—not the women, anyway.'

She looked at him coldly and he rose and went to the window to inspect the altar-cloth.

He had thrown the stone; the ripples would spread.

'This is almost finished, I see,' he said. 'It is a magnificent piece of work. It really is extraordinarily good of Miss Barlow to do it for us.'

'Us!' exclaimed Louisa to herself. 'You know very well she did it for you.'

'I only hope the congregation won't find anything Popish in wistaria blossoms.' He was voluble in order to cover Louisa's silence, which discomfited him. 'Or denounce it as too beautiful for the altar.'

He began to walk about the room, with his head

thrown back. Louisa's eyes followed him gravely over her spectacles. A celibate priest ! Poor Kate !

'You know, Mrs. Ashton, I verily believe some members of St. Anne's would, like Cromwell's soldiers, stable their horses in the house of God. . . .'

Whatever was he talking about, Louisa wondered. A celibate priest. . . .

'Ah, Miss Barlow,' cried the Vicar, breaking off his monologue. 'How are you ? '

Kate had come into the room looking extraordinarily handsome in her new frock of deep but bright blue.

'It's a shame ! ' cried Louisa to herself. 'She knew nothing about his vows of celibacy, I'll be bound.'

She watched them as they went to the window together to look at Kate's work ; she shook her head when their backs were turned. This meant more trouble for Kate. The thought of it sickened her. She was filled with indignation.

'If they take these vows, they should behave differently,' she thought angrily. 'They shouldn't go about making themselves charming to poor women.'

Bella brought in tea, and Louisa laid aside her knitting to pour out. But she could not be beguiled into conversation ; she held off. Kate's ways and looks, the tones of her voice, warm and unlike those she gave to anyone else, made Louisa wince. But she had not long to bear it. As soon as he decently could, Mr. Northcote excused himself and went. Kate went at once to her embroidery frame to put the last stitches in.

'In less than an hour,' she said to Louisa, 'I shall have finished this.'

Louisa went upstairs to Rachel, who was working in her little room.

'Hello, darling, what's the matter?' she said, at the sight of her grandmother's troubled face.

'Well, love, it's this—am I disturbing you?'

'No, I've finished,' said Rachel.

'You know Mr. Northcote's been. I thought he might have come to propose to Kate, but it was something just the opposite. He came to say he was a celibate priest.'

Rachel gazed at her grandmother in astonishment.

'You thought he'd come to propose to Miss Barlow! Grandma! Has he ever shown any signs of it? You don't mean to say she's in love with him? I thought you said she was forty! Besides . . .'

Rachel's cheeks went red, her eyes wide with amazement.

'I'm afraid Kate *is* in love with him,' said Louisa.

'Good heavens!' murmured Rachel. In love at forty! You'd have thought it would be all over by then. Rachel felt it was vaguely indecent that John's mother should be falling in love at forty. She tried to rearrange her idea of Miss Barlow.

'Is that why she's been different lately, d'you think? Having new frocks and going to church? Has going to church been all for love of the Vicar? It seems pretty awful—that, doesn't it? Using God as a sort of smoke-screen.'

'Oh, no, no,' protested Louisa. 'I think Kate has genuinely changed her views. And I think the Vicar meant to help her. I think he was quite sincere in that way.'

'You think he tried to save her soul and forgot she had a body attached to it?' said Rachel.

'I should think that's how it began,' said Louisa. 'But I am very worried, love,' she said, her eyebrows

climbing higher. ' I'm afraid it means trouble for
Kate. I shall have to tell her. I can't let her go on
thinking he'll marry her.'

She sighed and absently straightened the fringed
mats on the dressing-table.

' You see now why she refused to have anything
to do with the boy—with her son, don't you ? ' she
asked Rachel.

Rachel's cheeks, which had resumed their normal
hue, were dyed again by a recurring blush. She bent
to the floor in search of something that was not there,
and cooled her face in the shadow of the chest of
drawers.

' Grandma,' she said when she came up again.

' Yes, love,' said Louisa, turning at the tone in
Rachel's voice.

' Er——' said Rachel. The blush came back and
made her frown. She took a little comb from the
side of her hair, shook her hair back and put in the
comb again. ' Well . . .' she began again. ' I've
been seeing a good deal of John . . .'

' What ! ' cried Louisa. ' And you never told me.'

' No, but I was going to . . .' said Rachel lamely.
' But listen, darling ! We've got a plan, John and I.
We thought we'd try another meeting between him and
his mother to see if it would be any better this time.'

Louisa cried out in alarm.

' But, Grandma, don't you see—now that this has
come out about Mr. Northcote, it will make her much
more ready to welcome John, won't it ? I thought
I'd bring him to-morrow afternoon. It's rather opportune, really, isn't it ? She's lost the Vicar and gained
her son. It will break the loss a little, won't it ? '
reasoned Rachel.

' Eh, dear me, I don't know,' said Louisa anxiously.
' I never know how to treat Kate, and I'm afraid to
risk anything. I don't think it will do any good
your bringing him here, love. I don't really.'

' Oh, I do, darling,' said Rachel persuasively.
' And we can only try. After all, a big thing is at
stake. We ought to try once more. John is as nervous
as a cat, but he thinks he'd better try. And if she
won't accept him, well, she won't, and it will all be
over. But he will have tried, anyway. Poor John!
It's so awful for him, and you would be sorry for
him, and like him if you knew him. I know he's had
that money and the Macdonalds have been awfully
kind to him—but year after year he had to stay at
school for the holidays, and he let out the other day,
meaning it as a joke, that he often used to send for
shop catalogues to make himself a bit of correspondence. Oh, darling, I could have wept when he
told me that,' said Rachel, her eyes rather too bright
even now. ' He'd nobody to write to him, nobody
to love him ; people were good to him, but he didn't
really *matter* to anybody and he's such a diffident
creature ; he doesn't expect to matter to anybody
now. His mother ought to be decent to him. It's
too bad ; it's disgusting.'

Rachel's breath came rather fast ; she pulled down
the cuffs of her jumper, her eyelids lowered stormily.

' I know, love,' said Louisa soothingly. ' I know
all that. I'm very sorry for the poor young man. I
do like him. I thought he was a sweet-natured boy,
and a son any woman might be proud of. But if
Kate won't have him, she won't, and we can't make
her.'

' We can try once more, anyway,' said Rachel.

'And you'll help, won't you, Grandma ? You'll break it gently to Miss Barlow to-morrow morning—not before, mind—that I'm bringing John home with me in the afternoon ? Then she can be a little prepared, and not go off the deep end again. I want to spare him as much as possible.'

'Eh, dear me,' sighed Louisa. 'You do give me some uncomfortable jobs. . . .'

'We do, don't we ? ' said Rachel, laughter in her eyes. 'We lead you an awful life. But what we should do without you I can't think ! Everybody depends on you, precious ! Deserted husbands descend on you, defaulting wives apply to you for divorce, vicars, who go too far, place the onus of their celibacy on you, and now you have to prepare an unaccommodating mother to receive her son ! And you're such a little mild thing, darling ! I could laugh at the sight of you, bless you ! '

Rachel threw her arms round her grandmother's neck. Louisa, smiling, let herself be kissed, then straightened the little lace erection that had long ago replaced her 'switch', and felt herself ready to do anything for anybody, within reason.

'Now remember,' whispered Rachel, as they went downstairs together. 'In case I don't get another chance to remind you, don't say a word about John before to-morrow morning. But you'd better say something about the Vicar to-night, hadn't you ? '

CHAPTER TWENTY-SIX

I

LOUISA was horrified to find herself going to bed without having said a word to Kate about the Vicar.

Kate had spent the evening in the kitchen, first unpicking the altar-cloth from its canvas and calico mountings over a clean sheet spread on the table, and then pressing the work on the wrong side to raise the embroidery. She took a long time over this task, leaning on the iron, waiting for it to do its work, with satisfaction in her dark eyes.

Perkins, the parrot, who had long outlived his master and showed no signs of age, watched with a wicked eye and from time to time whooped out : 'I don't know why I love you, but I do—oo—ooo ! '

Bella was so tickled by his perspicacity that, every time he did it, she disappeared into the back kitchen and hid her face in the roller-towel to stifle her laughter. But in the end she thought it had gone far enough and threw the green cover over his cage.

'Be quiet with you, you knowing old thing ! ' she said.

'What ? ' inquired the parrot in a muffled voice.

'Go to sleep ! ' cried Bella. 'Isn't he yuman ? ' she said to Louisa.

Louisa hung about, waiting uneasily for her opportunity, but Bella, who liked company in her kitchen, hung about too ; there was no getting rid of her and her exclamations of admiration.

At last Kate could find nothing more to do to the altar-cloth ; she packed it up in the new sheets of tissue paper she had bought from the stationer's, and bore it into the drawing-room. Louisa followed her, and gave a cough or two which Rachel rightly interpreted as a hint, and complied with by going upstairs to bed.

Louisa gave another preparatory cough and rehearsed her opening, but before she could get a word out, Kate herself said good night and followed Rachel out of the room.

Louisa was left alone with her unsaid word about the Vicar. She made a funny little figure of perplexity, as she sat on the edge of her chair, her fists folded on her knees, her cap slightly askew, giving her a deceptively rakish air. She sat for some time, her eyebrows high, looking over her spectacles at the dying fire.

' Well, it's no good sitting here,' she said at last. ' I can't get Kate told by sitting here. Dear me, she's setting such store on giving him that altar-cloth, I can see.'

She sighed, and got up to make her usual round of the room. She straightened the chairs, shook up the cushions, closed the piano with a thought of Charles as she did so ; she pulled back the silver-green curtains, thinking that the rings must be worn, or her hands not so strong as they used to be. Then she turned out the lights, and, holding up her dress before her feet, slowly climbed the stairs.

Before the three steps leading down to Kate's room she paused. She saw the yellow line of light under the door. Should she go in and get it over now?

But no, she thought, she must bring it in casually as if she attached no significance to it. Poor, proud Kate was going to be humiliated again, and Louisa knew that at all costs she must seem to notice nothing of it.

She went on to her bedroom and at once Rachel called out from the little room adjoining.

' Grandma ! '

' Yes, love ? ' said Louisa, opening the door.

' Did you tell her ? '

' No,' confessed Louisa.

' Oh, dear, what a muddle it is ! ' said Rachel. ' Why can't people behave as we want them to, without giving us all this trouble ? Never mind, darling. You'll get it said in the morning. Go to bed and sleep well.'

Louisa came to tuck her up.

' Are you warm enough ? '

' Yes, I'm most snug, but I can't go to sleep.'

Louisa's practised hands busied themselves with the bedcovers, she pulled up the sheet and smoothed it under Rachel's chin.

' There, that's better. Now turn on your right side and close your eyes.' She stroked back Rachel's dark curling hair and lingered a little longer. ' Now you'll soon be off, I know. Good night.'

She undressed slowly and climbed into her great mahogany bed.

Next door, Rachel, soothed and smoothed, had gone to sleep. But Kate, in her room, had the altar-cloth undone again and pored over it, thinking that she would give it to him to-morrow. She burned with impatience to see him again. On Wednesday night, in his study, he had come very near to saying he loved her. She had seen the words trembling on his lips, at that moment when he took her hand in his and came close. What had kept them back, she wondered? What had made him hold off? A moment of panic, of hideous doubt, seized her, but she reassured herself. He had shown in so many ways that he loved her; he had only to put it into words now. And he would, to-morrow, she was sure. It was strange, and perhaps foolish, she told herself, but she had always felt that the finishing of the altar-cloth would bring the climax of her love.

She folded it again with careful hands and laid it in its box.

She began to undress. Should she wear the blue or the red dress to-morrow? She wondered which he liked best, and smiled at herself for thinking of such things, as if she were a girl again. When she stood before the mirror, knotting her thick dark hair for the night, she noticed how white her neck was, her shoulders too. She closed her eyes and stood with her hand at her throat. To be lovely enough still for him to love . . . what unlooked-for respite, what happiness!

II

By two o'clock on Saturday afternoon Louisa had still not spoken to Kate about the Vicar. Never had anything been so hard to say. She simply could not get it in among the ordinary domestic conversations of the morning. Then suddenly, in the drawing-room, Kate gave her an opportunity.

' I think I'll take the altar-cloth to the Vicarage to-night, if you can spare me,' she said.

' Oh, certainly, dear . . . yes,' said Louisa hurriedly.

Then she laid down her knitting and took the plunge. A tense look came over her face, her eyelids batted a little. 'D'you know, Kate,' she said, thinking how foolish it sounded, 'd'you know, he told me on Thursday when he was here, that he was a celibate priest; he said he'd taken vows of celibacy and could never marry. I was surprised, Kate . . . I never thought . . .' Her voice fluttered away, and she seized her knitting with damp, trembling hands. She dared not look at Kate, but she felt the chill, the silence that succeeded.

The silence was long, but Louisa kept her eyes glued with desperation on her knitting.

At last Kate spoke.

'He said what?'

'He said he was a celibate priest,' said Louisa as if she was repeating a lesson. Ever since he had used the term 'celibate priest' it had stuck; she could not call him anything else, or find any other way of passing on what he had said, to Kate.

'Are you sure?' asked Kate harshly. 'You know you often get words wrong. Are you sure?'

'Yes, I'm sure he said that,' said Louisa miserably. 'He said he couldn't marry. They do take these vows, it seems,' she finished as casually as she could.

The room was intolerably quiet. At last Louisa stole a glance at Kate. The expression of Kate's face made her want to exclaim with pity, but she kept her lips tightly shut and looked away again. She knew she must seem not to notice; she knew Kate too well.

She knitted on; she made a few remarks that needed no reply. Kate did not stir or speak. Bella came in with the after-lunch cups of tea, and Louisa watched

Kate take hers with a shaking hand. She did not
drink it, but put it down and forgot it.

An infantile, silvery note from the clock on the
mantelpiece made Louisa look up with a start. It was
half-past two. Rachel and the young man would
soon be here. Panic beset her again. Why, oh, why
had she allowed Rachel to bring him to-day ? It was
too much ; things were piling up too high for Kate.
How would she stand it ? How would she behave
to him this time ?—Worse than ever, Louisa feared.
And she had got to be told he was coming. Louisa
pressed her handkerchief to her lips, and looked
imploringly at Kate. But Kate did not notice her.

Louisa suddenly thought that perhaps the coming
of Kate's son might act in the same way as a blister
applied to the chest draws the sufferer's attention from
a pain in the stomach. The idea gave her such courage
that she burst into speech.

'Kate . . . Kate, my dear, I do hope it will be
all right to you, but Rachel has been seeing a good
deal of your son in Liverpool lately, and it seems he
is very anxious to see you again. . . .'

Kate's eyes, turned unseeingly on Louisa when she
began to speak, now hardened their gaze.

'Rachel is bringing him here this afternoon,' faltered
Louisa. 'Though of course you don't need to see
him if you would rather not.'

The blister was having its effect. Kate's pallor gave
place to a deep flush of anger, her eyes blazed at
Louisa.

'Rachel is bringing him here ? How dare she !
How dare he come ! Didn't I make it plain that I
won't have anything to do with him ? How dare he
force himself on me again ! And you—Mrs. Ashton

—I expected better from you than to expose me to this kind of thing. I shall have to go. I won't stay here to be interfered with like this. And my son knows he's no right to meet Rachel in Liverpool or anywhere else. How far has it gone?'

Poor Louisa went pale at this outburst.

'I don't know, Kate. But don't distress yourself. They'll soon be here, and you can just make the position clear to the young man. I don't suppose he'll ever trouble you again afterwards. Only tell him as kindly as you can . . .'

'How dare they come here together!' interrupted Kate furiously. 'Rachel's arranged it. But I'll show her what a mistake it is to interfere in other people's affairs. . . .'

Kate got up and went swiftly from the room.

Louisa sat helpless where she was. She wondered what Kate meant to do. She wondered with distress what would happen now.

Kate came back.

'I've telephoned for her father,' she said, as if she had got the better of Louisa.

'Oh, dear me!' cried Louisa, throwing up her hands in despair. 'I didn't want Ambrose here! There'll be such a scene!'

'Don't you think I'm sick of scenes too?' asked Kate fiercely.

Louisa quailed.

'Do calm yourself,' she besought, as Kate began to walk up and down the room in agitation.

But Kate flashed such a look on her that Louisa decided to get out of the way for a while.

If Letty had her new car out ready, Ambrose would be at Greenbanks in a very few minutes, she thought.

She was right. It was not long before there was a crunch of wheels on the back drive, and the door opened to admit Ambrose, who looked at her angrily from under his bushy eyebrows and asked at once for Miss Barlow.

' She's in the drawing-room,' said Louisa, presenting a flushed cheek to Letty, who came behind.

' Isn't it a lovely afternoon? ' she added plaintively, looking through the glass door at the garden flooded with sunshine.

It was far too lovely an afternoon to be wasted on scenes in the drawing-room.

III

As Rachel mounted the steps she saw the faces of her relatives showing white through the drawing-room windows.

' Oh ! ' she said, drawing back a little.

' What is it? ' asked John, looking not at the windows but at her.

' Nothing really—except that Father's there. We shall have to face the music.'

She smiled over her shoulder at him as she opened the front door.

' Come on,' she said. ' It will soon be over ! '

There was significance in the hush of the hall. They felt it and spoke in whispers.

' Shall I hang my hat here? '

' Yes, and I must take mine off, too.'

Bella watched them through the crack of the green-baize door.

' What a bonny pair they make,' she thought admiringly. ' Him so tall and strong, and her so pretty in that yellow jumper.'

John and Rachel whispered together for a moment longer, then Rachel opened the door and they went into the drawing-room. She smiled tentatively as she advanced, then became suddenly serious. John and she halted by mutual consent, in the middle of the green carpet with its faded terra-cotta garlands.

Ambrose broke the silence.

'What is the meaning of this?' he asked. Letty knew he would.

Before Rachel could think of an answer, Kate Barlow spoke to her son.

'Why have you come here? Didn't I make it clear enough that I never wanted to see you again?'

Her voice was cutting. John flushed.

'What do you want?' asked Kate with sharp impatience. 'Say what it is and let's have done with it.'

'She looks appalling,' thought Letty. 'I don't like her. I never did.'

John Barlow looked wretched. He faltered out :

'I thought I'd have one more try, Mother . . .'

Mother ! The word startled them all—even Rachel. They thought of her as Miss Barlow, or Kate, but he thought of her as 'Mother'! Kate closed her eyes at the word. She loathed this scene she was forced to take part in. She was desperate to get it over, to be alone. While this boy came here calling her mother, and Rachel furthered some plan of her own, and Ambrose Harding seethed with words, Kate felt herself bleeding inwardly from the wound the Vicar had struck her through Louisa. Let them deal with her son themselves ; she had nothing more to say. She turned from him with a sick look and left the field to Ambrose.

Ambrose had already taken it.

'You realized your own position, I presume,' he was saying, with his head lowered at John Barlow. 'You must have known any association with my daughter would be distasteful to her family.'

'Father!' cried Rachel, angry colour running up into her cheeks.

'Did it not strike you that you were making a poor return to the family that had shown kindness to your mother?'

John blenched.

'Yes, it did . . .' he began, but Rachel interrupted him.

'Father, how can you talk like that? It makes me so ashamed.'

'And so it ought,' cried Ambrose. 'You ought to be ashamed, both of you.'

But that was not what Rachel meant. She looked at John, mutely imploring him not to mind.

'Can't we discuss this reasonably, Father?' she asked. 'Can't we sit down?'

'No,' thundered Ambrose. 'That young man must leave the house. His mother doesn't want him. His presence is nothing but an annoyance to her. She has provided for him very generously. There's nothing to keep him here. Let him go. And kindly keep out of my family, sir. I absolutely forbid you to see my daughter or communicate with her in any way whatever.'

Rachel stepped swiftly in front of John, facing him.

'Don't listen,' she cried.

'What?' shouted Ambrose.

'Don't listen, don't listen!' urged Rachel. 'You have to see me. It doesn't matter what they say—it's between us—you and me. . . .'

'Rachel!' shouted Ambrose, beside himself.
'Stand away from that young man.'

But Rachel caught John by the lapels of his coat.
Her father's anger only moved her on.

'Don't let them separate us—at least, if they do now,
remember I love you. One day I'll be free—next
year I'll be twenty-one.'

'Rachel!' Ambrose was hoarse with fury.

He made no impression on the lovers. John had
leaned to Rachel to hear. He could hardly believe.
Was it true what she was saying? Had she said she
loved him? He forgot his mother, his birth, the anger
of Rachel's father. For a moment he heard nothing
but her voice saying she loved him.

'Letty!' Ambrose plunged to where she sat. 'This
is your daughter. Are you going to sit by and let her
talk about love to this fellow? Why don't you stop
her?'

Letty shook her head helplessly.

'What can I do? She must decide for herself,
Ambrose.'

'Decide for herself? Good heavens! How can you
say such a thing? She's out of her senses.'

He returned to the charge.

'D'you know what you are, sir?' he shouted, pulling
Rachel forcibly aside so that he could better present
his irate front to John. 'You're a bastard! D'you
think I'll allow my daughter to marry a bastard?'

Rachel caught John's hand again.

'Don't mind, John. It's only a word.'

'But it's true,' said John gravely. 'It's what people
will always say. You must realize that, Rachel.'

'I do,' said Rachel, her candid eyes lifted to him.
'But I don't care about it—except for your sake. But

what is all this fuss about illegitimacy?' she asked, turning in perplexity to her father. 'I don't understand it. You know all about John's parents. They were both healthy and normal. . . .'

'Rachel!' Ambrose's voice was thick with angry disgust. Healthy and normal! These frightful modern opinions to be voiced by a young girl, his daughter.

'Kate, dear,' interrupted Louisa. 'You go. I can see you're not well. Shall I come with you?'

Kate shook her head and went from the room.

'You ask that young man,' said Ambrose heavily, without pausing for Kate's exit. 'Ask him if he hasn't suffered from his illegitimacy.'

'I know he has,' said Rachel. 'But it's people like you who make him suffer. But why do you do it? I know illegitimacy was penalized to protect the legal wife and family, but there's no wife or family to protect here.'

'Bah!' said Ambrose. 'It's no use talking to you. You're an Ashton. You'll go for what you want if you've to trample on us all to get it.'

'You object to John because of what people will say,' Rachel charged him. She was getting very angry. She stood like a boy with her head back and her chin out. 'Public opinion—that's what you care about, Father.'

'Of course I care about public opinion,' said Ambrose. 'Who doesn't?'

'I don't,' said Rachel. 'I don't care tuppence, and if John and I lived in a big town there'd *be* no public opinion. So what would you have to object to then?'

'You talk like a fool,' said Ambrose. 'You're a wrong-headed, silly, inexperienced girl. You don't know your own mind. You persuaded me to send you to Liverpool University. You made out you couldn't be happy until you got a degree and worked for your living, and now you want to throw all that up and engage yourself to a most undesirable young man. There isn't a father in England,' shouted Ambrose, with another spurt of fury, ' who wouldn't consider that young man undesirable ! '

' It's true, Rachel,' said John.

Rachel ignored this ; she answered an earlier charge.

' I don't want to give up the University,' she said.

Ambrose turned on her instantly.

' But you don't expect me to provide the money for you to go on there so that you can go against me by marrying this fellow in the end, do you ? '

' Well, if you won't give me the money,' said Rachel, ' I shall have to earn it myself. I shall have to teach in Liverpool and finish my course that way.'

Ambrose was utterly taken aback. She defied him at every turn. The stubborn, foolish creature. . . . A deeper flush of anger purpled his cheek.

' Ambrose,' said Letty, ' leave it alone now. Leave it till later and talk it over again.'

' Yes, Ambrose,' begged Louisa, in distress.

' No,' said Ambrose thickly. ' This business shall be settled once and for all. If Rachel defies me, she'll have to choose between me and this young man.'

' Tch,' exclaimed Letty impatiently. He *would* force things up to impossible heights.

' Which will you choose,' said Ambrose to Rachel, who had gone rather white. ' Your parents who have loved you and given you all you have, or this stranger of whom you know next to nothing ? '

Rachel looked at John.

'Will you have me?' she asked, with a shaky smile.

His eyes answered her with steadfast tenderness. She put her hand in his.

'You make me choose, so I choose John,' she said. Colour came rushing back into her cheeks making her so lovely that tears sprang to Louisa's eyes.

Then she turned to her mother.

'You won't cast me off, will you, Mother? And Grandma won't?' Her eyes questioned like a child's and she smiled like a child at their reassuring faces.

Ambrose made a strange, inarticulate sound and they all looked at him in apprehension. The red had run out of all the little veins that made up Ambrose's ruddy complexion. He looked suddenly blue, defeated. He was alone; they were on one side, opposed to him, and he was alone on the other. First his wife had forsaken him, and then his daughter. He was nothing to them. After all he had done, after all these years, he was nothing to them. He could do nothing with them; Letty had her money, Rachel her young man. Money and a stranger had ousted him. All these years he had loved them, but they had not loved him. And what had he done not to be loved by them? His eyes asked them that question, and some of Rachel's exhilarating defiance left her.

'Father . . .' she began, starting towards him. 'Why must we quarrel like this?'

Ambrose raised his hand to keep her off. He turned on John Barlow.

'Get out,' he said briefly. 'At any rate, I have jurisdiction over my daughter until she is twenty-one. Get out.'

John unclasped Rachel's hand.

'I'm sorry for this, sir,' he said, looking at Ambrose with troubled eyes. 'I know it's been a shock to you and I understand your objections to me. But, as Rachel says, in Liverpool or London no one will bother about my birth and we can't let possible public opinion ruin our lives. There's a much more serious objection you could have made. You don't know anything about me personally. Will you fix your own conditions for a year, and see what you think of me then?'

'Get out,' repeated Ambrose.

'Very well,' said John, setting his jaw. 'Good-bye, Rachel.' He pressed her hands very hard in his.

She looked desperately at him.

'Oh, John . . .'

'Stick it, stick it . . .' he whispered.

He bowed gravely towards Letty and Louisa—he did not know whether they would want to shake hands with him—and went out of the house.

Rachel ran to the window to watch him go down the steps. When he was out of sight she turned back into the room.

'Father,' she said, as if she was going to begin all over again. But Ambrose strode past her to the door.

'Wait, Ambrose,' called Letty hurriedly. 'I'm coming. I'll run you home.'

He raised his hand as he had done before, to silence her. There was dignity in Ambrose for the first time in his life. He went out of the front door and down the steps in his turn.

'Oh, dear,' said Letty, collecting her things. 'I must go after him. This is too much, poor old chap. Botheration. I'm afraid I'm going to have to take him to Africa!'

'Africa?' exclaimed Louisa in amazement.

'Oh, I'll tell you later, Mother,' said Letty.

'Mother, may I stay here for the night?' begged Rachel. 'I couldn't face Father again just now.'

'Yes, you'd better stay here,' agreed Letty grimly. 'All this upset. . . .'

She hurried out to her car.

'Oh, Grandma!' cried Rachel, flinging herself down by Louisa's knee.

IV

It was past eleven o'clock. The garden, still warm from the sun, was silver and black in the moonlight; black under the bushes and the trees, silver on the lawns and the steps.

The house was dark below, but upstairs lights still burned in Kate Barlow's room and in Rachel's.

Rachel could not bring herself to go to bed. She moved restlessly about her little room in various stages of undress. She was filled with longing and dissatisfaction. John loved her. He loved her but he had gone away, before they had been alone together at all, before they had time to kiss or to promise anything.

'Oh, John . . . John . . .' she murmured, pressing her face into her bare arms.

How long would it be before she saw him again? Would they have to go without a sight of each other until March, until the law released her from parental bondage? Six months?

'I can't bear it,' said Rachel.

She sank on the rug before the dressing-table and stared at herself in the glass. Houses, rooms, bodies —they were prisons. Some part of her had gone with John—would always now be with John—but the rest of her remained, caught, penned.

'If it wasn't for Father . . .' she said, her face darkening in the mirror. 'Tyranny . . .' she said between her teeth.

She shook back her hair, which just brushed her bare shoulders.

'Of course, I'm sorry for Father,' she said mechanically. But, with the egoism of youth, she was much sorrier for herself.

'Oh, John . . . John . . .' she said desperately, pressing her cheeks with the palms of her hands.

She got up from the sheepskin rug and pulled her petticoat over her head. She stood about with her long, slender legs revealed and her hair on end. She was charming in the mirror, but she did not look at herself. She leaned on the mantelpiece and sighed :

'What a day !'

And what was going to happen?

She went through it all again, but could find no way out.

She reached at last for her nightgown and turned off the light. When the yellow electricity had gone, the quiet moonlight stole into the room through a gap in the curtains.

Rachel drew them back from the wide-open window.

'I won't shut that out,' she said. 'The moon will move over me when I'm asleep. I'll lie in the silver and dream of John.'

She looked out into the garden.

'I love the rustle of a garden at night,' she thought. 'Why do we keep going to bed and missing things?'

But her nightgown was thin silk, and the floor was cold to her bare feet. She took a running leap into the despised bed.

'John, John !' she said, pulling up the covers. 'Do

you know I adore you? I adore you!' She bit her pillow ecstatically.

She arranged herself to her liking with care, then upset all by emerging suddenly to kneel up in the bed.

'God,' she said, 'you know I don't understand about You at all. But in case You can hear me, I thank You for John, and please let me make up to him for all he has missed, and let us love each other as long as we live.'

She lay down again, and covered herself up once more. Before the clock on the landing had struck twelve she was asleep.

The moon woke her. When it reached her window and bathed her in its full flood of light, she awoke and lay in it.

'Now I'm in the moon,' she thought, and lay on her back with her arms outstretched on the pillows.

'How lovely it is—all illumined. . . . I wish John was here.'

As she lay there a strange conviction grew in her that he was there in reality. She sat up in bed.

'No,' she told herself. 'This is not St. Agnes' Eve. He isn't hiding in the curtains.'

She looked hopefully at them. But they were short and could hide nothing.

'But I feel he is here,' she said. 'So close. I'm certain he's here somewhere.'

She leaped out of bed and ran to the window. She leaned far out into the garden, holding her breath. Then she called softly:

'John. . . . Are you here? Or am I dreaming? John!'

Miraculously he was there. He moved out of the

shadow, crossed the moonlight, and stood under her window.

'Oh, John . . .' breathed Rachel. 'Is it really you? Haven't you gone after all?'

'No, I couldn't,' he whispered. 'Not to-night. Was it true this afternoon? Did you mean it, Rachel? Do you really love me?'

'I love you,' said Rachel, kneeling down on the cold floor to bring herself nearer to him.

'Oh, Rachel. . . .' He strained upwards.

She pressed her lips against her hands on the window-sill. They were silent, gazing at each other, immensely separated, yet very close.

'I'm coming down,' announced Rachel.

'Oh, can you?' asked John, rather fearfully. 'I don't want to get you into another row.'

'Pooh!' said Rachel. 'Wait.'

She turned from the window and snatched her coat, belted it, thrust her feet into her soft slippers, and with infinite caution opened the door between her grandmother's room and her own. Louisa's tranquil breathing made itself heard.

'It's only me, darling,' whispered Rachel reassuringly, if unnecessarily, as she stole through the room, down the dark stairs, to the back of the house, where she could escape noiselessly into the freshness of the night, round the side of the house, into John's arms. She sprang straight into them, and he closed them round her. Their lips met in the heavenly solace of their first kiss. They did not speak. They kissed, and kissed, pressed close, enwrapped.

'Oh, Rachel. . . .'

'Oh, John. . . .'

Later she said : 'But let's move from here. Let's

go round the other side of the house. These are Grandma's windows and anyone passing the gate might see us.'

Hand in hand, they stole round the house. Kate Barlow's window was dark, and they did not think of her.

' Rachel, you'll get cold,' said John apprehensively. ' Haven't you got a dressing-gown under that coat ? '

' No, this is my nightgown. I expect I look like a cracker, really ! ' said Rachel. ' No, I'm not having your coat. I should be weighed down. Can't you take me inside it ? '

He took her inside his coat, enfolding her with ecstasy. The wall of the house was in such deep shadow beyond them that they did not see a head look out and withdraw cautiously.

They kissed again and again. Rachel pressed her head back against his supporting hand, tilting up her face in the moonlight.

' Rachel, you're so beautiful ! '

' No, I'm not. I'm quite ordinary really, but don't let's admit it ! '

' My darling, you're beautiful,' insisted John fervently.

She made a place for her hands on each side of his tie below his collar.

' I love you,' she whispered.

He did not let his hands wander, except to her little neck which he could almost span with one hand, and to the lobes of her ears which showed pearly under the ends of her dark hair. He held her tenderly ; she was pliant and slender against him ; and the feel of her body, with its little bones, reminded him of a young lamb he had once carried in a field.

'You mustn't stop long,' he said. 'You'll get cold.'

'You know, we've got an awful time in front of us,' said Rachel, suddenly grave.

'Awful,' he agreed. 'I suppose I shan't be allowed a glimpse of you, I mightn't even be able to get a letter to you. Will you be able to go on loving me through that?'

'Shall I ask you the same thing?' mocked Rachel.

'No—don't. It would be such silly waste of time.'

Their lips met again.

'How am I going to take my exam,' groaned Rachel, 'with you in my head all the time?'

'You must chuck me out. I'll allow you to do that for the time being. I know very well I oughtn't to have sprung myself on you just now,' said John self-reproachfully.

'You couldn't help it,' said Rachel. 'It was me. I made you.'

'You didn't make me,' said John. 'You *let* me, perhaps. I didn't need any making.'

'No, but I ran after you,' said Rachel. 'I ran after you, now didn't I?'

'No, of course you didn't,' said John indignantly.

'I did. I ran after you!' laughed Rachel, burrowing closer under his coat. 'I don't mind admitting it.'

'You showed me I could try,' corrected John. 'Shall we say you didn't run away?'

They shook with laughter, and when they tried to kiss their teeth clashed lightly and made them laugh more.

They kissed and laughed, and in the shadow above, Kate Barlow listened and trembled.

Hideous, hideous, this old game! Once she had played it; once she stole out to her lover in a garden at night, and kissed and murmured like this. Oh, it was hideous ! Other people's passion was hideous, nauseating ! She loathed these kisses and murmurs under her window, but she could not leave them. They inflamed an old nerve, but she went on exposing it.

All physical love was ugly, she told herself ; all—her own, too. She was humiliated at having giving way to it again, humiliated to the earth to have been repulsed. She pressed her knuckles hard against her lips and moaned to herself.

Oh, he was right, he was right to deny the body. It brought the soul low, it degraded, it betrayed. She had finished with it.

'Never again,' she said to herself.

Never again would she let love move her to warmth ; never would she put out a hand to another living creature !

And he had known ! He knew what he was doing ; he knew she was loving him. He went as far as he could. Kate looked at the Reverend Cyril Northcote as he was ; but she did not blame him much. It was the body that was to blame ; these cursed bodies, his and hers, and the bodies of these two under the window, putting on lovely-seeming guises to lead them to destruction.

Well, she would conquer hers once more. She would tear this love out of her heart, steel herself, and go on, as she had done before—but not here. Not in this house, under these observing eyes, no matter how kind. The kinder the eyes, the more she resented them. Kindness meant interference ; and, if no one was kind, no one intruded into her isolation and she could keep on her way with a grim satisfaction at being able to do without everything that made up the happiness of other people. The lust for saying ' no ' grew and flourished when she fed it daily ; it could dominate her life again, as it had dominated it before.

Her mind was made up. She only waited for these two under her window to have done.

They were parting now.

' Oh, John . . . I can't go. Don't make me.'

' You must, Rachel. You must, darling. . . .'

' Oh, John, perhaps Father will give in before March. He often gives in suddenly when you don't expect him to.'

' Let's hope he'll give in then. We're at his mercy. But you must go, darling. You're cold and it's very late.'

' Perhaps Grandma will help us. Write here to me. We can write until he stops us, surely.'

' Yes—well, I'll write to him first. But go in now. Kiss me once more, little beautiful one. . . .'

' Oh, John.'

' Oh, I love you, Rachel, I love you ! D'you know how much I love you ? '

They tore themselves apart at last.

Kate Barlow heard the slight crunch of the gravel under John's feet. Later she heard Rachel lightly pass her door. But when she looked out into the garden again, she could make out John's figure standing under the birch tree at the end of the left lawn, turned towards Rachel's window still.

' Oh, go ! Go away ! ' Kate murmured angrily.

Was he going to stop there all night ? She couldn't put on the light until he went. She paced the room in the dark, but she was impatient to be getting ready, and began to take things from the drawers and lay them on the bed.

At last, looking out, she saw that he had gone. She dropped the dark curtains across the window and turned on the light. Then she set about her preparations in earnest. She drew the small, flat, worn leather trunk from under the bed. She had taken it from the box-room earlier in the evening, while Rachel wept in the drawing-room and Louisa consoled.

Kate turned out the light again and opened her door. The house was now still. She waited a moment, then lifted the trunk and carried it cautiously down the stairs, through the baize door and into the kitchen. She returned to her room to fill her arms with clothes, and felt her way down the stairs again. She made these journeys in the dark, without a sound. She did not have to make many, because her possessions were few.

When the trunk was filled, she closed and strapped it. Then she went back to her room and completed her preparations.

She wrote a note to Louisa to thank her for the long shelter at Greenbanks, and to ask her forgiveness for this sudden departure, which, in the circumstances, she explained, was the best, the least embarrassing for them all. She was so sorry, she said, that her son should have brought trouble into the family; she hoped some happy way out would be found. She wrote all the things she would never have said, but ended:

'Please make no attempt to discover my whereabouts, dear Mrs. Ashton. I am better alone. I want to be alone. You have been very kind to me, but I want to be alone now.'

Then she signed herself: 'Yours affectionately, Kate.'

She put the letter in an envelope and laid it on the dressing-table. There was still much of the night left, so turning back the embroidered bedspread from habit, she lay down, fully dressed, to wait.

The darkness would not lie restfully on her lids, but blazed with red and yellow lights and fantastic squirmings. Once she rolled over convulsively, and a sob broke from her. But she stifled it ; she straightened herself out and lay stiff with her hands clenched at her sides. The dark went on beating redly against her eyelids, and it was a long time before, lifting them, she saw a greyness between her magenta curtains.

She rose then, straightened the bed, laid the altar-cloth on it for the Vicar, and having put on her outdoor things, she opened the door of her room. The house was still. No sound but the near-by tick of the clock on the landing, and the remote tick of the clock in the hall. She stole down the stairs with her cardboard case, and placed it with the trunk in the kitchen. She went into the cloakroom, and, speaking very quietly, telephoned for a taxi. Then she opened the back door and stood in the grey morning, waiting. She looked round the garden, which smelled of chrysanthemums. She had loved it, but she was leaving it and would not permit herself to feel regret. Soon she heard the whirr of the approaching taxi, and went out to stop it at the back gate. The chauffeur followed her into the kitchen to carry out her trunk.

' Be as quiet as possible,' said Kate. ' I don't wish to disturb them.'

The man, unshaven and surly from sleep, looked suspiciously at her. But she waved him imperiously out before her, and closed the back door.

' The station,' she said.

In the taxi, she took a time-table from her handbag to look where she could go to until she found another situation.

At Greenbanks the house remained still for some time. Louisa woke early as always. Often between sleeping and waking, she was as conscious of Charles as if he were actually in the room. A precious reassurance came to her in these hours, a sense of God. Louisa, in the early morning, made her meditations.

In the little room adjoining, Rachel slept with traces of tears on her cheeks and a smile on her lips. The lobes of her ears showed rosy as if from John's kisses in the garden.

And by and by Bella's alarm-clock went off in her attic and brought her to the dormer window in the old roof to look out.

'Another nice day,' she said.

For some, yes ; for others, no. But in that it differed from no other day that had gone before or would come after.

AFTERWORD

❋❋❋❋❋❋❋

The final sentence of *Greenbanks* confirms the exceptional tonal consistency of the entire book. In the same way the opening conveys only whatever is needed to draw the reader in, and even that seems reluctantly spared in the first sentence: 'The house was called Greenbanks, but there was no green to be seen today; all the garden was deep in snow.'

This is flat, yet there is craft in the flatness. First choose a name for the house, then use that name as the title of the novel; introduce the name in the very first sentence, and then observe that actually it is not particularly appropriate, if not, at this season, misleading. Should a reader pick this novel up on account of its title, the opening is hardly designed to encourage. There is something comparable going on in the first sentence of *The Small House at Allington* by Anthony Trollope: 'Of course there was a Great House at Allington. How otherwise should there have been a Small House? Our story will, as its name imports, have its closest relations with those who lived in the less dignified domicile of the two.'

Thus with elegance and wit Trollope sets up a tension between the two houses which will be resolved, as far as the reader is concerned, in favour of the smaller. Looking again at the opening sentence of *Greenbanks* we can see how concisely and economically the green has been set against the snow. And the opening paragraph concludes with a repetition that borders on the trite: 'Snow muffled the old house, low and built of stone, and of no particular style or period, and made it look like a house on a Christmas card, which was appropriate, because it was Christmas Day.' Introduced thus, the reader is likely to expect the narrative to pursue its course through the seasons until 'in the end' the house will be happily presented in a verdant state appropriate to its name.

The understated quality of Dorothy Whipple's style is a special gift; an even greater gift is to know how to maintain that quiet steady tone against all temptations to introduce variety. For there is nothing spectacular in the manner of Dorothy Whipple: not the stylistic eccentricities of Ivy Compton-Burnett, nor the sophisticated wit of Rose Macaulay, nor the intellectual or psychological brilliance of Elizabeth Bowen, nor the exotic blend of all those qualities in Whipple's exact contemporary (born 1893), Sylvia Townsend Warner. It is her lack of showiness or obvious stylishness that must account for Dorothy Whipple's years of neglect, for the ill-informed dismissal of her name, on those few occasion on which it might have been raised. Amongst those who can sense the quality of Whipple's style there is a clear case for mounting a campaign to rewrite English literary history so as to give due recognition to the author of *They Knew Mr Knight* (1934), *They Were Sisters* (1943) and *Someone at a Distance* (1953). (She was rather good at titles.) By reissuing a number of her works – *Greenbanks* (1932) is the seventh on their list – Persephone Books has performed a great service for Dorothy Whipple, and then for those who have thereby come to count themselves her admirers.

Dorothy Whipple's understatedness is addictive. Once the reader has found its measure, caught its tone, tuned in to its frequency, there is an attentiveness to one's reading, not in anticipation of surprise and delight, but a keen vigilance in which one waits for a slip, a disruption of tone, a false note. And as the tone is held for hundreds of pages, so one's admiration grows. The narrative voice seldom gets excited, or philosophical, or sentimental, or indignant, but quietly edges along in an inconspicuous, daily sort of way.

The artful flatness of Whipple's style is well suited to her analysis of how families communicate through words suppressed and unspoken. Other writers make stories of interesting, rebellious or extreme characters. Whipple's characters have their moral lapses, but the most scandalous events are presented as if nothing much had happened, and are seldom spoken about. There are two heroines in *Greenbanks*, Louisa and her granddaughter Rachel; Louisa's husband dies in compromising circumstances, and the shame felt throughout the family is such that the event is hardly mentioned again. If an English middle-class family were to be permitted to tell its own story, this might be their version. In a story told through a child's awareness, such as Henry James's *What Maisie Knew* or Elizabeth Bowen's *The Death of the Heart*, the reader can infer and understand more than the narrative presents. So in Dorothy Whipple's novels, flat and uneventful

✳✳✳✳✳✳✳✳✳✳

as they seem and, if eventful, apparently indifferent to those events, we find a view of middle-class family life that might at first seem entirely comfortable, complacently in league with the values of that world. Only gradually does the reader sense a critical and even disillusioned gaze; what had seemed so reassuringly solid is gently exposed in its malice and hypocrisy.

Long ago Dorothy Whipple was described as 'the Jane Austen of the twentieth century'; the source of that epithet was J B Priestley who, immensely influential in his day, carries little weight now. To recall such a comparison is almost inevitably to summon disappointment, yet Priestley had a point: there are very few novelists who can carry flatness off, and not even Jane Austen displays such apparent indifference to its effect. There is a coolness in Dorothy Whipple's lack of interest in whether the reader follows what is going on. There are very few asides. Sympathies are not solicited, nor opinions sought. The reader's reactions seem to be a matter of complete indifference to the world of the novel. The absence of narrative coercion is rare and refreshing, and thanks to this quality of cool detachment – suggestive of E M Forster – the reader's involvement and feelings of indignation will be only the more engaged, and the more heated.

The story traced in *Greenbanks* is that of the relationship between its two heroines, grandmother and granddaughter, set across and against the generation inbetween. The sympathy that binds Louisa and Rachel is all the more convincing in its presentation because their shared disapproval of the behaviour of the one's children and the other's parents (and aunts and uncles) is so seldom given voice; they can signal impatience or irritation without using so many words. Their relationship is founded on implication and slightest gesture, established indeed as such relations are – and need to be, if they are to flourish – on a mutually recognised code of suppression.

This code of suppression is one we admire, for it serves a good purpose. Nobody else in the Ashton family comes through the story with much credit; for them suppression is an instrument of concealment, deception and manipulation. The novel is the story of Rachel's growing up, and her assertion of independence against her father's wishes and commands, but with the help of her grandmother's tacit encouragement. Selfishness, cruelty, bullying, authoritarianism: all of these are presented as entirely normal. This is how a middle-class family gets along and stays together: staying in the family being explicitly what is demanded of Rachel.

The comparison with Ivy Compton-Burnett is inevitable: of course, her novels are among the comic classics of English literature, but their comedy depends on the outspokenness of the characters. The dynamics may be familiar to any family, yet the way the behaviour is manifested, through those conversations, is far from realistic. By contrast, in Dorothy Whipple, what is suppressed and goes unsaid in family life is left unsaid in the novels. The attentive reader learns to listen out for the silences between the words.

Dorothy Whipple died in 1966, having published her last novel in 1953. In the following decades she was considered a plain and unsubtle novelist, sharing the values of those she wrote about. Yet today we can see that she is a writer whose accuracy of perception and recording is so sharp as to need no overt commentary or supplementary criticism. The doubleness of our narrative focus in *Greenbanks*, on Louisa and Rachel, is matched by a doubleness in our reading, for each reader is liable to be both entranced and appalled by Whipple's world. There is a thoroughness of description in Whipple's towns and houses and villas which lends them the simple charm of being solidly there; that description is furnished by details of social life and domestic customs. To those familiar with such doings, Whipple's novels may well have seemed merely and tediously realistic; to us they give us access to a world that though well lost is pleasing to revisit.

One of the things that first entrances the reader is the 'artless' accuracy with which speech is represented. There is something entirely convincing about the way these people speak, simply because their author is not trying to make them sound clever or witty, or even interesting (unlike a contemporary such as Aldous Huxley). Whipple's hearing is acute; through all her novels she displays an exceptional sense of the transience of idiom, and of the date in which phrases come into use. Louisa's officious, self-important, and incompetent son-in-law, Ambrose, takes it upon himself to regulate her bills and invest her savings: 'He had talked a good deal about the expense of upkeep lately, and urged her not to consume so much gas. He always said "consume" in relation to gas; and Louisa smiled to remember that Rachel had inquired if they ate gas at Greenbanks.' The narrative is at this stage set in 1910, and will close in the mid 1920s; we can trace the shift in idioms over the decades. The noted oddity of Ambrose's use of 'consume' must prompt us to wonder at the process by which the subjects and citizens of a hundred years ago became the consumers that we know, and are.

Similarly, Louisa's son Jim has insisted on installing a telephone, although she dislikes it: 'When she had to answer it, she spoke in a voice without expression and could not be beguiled into giving any information other than that asked for.' On a rare occasion, we are told, 'she went to the telephone of her own accord' in order to speak to her son-in-law:

> After gripping the receiver with blenched fingers for what seemed to her an unaccountable time, she heard Ambrose himself saying: 'Hello, hello' over and over again with great rapidity and cheerfulness. When she could manage it, she got in her own 'Hello'; not a very loud one, because she thought it a foolish mode of address for a woman of her age.

That sort of detail seems entirely reliable, for Dorothy Whipple is not a novelist who strikes one as ever needing or wanting to make a point. Born in 1893, she is some fifteen years older than Rachel and forty years younger than Louisa; we must admire her ability to understand and sympathise with the sensibilities of both while carefully distinguishing their attitudes and habits, above all, their words and idioms. Putting the receiver down while Ambrose is in full spate, Louisa reflects: 'The telephone had its merits, after all; Ambrose could be cut off'. The phrase 'cut off' suggests the supplementary phrase 'so-and-so without a penny', which was the fate of disinherited feckless relations, perhaps especially in the generation before the telephone. Both Ambrose and Jim would like Louisa to 'cut off' Charles, who is irresponsible and gullible, yet his mother's favourite child. The telephone offers Louisa the opportunity to 'cut off' Ambrose: this might be termed 'revenge by idiom'.

Charles has been packed off to Malaya, where he is to take a post on a rubber plantation run by a friend of Jim's: 'The family was sick of him, and would see to it that no more money reached him from his mother.' Just in that sentence we can hear 'the family' shift from the flatness of shared assumptions to the phrase that Jim and Ambrose would use in order to suppress and exclude Louisa's quite different view. Then, having got Charles off:

> 'I'm by no means certain that we've seen the last of him,' said Ambrose, turning in his collar to Jim when Charles had been got off. 'By Jove, if he dares to show his face here again . . . ' exploded Jim. But he didn't finish the sentence, because he didn't know how to. Speech is so useful; you can leave off anywhere.

This has the look of a general observation, until one realises that the very idea of 'leaving off' speech might be derived from the new modes of speaking and speech etiquette associated with the telephone. And while women have been traditionally judged for their failure to complete a sentence, on account of their susceptibility to the emotional and the hysterical, men who entered into the professions were qualified precisely by their unfailing skill in speech. Rachel, we are told, had a passion not only for reading but also 'for declamation, in secret.' She has to create the circumstances in which her declaiming will go unheard, as when the bath is being filled and the taps are running loud: 'the covering noise gave her a splendid opportunity to let herself go.' Compare Rachel's guarded enthusiasm with the sentence not clearly attributed to Jim: 'Speech is so useful; you can leave off anywhere.' This sentence bears re-reading, and re-hearing, until general flatness turns to gendered sharpness.

There is plenty of material in the plot to make this a 'feminist' novel. Rachel is awarded a State Scholarship to go to either Oxford or Cambridge; her father, Ambrose, insists that her place is at home. After a miserable year, in which Rachel's frustration is exacerbated by the company during university vacations of a friend who is now at Westfield (the women's college of the University of London), Ambrose allows her to study, but the State Scholarship has been forfeited and so she attends the University of Liverpool. There is a subtly noted discrepancy between Rachel's pleasure and the reader's awareness that, even in relenting, Ambrose has offered her a poor substitute. And there is the story of Kate Barlow, ostracised for having a child outside marriage, and restored to a limited respectability by Louisa, who takes her on as a companion; Kate is then crushed once more by the new vicar who, after having led her on, cuts her off by letting it be known that he has taken vows as a 'celibate priest'. A wide range of masculine failings is on display.

It is in the language of the novel that one finds feminist thinking doing its most critical work. By 1932 there were many novels protesting about the obstacles faced by young women. There are still not many novels that can so stealthily take down male pretensions and presumptions. Throughout Whipple's works the signs of independent female thinking are presented indirectly, not through what the girl or woman thinks or says or does, but rather by the description of what she is reading. Reading is a general good, evidence of intellectual independence. Rachel reads 'with rapture' a story by Katherine Mansfield, though it is not necessary that the book read should be by a feminist or a female author.

Towards the story's end, Rachel, studying English at Liverpool, thinks about the seriousness with which students read: 'Funny all these ordinary little people picking Shakespeare, Milton – the great ones – to pieces for examination purposes. Pick, pick, pick with their perky question-and-answer beaks, like hens at a rose'; and then we are surprised that this is ultimately not condemned because 'after the rose was picked to pieces it all came together again and presented its lovely whole unimpaired.' No less surprising and refreshing is the conclusion of the description of what Rachel reads:

> Rachel had a passion for reading, shared by no member of her family. None of the Ashtons read much; Ambrose read the papers; London and local papers, morning and evening papers took up all his spare time. The boys progressed from Sexton Blake to Sherlock Holmes

and historical romances, and seemed to stop there. But
Rachel . . . read the classics with avidity, not knowing
them to be classics, but she read with equal avidity
St. Hilda's, *Brenda Shows the Way*, *The Hockey Heroine*
and other school tales. . . . She read, too, the penny
novelettes she found in the kitchen. . . . She made no
discrimination between these literatures; she read and
enjoyed them all.

The casual reader of *Greenbanks* might, in her or his
enjoyment, wonder what has become of those critical standards
by which we distinguish the great from the mediocre. And
then that reader might think, rather enviously, that it must be
a rare pleasure in adult life to read a classic without knowing
that it is a classic. It is a pleasure we suspect might be ours when
we read a novel by Dorothy Whipple.

Louisa does not read at all, yet this only increases Rachel's
admiration for her, that she should be able to find strength
and resolution and wisdom without the help or consolation
of books. There are interesting generational questions, hardly
'raised' but gently suggested, as to the changing roles of
reading in the formation of a woman's identity. It is not a
criticism of Louisa that she reads nothing, but it is a criticism
of her daughters that they read only magazines and romances.
It is as though society, or the family, had once provided
sufficient sources of understanding, perhaps above all of
sympathy; and that, for Rachel's generation, reading supplied
something that the family could no longer give. Ambrose's
objection to his daughter's reading is founded on his mother-

in-law's own book-less contentment. If the family is happy, reading can only create trouble, leading girls to imagine a life elsewhere, lived differently. What in reading habits and education was acceptable to Louisa in her generation is respected by Rachel, while she reckons it quite unacceptable in hers.

The 'sympathetic difference' between these two generations is evident throughout *Greenbanks*. Charles, home on leave during the Great War, speaks for the generation between. In response to his mother's protesting her lack of cleverness, her inability to keep up with her children, Charles teases her, affectionately:

> 'It's better to be wise than clever, and that's what you are, darling. . . . When I think of you sometimes at the Front, I roar with laughter. Just remembering how you look over your knitting, or those priceless sort of flat remarks you take people down with.'

The son's memories of his mother are never of her reading, as ours of Rachel might well be. Yet one might see in 'those priceless sort of flat remarks' an all but unnoticed image of the author, as she looks, over her writing rather than her knitting, winking as it were at her own carefully concealed reflection.

On reaching the end of *Greenbanks*, the reader will take special notice of the closing paragraph, in which no green shoots emerge from under the snow; there is no sign that the title of the novel is of any lasting significance. Flatness must, by definition, shun the heights and the depths; it recognises

****

no conclusion, no resolution, no satisfaction even, beyond the wisdom of realising that the days go by, bringing joy to some, sorrow to others. A more understated conclusion could hardly be reached, nor one that displays a greater indifference to its effect on us. For the reader there is the complex satisfaction of a riddle not quite solved, in this as in Dorothy Whipple's other novels: they not only need to be read but – the mark of the best – they need to be read again.

Charles Lock
Professor of English Literature,
University of Copenhagen,
2011